For the Ones
Who Rebel

R. Collins

Samsara Fleet | Book Three

Books By Riley Collins

To learn more about Riley Collins, see an updated list of titles, and join his mailing list go to his webpage at www.rileycollins.info.

Samsara Fleet Series

Book One: For the Ones Who Remain
Book Two: For the Ones Who Are Forgotten
Book Three: For the Ones Who Rebel

Copyright © 2021
All rights reserved.
ISBN: 1-7359029-5-0
ISBN-13: 978-1-7359029-5-1
Print Edition

Cover Art by: 17 Studio Book Design
Editing by: Lisa Binion and Rosaire Bushey

For Mom and Dad with all my love.

Chapter One

Brigadier General Kal Norman rushed to the bridge of the *Ofira* with Lieutenant Colonel Nicole Bergeron fast on his heels. The wailing sound of the ship-wide alert rang through the sterile hallways and soldiers rushed around them heading to battle stations. Kal gave a silent word of thanks that his cabin wasn't too far from the bridge as a soldier bounced into him.

He and Nicole had been in laying in their cabin when they received word from General Samaha that a Jadid fleet had arrived in the system. Initially, she'd ordered them to her flagship, the *Gedorhan's Return*. But Kal convinced her there wasn't time for them to move from the *Ofira*. He wasn't sure what the Jadid wanted, but he doubted it was good. When he'd left their home world, Altterra, it had not been on the best of terms.

"Why do you think they're here?" Nicole panted as they waited for a lift door to open.

"No idea," Kal replied. "I doubt they are my biggest fans." That was putting it mildly. Kal and Major Garcia, the head pilot on their ragtag scout team, the Skulls, had barely left with their lives.

The officers rushed into the small lift as the doors opened. It felt like ages before they closed and the cabin started moving. The machine sped them through the ship, traveling both laerally and vertically toward the bridge. There was no sensation of movement. The only sign the lift was working was a small screen next to the doors that showed their position moving within the *Ofira*.

1

"Maybe they're here to help," Nicole suggested, averting her crystal blue eyes.

"Maybe…" but Kal doubted it. The Jadid had shown no desire to help anyone but themselves.

They stood quietly; the seconds felt like years as the lift reached the bridge and the cream-colored doors opened. Kal tried to ignore the gnawing in his chest and assure himself that the Jadid wouldn't hold grudges. The happiness he'd felt only a few minutes ago, as he was laying with Nicole was a distant dream.

The *Ofira's* bridge was a hive of activity. Human and alien soldiers scurried between the battle stations. Initially, Samsara Fleet had been made up of only a few Human warships. However, they had taken on other survivors of the Nasi invasion, and the fleet was now composed of several species: Humans, Kurz, Tounous, and Qudoru.

Colonel Irina Petrov gave a small sigh of relief when she saw Kal and Nicole step off the lift. The middle-aged officer rose from her command chair and briskly walked toward them.

"Sir. Colonel Bergeron." A small sheen of sweat glistened on Petrov's brow. Normally the senior officer could have been carved out of granite for all the emotion she displayed under stress. "Three ships just appeared a few minutes ago. As soon as they arrived, they hailed us on an open channel, demanding to talk to you."

Kal studied the large viewscreen that dominated the far wall of the bridge. Their vaguely ovoid shapes were twisted and covered in alien bumps. They looked like fruit that had been left in the sun for days with dimples and craters marring their ashen surface. Kal couldn't tell the difference between these ships and the Nasi ones which had laid waste to Earth and much of the galaxy. But they brought back memories of Humanity's home world being wiped away in hours. Memories he would rather forget.

The Nasi were a sect—a cult—that had sprung from within the Jadid. The Jadid were descendants of unwilling Human test subjects who'd found themselves stranded in a different universe after the experiment—testing faster-than-light travel—had failed. After arriving in their new universe, it had taken everything they had to survive the strange and hostile environment. But they had survived and even flourished, creating a new civilization that grew more advanced and powerful than Humanity. Most of the Jadid grew to accept and even like their new home and focused on continuing to advance and grow. However, a portion of them, the Nasi, never accepted it. They became fixated on developing a way to return to Earth.

When the Nasi returned hundreds of years later, they laid waste to Earth and several other home worlds in the galaxy. Their dreadnaughts folded into the systems without warning and fired on their central stars. The weapons disrupted the stars' fusion reaction, causing them to destroy everything in the system in a supernova.

Although they had captured a few Nasi, Kal didn't truly understand why they had done this. They professed to care for Humanity. They said they wanted to help lead their ancestors to a new age of glory. It made little sense for them to destroy Earth without warning.

Since the Nasi returned months ago, Kal—and Samsara Fleet—had been struggling to defeat them with scant success. That they were still living was a major victory. The Nasi were ruthless, intelligent, and had them on the ropes.

"How do you know the ships are Jadid?" he asked, unable to look away. "Maybe it's just a Nasi trap."

"Not very likely." Petrov cracked her knuckles. "Also Bo confirmed that they're Jadid." Bowen Nguyen was a Jadid scientist that Kal's team had freed from Nasi captivity. Kal wasn't sure he completely understood him. But he trusted him.

"We decided not to deploy our fighters. Samaha thought it'd be too aggressive," Petrov continued. "But damn if I won't have every pilot in their cockpit and every soldier at their battle station."

She turned to look at the three ships on the viewscreen. He could see the muscles in her face tense as she stared. They'd all been through so much. Kal knew she had a family before the Nasi came. Wounds that deep left scars.

"I need to speak with General Samaha before I talk to them," Kal said. The fleet commander had been clear on that point. Kal had become used to operating on his own, and she knew it. She wasn't about to let him go rogue if she could help it.

Samaha had moved her flag to the Tounous Carrier *Gedorhan's Return* as a nod to the multispecies makeup of the fleet. With four species in and a fifth, the Torgham, most likely about to join, she worked hard to overcome rivalries and

4

cultural differences. Kal didn't envy her job.

He used his neural implant to speak directly with General Samaha. Implants were small devices embedded directly into Humans' brain stems when they reached adulthood. They were as essential to interstellar space travel as the fold drive, providing a variety of capabilities including automatic translation, communications, interface with computers, and more. The implants interfaced directly with the optic and auditory nerves in the brain. Like most Humans, Kal's implant had become as important to his everyday life as his eyes or ears—more important, in fact.

Kal. Samaha's synthetic voice rang in his ears. To Kal her message sounded like a generic Human voice though no one around him could hear the message at all. *Took your time in getting to the bridge. Any idea what they want?*

No idea, ma'am. You know from my mission brief that Garcia and I didn't exactly leave on the best of terms.

Kal could have sworn she laughed. *That's one way to put it. You defied their government in front of the entire planet and then hijacked an experimental ship. Either way, they'll only speak with you.* Kal sensed her annoyance.

So I gathered. He felt the gnawing in his chest get stronger.

Remember, the Jadid can help us, Samaha said. *Perhaps even stop the Nasi in their tracks.* She was desperate for any help she could get.

He didn't need reminding how dire their situation was. Samsara Fleet was the only remaining resistance, and the Nasi outnumbered them more than five to one.

5

I doubt they'll do that. The Jadid didn't seem to feel any responsibility for some of their own starting this war. They saw themselves as neutral bystanders.

You need to figure out a way to get them to feel some responsibility. Samaha's tone softened. *You know as well as I do that we're running out of options.* The commander cut the line.

"Let's do this," he muttered. Kal turned to face Petrov. "Open a channel to the Jadid fleet."

After a few seconds, the three ships disappeared from the main viewscreen, replaced by a gaunt face. It was a dark violet with severe angular features and the coloration grew slightly lighter around the thin mouth and dark brown eyes. Close-cropped black hair framed a decidedly feminine face. The physics in the Jadid's universe was extremely different, causing them to have wildly different physiology from their Human ancestors.

"General Norman?" the Jadid asked.

Kal nodded.

"I am Section Chief Angelika Chin." She inclined her head. "I am here on behalf of the Ancients and need to speak with you." The Ancients were the original six Humans that all Jadid were descended from. They were the former prisoners and debtors that the Human government had forced into becoming test subjects in the development of the fold drive centuries ago. One of the major side-effects of their alternate universe was the gift of immortality, the Ancients hadn't aged a day since they had arrived on Altterra. Although they denied it, they were the ultimate decision makers and authority among the Jadid.

"I'm all ears."

"This needs to be in person. I will send a tender to bring you over."

"Wait." Kal stepped toward the screen. "I need to know a little more than—"

The external video sensor feed of the Jadid ships abruptly reappeared on the screen. She had cut the link.

"Looks like they're not ones for small talk," Petrov stated.

"I doubt they trust the security of your crew or your communications equipment," Bowen observed.

Kal tamped down his annoyance; it was understandable. The Jadid and the Nasi were decades ahead in many areas technologically. Samsara Fleet had started to catch up through reverse engineering Nasi wreckage they found, but they had a long way to go.

"We don't need them to talk. We need them to fight." Kal turned and walked into the lift, heading toward the landing bays.

Nicole took a sideways glance at Kal as the lift moved them through the ship. He furrowed his brow in concentration as he listened to General Samaha through his neural implant. It was a look she had almost memorized by this point. The dark skin, splash of gray hair, and faint lines told the story of a life fully lived. She knew he had seen more than his fair share of happiness and sorrow. They all had seen more than their fair share of sorrow at this point.

When Nicole had first met Kal, he'd interrogated her while transporting her from one space station's brig to another. Despite that, his appearance and demeanor had captivated her. There was something different about him. He had looked like hell with bags under his eyes, and his uniform was wrinkled except where it strained against his midsection. But there was an empathy in his eyes she hadn't seen in her other captors. Since that first encounter, Kal had grown and matured. He'd risen to the challenge before them and earned her faith. Hell, he'd earned everyone's. She just hoped it was enough.

Kal turned his head and gave her a look of exasperation, tapping on his ear. General Samaha was not someone who normally micromanaged her subordinates. But the stakes were high, and she was desperate. Almost everyone—generals included—needed to have the illusion of control. They had barely withstood the Nasi before. Now their enemy was four times as strong and had brought their entire fleet. Nicole didn't know how they could stand against them.

She had been in situations almost as bad though. Prior to joining Samsara Fleet, Nicole had served as an attaché for the United Earth Government. The UEG had been the civilian government of Earth and all of Humanity's colonies. It had its troubles: inequality, prioritizing Earth before their colonies, and a deep stagnation. Despite that, the last two decades were a period of prosperity and peace, something that Nicole only realized when the Nasi came and blew it all up.

When she'd joined the UEG's diplomatic corps, she left her family on Earth, went through extensive training, and then spent years working at the UEG's embassy on Gorash, the home planet of the Kurz. When Nicole had heard the corps selected her, she'd been ecstatic. It was her chance to see the galaxy, make a name for herself, and help her family escape Earth's communes. Nicole's family had been the lowest of the low. They were close and had been lucky in many ways. Nicole's parents protected her and her sister from most of the violence that permeated the dense clusters of buildings that made up the communes. But she'd wanted more. She knew that if she could escape Earth, she could change her family's fortunes. Only many years later while on Gorash, did she realize it was a lie. The UEG's system only let one go so far. She didn't know the senior officials within the UEG, and she didn't have the pull to find the plum assignments, the ones that would allow her to move her family into their own home. So, she had agreed to listen to a shadowy figure who called himself Two and betrayed her species, her government, and her family in the process.

It had been the biggest mistake of her life.

Over the next few years, Two used her to funnel information to the Nasi, who were already planning their assault. She hadn't realized what the information was being used for. She wouldn't have done it if she had known. But in the end, that was an excuse. Nicole had to live with the fact that she was at least partially responsible for everything they had been through. It was something she could never forget.

"I know she means well," Kal said, interrupting her

thoughts, "but Samaha needs to let go. This meeting is not something we can plan for."

"Just listen to her," Nicole advised. "She knows that. Even Samaha is Human though; it makes her feel like she has some control over events."

The lift doors softly parted, revealing the utility corridors of the landing bay area. The *Ofira* had several landing bays, all connected through a network of corridors. As opposed to the other decks, the hallways were darker with equipment affixed against the walls. Pilots and mechanics walked brusquely through the area, rushing to make sure they were at their stations if something happened.

As they walked into one of the bays, a small tender glided through the energy shield that kept the atmosphere within the bay while also allowing ships to exit and enter. The ship was dark with a rainbow-colored patina covering every surface. It was about fifteen meters long and reminded Nicole of a misshapen ball of clay. Protuberances and nacelles jutted out of the hull at irregular intervals. *JHF BAGHDAD* was emblazoned on the front and aft of the ship, the words embedded in the bulkhead material itself rather than painted on.

After it had gently set down, a small door on the side of the ship dilated open and a tall Jadid woman glided out. The opening was slightly shorter than her frame, forcing her to exit legs first and duck her head as she strode through. As the alien woman walked toward them, Nicole admired her grace. She looked like a dancer slipping across the stage. Each step was smooth and deliberate with a sense of strength and purpose. She wore a tight-fitting green uniform, the colors clashing with the violet of her skin. The uniform accentuated the lean musculature of her frame, enhancing Nicole's impression. As the Jadid got closer, Nicole realized she was looking at Section Chief Chin.

"Welcome to the *Ofira*," Colonel Petrov said as Chin came to rest in front of them. With a start, Nicole realized two Jadid guards were flanking the section chief. She had been so captivated she hadn't even registered them.

"Thank you." Chin placed her hands on her chest, one on top of the other. After a brief pause, she turned to face Kal. "Come with us, General Norman." It was somewhere between an order and a question.

"Of course." Kal cleared his throat. She wasn't the only one caught off guard by this woman. "This is Lieutenant Colonel Nicole Bergeron." Kal inclined his head toward Nicole. "She'll be coming with us."

Chin turned her head to study Nicole. "I am sorry, but that will not be acceptable."

Kal's eyes narrowed. Nicole knew that look; either she was going, or no one was. "If you want to talk with me, then she comes. I trust her completely." It wasn't clear if it was just posturing or a calculated move. Either way, as a diplomat she approved. The Jadid had to know that they could not dictate the terms of this relationship.

Chin matched Kal's stare for several seconds before giving a short grunt. "Very well, let's go." Without another word, Section Chief Chin strode back to the *Baghdad*. Kal looked at Nicole, gave a small shrug, and followed. As the

11

two Humans walked side by side toward the ship, the two Jadid guards stayed a pace behind them.

General Norman, I hope you know what you're doing, Petrov said over the neural net.

So do I, Kal replied as he and Nicole walked through the door and into the Jadid ship, not needing to duck as they entered.

The inside of the *Baghdad* was a single spartan compartment with a few rows of seats. At the front was a small viewscreen that gave the illusion they were looking at the *Ofira's* landing bay through a window. Like every other species, the Jadid used viewscreens to relay a live video feed from outside the ship. There wasn't a transparent material which could match the strength of a composite metal hull. Instead, most ships were covered in sensors which fed into high resolution viewscreens in the interior. It gave the impression of looking out a window but had none of the structural vulnerability.

Nicole had been in a few Nasi ships and buildings. This Jadid ship had the same organic feel she remembered from them. The bulkhead was made from a thin fabric-like membrane. Small threads of luminescent material were woven into the material, creating the impression that the surfaces of the ship were glowing. Despite their fragile appearances, these walls could handle almost anything thrown at them. It was one of the mysteries of the Jadid and Nasi. How did they build ships and buildings like this?

She was comforted to see some differences as well. Small placards, written in Human Standard, were affixed around the cabin. Although still dark by Human standards, the interior was lighter than the Nasi ships and buildings. The chairs were also padded, a nod to comfort that she would have never seen with the Nasi.

Chin gestured to a row of chairs, and Kal and Nicole sat down.

"Please fasten your restraints," Chin instructed as she sat across the aisle from them.

The chairs were intended for the longer, thinner Jadid frame. Nicole had to slide down so that her legs could touch the floor, which left a space between the seat and her back. The restraint straps dug into her shoulders and midsection as they self-tightened across her chest.

More Jadid were already in the two chairs at the front. The pilots, Nicole assumed. As the passengers fastened themselves into their chairs, their hands flew across the switches, knobs, and controls scattered below the viewscreen in front of them. The *Baghdad* slowly drifted upwards and coasted through the energy shield and into the vacuum of space. Nicole felt herself being pushed back into her chair as they began to accelerate.

"I'm eager to hear what you have to say," Kal said after the pressure had lessened. "You must have gone through a lot of trouble to get here."

"Indeed," Chin replied. "I just hope it will be worth it." She stood up and walked to the front of the ship, cutting off any further questions.

"How do you think they found us?" Nicole asked. After their loss to the Nasi at New America, Samsara Fleet had fled

13

to Keerloa. The small desert planet was one of the Torgham colonies. They had colonized the planet almost a hundred years earlier because of the deep mineral and water deposits beneath the sands. Although Kal had not been to the planet's surface, he'd heard stories of people dying just minutes after getting stranded.

The fleet had not intended to end up there. Samsara Fleet had entered the Patagonia system expecting to recapture the planet from the Nasi. Instead, they'd found a fleet several magnitudes larger than they expected. Kal and Major Karl Garcia were the only reason that she was still alive; they'd destroyed the anti-space defense system on the planet and allowed the *Ofira* to escape.

Nicole had an unsettling thought. If the Jadid could find them, the Nasi could as well.

"I don't know," Kal replied, "but it isn't good." He must have had the same thought as her.

After fifteen minutes, the small tender reached the Jadid fleet. The pilots and Chin's lanky forms partially obscured the viewscreen. She felt them decelerate and saw glimpses of the Jadid ship looming before them between the three profiles. The tender drifted into the dark landing bay of the ship and came to a rest against the ground.

"Come with me." Chin led them out of the *Baghdad* and into a landing bay made of the same fibrous material as the tender. The faint glow from the wall and ceiling cast ominous shadows throughout the large room. Combined with the sloping irregular ceiling overhead, Nicole felt like she was exploring an underground cavern. Tender ships and fighters filled the bay, arranged haphazardly. The strange layout of the room highlighted the alienness of the Jadid; only they would organize a bay like this.

Kal and Nicole followed Chin through the sinuous corridors of the ship. As they walked, they passed small groups of Jadid calmly walking and talking in tones that were too soft for Nicole to hear. She idly wondered what Jadid said to each other. Did they even have personal conversations? They arrived at a circular portal and Chin tapped on her wrist computer, which was the Jadid and Nasi equivalent of a neural implant. The door opened revealing a lift and the three of them stepped in. The two guards that had flanked them on the *Ofira* were not trailing them. Probably because two unarmored Humans presented no threat to the physically superior Jadid.

"So when are we going to talk?" Kal asked.

"We are not going to talk." The chief didn't bother to turn her head. "You are here to speak with someone else."

Nicole grunted in frustration. The chief couldn't possibly be less forthcoming. Kal gave her a sympathetic smile and turned back to face the lift door.

After the door opened, they followed their guide through another set of hallways before ending at another one of the strange doors, this one larger than any of the others they had passed. Something or someone important must be behind it. Chin held a hand out as the door opened, inviting them to enter.

Nicole and Kal stepped through the door as one. Nicole almost gasped when she saw who was on the other side. It

15

was a man—a Human—who looked to be in his mid-thirties. His dark black hair was slicked back, with two wings of gray radiating from his temples.

"Kal Norman," the man said as he stood up from what looked to be a desk. "I wasn't sure you'd survive." He gestured toward a few chairs in a corner of the room. "Sit down. We need to talk. I've come here to help."

Chapter Two

Bao Wang smiled as he moved from behind his desk. It had only been a couple of weeks since Kal had seen the Ancient, but it felt like years.

"You look surprised." Bao's grin remained plastered on his face a touch too long. Nicole saw the effort he was making to maintain it from the lines around his eyes.

"Well, we didn't exactly leave Altterra in the best of conditions." Kal looked apologetic.

Bao's grin grew wider.

"No," he agreed, "that's true. You left a guard unconscious and stole an invaluable experimental ship. Of course, that was after you went against our direct orders."

"To be fair"—Kal held up a finger—"we'd brought the ship."

The Ancient shook his head and waved at Section Chief Chin. "Chief, you may leave. I will notify you if you are needed."

Chin nodded and stepped back through the door, keeping her eyes trained on Kal and Nicole.

A small set of chairs surrounding a serving table was in the corner of the room. A steaming pitcher of coffee—Nicole guessed based on the smell—sat on the table with several empty mugs.

As Nicole and Kal sat down, the Ancient strode to the table and poured three cups of coffee which he offered to them, giving a small nod of his head as he placed it in their hands. It was a gesture that reminded Nicole of some of the ancient Asian cultures. Though it could have been a Jadid ceremony just as easily.

"So…you lit a powder keg when you begged for our help," Bao said. Although Human, the Ancient spoke in the archaic dialect that the Jadid and Nasi used. Since it was in Human Standard, Nicole's implant did not translate for her. She heard the Ancient's formal speech through her own ears.

In order to avoid them being destroyed, Bowen had taken Kal and Karl to Altterra, the Jadid home world. Of course, Karl had been his normal impetuous self and done everything the Jadid had told them not to. That included leaving the secure compound of the Ancients and walking into a public square. Seeing Humans, the Jadid's almost mythical ancestors, had sent shock waves through their society. Later, as the Ancients attempted to quell the unrest, Karl had continued to defy their commands and pleaded for Jadid assistance in fighting the Nasi.

To see that your long-lost ancestors were not only alive but fighting for survival against your own people must have had a deep impact on the Jadid. Bao Wang's presence in their universe certainly indicated there were major changes going on among them.

"It worked though," Nicole said. "You're here after all."

Bao's mouth curled slightly as he turned to look at her. "Not quite. It created the largest crisis our people have seen since we left Earth. It resulted in unrest and divisiveness."

"So why are you here?" Kal asked. Nicole sensed the frustrated tinge in his voice.

Bao took a languorous sip of his coffee. "When the Nasi distanced themselves from the Jadid, we were not surprised.

18

Esma was always focused, laser-like, on her goals. We maintained a balance over the past decades; the Nasi pursued their goals, and we let them." He spread his arms. "Thus, peace is maintained."

Esma Baykara had created the Nasi so that the Jadid could return to Humanity's universe. She'd been an Ancient—maybe she still was—but unlike the others, had never been able to accept their fate.

Nicole wanted to point out that the Nasi had kidnapped several top Jadid scientists, including Bowen, but held her tongue. The Ancient clearly knew his description of their situation wasn't true, otherwise, why would he be talking to them?

"What exactly happened after our people left Altterra?" Nicole asked.

"At first? Chaos." Bao held his hands out on either side of his body. "Our people were divided into two camps, those that wanted to leave the entire situation alone and those that were eager to help in any way possible." He put his hands down. "Your visit set things into motion. Big things. I don't know where they will take us."

"What about you Ancient Wang?" Kal asked. "What do you think?"

"I'm," he hesitated, "undecided. I don't harbor the animosity toward Humanity that some of the other Ancients do. But I don't trust you either. Humanity left us to rot. And you quickly broke your vows to remain silent when on Altterra."

"Fair," Nicole admitted begrudgingly. She didn't trust

19

her fellow Humans that much either. But she trusted them more than the Nasi. "But you're here."

Bao nodded, his eyebrow raised. "Officially, I am here only to observe. The Council of Ancients felt we needed our own eyes and ears here to see what exactly was going on." He let out a low sigh. "Unofficially, I can't help but do more. I do not feel I can remain on the sidelines while the Nasi commit atrocities. At some point, our inaction becomes culpability."

"Do others feel this way?" Kal asked.

"Yes. But," he leaned forward conspiratorially, "I am the only one who can help. The same divide that separates our people separates the Council too. We will see where the others land. But I am here right now."

Nicole tried to quell her excitement over these words. The Jadid were powerful, perhaps more powerful than the Nasi. They were also indecisive and reluctant to act against their own people. She doubted Samsara Fleet could rely on anything more than Ancient Wang's small fleet.

Bao seemed to read her thoughts. "We cannot provide much help—at least not at first. My fleet of three destroyers cannot stand against what the Nasi have brought here. Our weapons and systems don't work in this universe anyway. However, we can provide some cover and help you understand the Nasi and their tactics."

The Jadid's universe operated on a different set of principles. In addition to transforming the Jadid's physiology, it meant that many things that worked in one universe would not work in the other.

Kal studied his coffee mug intently as he rotated it in his hands. Finally he sighed. "I'm not sure what we can do with you. I'll be honest, we need something big if we're going to survive this war. The Nasi fleet outnumbers us eight to one and they have the technical edge as well."

"Perhaps we should see this as an opportunity to further our relationship with the Jadid," Nicole offered. "We can use this as an opportunity to normalize relations. Through our work together we can make them invested in this fight."

Kal raised an eyebrow. She knew his doubts about the Jadid.

"Honestly, Kal," she said, "we need the support of the Council and the Jadid. It's the only way we'll survive."

"I've been thinking about that." Bao got up and stood behind his chair. "We need some way to travel between the two universes. A steady line of communication. We need another one of those experimental ships."

He was referring to the *Park*, the experimental skip ship the Skulls had stolen from a Nasi facility on Patagonia. Skip ships were the only ones that could routinely fold between Humanity's universe and the Jadid's. There were other ways to travel between the universes: through one-time-use fold drives or the gateways the Nasi had built. But both were out of the question for Samsara Fleet. If they could get a few of those small ships, they could establish regular relations with the Jadid and seek out their help.

"That's a tall order," Kal said. A picture of Kal's agonized face, covered in the blood of a Jadid soldier, flashed through Nicole's mind. It had cost them so much to get the first ship.

Bao leaned over his seat and nodded. "I am sure it is. But I don't see another option. I would bet my next meal there are other experimental ships on Patagonia." He gestured around the room. "Also, we can assist you in getting through the Nasi perimeter. My fleet may not face the Nasi directly. But we can still aid you."

"You mentioned that before," Kal said. "What kind of help?"

"This fleet contains four cutting-edge destroyers. We also have intimate knowledge of the personnel, equipment, and tactics of the Nasi." Bao raised a fist. "We can get you into and out of any Nasi controlled area quickly. Also, we can act as scouts and report back on the location and strength of the Nasi fleet."

Nicole and Kal fell silent. He was right. They could help them, but Bao himself felt as slippery as an eel. There was something amiss, a subtext Nicole could not decipher. An itch she wanted to scratch but couldn't.

"They're going to know you're helping us." Kal raised his head to meet Bao's gaze.

The Ancient smiled and gave an uncharacteristic wink. "Yes, they will. But they won't be able to prove it." He walked next to the Human officer. "And more importantly, neither will the Council."

"Plausible deniability," Nicole said. Bao pointed at her but kept his eyes on Kal.

"Which is why we have to meet in person," she continued. "There's no record of this conversation."

"Bingo," Bao replied to both Kal and Nicole's confusion. It must be an ancient Human word; from its context, it must mean agreement.

The itch came back. There was more going on here than Bao was letting on. As they learned more, they learned how little they fully understood. The last six months had been a struggle for survival. If they wanted to do more than survive and win, Samsara Fleet would have to operate in two universes where they were a piece on a chessboard, being maneuvered by mysterious powers.

Although the Ancients had been Humans, Nicole didn't think that was an accurate description anymore. They were hundreds of years old and had been through more than she could imagine. In some ways, they were even less Human than their offspring, the Jadid and Nasi. Ultimately, she knew they had little choice. They had to trust Ancient Wang.

"We'll need our fleet commander, General Samaha, to hear your proposal," Kal said. "We can't do anything without her."

Wang nodded in agreement.

❖

General Samaha leaned back in her chair and eyed Kal and Nicole. The meeting with Ancient Wang on the *Galaxy's Edge* had gone about as well as Kal could have expected. He'd met General Samaha's fiery demands for help with the same cool demeanor he had shown Kal and Nicole. Samaha was too professional to let her frustration be plainly visible, but Kal knew her well enough to tell.

In the end, they had agreed upon a plan. The Skulls would travel with Wang's fleet to Patagonia. There they would infiltrate the planet and attempt to retrieve another experimental skip ship. Failing that, they would try to steal the schematics so their engineers could build one of their own. Then they would rendezvous with the fleet within Nasi space.

Samaha let out a long breath, and Kal could almost see the tension leave her body. She cracked her knuckles absentmindedly as she stared at the stars displayed on the room's viewscreen. They sat in one of the briefing rooms of her flagship, the *Gedorhan's Return*. It was a Tounous ship, and the cabins and features were uncomfortably foreign for a Human. The room was oval-shaped with benches lining every wall and viewscreens placed above them. Kal, Nicole, and Samaha sat on the benches facing each other as they talked.

"You know, I was about to retire," Samaha said to no one in particular. "Two days before Earth was destroyed, I told my commanding officer I was done. My husband and I had bought a farm on Earth, outside of Sao Paulo. We were going to grow coffee." She gave a chuckle. "We knew nothing about it. Our kids thought we were nuts. They were probably right." Her voice trailed off.

After a moment, the general turned to look at Kal. "What do you think? There's something about Bao Wang I can't place my finger on."

"Doesn't matter," Kal replied. "When you're stuck in a cave, you'll grab any light you can even if it's a Zrygle." Zrygle were small but extremely venomous creatures native to Kal's home planet of Mariga. They lived inside small ice caves feeding off the algae.

Samaha steepled her hands as she chewed on Kal's words.

"General," Nicole said, "I agree. There's something off about Ancient Wang. But I think — at least for now — our interests are aligned."

"Yes. But I wonder what he'll do if they are no longer aligned." It was the same thought they all had. "Either way, this is our best option. But the fleet is not going to just sit around and wait for your return, General Norman."

Samaha told them that while the Skulls infiltrated Patagonia, Samsara Fleet would travel to the Z'Ta home world of T'kor'nuk in the H'Far system to enlist their help. The Z'Ta were a relatively peaceful species, but the naked aggression of the Nasi had to have them worried. It was clear the Nasi would continue to expand beyond the systems they already controlled. And the Z'Ta were in their way.

"General Norman, your team will be away from the fleet and any help for a long time," Samaha said.

"True, but that's why we're here," Kal replied. "I am prepared. Colonel Bergeron and I both are." Nicole nodded in agreement.

Samaha looked away for a moment. "About that," she said, "I am afraid we will need Colonel Bergeron for another mission."

Nicole's hand stopped over the tablet she had been manipulating. "Ma'am?"

"I'm sorry," Samaha said, "but I need your diplomatic

skills with me."

Kal started to speak, but Nicole cut him off with a wave of her hand. "Ma'am, I've been with the Skulls since this war began. You commissioned me to serve as their commanding officer when General Norman was missing in action—"

"Yes, I commissioned you to take over for Colonel Norman when we thought we'd lost him," the general agreed. "He's back though. As a former attaché, you have skills we need." She raised her hand. "It's not something I'm going to discuss. This war's bigger than any of us. You joined the fleet as a civilian and I commissioned you. You're no longer a civilian. This is an order."

"Understood." There wasn't anything else she could say.

Kal had over twenty years experience as an officer in the Earth Defense Force, the military that had supported the UEG before the Nasi destroyed them both. He knew that General Samaha was right. The mission always came first. In stories and holos, the heroes got to choose their battles. In real life, they were lucky if they got to choose how they would fight it.

Samaha awkwardly patted Nicole's shoulder. "If it makes you feel any better, this is a detail. I'm not reassigning you. You'll rejoin your unit when it's said and done."

Kal tried to make light of it. "You won't be missing anything anyway," he said. "We've already been to Patagonia. It won't have changed much." He hoped he was right but doubted it. He hated that planet.

❖

"So they're taking Colonel Bergeron from us?" Sergeant Ekon Kimathi asked. "They can't do that."

"They didn't do anything, Ekon," Nicole said. "General Samaha ordered me to assist her in establishing relations with the Z'Ta." Although Nicole was now an officer, she still routinely used soldiers' first names. She'd been diplomatically told by Sergeant First Class Jones that it wasn't proper etiquette for an officer, but she'd been using their first names for so long it was hard to change now.

"That doesn't make any sense, ma'am," Ekon said. "You've got more combat experience against the Nasi than almost anyone in the fleet."

"It makes a helluva lotta sense," Sergeant First Class Asif Jones interrupted. He fixed Ekon with one of his trademark glares. "Colonel Bergeron knows more about diplomacy and foreign relations than almost anyone in the fleet. If we can get the Z'Ta to join with us, it could change the war."

Nicole held up her hand. "Look, I want to stay with the team as well. But I've been part of Samsara Fleet long enough to know that what we want usually doesn't matter. I've got to go where I can make a difference."

"Truly inspiring, ma'am," Major Karl Garcia said, wiping away invisible tears. "I think I speak for all of us when I say dibs on your cabin."

"You sound inspired, Major Garcia," Kal deadpanned.

"I try, sir. I try." Garcia finished the beer in his hand.

Private First Class Sandra Chedjou stood up. "Anyone want anything to drink? Damn bots are takin' too long."

Nine of the ten members of the Skulls sat together at a

table in the *Ofira's* lounge. Their junior pilot, Lieutenant Hitesh Sampson, had declined the invitation. The Skulls was not their full name. Their unofficial *full* name was actually Not Norman's Numbskulls, a result of Sergeant Jones's desire to taunt Kal. Through a combination of luck, bad timing, and skill, they had become the most decorated reconnaissance team in the fleet. Their reputation had been hard earned, paid for by the loss of many of their comrades.

"Taisha, what about you?" Nicole asked.

Chief Taisha Kanumba was Nicole's best friend. Over the past several months, the two of them had grown close. However, the recent death of Taisha's fiancé, Captain Jae-Ho Park, had strained that relationship. Nicole tried to be there for her friend, but she knew Taisha was in a place where she couldn't follow.

The chief simply shook her head. She'd been slowly drinking her beer all night, holding the glass in her hand and staring at it between sips. She'd been even more distant than usual lately. Nicole felt she was punishing herself for her lover's death.

"Ma'am, what's the Jadid ship like?" asked Private Frederick Kinawadi.

"It's the same as the Nasi ships," Nicole replied. Then she realized that the young private hadn't been on a Nasi ship. As the youngest and second-most junior person on the team, he hadn't experienced the joys of fighting through a Nasi base. "The Nasi ships, they're...organic. Look almost as if they'd been grown in a lab. They take a bit of time to get used to."

The young soldier looked back at her blankly as if he were waiting for her to continue.

"You just have to see it," Ekon said, patting him on the back. "Don't worry, we'll be on it soon enough."

"True," agreed Kal as he drained his glass, "we'll be heading out in less than twenty-four hours." He turned to Taisha. "Any word on our new ship, Chief?" The Skulls' first ship, the *Oruc*, had been destroyed, like the one before it, by enemy fire. They had used another scout corvette called the *Keying* on their last mission, but Samaha had mentioned she had a new state-of-the art scout ship lined up for them.

Taisha looked up from her glass. "Yes, sir. The *Ofira's* tech crew has been working on a heavily modified reconnaissance vessel for us." She inclined her head toward Bowen. "It's the most advanced ship in the fleet, thanks to Bo's help." Several of the Skulls had started to call the Jadid by the nickname that Karl had given him, and the erudite scientist didn't seem to mind. In fact, he seemed to relish the new name.

Bowen was an expert in fold drive and interstellar technology. He had been working with Samsara Fleet's technicians prior to their attack on the Nasi fleet at the Torgham home world, Geerlok. Nicole guessed he was the most knowledgeable scientist in the galaxy, considering he was the top Jadid expert.

"I've examined the ship myself," Bowen added. "It—she—is advanced by even Jadid standards."

"I've checked her out too, sir." Karl whistled. "She's a beauty."

"Can't wait to see her for myself," Kal said. "If she's half the ship the *Oruc* was, we'll be set."

Nicole had come to understand why soldiers and pilots referred to their ships as people. The *Oruc* was like a friend who had passed away. The time they had spent on the ship bonded them as a team and, in many ways, saved her from herself. During those long months, she had learned to accept the part she played in the Nasi's attack. She knew it was juvenile, but she couldn't help missing the ship.

"It still won't be the same as the *Oruc*," Ekon said, echoing her thoughts.

Kal nodded. "True, but we'll get used to her. Besides, any advantage we can use in this war is needed."

The group fell silent and looked around the lounge. As they sat, Nicole's mind drifted to her mission. It would be hard to be separated from these people. She thought of them as a second family, her only family now that her parents and sister were dead. Her hand lingered on the starfish pendant around her neck, her reminder of a life that she had lost on Earth.

"Make sure you save me a bunk," she said to no one in particular.

"Of course, ma'am," Sergeant Jones replied. "We'll have it ready and waiting."

Their impending missions hovered over the group like a cloak, but through an unspoken agreement, they spent the rest of the night talking about other things: what they would do when the war was over, their home planets, funny stories about the people they had lost.

Several hours later, Kal and Nicole walked back to the stateroom they shared and enjoyed a last night together. The mission would be there when they woke.

❖

Kal whistled. "You weren't lying, Bo. This thing is a beauty."

Kal walked around the perimeter of the *Salamis*. He wanted to get one last look before heading back to his stateroom. Like the *Keying* and *Oruc*, the ship was a scout corvette, roughly fifty meters long. However, the *Salamis* had an almost predatory look the other ships had lacked. The slate gray ship had been modified so its wings swept forward with two deadly-looking plasma cannons perched on the tip of each wing.

Nacelles, containing the most advanced technology ever possessed by Humanity, dotted the ship's exterior. Bo led Kal and the flight team comprising Major Garcia, Lieutenant Sampson, and Chief Kanumba through the ship, going over the new features the maintenance techs had added. It was loaded with the best of Human, Tounous, and Kurz technology along with even more advanced technology that had been reverse engineered from Nasi wreckage or provided by Bo.

The interior layout was like their previous ships: rear cargo bay, bunks, and galley on the bottom level. The cockpit, two staterooms, and three cabins were situated on the top. Despite the familiar layout, almost every piece of equipment inside the ship was different. Even the battle suits that the Tac-1 squad used for missions were brand new. As they wandered through the ship's interior, Bo called out the various upgrades the engineers had made: advanced cloaking, upgraded fold computer, enhanced battle suits. The list went on and on.

Kal had been particularly interested in a new device called an optical screen. It not only allowed them to cloak the ship but transformed its appearance and sensor print. They would be able to make the *Salamis* appear to be a small transport ship or a large destroyer.

"Nice," Lieutenant Sampson said. "Finally we get some decent equipment."

"It's amazing," Kanumba said. She ran her hand along a nacelle on the ship's hull. "Bo, you did well."

"Really well," Garcia added, patting the Jadid on the back.

The violet hue of Bowen's cheeks darkened as he looked at the bay floor. "Thank you." Two weeks ago, Kal wouldn't have thought the taciturn scientist could feel embarrassed.

Sampson gestured toward the maintenance workers scurrying around the bay, refueling and repairing the host of ships in the fleet. "I'd say *our* engineers deserve the bulk of our gratitude, sir. They made this all happen. They actually built it."

"They did," Garcia admitted, "but Bo was the brains behind it."

Lieutenant Sampson screwed up his mouth and turned to look back inside the ship's bay. The door was open, allowing them to see the battle suits in their charging cradles lining the walls of the bay. Kal had made a special request to add enough suits so that every person on board would have one. On most Human ships, there were only enough suits for the Tac-I, the Tactical Insertion, squad members.

Tactical Insertion soldiers were the "elite of the elite". Before the Nasi had invaded and destroyed the EDF, Tac-I soldiers were required to go through some of the most difficult training in the fleet to become one of them. They had to be experts in hand-to-hand combat, battle suits, search and rescue, and a host of other things. Now, under Samsara Fleet, they were the soldiers that had proven themselves in combat.

"That one, he's got a chip on his shoulder for sure," Kanumba looked at Sampson and whispered so low that Kal almost didn't hear her.

"Well, I think we all do," Kal said philosophically.

"Maybe, sir. But I see one of three things happening: he gets killed, gets us killed, or he somehow figures out a way to change."

"Let's hope it's the last one," Kal said. "We've already seen too many people die." He thought of Captain Jae-Ho Park, Chief Kanumba's fiancé. One of the many people they'd already lost.

It was almost certain they would lose more.

Chapter Three

"Sir, we're ready to go," Garcia said as he finished the preflight checks.

The cockpit of the *Salamis* was almost identical to the other scout corvettes Kal had been in; a large viewscreen dominated the front bulkhead with small control screens for the pilot and co-pilot extending beneath. Behind their chairs was the ship's engineering station, where Chief Kanumba sat. She faced sideways and had a viewscreen of her own which she used to manage power levels, shields, and other systems. Kal sat in the back in the commander's chair, complete with a small terminal for his personal use.

"Do it," Kal instructed.

He watched through the front viewscreen as the ship slowly rose in the bay and floated toward the *Ofira's* bay door. Outside the open door, Kal saw clusters of stars tinged a bluish-green color by the force field that kept in the ship's atmosphere.

The image looked so real Kal almost forgot the screen was a live feed from a camera on the ship's hull.

When they arrived in the landing bay of the *Galaxy's Edge*, a small contingent of Jadid was waiting for them. As Kal stepped off the cargo ramp, he saw that Section Chief Chin was at the head of the group.

"General Norman, we are pleased to have you on board." Chin gave Kal the same two-fisted salute she had before. "I will take you to the Leader's Deck, where you will have your own stateroom. The rest of your crew will be housed in cabins on the Crew's Deck with our lower-ranking officers."

"I'll stay with my crew," Kal said.

Chin had already started turning around, but she stopped as she registered Kal's words. He saw emotion, probably annoyance, flicker across her face for a moment. "That is...irregular," she intoned.

"Maybe, but we'll be staying together," Kal replied. "At least for now."

"You do not trust us." Chin's words came out as a mixture between a statement and a question.

"Yes, that's true," Bowen replied as he strode down the *Salamis's* ramp. "We are also a team and dislike being separated from one another during missions; it causes anxiety. I would venture to guess that you do not trust us either."

Chin stood motionless for a moment, seeming to measure each of Bowen's words. "Interesting. Interesting." Kal could sense her confusion.

"Yup, a t-e-a-m, team." Garcia added, standing next to his Jadid friend.

"Very well. We will wait for the rest of your—team—and lead you to the Crew's Deck."

Several minutes later, the Skulls were being led through the eerily dim corridors and lifts of the *Galaxy's Edge*. The strange twists and turns, the weird lighting emanating from the walls, and the meandering path of the corridor made Kal feel like he was in a spider's web. The silence of their Jadid companions did not help.

They finally arrived in front of a grouping of oblong

doors. As they approached, Chin manipulated her wrist computer and the four doors dilated open simultaneously.

"Apologies, but we have only these four cabins prepared." Chin said. "General Norman, we will have another bunk brought for you."

Kal thanked the section chief, and the Skulls divided themselves among the four rooms. As Kal walked into the cabin he was to share with Garcia and Jones, he was impressed by how large it was. It was easily three to four times the size of his stateroom on the *Salamis*. Two bunks lay near the irregularly shaped back wall, and there was a small sitting area with four chairs and a table in the middle of the room. The furniture had clearly been fabricated just for them; it was too compact, too Human-looking, to be used by Jadid.

The group dropped their jump bags and inspected their rooms. There wasn't much else to look at though. By unspoken agreement, they gathered in Kal's cabin to talk.

"Did you activate the security protocols on the *Salamis*?" he asked.

"Yes, sir," Kanumba replied. "It would be secure against any species I know of in *this* universe. But the Jadid still may be able to hack it."

"I've added some upgrades to the system," Bowen added. "It would require some effort for them to infiltrate. I also upgraded the tamper alarms; we should receive an alert if they try."

"Sir, any chance you'll reconsider my offer?" Sergeant Jones asked. He wanted to have one of his soldiers on the ship at all times. Kal had decided against it; it sent the wrong message.

"Still no. Our mission is to recover another skip ship. But we also need to bring these Jadid over to our side. To have them sympathize with what we're going through. The only way to do that is to talk with them. Learn about them and have them learn about us. That may be even more important than the skip ship in the long run."

"Sir, if I may," Bowen interjected.

"We Jadid had only heard about Humans in the tales told to us by the Ancients," he said after Kal gave him a nod. "You are a great curiosity to us, a part of our past that we can now see before our own eyes. There is a," he paused for a moment, "connection I feel to you. One that I wouldn't have expected."

"You like us, moron." Garcia slapped the Jadid on the back.

"Maybe. But I think the general is even more correct than he realizes. I think we are drawn to you Humans."

There was a momentary pause as the group considered Bowen's words. It was one of the longest speeches Kal had ever heard from him that didn't revolve around scientific theory.

"Well," he broke the silence, "you heard the man. Get out there and make friends."

They'd been folding for three days towards Patagonia and the voyage was relatively uneventful, and they still had a little over two days until they reached the planet. The journey would have taken a Human fleet a week, but the Jadid had more efficient fold computers calibrating their drives.

The fold drive was perhaps the greatest invention in the history of Humanity and perhaps the universe. Theoretically, ships could fold to anywhere in space, but trying to fold too far increased the risk the ship would implode or appear in the middle of an asteroid field. To adjust for this, ships strung hundreds or thousands of folds together to travel between systems. The ship's fold computers calculated the proper power and direction for a ship to fold as well as automatically plotting their course. Fold drives were also limited by gravitational fields. If a ship tried to fold too close to another ship or planet, they risked implosion. The fold computer helped calculate where ships could fold from. The better your computer, the less likely you were to die and the farther you could travel with each fold.

Kal was sitting in his bunk in the Jadid stateroom reading a novel via his implant. He always had a few stored there for times like these. Sometimes a soldier's job was to wait. It still felt odd to be in the alien room, but he wasn't about to retreat to the comfort of the *Salamis* like Private Chedjou and Lieutenant Sampson. He had to lead by example even if he felt like he was continually being watched.

"Sir, you got a moment?" Garcia asked, standing in the doorway.

He was the one person in their group who had shown no discomfort at being on the Jadid ship. A natural extrovert, Garcia walked around the ship trying to engage the Jadid soldiers. So far, he had been met with either cold indifference or almost naked hostility. The rest of them had given up and stayed in their rooms or on the *Salamis*.

"Sure." Kal sat up. "What's on your mind?"

"I've been thinking about the mission," Garcia said as he sat down on his own bunk. "Sir, we barely—*barely*—made it off that planet alive last time." Kal's mind flashed back to Captain Park, to the young pilot's lifeless body prone on the ground, blood staining the area around him. "This time it's going to be worse. We've got a better ship and we've got that Jadid fleet to help us get onto the planet, but that won't do us a helluva lot of good when we're by ourselves."

"What are you saying?"

"We'll need everything we can get to help us. You know that I've got contacts. They might not live up to the moral standards of the EDF or Samsara Fleet, but they can help us."

"Your family," Kal said. Every planet had at least one syndicate, a criminal organization that dealt in drugs and other contraband. Major Garcia's family was one of the largest syndicates on Patagonia. Garcia had fled that life and joined the EDF to become a pilot. Kal doubted he'd ever thought he would have to return home.

"Yes, sir. My contacts, my family, can help. But we'll be operating in a moral gray zone." He ran his hand through his thick black hair. "How badly do you want us to find this ship?"

Kal paused. Before the Nasi had attacked and he rejoined the EDF and then Samsara Fleet, he had been a merchant, taking contracts and using the profits for drugs and alcohol. He'd lived in that gray zone for a decade. He wasn't

39

sure how he felt about reentering it, but it was a resource, and they couldn't waste it.

"We'll do what we have to," Kal said. Morals were increasingly becoming a luxury.

Garcia bowed his head. "I know that you have some contacts as well. From before."

Garcia was referring to Kal's work with the Alliance, a clandestine criminal organization that had its tendrils in almost every planet and station in this part of the galaxy. The syndicates operated on a planetary level, but the Alliance stretched across planets. No one knew how big it was or who ran it, but it had controlled the interstellar criminal trade before the Nasi came. When Kal had been an independent merchant, he'd done some work for them, transporting contraband. The Nasi had targeted the organization—most likely because they saw it as a threat to their control—and destroyed many of their fronts.

"I do." Kal admitted. "I don't know if they're still around, but we should check it out."

"Have you been able to meet with Ancient Wang yet?"

Kal shook his head. He had asked to speak with the Jadid Ancient several times but had been rebuffed each time. Section Chief Chin and the other Jadid officers on the ship were also unwilling to talk to them. They were cargo, just something the fleet was transporting.

"They almost seem scared of us," Garcia said. "But I've got some wonderful material. I even got Bo to smile once. But they just scurry away before I can get going."

"No one can resist your charms forever, Major Garcia."

Kal smiled. "Just stick at it."

"I could use a wingman, sir." The pilot eyed Kal hopefully. "I was thinking of going up to the Leader's Deck. Maybe check out the bridge." The Jadid organized their ships into various zones they called decks. The Leader's Deck contained the senior ranking officers' quarters, bridge, and high-level conference rooms.

"You don't need me."

"I think it would be good for the group, sir. The soldiers see you sitting in here. Makes them nervous too. They need to see you taking charge and trying to build the relationship."

Kal felt heat in his face. Of course Garcia was right. He'd been derelict in his duty. It shouldn't be Garcia walking the hallways and trying to talk with the Jadid. It should be him. As the senior officer, he should talk with every single senior Jadid officer aboard.

"Damn, you're right." Kal stood up. "Let's go."

"Excellent. I've been working on a few routines that you can borrow."

The Jadid had been partially successful at integrating the Humans' neural implants with the *Galaxy Edge's* net. The Skulls were able to pull up ship maps, access ship-wide communication, and operate the doors and lifts. With the aid of the ship's map and lifts, it didn't take long for Kal and Garcia to make their way to the Leader's Deck.

As they walked through the twisted corridors. they

passed several Jadid soldiers, never in groups, striding past them. Each time, Garcia called out a greeting, startling them, then chuckled to himself. The Jadid soldiers all wore the same tight-fitting uniform, which covered their torso from their ankles to wrists. The only differences were the colors and the insignias on the collars.

"General Norman. What are you doing here?" Kal and Garcia stopped as a Jadid stepped away from the wall and planted himself in front of them. According to the map in their implants, the ship's bridge was on the other side of that door. The soldier was short for a Jadid, almost Kal's height, and his uniform was a deep blue color. He had a silver insignia with four intersecting lines on his collar.

"I came to see the bridge and meet my fellow officers," Kal replied, ignoring the rude tone. He'd dealt with enough species to understand that niceties were not universal.

The Jadid looked down, tapped on his wrist computer a few times, and then looked Kal in the eyes.

"Very well," he said. "Please proceed." He stepped aside to let the two Humans pass.

"Thank you." Garcia had a grin plastered on his face as he held out his hand. "I'm Major Karl Garcia, pleased to meetcha." The greeting was corny, over-the-top. Kal guessed intentionally so.

The soldier regarded Karl's hand without moving.

"What's your name?" Garcia maintained the same overeager grin.

After a pause, the Jadid replied, "I am Senior Soldier Asger Weber." He abruptly mirrored Garcia's idiotic grin. He looked like a child trying on their parents' clothes; the smile was ill-fitting and seemed almost predatory. A shiver went down Kal's spine.

Garcia didn't miss a beat. He grabbed the Jadid's hand and pumped vigorously. "Pleased to meetcha. We'll talk to you later."

Asger remained frozen for a moment, the smile fixed on his face. Abruptly, he reverted to the same neutral expression and strode down the hallway, away from the bridge.

"Still got it." Garcia whistled. He extended his hand toward the door to the bridge. "Shall we, sir?"

As they approached the bridge, the door opened. The room was small for a vessel of this size, perhaps half the size of a similar bridge on a Human ship. The far wall, where there should be a large viewscreen, was empty. Workstations were clustered together in groups of four, the backs of their viewscreens touching each other. The Jadid in the room stood behind their stations in a quasi-sort of attention while what Kal assumed was their commander stood in the immediate center of the room. With the dim light emanating from the fibrous walls and lack of monitors, the room seemed lifeless, a far cry from the action and bustle Kal had seen on most bridges.

"General Norman, welcome to the bridge. I am Section Chief Tyra Washington." She gave a Jadid salute, fists across her chest.

"At least one of them has some manners," Garcia whispered.

"Thank you for having us on board." Kal raised his open

hand to his forehead, returning with the standard Samsara Fleet salute. "You don't need to stop what you're doing on our account. We'd love to learn more about how your staff operates. If we're going to be working together, we each need to learn more about each other."

The officer gestured toward a door to the side of the bridge. "I will be happy to brief you on our procedures. Follow me."

She walked through the door. Kal and Garcia had little choice but to follow. On the other side was a small conference room, probably used for quick operations meetings during flight. Human ships often had this same type of operations briefing room.

Ten chairs were arranged in a semi-circle in the middle of the room. Washington tapped on her wrist computer as they sat down, and the wall they were facing suddenly turned black and a three-dimensional model of the ship appeared. The section chief immediately dove into a monotonous lecture on the capabilities and structure of the ship. While she talked, she used her wrist computer to manipulate the model in the viewscreen, highlighting various subsystems and areas.

After five minutes, Kal wished he were anywhere but in that small briefing room. Washington immediately cut off questions from her audience and continued along with the same dry tone for over an hour. When she finished, she suggested they return to their cabins. Kal desperately wanted to but remembered his conversation with Garcia. They needed to understand the Jadid better.

"Thank you for that…comprehensive overview of *the*

Galaxy's Edge." He tried to look sincere. "We'd like to stay on the bridge with you to better understand how your crew operates such a fine vessel."

"*I* am interested in understanding how you process 1,919 kilograms of feces every twenty-four hours." Garcia sat forward in his chair with a broad smile.

"Absolutely. I will have one of my officers give you an in-depth briefing on our waste recycling facilities," Washington replied, oblivious of the joke.

Garcia's smile faded.

"Maybe later," Kal said. "For now, we'd like to observe the bridge."

"I am sorry. That will not be possible." Without another word, the Jadid officer opened the door to the bridge and stepped through. The soldiers were all standing at attention behind their consoles, exactly as they had been when Kal entered the briefing room.

Without a choice, the two Humans left the bridge and began to walk back to their cabins on the Crew's Deck. Garcia had given up on trying to engage the Jadid they passed.

"They don't seem to trust us," Garcia observed as he flopped down on his bunk.

"Well, we don't really trust them either." Kal rubbed his fingers thoughtfully, "Perhaps we're going about this wrong."

"How so, sir?"

"Rather than trying to befriend the entire crew, we should focus on a few people. We need to build their trust and break down the barriers. Have each person on the team pair up with one of the Jadid and do their best to ingratiate

45

themselves."

"Bug the hell out of them?"

"Essentially...yes."

There was a small tone indicating someone was outside their door. Kal used his implant to open it. An especially lanky Jadid soldier wearing a yellow uniform stood on the other side.

"Major Garcia?" she asked. Garcia raised his hand. "I've secured a briefing room for us. Section Chief Washington asked me to give you an in-depth briefing on how we recycle fecal matter. Please follow me."

Garcia stood up from the bed and trudged through the doorway, giving Kal a look of pure misery.

❖

"Glad we're able to finally meet," Kal said as he held the warm cup of tea in his hand. He mostly succeeded in keeping the annoyance out of his voice. The Ancient had put him off for almost the entire journey.

Kal was sitting in Ancient Wang's office with the Ancient across from him, calmly sipping his own drink. The *Galaxy's Edge* was twelve hours out from Patagonia and Wang had summoned him, saying they needed to "confer prior to their arrival."

After the debacle that was their tour of the bridge, Kal had tasked each member of the crew to concentrate on making friends with one member of the Jadid crew. They'd tried their best to pair up by rank and position, selecting whichever Jadid officer or soldier would be most equivalent to their own.

Kal had struggled to establish some rapport with the ship's commander, Ship Chief Kevin Yoshida. The commander refused to talk to Kal for more than a sentence, always finding an excuse to shut a door in his face or walk away. The other members of the Skulls had mixed results. Private Sandra Chedjou had been the most successful; she'd even had a few meals with the Jadid soldier she had been paired with.

"Sure, no problem, Kal." He turned his head. "It's okay if I call you Kal, right?"

"Of course, Bao," Kal said with a forced smile.

"We'll be arriving at Patagonia soon," Bao began. "Based on our intel, we expect to see a sizable fleet there. We'll be able to get close to the planet, but you will need to get yourselves onto the surface."

Kal nodded. "We have an optical screen, so it should be no problem."

"As soon as you leave this ship, there can be no communication. The situation with the Nasi is tense. If you have to escape immediately, you'll have a couple of days. After that, it's up to you to get to the rendezvous point in time."

While the Skulls were on Patagonia and Samsara Fleet was at T'kor'nuk, Ancient Wang's fleet would travel to each of the known Nasi controlled worlds. Ostensibly, they were there to report back to the Ancients what was happening. However, they would also track the Nasi fleet disposition. The Nasi had just brought in reinforcements, tripling the size of their fleet, and Samsara Fleet did not know where the new ships were.

"Understood. Basically, we're on our own."

"Sorry, but yes." Wang leaned back in his chair and took a deep breath. "Tell me, what do you think of my children, the Jadid?"

Kal cleared his throat. "They're efficient. You can tell that they care about you, about the Ancients, and their fellow Jadid. I'm astounded by their intelligence." He hesitated to say anything more revealing.

Wang made a waving motion. "Yes, yes. That results from spending centuries in a universe that seems hell-bent on killing you. I've always felt we lost something though. We—us Ancients that is—did everything we could to survive. We instilled that same focus and determination in our children." He sighed. "We could have done a better job at teaching them *why* they should survive."

Kal looked the man in the eyes. "That's not something you can teach. How do you teach happiness or joy? People have to see it to understand."

Wang shrugged. "You're probably right. Maybe that's why they are so drawn to you Humans. We taught them how to live, and you're showing them *why* they live."

"I like that," Kal said with a smile; this time it was genuine.

A shadow passed across Wang's face but left almost as soon as it had come. As he looked at Kal, the soldier realized just how old the Ancient was; generations had come and gone during his life.

"As do I."

Chapter Four

"*Salamis*, you are cleared to depart." The Jadid's voice gave Kal a jolt. They'd been waiting almost an hour to receive clearance to leave the *Galaxy's Edge*. The Jadid refused to patch their sensors and communications into the *Salamis*, so the Skulls sat in the dimly lit Landing Deck waiting for clearance with their engines fully spun up. They didn't know what the Jadid and Nasi fleets were discussing nor what they would find when they entered Patagonia.

"Roger." Kanumba closed the line. From now on, they were on their own.

No one spoke while they waited for word from the flight crew. It had only been a few weeks since they were last in the Patagonian system. Last time they'd been there, Samsara Fleet had entered the system expecting to find a small Nasi presence, only to discover seventeen Nasi capital ships. They'd barely made it out alive. Prior to that, they had lost Kanumba's fiancé, Captain Park, while conducting a reconnaissance mission on the planet. No one was looking forward to returning; Patagonia was bad luck.

The scout corvette lifted off the deck and rapidly launched out of the bay. In front of them was the planet's bright blue ocean, striated with feathery white clouds; its single land mass was on the opposite side.

"Cloak up?" Garcia asked.

"Cloak up." Kanumba confirmed. The cloak *should* prevent them from being noticed by the Nasi. Unfortunately, they'd had trouble before with the optical cloak. It didn't fool the Nasi for long, but it was better than nothing.

They descended at a shallow trajectory. If the cloak failed and they showed up on the Nasi sensors, it would be harder to discern them from the many satellites orbiting the planet. This path also let them enter the atmosphere close to their first target, the same Nasi research facility they had infiltrated last time. The plan was to enter the facility, retrieve the schematics and details of the skip ship, and quickly escape.

Kal studied the battle map on his personal display. There were no less than ten Nasi ships orbiting the planet. It was enough firepower to destroy Samsara Fleet without breaking a sweat, and the Nasi had several fleets as big as this one on other planets. A cloud of fighters and assault ships buzzed around the enormous capital ships, a sign of growing Nasi strength.

Kal gripped his console during the entire thirty-minute descent into Patagonia's atmosphere. If the Nasi spotted them now, there was almost certainly no chance for escape— there were just too many of them. Finally, they entered the atmosphere and Kal felt the ship being gently buffeted by the atmospheric friction. He could breathe again.

"Switch to optical screen," Garcia instructed.

Kanumba turned on the optical screen, causing them to look like an atmospheric freighter. At the same time, Garcia reduced their speed to that of a slow-moving cargo freighter.

"We're about five minutes out," Kanumba reported. They were returning to the same research facility where they had stolen the first experimental skip ship, the *Park*. The facility was on the coast of Pangea, away from the capital,

Kasongo, and the other cities that dominated the continent. They flew nap-of-the-earth, low to the ground, so the dense undergrowth barely touched the bottom of the ship.

"Conducting long-range sensor sweep," Chief Kanumba reported. Kal looked at his console's viewscreen. The lab facility comprised three oblong domed buildings arranged in a circle with a wall surrounding the perimeter. There were faint signs of the battle that had been there weeks before, charred splotches along the perimeter walls and bent or dented equipment in the center. At first glance, the base looked completely abandoned.

"There's no shield." Kanumba observed. Kal checked his terminal; she was right. The energy shield that protected the facility from aerial attack had not been reactivated. The Skulls destroyed it to gain access to the compound. Not a good sign that no one had repaired it—there may be nothing left to protect.

"Proceed cautiously," Kal instructed. "Maybe they haven't been able to fix it yet. If there's anything still there, this could work to our advantage."

The *Salamis* landed in a small clearing a few kilometers from the Nasi lab. After conducting a detailed perimeter scan, the flight crew set up optical projectors around the ship that created a hologram which made it impossible to see unless a person was right next to it.

Kal, Bowen, Jones, Garcia, and Kanumba met in the ship's galley. On a ship as small as a scout corvette, the room did double-duty as a briefing room. A large table sat in the room's center with two viewscreens against one wall and a food fabricator against another.

"The place looks dead," Kanumba reported. She paused for a moment. "Scans show no sign of life in the compound."

"Not surprising. They must have moved everything to a more secure location. We need to get closer and get a team in there," Kal instructed.

"Agreed, sir," Sergeant Jones said. He stood up and used his neural implant to manipulate the viewscreens in the room. An overhead wireframe of the compound appeared on one of them.

As the noncommissioned officer in charge of the Tac-I squad, Jones was the leader on infiltrations and ground missions. Kal told them what needed to be done, and Jones decided how to do it.

The NCO outlined his plan. They would send the four-person Tac-I squad to examine the perimeter. If they found nothing, they would proceed inside the compound. Meanwhile, the rest of the crew would remain on the *Salamis* and be prepared to move.

"Any thoughts, Bo?" Kal turned to their teammate. "You know the facility better than any of us."

"I was a prisoner," Bo replied. "I don't know what security equipment it has."

"Not helpful," Jones said as he stood up from the table. "Well, I guess we'll find out." He walked out the door.

❖

Kal watched as the Tac-I squad inspected their battle suits. The four soldiers stepped into their suits and arranged themselves in a semi-circle, checking each other's readouts and walking around each other to make sure that nothing was off. The gray suits were the difference between life and death for Tac-I soldiers; they would double- and triple-check their suits to make sure they could rely on them in battle. The suits were incredibly complex and there were a lot of things to inspect. Besides the armor plating, they had thrusters, weapons, sensors, and a host of other advanced systems built into their frames.

Sergeant Jones inspected each member of his squad—no one would go on the mission without his approval. After each soldier passed this last inspection, he gave their helmet a rough slap.

"Good luck out there," Kal said after Jones slapped Private Kinawadi's helmet. Jones raised his arm in a salute and then directed the squad to move out. They left the clearing and slipped into the dense underbrush, silent except for the leaves brushing against the metal plating of their suits. The sergeant split the squad into two teams: Alpha and Bravo. Alpha Team comprised Jones and Kinawadi, and Bravo Team were Kimathi and Chedjou. Once they got close to the perimeter, the teams would split and circle the facility.

Kal moved back to the ship's galley, joining Garcia and Bo, who were already seated at the table. The viewscreens displayed a live feed from each team's battle suits. The squad's communications net was piped to the speakers in the room, allowing them to hear exactly what the squad said to each other.

We're not detecting anything, reported Kimathi.

Roger, nothing here either, Jones replied. *Stay on guard.*

Within the *Salamis's* galley, Kal watched in rapt attention as they slowly walked around the base. Occasionally, they stopped to take more detailed sensor readings, but there were no signs of activity. Chief Kanumba had gone to her cabin. To be back in the place where her fiancé died must be overwhelming.

After completing their recon, the teams used their thrusters to launch into the center of the facility. The scorch marks and twisted machinery from their previous battle were still untouched in the courtyard. In the center was where Park had fallen, a round through his chest. Was the stain on the ground Park's blood or the blood of the Nasi who had killed him? Strange to think that killer and killed were connected in such an intimate way.

The team swiftly made its way into the lab building. When the Skulls had been there before, lab workstations— computers and testing equipment—had filled the building. Now only the tables they had sat on remained; the Nasi had removed everything else. There was already a thin layer of dust on the tables that rose into the air as the Tac-I squad swept the room. Kal felt his heart sink as he saw the vacant room; their first mission seemed like a failure.

Double-check everything, Sergeant Jones instructed his squad. *They might have left something behind.*

Kal doubted it. The Nasi were not ones to be careless.

"Sir, we got a problem," Sampson's voice came over the galley speakers. "We've got multiple aircraft coming this way."

Damn it, Jones swore over the net. *Must've been a silent alarm. We need to move. Head back to the ship now.*

Kal switched one of the galley's viewscreens to the tactical map of the area. Three drop ships were heading toward the facility at a high rate of speed and were going to reach the facility before Jones and the Tac-I squad could extract themselves.

"You don't have time to get out." Kal said. "Get some cover and get ready for a firefight. We'll be in the air immediately."

Garcia ran outside to grab the optical projectors that hid their position while Kal barreled up the ladder and into the cockpit. Sampson had already strapped himself in and had all systems online while Chief Kanumba was in her seat, conducting quick checks of their systems.

"As soon as Garcia steps foot on the ship, we're off," Kal instructed. Sampson nodded.

Kal adjusted his console's viewscreen to watch the squad's live feed. The Nasi ships released about two full squads—twelve to fifteen total—of Nasi. The battle-suit-clad soldiers took the top of the wall and fired on the Tac-I squad below. Kal had a sickening sense of déjà vu. He wasn't going to lose another soldier in that compound.

"Obliterate the wall," Kal ordered. "Make sure those bastards aren't able to fire a shot. Once we get our people on board, destroy the entire thing. I never want to see this place again." He slammed his fist down on the console.

"Hell yeah," Kanumba whispered.

"Garcia's on board," Sampson called out. As he said the words, the ship launched straight into the air and the aft thrusters fired, shooting it toward the compound.

The four Tac-I squad icons on the tactical map were green; no deaths or injuries so far. It was a race against time. The squad wouldn't last long.

"The fighters are some sort of new design," Kanumba reported. "Unclear if they are only atmospheric." Ships fit into one of three categories: atmospheric only, space only, or ships like the *Salamis* which could operate in both. Their tactics would vary depending on which type of ship they were facing.

Kal was an experienced pilot. He gave Major Garcia leeway to operate the ship but was also willing to provide direct instruction at critical times.

"Target the three ships to buy us some time. Then strafe the walls with plasma fire. Looks like our team is holding on for now."

The *Salamis* let loose a salvo of missiles. They snaked forward, twisting and splitting off from each other as they locked onto their targets. The three Nasi ships abruptly spun away from the facility in different directions trying to avoid them.

Sampson skillfully turned the ship to orient the front plasma cannons toward the research camp and a barrage of bright plasma bolts crashed into the top of the wall, decimating the Nasi soldiers. Kal saw them jumping off or jetting away trying to avoid the deadly blasts.

Sampson circled the base, keeping the front of the ship facing inward, while Kanumba used her console to reign plasma fire down on anything that wasn't Human.

"Jones, you're clear for extraction," Garcia called out over the net. "We'll hold position until you're in."

Roger, Jones replied. *Bravo Team, you take lead. We'll follow behind and provide cover.*

"Open the bay gunnery position," Kal called out as he catapulted himself through the cockpit door and ran toward the bay. When he arrived, he was pleased to see the large kinetic machine gun online and ready to fire. Normally the weapon sat in the bay's ceiling, but when activated, it descended and the bulkhead opened, allowing clear fields of fire to the side of the ship. Kal jumped into the small jump seat and examined the firing console.

The four Tac-I soldiers were almost at the bay door. Plasma rounds buzzed past them, some missing by centimeters. The Nasi had abandoned the wall but were firing from beneath the jungle outside of it. The gun's targeting computer highlighted likely enemy positions, and Kal lit them up. He concentrated streams of metal into the dense foliage, unsure if he was hitting anything.

Kal blinked as he noticed a bright flash out of the corner of his eye. As he turned, he saw the twisting contrails of several anti-personnel missiles streaking toward the four soldiers. He held his breath as he watched the missiles snake toward his soldiers. The comms net was a jumble as they shouted out to each other to take evasive action. They shot away from each other, firing their thrusters to avoid the oncoming threat.

Kal let out a yell as he saw a missile connect with a soldier, launching them forward, toward the *Salamis*, a faint wisp of smoke trailing behind.

A guttural yell echoed across the net. It was Kimathi who'd been hit. Kal saw his icon flicker from green to yellow as the suit registered the damage. Amazingly, he was still flying toward the ship, somehow maintaining an even trajectory as he got close.

Kal shook his head and reoriented the machine gun toward the origin of the missile attack. His constant barrage of metal deforested the area, scything down shrubs and trees with ease. He could faintly see the twisted body of a battle-suit-clad Nasi soldier among the debris in the small clearing he'd made.

The other three Tac-I soldiers had recovered from their evasive maneuvers and landed gracefully on the bay floor. Kimathi followed soon after, hovered for a moment, and dropped like a stone, the bottom of his suit a melted jumble.

"Blow this place and get us out of here," Kal called to the cockpit. He saw several missiles streak toward the research facility before he finished his sentence.

The bay door closed with a thunk, and the ship's thrusters fired, propelling them forward. Kimathi lay on the ground, unmoving. Kal wanted to help but trusted Jones and his comrades would do everything they could. He ran back to the cockpit, using his implant to close the gunner's hatch.

"The Nasi ships are back," Garcia said. "And they

brought friends."

The "friends" were three fighters streaking toward them. In front of them were an array of missiles already locked onto the *Salamis*.

"Everyone. Get ready for evasive maneuvers," Sampson called over the ship's intercom.

Garcia pulled the ship up into a vertical climb. The maneuver pressed Kal against the back of his chair despite the best efforts of the ship's inertial dampeners. Without them, every single person aboard would be unconscious.

"Sir, we can't leave the atmosphere," Sampson said. "The Nasi fleet will destroy us."

"We'll have to deal with it when it happens." Garcia didn't look at his copilot.

"Sir, it's suicide!" Sampson yelled.

Garcia grunted but otherwise didn't respond. They continued to climb.

Suddenly the engines cut off, and the *Salamis* spun on its axis to face the ground.

"What are you doing?" Garcia turned and gave an angry look at his copilot.

"Sorry, sir. But you have to trust me." Sampson's face was the picture of pure concentration. Their thrusters came to life, immediately reversing their course and sending them hurtling back toward the ground and their three pursuers. Kal's vision went black. When he recovered, the impossibly green landscape of Pangea filled the cockpit's viewscreen.

Sampson launched several missiles directly in front of them and pulled back on the yoke. As they started to level off,

Kal could hear small metallic pings from throughout the ship and felt lightheaded as he was ground into his seat. The equipment in the cargo bay made a thunderous crash as it was thrown around and he could hear faint cries from the Tac-I squad. They slowly reached horizontal flight and Kal exhaled. The *Salamis* was now literally brushing the tops of the trees, their branches and leaves making a soft patter on the alloy metal hull of the ship.

Behind them, the missiles impacted into the ground, creating a bright fireball that rose from the undergrowth.

"Please activate the optical cloak," Sampson called. His voice even and calm, he could have been asking for breakfast.

"Activated," Kanumba responded.

Sampson pulled their nose up slightly, putting an additional meter or two of distance between them and the forest below. After a few minutes, they found a small clearing by a stream and the *Salamis* gently touched down.

"What the hell were you thinking?" Garcia grabbed the junior officer by the shirt and shoved him back in his chair.

"I was thinking that I want to live, sir." Sampson met his superior's eyes with his jaw clenched.

"You almost killed us."

"*Almost*, sir."

Garcia let go of his copilot and bent down, placing his head between his knees, letting out a sigh. "Chief Kanumba, we need to check and see if there was any damage from that little maneuver. Can you inspect the frame? Sampson and I will check the systems." He turned back to the lieutenant. "We're not done yet. I promise you."

Kal stood up. "Kimathi was hit, and it looked bad, I'm going back to the bay." He strode out of the cockpit toward the cargo bay, dreading what he would find.

❖

Peals of laughter greeted Kal as he reached the bottom of the ladder. He stepped inside the bay to find the Tac-1 squad outside of their battle suits. Ekon Kimathi lay in the center of the bay, the bottom of his suit a charred mess.

"General Norman!" Sergeant Jones shouted as he noticed Kal staring.

Kal looked back in shock. What was happening?

"Sir, you look surprised," Ekon said with a smile. "Is it my new look?" He waved his arms across the charred stumps where his legs had been.

"Sir," Sergeant Jones placed an arm on Kal's shoulder. "Remember, this isn't the first time."

A wave of realization and relief flooded through Kal. Ekon had lost his legs during a firefight with the Nasi when they were escaping New America. The Nasi had destroyed his prosthesis, not his actual legs.

The others noticed Kal's realization. "Sir, your expression was priceless," Private Chedjou called out. "If it makes you feel better, we all had the same reaction. This jerk," she pointed at Ekon, "even played it up before Sergeant Jones remembered." She playfully kicked her friend in the side.

"It takes a lot to get a leg up on me." Ekon slapped the

metal floor at his own joke.

"I was going to say that I'm glad you're not hurt, but now I'm not so sure." Kal stepped forward, leaned over, and gave Ekon a light punch in the chest.

"Chief Kanumba stocked our medical supply bin with cybernetic limbs," Jones explained. "We've got replacements available. We even have replacements for your arm if needed. Unfortunately, we lost the suit though." Kal's arm was also cybernetic. Again, a result of combat against the Nasi.

"I'll take that," Kal said with a smile. As he was about to leave, he noticed Ekon's hand shaking. Among soldiers, it was hard to admit when something rattled you. You didn't want to let your fellow soldiers down, didn't want them to realize you were hurt, especially when it wasn't physical.

He glanced at Ekon, whose face lit up in a smile, and his hand with tiny tremors running through it pressed against the floor. Kal remembered when he had first met him. Kal had still been a civilian, still operating in the haze of his own sorrow combined with drugs. Ekon had been fresh from school, angry that his once simple life had been destroyed and looking for someone to hate.

They both had changed so much.

Chapter Five

"Damn," Ekon cursed as he kicked a stray piece of trash.

Kal, Ekon, and Sergeant Jones stood in the middle of an abandoned space defense facility buried in the Patagonian forest. Last time they were there, it was the headquarters of the Patagonia Front, a group dedicated to resisting Nasi rule of the planet. Now it was a trash dump.

"No signs of a fight." Sergeant Jones knelt down and picked up the trash that Ekon had kicked. "It looks like they left in a hurry."

"Sergeant, we've found something," Kinawadi called out. The Tac-I squad was conducting a sweep of the base's perimeter.

They walked toward Kinawadi's location to find something had completely leveled a large swathe of the forest. Craters cluttered the ground, outlined by telltale plasma scorches. What had been a normal Patagonian forest was now a hellish wasteland. Bloated bodies with bloody foam leaking from their noses were scattered across on the ruined forest floor. The faint acrid smell of the battle still hung in the air.

"Okay, there was *some* fighting here," Jones admitted, picking up a piece of shrapnel.

Kal studied the battlefield. The question was, who had attacked the Front?

The Nasi invasion had fractured Patagonia's power structure. In the absence of a planetary government, multiple factions had seized control and begun a devastating civil war. The Nasi didn't care. As long as they got the materials they needed, they were content to let the Humans fight each other. It meant that there were many groups who could have conducted this attack.

"One of the other factions found 'em," Jones said. "There was a firefight, and some of the Front escaped. The rest..." he waved toward the corpses.

"Looks like they were doing a retrograde maneuver," Kal said. "Sacrifice the few for the many."

"Question is," Ekon asked, "who attacked them?"

"It wasn't the Nasi," Jones said. "This isn't like them. They would encircle the whole camp to prevent any chance of escape."

"They would," added Kal, "also make quick work of the Front in a head-to-head battle. These guys look like they gave as much as they got." He gently untied a band from around the arm of a body, trying not to look at the disfigured face.

The band was faded red, with a stylized letter F stitched in yellow. Several of the bodies had the same armband. "Not trying to keep a low profile, are they?" Kal said.

"Why would they?" Jones asked. "It's a show of force. They've proven they're the biggest kid in the commune. It's a statement."

"Garcia may know what this is," Kal said, tucking the band in his cargo pocket. The pilot was from Patagonia. "I'm going to check out the buildings."

"Roger, sir, we'll continue our sweep," Jones replied.

Kal walked back to the center of the abandoned base. When they had been there before, the Patagonia Front had tents set up around the hardened bunkers and buildings of the base. They now lay flat on the ground, ripped to shreds, and their contents strewn across the ground.

Kal meandered through the buildings, looking for anything amid the broken equipment and refuse littering the floors. There was nothing interesting. Whoever had been there had done a thorough if somewhat chaotic job of retrieving anything of value.

"Anything?" Kal asked Sergeant Jones, after the squad had completed their inspection.

"No, sir. Just bodies and destroyed equipment." He looked back for a moment, shook his head, and then regarded Kal. "Anything inside the base?"

"Whoever was here cleaned it out," Kal replied. "There's nothing left but junk. I'm calling it. I'll have Sampson land here in the perimeter."

The *Salamis* arrived a few minutes later from its position several kilometers away. The team had entered the base using their battle suits to avoid detection and keep a low profile.

"Looks a little different from when we were here last," Garcia said as he sauntered down the ramp.

"Someone came in and cleared the place out," Kal said. "Looks like the Front had their forces hold off the attackers over there," he pointed in the battlefield's direction "while the rest got out."

Kal pulled the armband from his pocket and held it out to the pilot. "There were a bunch of bodies with this on their arms. You ever seen it before?"

Garcia paled slightly and nodded. "Yeah, that's my families' sigil—Foyleton. The troops that attacked that camp

66

report to my brother Lukas."

❖

The Skulls strode through the hilly streets of Kasongo. The large city was an assault on the senses. Jumbled buildings climbed the undulating landscape and jutted into the narrow, twisting roads. Blockades in the streets, buildings scarred with plasma fire, and trash and discarded equipment piled up in the gutter were all evidence that the civil war had reached the city. They passed several patrols of the Planetary People's Front, the paramilitary faction that currently controlled the city. Despite the chaos, people were still in the streets: vendors selling cheap electronics, kids running around, and groups of citizens laughing as they walked together.

They had left the *Salamis* outside the city in a dense copse of forest far away from any roads or fighting and then entered the city on foot. Jones had split the team into three groups to be less conspicuous and ordered them to arrive at their objective using multiple routes. He'd grouped Kal with Garcia and Chedjou.

"So you lived here?" Chedjou asked as she examined a large spherical building that rose over the road.

"Patagonia, yes. Kasongo, no," Garcia replied. "I know the city though. We came here a lot with my parents."

"It's...a lot," observed Kal.

"Yeah," agreed Garcia as he stepped over a woman passed out in the street, "it's not the most charming city."

Kal saw their destination ahead of them—a large pyramid with iridescent sides. In any other city it would have been out of place. In Kasongo it fit with the unruly nature of the city. The building belonged to Garcia's family, one of their many houses.

Kal was reluctant to use Major Garcia's family. After they'd left the abandoned Patagonia Front base, Kal tried to contact the Alliance using the coded signal he'd used before. After several hours of waiting for a response, he'd given up. It was time to go to Plan B.

Bowen confirmed the Nasi had almost certainly moved all their work to the Foothold, a heavily fortified city-within-a-city in the middle of Kasongo. The Nasi had built one on each of the Human colonies. It was the center of their power and there was no way the Skulls could infiltrate the base on their own. They would need help, and lots of it.

The entryway of the house could not have been more at odds with the modern and eccentric exterior. It looked like a scene from an ancient Earth ruin that had been dipped in gold. Fluted golden columns rose from the marble floors to meet a vaulted ceiling adorned with an ornate golden chandelier. The style was conspicuously expensive rather than elegant.

"Master Karl," an attendant bot said as it rolled into the room. "We are glad to have you back."

"Thanks." Garcia idly looked around the room. "I'm guessing you already notified Lukas I'm here."

"Of course," the bot replied. "He's currently indisposed, but I am sure he will be here to welcome you as soon as possible."

"Yeah, great," Garcia muttered. His brother Lukas had become the head of the Foyleton crime syndicate when their parents died. From Kal's brief experience with the man, he understood why the pilot had wanted to leave the planet when he'd come of age. "We got six more people coming in here. Can you make sure the doors are unlocked until they get here?"

"Of course, sir. Anything else?" the bot asked, raising one of his holographic eyebrows.

"We still have food?"

"Of course, sir." The bot seemed affronted. "Our larders are fully stocked with whatever you may need."

Kal's mouth started watering. The "food" they ate on ships was a chemical concoction manufactured by the food fabricators. The machines did their best to mimic actual food, but it was no match for the real thing.

"Okay, put something together. We'll have nine in our party for dinner."

The bot wheeled away and left the three soldiers pacing the entryway, waiting for the rest of their group. In less than ten minutes, they were all present and accounted for.

"Follow me." Garcia led them to a sumptuous dining room. The walls were a deep red with gold framed pictures hung in even intervals. The rectangular marble table in the center of the room could seat at least twenty people. Kal felt his mouth water even more as he smelled the steam wafting from the countless trays filled to the brim on the table. The Skulls sat down and dug in with little fanfare except for a few

69

"thanks" directed at Garcia between bites.

As he enjoyed the feast, Kal couldn't help but think of the citizens who were homeless or starving because of the war. The food was exquisite—a combination of local Patagonian delicacies mixed with some of the finest dishes from Earth. It had to be the most extravagant meal Kal had ever eaten. After they made a small dent in the mountain of food, they all sat back in the chairs, groaning pleasantly to themselves.

Kal looked up from his plate as an attendant bot wheeled into the room to face Garcia. "Master Karl, your brother would like to speak with you." Before Garcia could respond, the face of Lukas Garcia replaced the bot's holographic face. The familial resemblance was immediately apparent, except for the air of menace that Lukas wore like a cloak about him.

"I've locked all the doors this time, brother." Lukas smiled. When the Skulls had been there before, they had left against Lukas's wishes. He'd been furious. Kal couldn't wait to meet the man in person.

Garcia gave a broad smile. "Don't worry, brother. I'm here for good. The war stuff wasn't working out for me." He shook his head. "So I've come back to help with the ole family business."

Lukas guffawed, small bits of spittle flying out of his mouth. "You're full of it, Karl. Don't try anything. Otherwise, I might get upset."

The feed switched off and the bot's smiling holographic face reappeared.

"Ah, family," Garcia sighed. He let his head drop against the table with a bang.

❖

Lukas Garcia was a man who didn't fit together quite right. His round head with its enormous nose looked off perched on his thin, wiry body. His clothes were opulent and garish, perfectly matching his home in Kasongo, but draped across his frame like a curtain.

He walked through the small door in the house's basement trailed by four bodyguards, each outfitted with the most modern ballistic armor and carrying high-powered kinetic rifles. Chief Kanumba had patched into the home's security network, allowing the Skulls to watch as Garcia's brother made his way to the central hallways.

"Karl!" Lukas yelled his brother's name, exaggerating each letter. "Kaaarrrrrlllll!"

"I'm right here, brother." Garcia stepped out from dining room. "Tell your crew to put down their weapons."

Lukas snickered but was interrupted by a cough behind him. The five Patagonians turned around to find Sergeant Jones and the rest of the Tac-I squad with their weapons pointed at them. If Lukas's men were any good, they would know the rifles the soldiers held were military grade and could pierce their armor like it wasn't even there.

"Put the weapons down, Lukas," Garcia ordered as he walked next to the squad. His brother snarled before finally motioning for his guards to comply. "Kick 'em to my friends over there," Garcia said. The guards again complied.

"I see you've gotten smarter," Lukas said. "You hacked the home's security system."

"Yup. Any system can be hacked. That's why we need pilots after all."

"So, now that you got me," Lukas gave a theatric yawn, "what do you want?"

"I told you. We want to join," Garcia said, eliciting a chuckle from his brother.

"You come back after almost twenty years and expect to just slide back in?"

"Yes." Garcia stepped toward his brother. "It's my birthright, same as you. It's what Mom and Dad would have wanted. I've been up there"—he pointed toward the sky—"and I know there's nothing for me."

"How can I trust you?" Lukas asked. "I mean, you've got me at gunpoint." Kal looked at the four rifles sitting on the ground in front of the Tac-I squad and bit his lip.

"Jones," Garcia said, "lower your weapons." The sergeant looked at him dubiously. "It's the only way."

"Lower 'em," Jones told the squad as he lowered his rifle. After a brief pause, the other three slowly lowered theirs as well.

"We can help you out, brother," Garcia said. He waved his arms toward the other members of the Skulls. "We've got trained pilots, computer experts, the most lethal Tac-I squad in the galaxy, and"—he pointed at Bo, who had stepped out from a darkened side room—"we have him."

There was an audible gasp from the Patagonians and Kal

could hear a couple of them murmur 'Nasi'. Two of them stepped back in fear.

"What's he doing here?" asked one of Lukas's guards.

"Long story, but I can tell you all about it later. No matter what he looks like, he's not a Nasi. But he *is* a genius. He can make things you've only dreamt of."

One of the guards whistled. "Never seen one up close before."

Lukas scratched the back of his head sheepishly. "That's pretty impressive, I have to admit." He put his hands on his hips and slowly scanned the room, studying the Skulls. "What about that guy?" He tilted his head toward Kal.

Before Garcia could respond, Kal unholstered his pistol, aimed, shot out a light on the chandelier, and reholstered it.

Lukas whistled, "Okay, not bad." He turned and looked at his brother. "So how'd you get back here? You got a ship with ya? Anything that can fold?"

"No, the Nasi destroyed our ship on entry," Garcia lied, "and that was the final straw for us. We've been fighting them, but nothing seems to matter. For every ship we destroy, they destroy two. We could see the writing on the wall." That hit a little too close to home for Kal.

"So not so altruistic after all," Lukas laughed. "Sounds like we're your last chance."

"Oh, we've got choices. Anyone would want us. You know that." Garcia held his hands to his side in a pleading gesture. "We've had our differences, I know, but I've never let you down. You know that too."

Lukas harrumphed. "I'm in charge though. You got that?

73

No more coming in as the golden child."

"Of course, brother. You're the boss. We're just the help."

"You're gonna have to trust me. You ready for that?"

Garcia's facade flickered for a moment.

He's scared to death, Kal realized.

"Yeah, we trust you," Garcia answered.

"Okay, let my crew get their weapons then."

Garcia nodded and the four Foyleton guards cautiously walked to where their weapons were, picked them up, and then returned next to Lukas.

Lukas smiled. "Now we're gonna need you to put down your weapons and kick 'em over to us. They'll be your first donation to the cause."

"No way," Private Chedjou declared. No emotion, just a statement of fact.

"All of you do what he says," Garcia commanded.

The other eight members of their squad slowly put down their weapons and kicked them over to the four Foyleton guards. As soon as the Skulls' weapons were by their feet, the guards immediately trained their own rifles on the squad. Only Chedjou remained. The young private looked around the room with eyes wide in disbelief.

Kal could feel the situation spinning out of control. If she didn't do it soon, one of Lukas's crew could get spooked—he'd seen similar things happen. "Do it," he said. Chedjou turned to stare at him. "Sandra, do it!" Kal yelled.

She jumped in surprise and then placed her weapon on the ground and kicked it to Lukas. He picked up the rifle and admired it for a moment.

"I gotta say, these military rifles are beautiful. So hard to find."

"What's next?" Garcia's facade had completely faded. Kal could see the beads of perspiration dripping from his forehead.

"What's next?" Lukas said the words slowly like he was tasting each one.

"Lukas, we've proved you can trust us," Garcia said.

"Yes, you have, brother," Lukas agreed. "But I'm not sure how far yet." He turned to his four soldiers. "Tranq 'em."

The Foyleton guards pulled out their pistols and started shooting.

❖

"General Norman. Wakey, wakey, sir."

At first, Kal could only feel pain. It started in his head and then radiated down to the tips of his fingers and toes, ending in a fuzzy numbness. He tried to open his eyes, but they refused to budge.

"Ah, he got it bad." Kal couldn't place the voice.

"Sir, I hope you don't mind me saying that your brother sucks." That was Sergeant Jones.

"No offense taken, Sergeant. You are spot on as always." Garcia seemed to have recovered his sense of humor.

Kal could hear a small hum of some sort and realized they were moving. Lukas was taking them somewhere.

75

"This is not one of our better ideas." That was Bo.

"None..." Kal tried to speak, but his mouth felt like sandpaper. The rest of the team stopped talking. "None of them..." He tried again.

"What's he saying?" Kinawadi asked.

"None of them are very good to begin with." Kal finally got the joke out. He heard soft chuckles from his team. It gave him enough strength to open his eyes.

Wherever they were, it was almost pitch-black. The only light was a soft glow emanating from beneath the benches that lined the walls of the small compartment they were in.

Kal realized his hands and legs were bound, and he was tethered to the wall, unable to do much except shift his weight slightly.

"Well, another story to tell the kids," Garcia quipped. His spirits were surprisingly high, considering their predicament.

"Why are you so happy?" Kal asked.

"If my brother was going to kill us, he'd have done it at the house. It has features that are designed for things like that. He's taking us back to Foyleton. Not sure what he'll do to us there, but he won't kill us." He paused. "Immediately."

They spent the rest of the journey in silence.

For a reason he couldn't understand, Kal thought of his family. He wished he could grab the small picture of them out of his pocket and look at it. It was strange to think that Lan Fen and Stephen would almost be adults now. If the accident hadn't happened, where would they be? He and Li Na had always talked about what they would do when Kal retired. He had always wanted to explore the galaxy, but Li Na had wanted to live on Earth. Perhaps they'd all be dead from the Nasi invasion. Perhaps not.

The feeling of the vehicle decelerating and descending distracted Kal from his thoughts. He felt the telltale bump of the ship touching down. A door opened at one end of their compartment, revealing the glimmering city of Foyleton. They had landed on top of a building. It was night, and the city was spread out before them.

Several guards came in and unshackled the Skulls from the vehicle, removed the restraints on their legs, and pulled them out of the vehicle. The guards marched them through the corridors of the building. Kal staggered frequently as they guided him through the hallways; the effects of whatever had knocked him out still hadn't dissipated. The building must have been enormous. The off-white utilitarian hallways stretched on forever, and countless Foyleton soldiers walked past them. Each one was wearing the same red armband that the Skulls had recovered on the battlefield.

Finally, they stopped in front of a large unpainted metal door. It swung open to reveal a small bright white chamber, and the guards instructed them to enter. After they obeyed, the door swung shut and a small receptacle slid out from the wall. "Place your hands in the box," said a voice emanating from a speaker in the room.

"How?" asked Garcia. "You've got them tied behind our backs."

"Figure it out." The speaker went dead.

One by one, with some difficulty, they placed their

hands in the receptacle, which removed the bindings. After the last person had been released, a door on the other side of the room opened, revealing a larger holding cell.

Taking the hint, the team stepped into the room. It was completely bare except for a small toilet in the corner. Around fifteen people sat slumped against the sterile walls, each sunken in a posture of defeat—head in hands or staring across the room at nothing.

"General Norman!"

Kal turned around to see Commander Bohai Kinkaid, leader of the Patagonia Front.

"It seems all is lost," the commander said.

Chapter Six

Kal shook Commander Kinkaid's hand. The elderly man had aged since Kal had seen him last. His cheeks looked more sunken than before, and his hand felt waxy and fragile in Kal's grip. "We haven't lost everything," Kal said. "We're still alive after all."

"What are you doing here?" asked the commander. "I never expected to see you again."

"We had to come back," Kal said. "Unfortunately, the Nasi shot us down on entry." He was sure every word they said was being recorded and analyzed.

"Why would you come…" Kinkaid's eyes widened as he noticed Bo walk through into the cell. "What's that?" Several of the people in the cell looked up and blanched as they saw the Jadid.

"What's that doing in here?" asked a man as he pushed himself away from the door.

"It's okay," Kal called out, "he's not a Nasi."

"Sure as hell looks like one to me," sneered a woman. She stood up and eyed the scientist.

"I'm a Jadid," Bo explained. "I'm fighting the Nasi, same as you. And I'm trapped here, same as you."

"Except he's about ten times smarter and stronger than any of us," said Ekon, eyeing the woman. "I've seen him kill people with his bare hands, so I'd steer clear." The woman stopped advancing and fear flickered in her eyes.

"What's going on?" Kinkaid asked. "How did you end up here?"

Kal launched into the fictional story the Skulls had

invented before leaving the *Salamis*. Like any good lie, they based it on some truths. They had visited Altterra, the Nasi were a faction of the Jadid, the Nasi had secured their hold on this part of the galaxy. But he also said they'd given up and that they were deserters. He didn't reveal their real mission, that they'd requested to join Foyleton, or Garcia's relationship to the group. They might not make it out of the cell alive if he did.

As Kal talked, the rest of the prisoners picked up their heads and looked at him. By the time he finished, every single eye in the room was on him.

"So you've abandoned the fleet." Kinkaid looked each of them up and down. "Now you're here, captured by these scum." He slowly studied them. "Hm."

One prisoner, a large man with a small patch of hair on his otherwise bald head, stepped toward them and spat on the ground. "That's what I think of ya. Bunch of traitors." There was a general murmur of agreement. Several of the formerly docile prisoners stood up and eyed the Skulls.

"Leave them be," ordered Kinkaid, holding out his arms. "We've all done things we're ashamed of. There are no heroes in war."

They listened to their commander's orders and backed away. Kal wondered how long the Skulls would be in this cell with them. They would need to be on their guard.

"Commander, what happened to the Front?" asked Kal.

"We were betrayed," Kinkaid replied. "By whom? I don't know. Foyleton attacked in the night. Luckily our defense systems alerted us before they landed. We held them off while the bulk of our forces retreated."

"How long have you been here?" Kal asked.

"I don't know," Kinkaid replied. "They disabled our implants. Maybe two weeks. Maybe three."

Kal tried to access his own implant with no success. Implants could be disabled by implanting a compact disc under the skin, which temporarily disrupted the connection between the implant and the neural pathways. Kal ran his hands over his curly graying hair but felt nothing.

"That's strange," Kal muttered to himself.

"No disc," Kinkaid said. "They use some sort of field or something."

"That shouldn't be possible."

"Well, I've seen a lot of things that shouldn't be possible." His demeanor shifted. "Like you betraying your oaths." With a flourish, Kinkaid walked to the other side of the cell. It was behavior that was uncharacteristic of the commander.

Kal walked back toward the rest of the Skulls.

"Norman's Numbskulls back in prison again." Garcia pumped his fist in the air.

Without his implant, time passed slowly in the Foyleton cell for Kal. The Skulls kept a watch to ensure an overeager fellow prisoner didn't try anything. There didn't seem to be a need though. The other prisoners had lost interest in them and were more focused on their own internal sorrows than anything else. Occasionally, a muffled sob or someone using the latrine in the corner interrupted the silence.

Knowing they were being listened to, the Skulls acted the part of hopeless deserters. Unfortunately, it wasn't too far from the truth. Kal would occasionally check on his soldiers but mostly kept to himself and waited to see what Lukas would do.

He spent much of the time reflecting on what they had done to end up there. Had they made the right choice in trusting Garcia's brother? Again, he thought about his family—his wife, Li Na, and their children. Even a decade after their deaths, they were never too far from his mind. It gave him some solace to think that if this didn't work, they would be waiting for him. To think that the dedicated family man and military officer had transformed into whatever he was now. Scout? Freedom fighter?

I hope you'd be proud of me, Kal thought to himself as he held the small paper photograph he always carried with him. It was all he had left of his family that he could touch. Thankfully, the guards let him keep it.

"Karl Garcia, step into the vestibule and place your hands in the receptacle." The voice from the speaker caused Kal to jerk. He looked at the pilot. Garcia gave a subtle thumbs-up and dutifully stepped through the door that had just opened. The other prisoners watched and then shook their heads ruefully as the door slid shut with a soft hiss.

Kal estimated Garcia was gone about an hour when he stepped back into the cell. His face was moist with perspiration, and he gave a wan smile as he saw Kal looking at him. The other people in the cell regarded him suspiciously. "No one's ever returned," whispered the man next to Kal.

Kal sat next to the pilot, who slumped down against the wall.

"What happened?" Kal whispered.

"They're deciding whether to turn us in."

"To the Nasi?"

"Yeah." Garcia sighed. "My brother's changed. He got rid of all the people who'd worked for my parents. He never was the nicest guy, but now..." Garcia looked away.

"We've been in worse situations," Kal said. "I think your brother's just trying to scare you to see if we're telling the truth."

"I hope you're right, sir." He didn't meet Kal's eyes.

"The rest of you, Karl's friends, come on." The speaker crackled back to life.

One by one, the Skulls entered the vestibule, and the door closed behind them. Kal was the final one out, leaving Garcia alone in the cell with the other prisoners. He stepped into the small chamber and obeyed the commands, placing his hands in the same receptacle that had removed his restraints. The flexible alloy bands wrapped back around his wrists, locking them together behind his back, and the door opened, revealing a guard with a rifle at the ready.

"Get out," she ordered.

The guard led Kal to another room with bare white walls and a large table in the center. The others were already there, sitting uncomfortably on bare metal chairs, hands behind their backs and feet fixed to the floor. There was a single chair on the opposite side of the table, empty for now.

"Glad to see you made it, sir." Jones nodded his head as if they were meeting for tea.

"Wouldn't miss it for the world," Kal replied.

The guard roughly shoved Kal into a chair at the end of the table, placed his legs into clamps attached to the floor, and walked out. They sat in silence, staring across the table at the door, waiting for someone to enter.

"This is one hell of an interview process," Ekon said.

"These are actually pretty standard interrogation procedures," Bo said.

"Bo, that's not what—"

The door opened, interrupting Sergeant Jones's response. Lukas walked into the room with a condescending smile. Two of his crew positioned themselves on either side of him carrying the Skulls' own military-grade rifles.

"Well, well, well," Lukas sauntered to the chair facing them and sat down, leaning backwards slightly. "Seems I have all the Skulls here now."

No one responded.

"I talked to my brother," Lukas stretched and placed his hands behind his head. "He's a good kid. He was young when he left though, never really got involved in the family business before he ran away."

"Good for him," Jones said.

Lukas swiveled his head to look the sergeant in the eyes. "Maybe. But he never understood what they did. He got to leave with his innocence intact. I had to get my hands dirty."

He lifted his hands in front of his face and wiggled the fingers. "He told me everything."

"We already told you everything," Kal said.

Lukas laughed. A large guffaw that made his entire wire frame shake. "No, you see he told me *everything*."

Kal felt his heart drop for a moment but controlled his expression. It was a tactic; it had to be. As a pilot, Garcia had been through the EDF's interrogation resistance course. He wouldn't break, not in an hour at least.

"What do you have to say?" Lukas leaned forward in his chair, studying them. He saw something that he liked and leaned over the desk, stopping with his face centimeters away from Private Kinawadi.

"What!" He pounded the table with his hand. "Do!" Pound. "You!" Pound. "Have!" Pound "To!" Pound. "Say!"

Kinawadi returned the gaze without flinching. He had grown in the months since he'd joined the Skulls. Lukas stood, leaning his gaunt frame across the table, quivering with rage for several seconds. Suddenly, a smile broke across his face and he fell back into his chair.

"Ha!" The warlord laughed, his eyes remaining focused on Kinawadi. "Had to make sure." He turned to a guard. "Grab Karl and bring him in here."

A couple of minutes later, Garcia entered the room and stood behind the table next to his teammates. Lukas stepped behind his brother and pressed a small device against his restraints, causing them to fall to the ground.

"Well, brother, either you're telling the truth, or you've become a much better liar." Lukas wrapped his arms around

85

his brother's shoulder. "You and your crew ready to get to work?"

"What about the Nasi?" Garcia asked.

"What d'you mean? Will we turn you in?" Lukas laughed. "That was just to make you sweat. I had to know what I was dealing with. The Nasi don't pay well for snitches as far as I can tell anyway."

Lukas raised a finger into the air and the clamps holding the Skulls' feet to the floor sprang open. The two guards walked around the table and methodically released the restraints around their wrists.

"So what happens now?" Kal asked.

"Now you are members of Foyleton," Lukas announced. "We can use your skills."

"I told you, Lukas," Garcia said, "we'll do whatever you need."

"Good," Lukas smiled, "because we need a lot. We're stuck between the PPC and the People's Movement. The PPC is pushing toward Foyleton, trying to take us out of this war. Then they can just clean up the People's Movement." The Planetary People's Council was the largest faction on the planet. They had the capital and largest city, Kasongo, while Foyleton held the area around Chengdu.

"It wasn't too hard to eliminate them." He chuckled. "Bunch of cowards. They were hiding in the woods and most of them ran when we attacked. But we're still facing two enemies, one to the west and one to the south."

"What do you want us to do?" Kal asked. "We're recon soldiers."

"You're going to be my secret weapon," Lukas said. "You can get into places my soldiers can't. Do things my soldiers can't. Kill people my soldiers can't."

Lukas stepped toward the door, which slid open. "You're free men and women now. When you work for me, you only get the best. First, you've earned a break. My crew will show you to your rooms. And," he held his nose, "take a damn shower. You stink." Lukas laughed at his own joke as he walked out the door.

❖

The Foyleton headquarters building was even larger than Kal had realized when they'd entered. Easily the size of several city blocks, it was the tallest building in the city and extended several hundred meters into the ground. The guards told them it had been an EDF command base before the Nasi took over.

Foyleton updated the utilitarian building by painting murals and setting out ornate furniture and carpeting throughout the common areas. To Kal, the effect was strange, like adding exotic woods and gilt to a cargo freighter. Foyleton seemed to want to create a screen of luxury and sophistication to cover their criminal behavior.

There was little evidence of discipline as Kal wandered the hallways. Groups of soldiers sat drinking, taking drugs like Kuaile, and gambling. Courtesans, men and women dressed in low-cut cheap outfits, sashayed through the hallways, glassy eyed from whatever drugs they'd taken to survive the night.

This was a force driven by greed and self-interest. Kal had seen it before. They would fight the weak and the helpless, take pleasure in others' pain. But if someone really challenged them, they'd run and hide in a second, telling themselves there was nothing they could do.

After failing to contact the Alliance and Patagonia Front, Foyleton was their last hope. Originally, Kal had hoped they could infiltrate the group and recruit soldiers to join them to assault the Nasi Foothold. He knew Lukas would never agree to their plan, but perhaps they could find a few former EDF who still cared about something other than themselves. After a five-minute walk through the headquarters, he was second-guessing his assumptions.

Their guides led them to a large, finely detailed door at the end of a short hallway. Kal's implant was working again, and he saw they were in the very center of the compound. The door opened to reveal a circular room with ten doors radiating out from it. In the center was a circular maroon rug embroidered with a silver and gold F.

"This is where you'll stay. Take whichever room you want," said the Foyleton soldier. "They're all the same." He walked away, not even waiting for an answer.

The guard was right. Each room was essentially the same with overstated maroon carpeting, an enormous bed, a dresser, and a viewscreen hanging on each of the walls. Each room also had its own private bathroom, complete with shower. The walls between the rooms were flimsy, not built to the same standards as the rest of the building. Foyleton must have divided a larger room, perhaps a storage area, and made it into these small suites after they took over the base. The rooms were significantly nicer than anything Kal had seen when they were walking through the halls. Lukas had been good to his word; they appeared to be the guests of honor.

He stood back while the rest of the team picked their rooms and took the remaining one. He walked around his room, examining each piece of furniture and the screens. The dresser was empty—he would need to get some new merchant clothes fabricated—but there was a red Foyleton armband laying on top. After putting on the armband, Kal met with the rest of the Skulls in the central hallways.

How much can I say? he thought. *They'll be listening and watching.*

"Good job everyone. We've finally been able to find a place to land. I know you're all not happy about this, but remember to keep your thoughts to yourself." He looked each one of them in the eye as he spoke. "We may have to do some things we don't like, but remember it's for a good cause, our survival."

"Sir," Kinawadi's voice wavered for a moment. "Are you sure about this?"

"No, I'm not." The young soldier deserved honesty. "But we can't fail. It's just too important."

Lukas Garcia had spent decades working for his parents. They'd been shrewd, but he'd come to realize they lacked vision. For them, the Foyleton Syndicate had been an end unto itself. They had all the money they wanted, and as long as they didn't cross certain lines, lines set by the Alliance and the UEG, they kept their place.

Lukas wanted more. That's why they'd needed to go.

The Nasi had shown him how much more he could have. When they destroyed the UEG and Alliance, they opened a path for him to control the entire planet. The PPC and People's Movement were now the only things in his way.

When Karl had arrived with his friends, Lukas hadn't been sure what to do with them. He'd done his research and learned enough of their backgrounds and exploits to know the Nasi would be very interested in them. But the evil purple bastards weren't exactly the most generous masters. They were more than happy to leave the Humans on the planet alone as long as they got the resources they needed—which suited Lukas just fine. However, he doubted he'd get more than a thank-you if he gave them the Skulls.

"You know, brother," Lukas said as he paused the video on the viewscreen, "your team is excellent. Most people wouldn't know they're lying."

"You wouldn't know either unless I told you," Karl retorted.

Karl still had that irritating trait, that quality that made it seem like he was above it all. He was the fat kid who ate the steak without ever thinking of the person who had slaughtered it. Lukas had spent his entire life slaughtering the weak and foolish to help his family. He was tired of his brothers and others taking him for granted.

"What are you going to do to them?"

90

"It's unfortunate, but we'll have to turn them in." Lukas frowned. "I hate it. And not just because we'll be throwing away some great resources. They tried to do something good for Humanity and for the galaxy. Their battle was futile though."

"I wish there was some other way," Karl looked back at the viewscreen. "This is betrayal. I'm betraying everything I believe in."

"Don't feel that way." Lukas put his hand on his brother's shoulder and rested it there. "You made the best decision you could. Same as them. None of us are perfect, but we make what we can with the parts we're given."

"What'll you have us do?" Karl asked.

Lukas covered his mouth to hide his smile. He wanted to jump with joy. His brother's return presented so many opportunities. The Skulls *were* the most elite recon team in Human space. They would help him solidify control over the planet. Then he could give them over to the Nasi and earn their gratitude. Finally, he would turn his self-righteous little brother over as well and eliminate the last part of Foyleton that held any allegiance to his parents. It was perfect.

And Karl had just handed it to him. Lukas had expected to have to torture his brother and his friends to make them talk. Instead, Karl had simply handed them over. Of course, Lukas didn't trust his brother completely. He didn't trust *anyone* completely, but he did trust fear, and he'd seen that in his brother's eyes earlier.

For now, Lukas Garcia had to act the part of the concerned older brother and let Karl think he'd welcomed him back. Act as if the brat hadn't had everything handed to him while growing up. Karl's treachery would only help Lukas. In the end, he would join his former friends in the Nasi cells, and then Lukas would be the most powerful Human on the planet and potentially in the Galaxy.

Chapter Seven

"Ah, Nicole, you've come back to see me." Salah Badu leaned forward in his chair, his hands bound behind him to the wall and his legs bound to the floor.

Samsara Fleet was en route to the Z'Ta home world T'kor'nuk, a voyage that would take around two weeks. At first, she'd spent her time diving into any materials she could find on the Z'Ta. As the voyage dragged on, she'd run out of material to read and remembered the Nasi prisoner the Skulls had captured months ago. As their only prisoner so far, he intrigued her. Bowen had taught her a lot about the Jadid, but she realized that even the Jadid did not fully understand their cousins.

With effort, Nicole met the creature's even gaze. "Yes, I thought you might be lonely." He gave her the same eerie, toothless smile that appeared in her dreams since they'd first captured him on New America.

"No, I've talked to so many Humans now. They're always asking what do the Nasi want. What are our plans? As if the answer is not already obvious." He tilted his head. "But you're still the most...pleasant...that I've talked to."

Nicole sat in the chair across from the prisoner. His voice and tone had changed in the past couple of months. His words were no longer in the stilted, archaic version of Human Standard that most of the Jadid and Nasi used.

"When we talked last time, you lied."

"How so?" Salah tilted his head.

"You acted as if there were only Nasi. You never talked about the Jadid. Never said you were part of the Jadid."

He gave her another toothless grin. "Are we part of the Jadid or are the Jadid part of us? The Jadid are just Nasi that have yet to realize the truth. We're the same—same as you Humans even. Eventually we'll all be Nasi."

"Once you 'help' us?" Nicole asked.

"Exactly," the prisoner said, his tone one of speaking to a child. "When Humanity abandoned us, we had to struggle to survive. In that struggle we planted the seeds of Humanity's salvation. We—"

"You've said that before. You're here to help. You've also destroyed planets and killed billions. I can't reconcile the two."

"Then perhaps you are too...simple." Nicole grated her teeth as he said the words. "You should realize that sometimes we all must do bad things to achieve a good result. Humans have been doing this forever, even before you cast us out."

Nicole could tell he was teasing her, but her frustration couldn't permit her to leave it alone. "Humanity didn't cast you out. Your entire civilization—Nasi and Jadid—seem to believe that you were victims. It was an accident."

"Was it? When the Human governments began experimenting on their own citizens, trying to perfect the fold drive, do you honestly think they thought of the subjects?"

"It was—"

"Do you think they looked for us? They created a system of willful negligence, and we were the victims." His voice rose.

"You weren't even there." Nicole said. "When were you born?"

94

He turned his head. "I know the stories. I know the truth. All of us Nasi do."

"Don't you want to reconcile with the Jadid?" Nicole asked. "From what I can tell, you're outcasts. Something you seem to have done to yourselves."

"We will reconcile when they understand that we're right. The Grand Ancient has always been correct. She is the strongest of them. Once the Ancients understand, the rest will follow."

Nicole wasn't sure what she'd hoped for from this conversation. Perhaps a bit of killing time, perhaps to convince the Nasi to cooperate. She'd talked to fanatics before. For instance, the Qudoru were almost fanatical in their religious beliefs. But he was beyond reason, beyond change. She'd come here to question him; instead, she was arguing with him. Nicole changed topics and peppered the prisoner with questions about the Nasi: their strategies, command structure, specific objectives that they had. Each time he turned the conversation back to the Nasi and their plans to "educate" Humanity and "restore their rightful place in the galaxy."

After an hour, Nicole gave up. Using her implant, she paged the guard to take away the prisoner. A few seconds later, the door opened and a lanky man in a disheveled uniform strode in.

"Sal, you causing trouble again?" the guard asked with a smirk as he casually bound the Nasi's hands together and then disengaged them from the wall. The guards could see everything that happened in the room.

Salah's demeanor shifted abruptly. He relaxed, his face losing the steely intensity. Instead, a sheepish smile replaced it, mirroring the smile of the guard.

"I've told you Amer. You must realize that we only want to help."

"Yeah, yeah." Amer pulled the Nasi into a standing position and guided him out the door. "Well, you believe in what you believe, and I'll believe in what I do."

Nicole watched as they departed the room and then went into the ship's corridor. Another guard waited to escort her to the brig's reception station.

"Who was that?" Nicole asked.

"The guard, ma'am?" asked the petite blonde-haired soldier. "That's Private Davies. Did he do something wrong?"

"Wrong?" Nicole paused. Had he? Why was Salah so friendly with him? "I don't think so. He just seemed so friendly with the prisoner."

The woman shrugged. "Well, Davies is an odd duck and a bit of a talker. The Nasi, well, he ain't one. So, I guess they just fit together. Yin and yang, ya know?"

Nicole nodded. "I thought you were forbidden to talk with the prisoners."

"Yeah, that's true. But since Davies doesn't have the stomach for the treatments, he always ends up being assigned for recuperation. Can't leave Davies in a room with someone for hours like that and expect him to keep quiet. It's not in the guy's nature."

"Wait, what *treatments*?" Nicole asked. "What do you mean?"

The guard reddened. "Damn. I shouldn't have said anything. I really can't talk about that."

"On whose orders?" Nicole asked.

"I can't say, ma'am." She looked around nervously.

Nicole felt the blood rise in her face. They'd been torturing him. How could they?

Nicole spun around and marched out of the brig facility, the doors closing behind her. Behind her, the young woman yelled, asking her to come back. Nicole ignored her; she had someone else she needed to question.

"The general is in a meeting, ma'am," the aide said as Nicole burst into the waiting room of Samaha's office. "Ma'am, you can't go in there." Nicole stopped. The door to the general's office wouldn't open.

"Tell her I need to talk *now*," Nicole said as she brushed the aide's hand off her arm. Samaha needed to explain what she'd done.

Nicole paced in a small circle while she waited. After a minute, a group of Kurz officers left the office, and Samaha stood in the doorway, an annoyed expression on her face.

"Colonel Bergeron, you demanded to see me?"

"Yes, ma'am." Nicole brushed past the general and stomped into her wood-lined office.

"This had better be good. I was meeting with the Kurz general's staff."

"I was with Salah, the Nasi prisoner, just now."

"Really? What did you learn?" Samaha's anger faded, and there was an eager tone in her voice.

"What have you been doing to him?" Nicole asked. She hoped there was an explanation. General Samaha had trusted Nicole and made her an officer. She hoped the general would be as surprised and as angry as she was. Together, they could find the evil person responsible. It was a faint hope, but she clung to it.

"What do you mean? What did he say?" Samaha stared at Nicole with a raised eyebrow.

"He's being tortured. The guards—"

"You can't trust anything that creature says, Bergeron. The Nasi will do anything to win. You know as well as I do what they're capable of."

"It wasn't him who told me, General."

"Ah, I see." The general let out a long breath.

She'd known. She'd probably ordered it. Nicole felt her heart sink. "What are you doing to him?"

"Only what we have to. He was close to the New American governor. He had to have heard things."

"Are you torturing him?"

"I've directed that the guards use enhanced interrogation techniques, yes. I wouldn't call that torture." A red tint was rising in the general's face. "And I'll continue to do so until we think we've gotten every single piece of useful information out of him."

"That's barbaric. It's—"

"What's barbaric is destroying a peaceful world with billions living on it. What's worse than that is destroying several. The Nasi already did that. We're beyond barbarianism. My job—*our* job—is to make sure they don't do it again. If we have to do some things that are...distasteful, then it's a price I will pay. It is a price that *we* must pay."

Samaha stepped forward and looked down at Nicole. Her face was flush, and her hands balled into fists. Nicole half expected the officer to take a swing.

"What I will not do is tolerate you coming into my office and trying to lecture me on how we should fight this war. If you do this again, I will not only strip you of your position, I'll throw you back in the brig."

The general stood trembling for a moment, hovering over Nicole before brushing past her and sitting down at her desk.

Nicole felt a pang of fear at the general's words. When she'd first met Kal, she'd been a prisoner. She couldn't go back to that. Not because she feared jail, but because she couldn't leave her friends to face the Nasi alone. She had sworn to be a part of the fight, to redeem herself.

The two women stood looking at each other, neither saying a word.

"Ma'am, can I just say—"

"Not another word," Samaha interjected. "Do you understand?"

Nicole nodded.

"Now get out."

Nicole spluttered for a moment and then turned and walked out of the general's office. The aide tried to say something to her as she walked past his desk, but she brushed him off. She had to get out of there before she said something she would regret.

❖

"You wanted to talk to me, ma'am?" Private Amer Davies asked.

"Yeah, thanks for coming by," Nicole said. She gestured to the chair across from her. "Please sit down." The young private took the seat and asked the waiting attendant bot for a tea.

"How long have you been with the fleet?"

"Well, that's a great question, ma'am. For me it's a hard question to answer. Ya see, I actually joined the EDF eleven months ago. Before that…" Davies went through a detailed explanation of growing up an orphan, his time at Base Camp, the EDF training program, and his first tour. The other guard was right; he was a talker.

By the time he stopped talking, Nicole had already finished her first drink. She waved the attendant bot over and asked for another. Time to cut to the chase; otherwise, the war would be over before he told her anything useful.

"Seems like you've become friendly with Salah," she observed.

The young solder looked embarrassed. "Yeah. I mean, we're not friends, but I think I know him a bit better than the others I guess." He shifted in his seat. "I don't believe any of the things he says though. It's just that we end up spending time together. I kinda feel sorry, I guess for—"

"Why sorry?" Nicole interrupted.

The soldier squirmed in his chair. They were getting close to things that he shouldn't be talking about.

"It's okay." She smiled reassuringly. "I've talked to General Samaha and know about the treatments."

Amer looked relieved. "Well, you know, after each session, it takes a while for him to recover. I just don't have the stomach for the treatments themselves, so I'm always the one that minds the medbot. They need someone to supervise it since the Nasi bodies are different."

"How bad are the...side effects of the treatment?" Nicole dreaded the answer.

"Errr." Private Davies looked down at his empty glass. "They're not good. Sometimes I think that he's dead when they drag him out of the room." The private shook his head as if trying to shake a memory.

It was as she'd thought. Nicole wasn't naïve. She knew that there were species for which torture was a perfectly acceptable technique, but she'd always thought that Humanity was not one of them. The UEG had banned it centuries ago.

"So, you talk to him while he's recovering?"

Amer told her how he regularly sat next to Salah, monitoring the progress of the medbot as it healed the wounds he'd sustained from Samaha's torture. At first the young private said nothing, but as his natural gregarious nature won out, he'd started talking at the Nasi. After a few sessions, Salah talked back. It seemed like the two of them had a lot in common; they were both soldiers, both orphans, and, as it turned out, both eager for the war to end.

"Sure, Sal is a bit nuts," Davies admitted, "but he's still a living being. Still has thoughts and feelings. I'd never do anything to help the Nasi, but I figure it didn't hurt to just talk."

"Of course not," Nicole reassured him. "Can you do me a favor?"

"Of course, ma'am." He looked at her eagerly.

"This needs to be between us though. I'm not going to ask you anything wrong, but it's sensitive."

"I can keep a secret, ma'am."

"Ask Salah—Sal—about his job. Nothing specific, just what did he do, what his boss was like. If you find out anything, just let me know."

Davies nodded his head. "Sure ma'am. I can do that." He paused. "These Nasi aren't much different from us. They're just brainwashed. We just need to get through to them, show 'em a different way."

It was a sweet thought. The young soldier saw a species hell-bent on conquering the galaxy and he seemed to think that they could talk it out. *But was he completely wrong? Could they win only militarily? Was there a way between victory and defeat?*

The young private began talking again, this time about his first voyage as a recruit. Nicole pretended that she'd received a priority message via her implant and excused herself. "Thank you for your time, Amer. We might win battles with large battleships. But it's going to take more than that to win this war."

❖

Nicole walked into Samaha's private briefing room aboard the *Gedorhan's Return* to find it was already full. In addition to the general, there was a senior officer from each species in the fleet—Human, Tounous, Kurz, and Qudoru—as well as a Torgham liaison officer. All of them, except the Qudoru officer, who just stood in a corner, sat along the bench along the wall of the room; the Qudoru were not bipedal.

Samaha sat in the middle, murmuring to the Tounous officer seated next to her. The short alien was waving its bifurcated arms in the air, clearly making an impassioned plea of some sort to the general. Samaha had on what Nicole thought of as her "business face"—mouth pressed together in a line, brow furrowed in concentration.

The general didn't react to Nicole's entrance. However, after a few seconds, she wrapped up the conversation with the Tounous and turned to face the room.

"Since we've stopped folding to prepare for our entry into the H'Far system, I thought it would be beneficial for us to meet," Samaha said.

"As I was saying to the general," said Grand Admiral Zzyrian, the Tounous officer. "The Z'Ta are not to be trusted. We'll have to be careful." Nicole's implant seamlessly transformed the alien's clicks and chirps into Human Standard.

The Tounous and Z'Ta shared a common boundary. As a result, they had a history of mistrust and conflict. Ironically, the two species were very similar. Both were hive creatures with a relatively small stature, about a meter tall. Both also tended to be headstrong and impetuous as well.

"We'll need to be careful, for sure," Nicole advised. "The Z'Ta are unlikely to enter into an agreement unless they think it truly benefits them. They will go where their interests lie and will not have an issue ending that agreement if the situation changes."

"They would betray us?" asked the Kurz officer, Field Marshal Krunalt. The Kurz felt all agreements were unconditionally binding. If you went back on a deal with the Kurz, you had to be prepared to fight a war of survival.

"Not betrayal exactly," Nicole replied. "They would inform us they were no longer interested in being allies. Then they would attack."

Krunalt grumbled deep enough that Nicole felt it reverberate through the bench.

"The key will be to ensure that we help make them understand that no matter what the Nasi offer, they are better off staying with us," Nicole said.

"How do we do that?" Colonel Petrov asked. "We're in a fight for survival. Do we really have much to offer?"

"We do," replied Samaha. "First, they must realize that the Nasi will come for them soon."

"All the more reason to for them to join with the Nasi now," said General Nervaan, the Qudoru representative. "They can come as allies rather than as the subjugated. Perhaps keep more autonomy and control."

Krunalt let out an even louder rumbling sound. He did

not like what he was hearing. "I am not saying I agree with it, but this would make sense to them, would it not?"

"It would," agreed Nicole. "That is why we have to show them we have a *good* chance of winning this war."

"I don't know if we have a good chance," Admiral Zzyrian quipped. "I think we'll need to lie."

"Lie? During negotiations for an alliance? We cannot enter an alliance on such grounds." Although the Kurz's voice was too high for Nicole to hear without her implant, the deep rumblings he produced from his body were enough to let her know he was extremely angry.

"It won't be a lie," Samaha said, holding her hands up in a placating gesture that was most likely lost on the Kurz field marshal. "I've talked with Ancient Wang, the Jadid leader, and he said they will join our fight. I think they're just preparing their fleet."

Nicole had not been present at the meeting with Wang, but Kal had told her about it. Samaha *was* lying.

"We can let them know this," Samaha continued. "When we show them what the Nasi have done, and what they're going to do. Well, I think that should convince them." She laid her hands down on her lap. "Now let's talk protocol."

The conversation progressed into a discussion of how they would engage with the Z'Ta. As a former diplomat and student of anthropology, Nicole had a deep understanding of how important social niceties could be in a tense situation. Offend the wrong person or start off from a position of weakness, and the rest of the conversation could be useless.

Nicole, with the help of Zzyrian, briefed the group on

how best to engage the Z'Ta once they arrived at T'kor'nuk. They settled on a plan that would show strength while also being respectful of the Z'Ta. After they all agreed on the plan, General Samaha concluded the meeting. They would continue their journey soon and would need to be ready to meet with the Z'Ta upon arrival. It would be rude not to request a meeting with their leadership as soon as they arrived in the system.

Minutes later, Nicole sat in the tender back to the *Ofira* and stared at the stars on the passenger viewscreen. With the Skulls, everything had been black and white. Here with the fleet, it was more complex. Samaha seemed more than willing to cross lines that Nicole wouldn't have dreamt of. Nicole couldn't decide how much she would give up to ensure their victory.

Chapter Eight

Waiting often was the worst part of any mission in Nicole's mind. She, along with everyone else in Samsara Fleet, was waiting for the return of one of their scout ships which was conducting a staged approach to T'kor'nuk to recon the planet.

Since fold drives allowed ships to move instantaneously, they could approach planets in a series of smaller jumps. As they got closer to the planet, their sensors detected light from weeks or months before, allowing them to peer back in time to see the situation in the planet from that time. For a large fleet, this maneuver, called a staged approach, could be extremely dangerous. Having enormous capital ships folding in close proximity multiple times risked one or more of them imploding from gravitational interference with the fold drive. Instead, a scout ship folded ahead of the fleet to see if there was any danger present and then report back.

After the debacle at Patagonia where Samsara Fleet had folded to the planet to find an enormous Nasi fleet, General Samaha had ordered that they use a scout ship to recon planets before sending the full fleet, except in case of emergency.

Nicole sat on the *Ofira's* bridge as she waited. The ship's crew had assigned her a small console near the back so she'd be available in case the commander needed diplomatic counsel. Normally the room would be humming with energy. However, there was nothing for them to do except wait. The crew sat at their stations, idly talking or performing their thousandth check on one of the ship's systems.

"Waiting. It's always the worst part," Frederick Zhou said as he walked next to Nicole. She turned her head to find the round face of the middle-aged officer looking earnestly at her. Then she saw the silver star pinned to the man's collar.

"Congratulations! Brigadier General Zhou has a nice ring to it," Nicole said with a smile.

He gave a brief smile in response. "Thank you. I'm not sure I deserve it. It's certainly not the way I expected to get it."

"You deserve it, sir." Nicole had known General Zhou since he was a lieutenant colonel on Kapustin Station and she'd still been a prisoner there. The war had changed him—it had changed all of them—and made him a more compassionate leader. Since leaving the Skulls and joining Samaha's operations staff, Zhou had distinguished himself and become indispensable. It wouldn't surprise her if he was promoted again. Samaha clearly had big plans for the officer.

"That's the thing about war. Waiting is such an integral part of it." He waved at the large viewscreen that dominated the bridge. "Now we sit here for hours watching the stars and waiting for word that we can go."

"There are worse things," Nicole replied, thinking of her friends trying to infiltrate Patagonia—again. She wished she was there with them.

Frederick sighed. "I guess there are."

As General Samaha's operations officer, General Zhou knew more of Samsara Fleet's strengths and weaknesses than anyone else. Samaha must have consulted him about how they could best use the Z'Ta in the fleet. "What do you think about the Z'Ta?" Nicole turned her head to gauge the general's reaction.

"I think that when you're about to fall off a cliff, even the smallest branch can help you." He chuckled mirthlessly. "The Z'Ta are one of the most advanced fleets in this part of the galaxy. They're also one of the most unreliable."

"That seems to be the consensus."

"Yes, because it's true." He winked at her playfully. Definitely a far cry from the career-focused, ramrod-straight officer she'd first met.

Before Nicole could speak, an alert sounded throughout the bridge. The scout ship had returned. The Qudoru scout's crew hailed the fleet over an open channel and reported that the planet was clear, no signs of the enemy.

Five minutes later, Colonel Petrov gave the helm the command for the *Ofira* to fold. The stars blinked on the viewscreen and T'kor'nuk appeared on it.

At first glance, the planet looked dead—a lifeless brown-gray rock. Looking closer, Nicole could see a few structures dotting the planet's surface. The Z'Ta lived in large hives underneath the planet's rock exterior. The only structures on the surface were landing pads.

It took several minutes for the Z'Ta to respond to General Samaha's request to meet with their Leadership Council in person. The Z'Ta council was a triumvirate of their top three political leaders. They believed in ruling through a council of three rather than having a single decision maker or commander. As part of their planning, Samaha had agreed that Samsara Fleet should come to the first meeting with three representatives as well: Samaha, Nicole, and the Tounous Grand Admiral Zzyrian.

Thirty minutes later, Nicole sat in a plush seat on Samaha's personal shuttle. A fleet commander's shuttle was designed to impress. The interior was lavish with cutting-edge technology complemented by gilt inlays and exotic wood finishes. If she hadn't been so nervous, Nicole would have loved to try the miniature food fabricator next to her.

Instead, Nicole kept her eyes focused on the viewscreen as they slowly dropped through the planet's atmosphere. As they got closer to the surface, she could see chasms, craters, and deep gorges marring the rocky surface of the planet. There were some animals that could survive on the planet's desolate terrain, but the majority were like the Z'Ta and lived in the network of tunnels and caverns beneath.

"Ma'am," the pilot's voice came over the speaker, "we're having some issues with landing. Their port operations have ordered us into a holding pattern. Something about mechanical issues."

"Strange," Zzyrian chirped, "they are delaying us. That is not like the Z'Ta."

The shuttle circled a few kilometers above the landing pad and waited for permission to land. Nicole used the viewscreen to look at the pad and figure out what was causing the delay, but it looked like it was operating normally. She saw several small atmospheric craft on the pad and small dots of the Z'Ta workers scurrying between the ships. She even saw a few small civilian craft take off.

Shuttle One, this is Ofira, said Colonel Petrov over the

command net. *Multiple Nasi ships have just folded into the system. Return immediately.*

The pilot must have also heard the warning because she immediately began climbing from the planet in an almost vertical trajectory. Nicole was pushed back into her seat by the acceleration combined with the planet's heavy gravity. Due to its immense size and density, T'kor'nuk had a much stronger gravitational pull than almost any other inhabited planet.

"Open the cockpit screen," Samaha shouted to the pilot, "I want to see what's going on." The barrier between the cockpit and passenger area dropped, and the general climbed from her seat to peer into the cockpit. Nicole used her implant to adjust the side viewscreens so that they were displaying a tactical map of the area and the view from the shuttle's front cameras. She could see almost as much as Samaha without having to drape her body through the passageway to the cockpit.

Six large Nasi capital ships had entered the space around the planet. The ships had already disengaged their fighters and released salvos of missiles at Samsara Fleet. Nicole couldn't see the ships due to the vast distances of space, but the tacmap told a grim tale.

"They've got to get out of here," Nicole said. "Why aren't they folding away?"

Zzyrian waved his arms. "They can't. The gravitational fields there won't allow them to fold. They're going to have to split up and try to find fold points. The Nasi are trying to block them, and they're positioned pretty well. It's like they knew we'd be here."

"How?" Nicole asked. "It can't be pure luck. There's no way to follow a fleet while they're folding."

"No, but the Z'Ta could have told them." The alien's ears flattened against his head in anger.

Samsara Fleet consisted of eight cutting-edge capital ships and hundreds of fighters. Against a normal enemy, they would have the advantage. However, the Nasi had caught them off guard and had the most advanced weapons and technology in the galaxy.

Thankfully, the initial Nasi barrage had been mostly ineffective. Samsara Fleet's engineers had been working continuously to upgrade the fleet's ships while they had been folding to T'kor'nuk. Thanks to the raw materials they had unloaded at Keerloa, their work in reverse engineering Nasi technology, and Bowen's help, the fleet was already significantly more effective than it had been just a few months before.

Samsara Fleet split up, each of the eight ships moving to a different fold point. The maneuver forced the Nasi fleet to scatter as well. They continued to harass Samsara fleet, firing salvo after salvo of missiles. Thankfully, they mostly missed their targets, thrown off target by the fleet's counter measures. Samsara Fleet also released their fighters who met the Nasi fighters head on, preventing them from closing any more distance.

"How's it looking?" asked Nicole.

Zzyrian whistled. "At least we're not all dead. This battle favors the Nasi though. They have ships and time. We have neither." The Nasi now had a massive fleet in this universe and a rapidly growing industrial base. They could afford to take losses that Samsara Fleet with its eight ships and piecemeal supply lines could not.

"Look at them," the Tounous admiral pointed at the Z'Ta ships on the tacmap. "They're doing nothing. Just sitting there." Zzyrian was right, the Z'Ta must have joined the Nasi or at least made some deal with them.

General Samaha turned around and looked back into the passenger compartment. "We won't be able to get back to the fleet. The Nasi are blocking our approach."

"We'll have to—"

An impossibly bright light erupted in the distance. As it grew, the explosion washed out everything else in the viewscreen.

"What was that?" the general called into the cockpit.

"The *Flight of the Tokras*, ma'am," the pilot responded. The Tounous battleship must have gone critical.

Zzyrian let out a loud screech causing Nicole to press her hands to her ears. Despite the difference in species, the pain and sadness were clear.

Samaha looked at the Tounous admiral. "I'm sorry, Zzyrian." She paused for a moment and then turned so she was looking at them both. "I've ordered the fleet to leave the system and head to one of our rendezvous points. We're going to have to figure out a way to get to them."

The small shuttle did not have a fold drive. Without Samsara Fleet, they were trapped in the H'Far system. Trapped under the Nasi's thumb.

"Ma'am," the pilot called from the cockpit. "We've got an incoming message from the planet. Voice only."

"Route it into the passenger area," Samaha ordered. "I can't keep sticking my head in there."

"Hey, General Samaha." Nicole could hear the voice beneath the Standard Human translation from her implant. It sounded like the burbles and glops of a small stream. The speaker was a Z'Ta. "We gotta talk. Don't worry. We're not working with the Nasi. I'll send some coordinates, and we can help ya out."

"Transmission cut off," the pilot called out. "There are coordinates embedded at the end of the message."

The coordinates the Z'Ta had sent were for a point on the opposite side of the planet from Samsara Fleet. Despite the offer of help, General Samaha had ordered the pilot to keep them in their current position, hovering just outside the planet's atmosphere. "No need to commit just yet," Samaha said after ordering the pilot to hold their position.

The three passengers sat in the small shuttle watching the battle play out. The Nasi continually hounded Samsara Fleet as they maneuvered to their fold points. Because of the gravitational interference of the planet and its moon, not to mention the capital ships in the area, there were only a few points where the fleet could engage their fold drives and escape without destroying themselves.

The Nasi fighters harassed the ships as they moved,

looking for a way to get close and launch their missiles. Nicole whispered a word of thanks under her breath to Samsara Fleet's fighter pilots, who miraculously held them at bay. The Nasi battleships continued to fire salvos of missiles at the fleet, targeting key systems like their shield emitters, thrusters, and fold drives. Luckily, the ships' upgraded point defense systems picked most of them off. The countermeasures fooled almost all the rest though there were some direct hits on several of Samsara Fleet's ships. Months ago, those missile strikes would have destroyed the ships. Now they were bad but not fatal.

The shuttle passengers watched the deadly dance between Samsara Fleet and the Nasi. One by one, the seven remaining ships disappeared as they reached their fold points and departed the system. There was a small cheer in the cramped shuttle after the last ship, the Kurz battleship *Lokryz*, folded away.

"Ma'am, the Nasi are going to head back toward T'kor'nuk. Are we going to the coordinates?" Nicole asked.

"I would not recommend that. We can't trust the Z'Ta. I think they've proven that today," Zzyrian said.

Samaha looked around the small passenger compartment for a moment and then sighed. "I don't know what choice we have. What else can the Z'Ta do to us? They've got us. There's no need for subterfuge on their part."

"I don't know what their plans are, but I'm sure it's better to stay away."

"Ma'am, the Nasi fleet is hailing us," the pilot called out over the ship's intercom.

"Don't answer," Samaha instructed. "Head to the coordinates that the Z'Ta provided." She looked at the two other passengers. "Sorry, Admiral, looks like we're out of choices."

Thankfully, the Nasi fleet had committed all their ships to chasing down Samsara Fleet. The small shuttle would be able to reach the planet well before the Nasi could detect or intercept them.

As they descended through the atmosphere again, Nicole's mind raced. Once they landed, they'd be trapped. T'kor'nuk had a few ports on the surface. It would be easy for the Z'Ta or Nasi to lockdown the planet and prevent them from leaving.

The shuttle pulled up from its descent and flew a few hundred meters over the planet's surface. In the distance, Nicole spotted their destination. It looked like a small crater but was too perfectly circular and smooth to be natural. The shuttle slowed and descended into the mouth of the crater. As they glided down, the natural rock transitioned into metal plating. The enormous shaft looked neglected; the edges of the metal plates were bent in places, and there were gaps where a plate had clearly fallen off, revealing the rock underneath.

"It's some sort of hidden port," Samaha observed. "Looks like it's abandoned."

The shaft opened into a large underground cavern. The bay floor had several landing spaces marked in paint—paint that was now chipped and faded. It was painfully empty; there were no other ships in the cavern. As the shuttle touched down, Nicole felt a deep thrum shudder through the ship and looked up to see that the ceiling was constricting shut.

Wherever they were, they were trapped.

❖

"Well, time to get out," Samaha announced dryly. The side of the shuttle opened, and a wall of moist acrid air struck Nicole in the face.

"Nice flying," Nicole said to the pilot as the four of them stood in the bay.

The young woman nodded her head, her dark hair sweeping forward in a curtain.

Nicole inspected the decrepit and rusted equipment scattered across the abandoned bay. No one had used it in years. As she walked around, she could feel the planet's heavy gravity weighing down her frame.

"Hey!" The burbles of a Z'Ta voice reverberated through the cave. "Over here! Come on, we gotta go!"

With the echo, it took Nicole a moment to figure out where the voice was coming from. Finally, she saw the dark silhouettes of three Z'Ta at the edge of the bay.

As the four of them walked toward the shadows, the smudgy outlines developed into three rocklike Z'Ta. Their brownish gray skin and short stocky frames blended into the rocky walls. The aliens stood on their hind legs with their front legs to the side.

"Hurry and follow us, will ya?" one of the Z'Ta shouted. The group sped up, almost breaking into a run. As they got close, the three Z'Ta went down on all fours, turned, and ran into a smaller corridor.

They crawled through the narrow twisting corridors, trying to keep up with the three Z'Ta. Both General Samaha and the pilot had the foresight to bring a light so the group could see a few feet ahead of them. Other than that, there was no light. The Z'Ta and the Tounous could use echolocation so there was no need. The tunnels were simple bare rock that appeared to have been carved out of the rock by hand.

For the three Humans, it was tough going. Nicole hit her head countless times on the low ceiling. She took some solace in the curses that she heard from the general and pilot ahead of her as they did the same. Zzyrian had been raised in tunnels like these and could move through them with ease, though he modulated his pace to stay with his Human companions. Nicole doubted he wanted to be alone with the Z'Ta.

The single tunnel intersected with multiple others, all of them empty and pitch black. Their path twisted from one tunnel to the next. They doubled back on themselves and undulated up and down until Nicole was hopelessly lost.

Eventually, the Z'Ta arrived at a small open doorway that had a faint light emanating from it. Nicole had to duck her head as she clambered through into the dimly lit room beyond. Inside looked to be an operations center with at least fifty Z'Ta inside. The room looked recently reoccupied. There was still a thin layer of dust covering almost every surface with prints and tracks where something had been drug through.

The Z'Ta had arranged dim viewscreens throughout the room and ran around talking to each other while they worked on the outdated consoles. As the Humans and Tounous entered, they stopped what they were doing and turned to stare.

Three Z'Ta stood in the center of the room facing them. They had four black eyes, two on each side of their head. Like the others in the room, they had collars around their necks with insignia to designate their rank and status. Nicole figured they were the three their group had just followed through the tunnels. She couldn't tell one Z'Ta from another though.

"What is this?" asked General Samaha, eyeing the room.

"Well, that's simple," replied the Z'Ta in the center, "this is rebellion."

Chapter Nine

According to Garcia, the Foyleton Syndicate had changed immensely since he'd left Patagonia to join the EDF. Back then, it had been a loose network of smugglers and thieves. Now it was a paramilitary force, complete with armored vehicles and atmospheric aircraft. They called themselves soldiers, and they had the equipment though not the training to back it up.

After Lukas had freed them, the Skulls settled into their ornate rooms and enjoyed their new freedom. Each member of the team spent the evening alone, appreciating the time spent in their sumptuous quarters rather than a crowded jail cell. The next day, Kal had them wander the headquarters in small groups, learning its layout and talking to the Foyleton soldiers.

The enormous building was divided into three areas—landing bays at the top, living quarters in the middle, and command and control systems at the bottom. The EDF had built it to support their fleet in space rather than to support a terrestrial army, so Foyleton had retrofitted much of the base since they had moved in. They'd added additional landing bays for smaller aircraft, quarters for soldiers, and facilities to support both.

Talking to the Foyleton soldiers did little to reverse Kal's initial poor opinion of them. Most of them had been civilians just a few months ago. The civil war had forced them to choose a side, and Foyleton was the most powerful faction in the area. Survival, money, and hedonistic pleasures appeared to motivate the vast majority.

During their second day, the group had split into three teams to conduct a recon of the city. Garcia stayed behind to "see who he remembered," and Bo stayed behind because he would probably cause a minor riot. Foyleton had been spared much of the fighting and destruction the large capital city, Kasongo, had faced. Lukas had quickly seized control of the city once the Patagonian government fell. The only violence had been small surgical strikes by rival factions trying to eliminate high-level Foyleton leaders or key infrastructure in the city.

On their third and final day of leave, Kal and Private Sandra Chedjou were scouring the eastern neighborhoods of the city—mostly run-down communes and small merchants selling homemade goods out of small storefronts along the winding roads. Whatever wealth the Foyleton Syndicate had won hadn't made its way there. Kal and Sandra were returning to the headquarters as the sun was setting in the east, spreading an orange warmth across the sky. The shops were closing, steel curtains coming down over their storefronts, and holo signs shutting down. The chem bars, brothels, and clubs were just opening, and loud music spilled into the street luring eager clientele to swagger in.

"This is so different from New America," Sandra said as she pointed to the surrounding streets. New America was a meticulously planned colony with each urban zone laid out in an efficient grid pattern and relatively homogeneous buildings. Foyleton was very similar to Kasongo with streets that seemed to twist and turn at every stop and no two buildings looking the same.

"It's a frontier town that's grown too big for its britches," Kal observed.

"I guess that's true." Sandra rubbed her arms.

"Do you miss home?" Kal asked.

Sandra was originally from New America. When Kal had first met her, he was a drunkard hauling cargo between systems, and she was a kid who'd just graduated from school. That girl was long gone. After the Nasi invasion, she'd joined a resistance movement on New America prior to being recruited by Kal to join Samsara Fleet and the Skulls.

"No—" she stopped herself. "In a way, I guess. I just worry about everyone left behind. The Domespat were hunting people down." The Domestic State Patrol was the police force of the authoritarian government that had taken control of the planet, the New American Empire.

Sandra continued, "What do you think is happening there?"

"I think your friends are—"

Someone bumped into Kal from behind. He stumbled, staggering into Sandra, before regaining his balance. As the person passed, he felt something shoved into his hand.

"Grab 'em," Kal yelled at Sandra, pointing at the person who had now broken into a run. They followed the dim silhouette as it turned into one of the many alleys that branched off from the road.

Kal heard the whine of a thruster as they turned the corner and saw the person lift off from the alley floor. Sandra had pulled her sidearm and began to take aim at the figure.

"No!" Kal pushed her arm down.

They watched as the figure rose over the tops of the buildings and disappeared. Kal looked down at his hand and saw that he was holding a chit. The card was standard sized—about six by four centimeters and a few millimeters thick. Its bare metal face had only a single mark on it, a circle about the size of a fingertip.

"What's that?" Sandra asked.

"Not sure," Kal said, "but I have a suspicion."

"What?" Sandra cocked her head.

"The Alliance. It's them or the Front, and I think the Front would just send an agent to meet us if they thought someone had compromised their communications. This is a little too dramatic for them."

He touched the small circle on the card with his index finger. A luminescent arrow appeared on the face of the card, pointing to the west of the city, the opposite direction from the Foyleton headquarters.

It would be great to let the rest of the team know about their find, but there was no way to reach them without potentially tipping off Lukas and Foyleton. Although the syndicate leader had said nothing, Kal was sure their every word in the headquarters was recorded. The planetary network might also be compromised by Foyleton, the Nasi, or both. It was now or never since they would be on a mission tomorrow.

Kal studied the glowing arrow hovering beneath the surface of the chit.

"Sir?" Sandra asked.

"Looks like we've got one more stop," Kal said.

❖

The arrow on the chit did not take into account streets or obstacles. It simply pointed in the same direction like an old-fashioned Earth compass. The rambling and chaotic pathways and roads of Foyleton forced them to circle back, climb over obstacles, and constantly check the map in their implants.

By the time they reached the building they were certain must be their destination, the sun had completely set. The only light came from the signs and windows of the businesses and homes around them. The few people they saw on the street were either selling drugs or clearly under their influence. When they saw the red armbands on Kal's and Sandra's arms, they averted their eyes, quickened their pace, and wordlessly moved to the other side of the street.

"I conducted a complete inspection, sir." Sandra said. "No sign of activity."

The faded green building had clearly seen better days. It was the only structure without light emanating from its windows at the end of an alley.

"Well, it's a great place to hide or a great place for a trap," Kal said, partially to himself.

"Or both," Sandra said cheerfully.

"Or both," Kal agreed.

"How do you want to approach this, sir? I can cover you." Sandra's voice never wavered. If she was nervous, it didn't show.

"No, let's go in together," Kal replied, "I don't think this is an ambush. Whoever gave me this chit could have shot us in the back an hour ago."

They climbed down from their rooftop observation post and slunk to the front of their destination. The wooden door was faded, the lacquer finish having worn away long ago. After a quick check for any alarms or triggers, Kal pushed on the door. After some initial resistance, it swung open.

They both turned on the small lights they carried with them and conducted a sweep of the room—Kal to the right and Sandra to the left. It was apparent this had been a shop of some sort a long time ago. There was only one room in the entire building. Empty display cases sat against the walls. Several cases sat in a small square in the center of the room with a dust covered attendant bot resting on its side in the middle of them. The bot's maintenance panels had been forced open, and someone had removed the circuits and wiring, most likely for salvage.

"Nothing here," Sandra said.

"Look close, this has got to be an Alliance front," Kal replied. He'd seen enough of them to tell.

They made second passes around the room, double-checking for some sort of clue. Kal looked closely at the bare walls and underneath the cases, looking for a switch or panel of some sort. Still, there was nothing.

Cursing, Kal awkwardly jumped over the cases in the center of the room. He examined the back of them without success. As he swept the room with his light, a small sparkle of light caught his eye. There was something on the deactivated bot in the center of the room. He bent down to examine it. Someone had attached a small rectangular box to the bot that was indistinguishable from the rest of the metal frame, except that its surface was almost completely clean. Not a speck of dust on it. Kal looked it over up-close. There were no slots or dials on it.

"Check this out," Kal called to Sandra. She gracefully leapt over the display cases, landing silently next to him.

"Show off."

Sandra bowed, raising her arms with a flourish at Kal's comment. "Check this out," Kal said, pointing to the box.

Sandra looked it over. "Press the card against it," she advised. Kal tried, but nothing happened. "Hm, press the bio reader on the chit," she said. As soon as Kal's finger touched the circle on the card, metal shutters slammed down behind the front door and windows, cutting off what little light was coming in from the street. The square floor that Kal and Sandra were standing on between the cases slowly started to descend. As soon as they were below the level of the shop floor, a metal door scissored shut above them.

Lights were embedded in the pristine white walls of the shaft every couple of meters, causing the elevator to get brighter the farther down they went. Finally, the floor smoothly came to a complete stop; Kal guessed they had dropped at least twenty meters. In front of them was an open doorway spilling a harsh white light into the passage.

"Damn," Sandra said, shielding her eyes.

After waiting several seconds for their eyes to adjust, Kal and Sandra stepped through the doorway and into a bright white hallway. A long royal blue runner ran the length of the hallway and metal sconces were attached at intervals along the walls. It was the kind of opulence Kal always associated with the Alliance. There was a hint of age and elegance to it as opposed to the garish displays of Foyleton.

"So this is the Alliance?" Sandra asked.

"This is the Alliance."

At the end of the hallway stood a small man, mid-thirties, with a shock of white-blond hair. He was dressed in an ill-fitting single-piece mechanic's uniform, a piece of rope around the waist as a belt.

"Finally!" he shouted. "I've been waiting for you."

"Alliance, I presume," said Kal.

"As if you don't know." The man gestured to the room behind him. "Sit. We've got a lot to talk about."

❖

"Glad you made it," said the man as he sat down across from Kal and Sandra. They were sitting in what looked to be a formal waiting room. The floor was dark hued with light complex inlays. The walls were light green with several pictures surround by ornate gold frames. Chaise lounges and chairs sat around a table that looked like it was carved from a single piece of wood.

"Who are you?" Kal asked. "The Alliance only uses bots."

"You know the rules," said the man, shaking his head. "No names. That's not how the Alliance works."

"Screw that," Sandra snapped. "There aren't any rules anymore. You're sitting in a cave and dressed like a beggar. You need us just as much as we need you."

Kal nodded. "You want to talk to us, then you tell us who the hell we're talking to."

The man grumbled. "Ah, fine." He leaned back in the sumptuous crimson chair. "Call me...Ishmael. I used to be—still am—the Alliance boss on Patagonia."

"What do you want?" Kal asked.

"To help. The Nasi took out all our fronts on the planet except this one. They hunted down every single one of our agents except me." He shook his head. "Not like we had many people anyway. But now all I have are my informants. I'm operating with almost no information either. The Nasi also destroyed our probe network, so I don't know what's going on with the rest of the Alliance."

"The Alliance has its own probe network?" Sandra asked, eyes wide.

Prior to the Nasi attack, a network of automated probes folded between systems in the galaxy. They would receive, store, and transmit messages between the various systems. It was how citizens, governments, and militaries communicated between systems. When the Nasi arrived, one of the first things they did was destroy the probe network, effectively eliminating communication between the planets and plunging much of the galaxy into darkness.

For the Alliance to have its own network of probes was amazing. It was evidence of how large and powerful they were—before the Nasi came.

"We did," answered Ishmael, "It lasted slightly longer than the public one when the Nasi arrived. But now it's down as well. The last thing I heard, General Norman, was that you were somewhere on New America." He leaned forward. "Bottom line, I *want* to help you. I've been given instructions to give you anything you need. When you activated your chit on Patagonia, I got the message, but there was no way I was gonna respond. The Nasi are tracking our signals." He nodded crisply. "So I had to get creative."

"So can you help us?" asked Sandra.

"I'll try. What do you need?"

"We need to storm the Nasi Foothold in Kasongo. There is something there we have to get. Or we think it's there."

Ishmael snickered. "Yeah, so, no. I can't get you that. I can get you weapons, but I'm assuming you already have them since you're working for Lukas Garcia now." He pointed at the red armbands. "In terms of people, the Alliance is bare bones under the best circumstances. And now, I have my informants but otherwise, it's just me."

"We're not working for Lukas," Sandra spat.

"Foyleton is the only way we can get the people we need to pull this off," Kal added.

Ishmael rubbed his hands together thoughtfully. "Probably right at that. But you'd better be careful. Lukas is as shifty as they come. And this is coming from a lifelong criminal. He's had people trailing you every day since you left his compound. It took me forever to find an opening to get you that chit without being seen."

Kal tried to hide his shock. He hadn't realized they were

being followed.

"I can help you one way though," Ishmael continued. "I heard the two people following you today talking. Guess when you're following someone you don't notice someone following you." He shrugged. "They've got plans for ya. They're gonna kill the two of you and then try to claim credit with the Nasi. Seems like they think they'll get some sort of bounty." He huffed. "Idiots."

"Where are they now?" Kal asked. "Are you able to track them at all?"

Ishmael placed his hand on his chest. "What do you think I am? Some wet-behind-the-ears two-bit thug? I'm an extremely skilled thug. Course I know where they are. This building may be a backup, but we still have a cutting-edge sensor system." As he spoke, a video of a man and a woman, both wearing Foyleton armbands, appeared in one of the frames on the wall. They were crouched behind a pile of crates with high-powered rifles in their hands. Another picture frame had a small overhead map, showing the Foyleton agents' positions outside the front. They had taken a position close to where Kal and Sandra had been, overlooking the entrance to the building.

"What do we do?" Sandra asked.

"Where's your back exit?" Kal asked. Alliance fronts always had multiple exits for just this type of situation.

"We've got a tunnel that exits here." Ishmael pointed to a spot about fifty meters behind the two Foyleton soldiers.

Kal stood up to study the map closer. The exit would take them to an alley a few blocks away from their would-be assassins. It was the perfect spot to take them from behind.

"We'll take them out," Kal said.

"We could just slip away," Sandra suggested. "If we kill 'em, that's going to be hard to explain."

Kal cracked his knuckles. "If we don't, then they or someone else will get us when we're not looking. Also, we led them right to the Alliance. They will almost certainly report where we went; that's an even bigger risk." They had to have Lukas think they were all in. If he thought they were working with the Alliance behind his back, he would have them killed.

"I suggest you take some new weapons," Ishmael said. As he spoke, the wall opposite the viewscreen opened up, revealing a room stocked with almost every type of armament imaginable. "Foyleton could trace their killings to you. Grab a burner, take 'em out, and dump the guns somewhere else. Make it look like a mugging."

"Good idea," Kal replied. He stepped into the small armory that Ishmael had revealed. All four walls of the room were covered floor to ceiling with shelves fully stocked with weapons. High-powered rifles, kinetic weapons, explosives, grenades—it was a cornucopia of death.

After carefully examining the shelves, Kal picked out two Gregov kinetic rifles. They were cheap, common, and would get the job done. Gregovs had flooded the black market; it would be impossible to trace them. Although he didn't look it, Kal was the best shot on the Skulls and an expert in small arms. He'd even been an instructor for several years in the EDF.

"Sir, should we take a few extra items for fun?" Sandra

asked, holding a small plasma grenade.

"Take a few things, nothing too large."

They grabbed a few grenades and proximity mines and stuffed them into the cargo pockets on their loose-fitting merchant pants.

"Take this," Ishmael said as he handed Kal a small black device that fit comfortably in his hands. The rectangular device was relatively plain with only a small circle on the side, identical to the one that was on the Alliance chit.

"This is an encrypted communicator." Ishmael held up a mirror copy of the one Kal was holding. "You can use it to reach me if needed. It doesn't use the local net, so there's much less chance of our communication being intercepted." Kal placed the small radio in his pocket. "This thing will reach me from almost anywhere on the planet."

"Thanks, I appreciate it. We'll be in touch," Kal said.

"Great. I'll be here when you need me," Ishmael said. "The Alliance is in hiding for now, but we still have resources."

Kal and Sandra thanked Ishmael and strode down the long utility corridor that led to the alternate exit. They climbed into the small lift was at the end of the hallway and shot up into a small sewer below the street. As the lift reached sewer level, it stopped abruptly, causing them to stumble forward.

"Okay, take the rear," Kal instructed. Sandra obligingly walked behind him, focusing on their sides and behind them, while Kal led them through the sewers and up into the alley. Several trash containers sat against the walls, perfect for scaling the crumbling buildings. They climbed onto the ramshackle roofs and carefully crept forward, keeping an eye out for weak points where they might fall through.

Kal caught sight of the two Foyleton soldiers, still in the same position they'd seen on the viewscreen. They were both laser-focused on the Alliance building and didn't bother to look around.

"Too easy," Sandra whispered as she raised her rifle.

Kal raised his own and began to countdown. "Three...two...one."

The sounds of their shots came out as one and the two Foyleton soldiers jerked and then slumped down as the rounds hit them in their backs. It was a cowardly kill, but Kal had learned early on that there was no valor in war.

"Now we just gotta—" One of the guards dragged themselves over the roof's ledge before the two Skulls could raise their rifles for another shot. "Damn it!"

Kal jumped from the roof, rolling into a ball to cushion his landing on the uneven street below. He heard a thump as Sandra landed next to him.

"Go left, I'll go right," Kal instructed as he took off. He ran down the small street and turned left around the corner of the building. Ahead of him he could see the Foyleton soldier, limping toward one of the large arteries that carried most of the traffic in the area. The road would almost certainly have security cameras set up around it, not to mention the citizens in their vehicles.

Kal raised his rifle and fired. The round hit the soldier in the back, but they continued to race forward. *Damn armor!*

Sandra had made her way around the other side of the buildings and was running as well. As she passed Kal, the silhouette in front of them disappeared. Sandra rushed forward and Kal saw her disappear as well. A few seconds later, several shots echoed from ahead. Kal saw an open sewer grate in front of him. Sandra must have foolishly dropped into the hole to chase their target. Without breaking stride, Kal latched his rifle to the holster on his back and pulled out his pistol. He dropped into the sewer, rolling to his side as he hit the slick moss-covered ground.

Several more shots reverberated through the sewer, and Kal could hear the metallic pings of slugs impacting the floor and walls around him. He dove behind a corner to get some cover.

"Stop or I'll kill her," shouted a female voice.

"Okay, okay."

"You're going to step out where I can see you with your hands up," the woman instructed. "If you don't, or if you try *anything*, I'll blow your friend's head to pieces."

Kal quietly holstered his pistol. "I am stepping out," Kal announced as he walked around the corner. The sewer tunnel was completely black, except for the halo of soft light that streamed in from the grate above. He could tell the sewer was still being used since the stench of decaying Human refuse filled his nostrils.

The Foyleton soldier stood directly behind Sandra, her gun pointed at the back of the woman's head. Kal could see a dark stain of blood in Sandra's brown hair. Her arm hung at her side limply, most likely broken.

"Throw your rifle down," the woman instructed. Kal slowly unhooked his rifle and set it on the ground.

"Now your pistol." Kal swore to himself. He'd hoped she hadn't noticed the holster in the dim light of the sewers.

Kal slowly took his pistol out of its holster, holding it by the barrel. As he bent over to place it on the ground, he noticed the whites of Sandra's eyes against the inky blackness of the tunnels. She gave a quick wink and dropped to the ground. At the same time, Kal used every bit of strength in his cybernetic arm to hurl the pistol at the surprised Foyleton guard. The pistol hit her in the chest, causing her to cry out in shock. She involuntarily stepped backwards, raising her arms out to steady herself.

Sandra somehow turned around and jumped toward the Foyleton soldier. Her fist connected squarely with the woman's eye, sending her falling backwards to the ground. Kal picked his rifle off the ground, flicked off the safety, and fruitlessly looked for any opening between the two women wrestling on the ground. Finally, Sandra wrapped her legs around the woman's neck and squeezed. After a minute, the woman went limp, and Sandra kept the pressure on for a few more seconds before kicking the now unconscious body away from her.

"You alright?" Kal asked.

"Been better, sir," Sandra replied, touching the bloodstain in her hair. "What do we do with her?"

"We can't let her go back," Kal said. "She's seen way too much."

"Are you saying . . ." Sandra trailed off.

135

What am I saying? Kal wondered. Could they kill someone in cold blood? Why had he been fine with killing her before and now the idea was so repellant to him? What was the other option though? Is this what he'd become? A cold-hearted killer? Someone who would put a slug between someone's eyes while they lay unconscious?

No.

"Restrain her," Kal instructed. "I've got another idea."

"First of all, you stink," Ishmael said. "Second of all, what the hell are you doing?"

Kal and Sandra had found several unused strands of wire in the tunnel and used it to haul her out of the sewer and drag her back to the Alliance front. Sandra's arm was broken, so Kal had to do most of the heavy lifting and dragging.

"You said you would help," Kal answered. "This is how you can help. Find a place to keep her."

"This isn't a prison, you dolt," Ishmael snapped. He ran his hand over his head and looked around.

"Don't you have a closet or something?" Sandra asked. "There's got to be some place you can keep her."

Ishmael groaned. "Fine, wait here. I'll see what I can do. And she stinks too." Ishmael disappeared into a different utility corridor than they had used to exit the base. Kal could hear the faint sound of metal scraping before the Alliance boss finally reappeared.

"Okay, follow me."

Several boxes and machines sat against the wall in the middle of the hallway. Between them was an open door that led to a small supply closet. Kal and Sandra dragged the body into the room and stepped back. She's young, Kal realized as he looked at her lying on the ground. About Sandra's age. Her blonde hair was matted and dirty. He guessed she cut it herself with a knife like he'd seen others do in the Foyleton headquarters. After a moment, Kal and Sandra stepped back into the hall and the door slid shut behind them.

"Okay, that should work for now," Ishmael said, "but you need to figure out what to do with her. Also, I have no more room. So next time you're going to have to kill them."

"Thanks," Kal said. "I hope there won't be a next time."

"Oh, there will be a next time," Ishmael said, patting Kal on the back. "There always is."

Chapter Ten

The bright Foyleton briefing room was comfortingly familiar to Kal; it was the same as any EDF base briefing room he'd been in countless times before. Rows of chairs with tables in front of them ascended from a wall covered with viewscreens. A holographic projector hung from the ceiling, allowing the briefer to call up three-dimensional representations of buildings, objectives, or anything else they needed.

So far, no one had said anything about Sandra and him coming back late and covered in sewage. The Skulls knew enough not to ask tough questions when someone could overhear them. So far, Lukas hadn't said anything either. He wasn't sure how much the warlord knew, but Kal guessed Lukas didn't want to admit he was having them trailed. He had to have suspicions though; one of his soldiers had disappeared and the other was dead.

"Welcome to your first briefing," Lukas said. "I have a few of you former EDF types, so I am going to warn you. We don't spend a bunch of time talking about courses of action. I'll tell you what you need to know and that's it. Short and sweet."

An overhead image of a large facility appeared on the viewscreens behind Lukas. "This is the People's Movement's headquarters in Chengdu. Not as nice as ours but still not bad." A three-dimensional blue wireframe of the base with a portion highlighted in yellow appeared in the air above Lukas's head. "A Tokamak reactor powers the entire base. It was one of the first reactors on the planet, in fact." He sucked air in through his teeth. "I need you to get in there and cause the generator to go boom. We can take out the base in one foul swoop."

"One fell swoop," Garcia corrected with a small smile.

"Whatever." Lukas waved his hand dismissively. "Point is, there should be nothing but a crater there when you're done." The holographic projection changed to a wireframe of the reactor with the parts labeled. It was a cylinder about five meters tall, according to the small ruler on the side of the model, with wires and tubes coming out of it. "Like I said, the thing's old. The modern safety precautions we have in place weren't around when they built this relic. Charges placed in these locations"—yellow highlights appeared over several areas on the reactor—"will cause the thing to go critical. The explosion should wipe out half their base."

Kal had only taken introductory classes in fusion reaction but knew that the explosion would probably kill tens to hundreds of thousands of people in Chengdu. His mind raced. How could they do this? Kill so many innocent people?

"I bet you're wondering how you'll get in there, right?" Lukas laughed. "I have no idea. That's why we let you live; you're the ones who'll figure it out. What I can tell you is that the People's Movement has checkpoints leading in and out of the base, as well as armed guards posted on the walls. You'll need to get past the guards, break through a biometric lock, and know the daily password."

"Why can't we just fly in there and blow the thing up?" asked Garcia.

Lukas shot his brother a look. "Oh, we never thought of

that. Maybe it's because the damn thing is behind meters of Ultracrete and sending all the missiles on Patagonia won't cause it to fail catastrophically. Oh, and because they have EDF anti-aircraft batteries positioned around the base."

"So what resources do we have?" Sergeant Jones asked.

"Finally, a good question." Lukas gave a mocking bow. "We have a few items: some atmospheric craft, some weapons, and other things in the armory. You can grab whatever you can find."

"I've looked at their armory," Garcia whispered to Kal. "They've got *some* decent stuff in there."

"So, let's recap." Lukas twirled his fingers. "You know the what, the where, and the why. Let's get to the when—a week from now. We need this mission to happen before our assault on the People's Movement's forces."

"Where?" Ekon asked.

Lukas tsked. "We already covered that. Weren't you listening? Anyway, that's need to know, and you don't." The screens went blank as he walked up the shallow staircase toward the back of the room. "Look, I'd love to talk with you all day. But I've got other things to do. And more importantly, so do you." He reached the back of the room and turned around.

"This should go without saying, but I'll say it anyway. Don't come back if you fail. You're here for one reason." He walked out of the briefing room, leaving the Skulls staring at the blank briefing screens.

❖

"Well, this is nice," Ekon said as he hopped out of the public transport that had brought them to Chengdu. The People's Movement was tracking any new aircraft in their airspace and the transport allowed them some anonymity. Foyleton had a private aircraft hidden in the woods outside the city for their escape.

Kal looked around. A cool breeze, soaked with salt, flowed up the large avenues from the coast. The evenly spaced square buildings of the city were a refreshing change from the crowded and chaotic jumbles of Kasongo and Foyleton. The Skulls stood in one of the many small squares scattered throughout the city. Small gravel paths wound through a carefully manicured garden filled with local plants.

Privates Kinawadi and Chedjou had arrived separately from the rest of the group. After Lukas's expedited briefing, Kal and Sergeant Jones had reviewed the security plans for the Movement's base and concluded there was no way to infiltrate it without someone on the inside—and a lot of luck. The two youngest members of the Skulls would be perfect for the job: young, talented, and no record to tie them to the EDF or Samsara Fleet.

"Let's find a place to lie low," Jones said, pointing away from the alluring blue waters of the ocean and toward the run-down area of town.

The six Skulls walked along the streets toward the small group of abandoned buildings and communes they had located during their map recon. They were posing as refugees from the fighting around Kasongo and had replaced their normal merchant attire with the tattered trousers and shirts they'd seen refugees wear in Foyleton.

Chengdu was filled with the mundane scenes of everyday life. Kal found it hard to reconcile the recent Nasi attack with the smiling children and haggling traders he saw around him. Occasionally he would see indications of the chaos that had consumed the planet: groups of refugees dressed in rags, damaged buildings, and armored patrols wandering through the streets.

"Why isn't this place a smoking ruin?" asked Sampson.

"Simple," Jones replied, "they're far away from the fighting. There hasn't been time for Foyleton or the PPC to build air forces; they only have light assault and transport craft."

"Give 'em time," Garcia said. "I know they're already working on it."

The elegant buildings started looking more faded as the group made their way from the heart of the city and into the slums away from the shore. Fresh paint gave way to facades that were cracked and peeling from years of being pummeled by the wind coming off the ocean. Graffiti tags started to dot some of the walls and increasingly large piles of trash littered the street.

"Looks like the citizens are taking care of it themselves," Kanumba said, eyeing one of the piles of trash.

They passed through a People's Movement checkpoint blocking the street. A small line of pedestrians and vehicles stopped and waited to be allowed through. A retrofitted civilian vehicle sat in the center of the street, blocking traffic on the ground. The ship had two anti-aircraft cannons aimed skyward, a warning to any vehicle that tried to fly over without stopping.

The soldiers manning the checkpoint seemed to be produced from the same fabricator as the Foyleton ones. They spoke in clipped surly tones as they checked the identification of citizens passing through and their uniforms, if Kal could call them that, were dirty and mismatching. Thankfully, the false identities Foyleton had provided allowed the Skulls to pass through without incident.

"This looks like a good place to hole up," Jones said, pointing to a large commune. The vast buildings were mazes intended to house people who didn't have homes of their own. For everyday citizens and most law enforcement, they were no-go zones and operated almost as cities in and of themselves.

Kal looked at the large masonry building. The salt-filled ocean air had cracked and spalled the plaster coating the block walls. Graffiti covered almost every inch of the building's facade, piles of trash lay scattered outside the windows and doors, and Kal could smell the distinct odor of urine.

"Beautiful, Sergeant." Ekon whistled. "All the inconveniences of home with none of the comfort."

"We shouldn't be here," Sampson complained. "I'm a pilot. I should be with the ship."

"So am I," Garcia retorted. "You don't see me complaining."

They entered the decrepit building and navigated through the twisting corridors. The inside looked even worse than the outside. Men and women lay in the hallway, looking like corpses in the dim light. Most of the rooms had makeshift barricades blocking the broken doorways. Whenever they found an uninhabited room, Jones would have the group wait while he checked to see what the escapes routes were. They had already been trapped once in a commune on New America—it would not happen again. By the time the squad leader found a room to his standards, Kal was completely lost.

The team hunkered down in the abandoned room and waited for the two privates to contact them.

Chedjou and Kinawadi were posing as two disaffected students from Foyleton who were looking to avenge their friend's death at the hands of the Foyleton Syndicate. They would visit several bars that were People's Movement hangouts and talk loudly about "how they wanted to make Foyleton pay." From the intelligence Kal had received, the Movement wasn't too picky on who they recruited. Like the other factions, they were low on soldiers and would give a gun to anyone who asked and then take it back when they died in the fighting.

The People's Movement was an offshoot of the local city government of Chengdu. Originally its goals had been benevolent—create a zone free from Nasi and other interference for the citizens of Chengdu. That had quickly changed when Elka Adams had seized control. She'd continued to espouse freedom and liberty while simultaneously recruiting people, mostly out-of-work young men and women, for her personal army. After a month, she'd gathered enough soldiers to drop any pretense and demanded tribute from the local citizens.

Jones set up a watch roster to ensure no one surprised them. He had someone always manning the radio to wait for word from their spies.

"Now we wait," Kal said.

"Ah, another mission where we get to hole up in a commune," Ekon sat next to the wall and splayed his legs out.

"This is crazy," Chief Kanumba said. "I'm getting some sleep while I can."

"Not a bad idea, ma'am," Jones replied. "I've got first watch. I suggest you all relax. We never know what'll happen next."

Over the next five days, they waited in their small room in the commune. Twice a day, they received updates from Kinawadi and Chedjou via an encrypted communication device provided by Ishmael. Communicating via implant was not an option.

Initially, everything had gone as planned. Shortly after they entered the second bar complaining loudly about Foyleton, a pack of People's Movement soldiers had approached Kinawadi and Chedjou. The soldiers were more than happy to listen and commiserate. They offered to introduce them to their squad leader at the People's Movement.

The next day, the privates showed up at the Movement's large headquarters building and were put through some rudimentary background checks and physical aptitude tests. Of course, both had easily passed. The greatest difficulty was hiding their skill with weapons and hand-to-hand combat. They needed to maintain their cover of being disaffected students.

Since then, communication had become spotty. They were going through the People's Movement's version of EDF Base Camp and were placed into separate training squads. The course wasn't something that was in the Foyleton intelligence briefing about the organization, so they must have only recently started putting recruits through it.

Kal admired the Movement's dedication to professionalism, but it threw a giant wrench in their plan. As trainees, their soldiers were under constant supervision and restricted to a small section of the headquarters. Nor had the cadre been forthcoming about how long the course would take, only saying, "as long as they need."

"This is ludicrous." Sampson sat with his back against the wall. After the last update, he'd launched into a diatribe about abandoning the mission. "We can't just sit around. We need to get out of here."

"Sir," Jones said, clearly straining to maintain his composure. "We need to wait it out. We have no way to recover our soldiers and no clear escape plan. We put our soldiers in there, we have to make sure they get out."

Sampson turned to Kal. "Sir, this mission needs to be scrapped. We can figure out a way to get Kinawadi and

Chedjou out, or maybe they'll just come back on their own. But to wait here for something magical to happen is suicide."

Over the course of the past three days, tempers had frayed. A dark shadow hung over the group. Concern about their comrades in danger and the frustration of not being able to do anything about it had led to several arguments. Lieutenant Sampson was the worst in Kal's opinion; he clearly had a chip on his shoulder, which he normally kept hidden behind a wall of deference toward his commander. However, time and familiarity were wearing it away.

Nicole warned me about that guy.

"We're going to stay," Kal replied evenly. "Sergeant First Class Jones has my trust. If he still believes we can do it, then we can."

"He's not facing reality, and neither are you—"

Ekon jumped up. "Don't talk to the general that way! You haven't earned that right, sir."

"We need to stay the course," Kanumba said from where she was sitting. "We can't keep having the same arguments over and over."

"All of you calm down," Garcia said soothingly. Ekon slammed his open hand against the wall and strode out of the room. "There's no need to yell. Sampson, the decision's been made. Relax!"

Sampson shot to his feet. "You want me to relax, sir? We're sitting in enemy territory. No, wait," he held up a finger, "we're in enemy territory that's inside of enemy territory. And we're waiting for something that won't happen. And you want me to—"

Kal didn't hear anything else as an explosion ripped through the room. The last thing he saw was Sampson's body being flung in slow motion across the room, his eyes wide with shock. Kal felt the pressure and heat from the blast, and then all went black.

❖

A line of fire seared its way across Kal's skull, down his torso, to his fingers and toes. He opened his eyes to find Sergeant Jones's head, only inches from his.

"Sir, get up," Jones said as he flung the ampoule he was holding to the ground. "We've got to move."

Kal shook his head and was rewarded with a wave of pain. He wiped at the strange warmth on his forehead and his hand came back covered in blood. Almost half the wall in front of Kal had disappeared, replaced by a smoking hole. Ekon lay in the prone position, his rifle pointing out and firing almost a continuous stream of plasma.

"Incoming!" Ekon yelled as a grenade flew over his head and landed in the center of the room.

For a split second, all Kal could do was to stare at the brushed metal cylinder sitting on the floor. *Fragmentary grenade, I think*, Kal thought. *That should do the trick.*

Ekon pushed away from the wall and twisted his body, trying to cover the grenade. Before he could reach it, Jones's hand appeared from out of nowhere and grabbed the grenade from the floor. The sergeant had pushed away from the wall and was falling backwards across the center of the room. He flung it back through the opening in a single motion. A few milliseconds after it cleared the wall, the room shook with the explosion.

The building took the brunt of the blast, which caused the ceiling and wall to collapse. Rubble streamed down, blocking the opening with a new mass of twisted concrete.

"Drag him out of here!" Jones yelled as he pointed at Sampson's limp form laying in a small pool of blood. Garcia shook his head as if trying to clear cobwebs and staggered up. He ran behind the unconscious pilot and pulled his torso up by the armpits. Chief Kanumba pulled herself from the floor and grabbed the pilot's legs.

"Let's go." Jones stood by the door, his rifle pointing down the hallway.

They staggered into the hallway, Garcia and Kanumba carrying Sampson, and Kal trying desperately to keep himself upright. Ekon was the last one out. He closed the door and then attached a small proximity mine to the wall directly across the hallway.

"Ready," Ekon shouted to Sergeant Jones. "The mine will arm in five seconds."

Jones was already halfway down the hall. He hurried with his rifle at the ready, stock pressed against his shoulder. As he moved, he remained close to the wall, quickly checking each doorway for hostiles before rushing past. Ekon brought up the rear, rifle pointed back toward the way they came.

A gigantic explosion from behind them caused a wave of dust to fall from the ceiling and knocked Kal to his knees. As he pulled himself up, he could hear parts of the building falling. Loud thumps sounded in the structure above them as pieces of ceiling rained down on the floors below.

"Let's go, let's go," Jones shouted. He pressed himself against the wall next to a doorway at the end of the graffiti-covered hall. Ekon rushed past Kal and pressed himself against the wall on the other side.

Jones nodded at the young sergeant then Ekon pushed away from the wall and kicked open the door. Jones rushed past him and through the door with his weapon raised. "Clear!" he shouted.

Kal hobbled through the doorway, desperately trying to focus on the person in front of him. On the other side was a large common area with an atrium overhead. It was night outside, and the flickering lights inside the room reflected off the glass above them. Kal could see the cracks in the glass. Squatters had set up makeshift tents in the area using rugs and other pieces of refuse. Small fires crackled in discarded metal bins or sat uncontained on the bare floor. The few people in the room huddled in their small sleeping areas, fearfully watching the Skulls as they pushed through the room.

Those eyes. Is that Stephen?

They were a light brown with a half-moon shape. The firelight sparked off them, small embers dancing across their glossy surface as if by magic. They were set in a dirty but solemn face framed by long bedraggled brown hair. The boy stood in front of his family's tent, unafraid, and returned Kal's stare. Slowly, he raised his fist in the air.

"Sir!" Kanumba shouted directly in Kal's ear. "We have to go."

Kal shook his head. He had stopped in the middle of the room, the worst possible place. The rest of the team was already at the other end. Kal finally had the sense to pull out his pistol. He ran to join the rest of the team, which had already started to spill through the door.

As he followed them through the doorway, Kal turned back to look at the boy a final time. His small fist was still raised defiantly in the air, his gaze focused on Kal and never wavering. Kal returned the salute and joined the rest of the team, closing the door behind him.

They were in a small maintenance room. Sergeant Jones had already pulled a grate from the floor, exposing an inky black hole. Ekon quickly climbed through the opening and climbed down the ladder, his feet making small pings each time they touched a metal rung.

"Clear!" Ekon shouted from inside the tunnel.

Jones pointed at the other three. "Go ahead," he said.

Garcia climbed down first, followed by Kanumba and Kal. Jones came down the ladder after them with Sampson's unconscious form draped across his arms and shoulders. As soon as the sergeant placed the pilot on the ground, Ekon stuck a bandage over the bloody mass on Sampson's head. It contained a cocktail of drugs that would help to promote healing and reduce the pain. It was the best they could do for now.

Jones climbed back up the ladder and replaced the grate they had come through, immersing them in complete darkness.

A light suddenly appeared, illuminating Garcia's grim

face. "I can't believe we're in the sewers again."

Their progress through the sewers was considerably slower than their flight through the communes. Using their small lights, the group trudged through the winding tunnels, taking turns carrying Sampson. Jones pushed them hard, calling out encouragement whenever he sensed they were flagging.

Throughout the journey, Kal's mind raced back to the young boy. What was his life like? Had anything changed for him since the Nasi had invaded? Probably not, he'd probably been born and raised in that commune. The only thing that changed was the uniform of the people he needed to hide from.

After an hour, the sewer tunnel opened, and the stars appeared above their heads. Ahead, Kal could see light reflecting off the water of the ocean and could hear the rhythmic pounding of the surf.

"Okay," Sergeant Jones called out, "we can stop. Let's see what we can do for the lieutenant."

The initial disorientation caused by the blast had faded, and a pain like a knife being driven into his skull replaced it. Kal made a cursory attempt to help with Sampson before laying down himself, resting his head against the cool culvert wall. Sergeant Jones walked to him and placed a small electronic syringe against his head. Immediately Kal could feel the pain recede somewhat.

"You've got a concussion, sir," Jones said as he examined Kal. "The cut to your head is superficial, most likely some shrapnel from the blast. But the shock wave messed you up real good."

"So, anything we can do?" Kal tried to remember the short primer he'd received decades ago in battlefield medicine. It hadn't been something he had needed as a logistics officer in the EDF.

"Nah, you're just going to feel like crap for a while. Can be dangerous though if you get any more blows to the head."

"Understood. I'll try to stop getting blown up."

Jones guffawed and punched his shoulder. "Good idea. You'll be alright, sir."

"I think now Sampson is right," Ekon called over his shoulder. "This mission is over." The sergeant huddled over the lieutenant, redressing his wound and injecting him with medicine, most likely painkillers.

Kal found it hard to argue.

"We can't end it," Garcia said, "I don't know if my brother will kill us, but we certainly won't be running missions anymore."

"What can we do, sir?" Ekon asked. "We lost almost all our supplies and weapons, we're wounded, and two of our soldiers are behind enemy lines."

"You don't understand," Garcia pleaded. "This mission fails, then our entire mission fails. We came to Lukas as a last resort. We've got nothing else."

Jones stood up. "Listen, we're not giving up on the mission. I've got a plan."

He led them out of the culvert and into a small copse of trees. They were on the periphery of the city. Small homes blended in with park and farmland. The only light came from the moon above their head. Kal was reminded of the small home he had shared with his family on Earth decades ago. It looked like the kind of place where parents raised their kids.

"I think we have to assume that Kinawadi and Chedjou have been compromised," Jones said. "We can't just leave. We have to get our people out."

He looked around, anticipating any argument, but none came.

"This mission has changed from an assault to a rescue. Luckily, we know where their prison is. We need a way to get inside though."

"We're gonna need a distraction," Ekon said.

Jones nodded. "Exactly, and I think I've got just the right one." He turned to Kal. "Sir, can you contact the Alliance?"

Chapter Eleven

The *Salamis's* thrusters pushed the undergrowth down and sent out a swarm of twigs and gravel as it set down in the field. The cargo ramp silently dropped to the ground and Bo gracefully strode out of the cargo ramp, weapon in hand, eyes scanning the area for danger. His large frame and sinuous movements made him appear awe-inspiring and deadly. Too bad the scientist couldn't shoot worth a damn.

"Bo!" Kal rose from the woodline and strode into the clearing, followed by the rest of the crew. "Glad to see you."

"Thank you, sir," Bowen replied with a smile. "Glad to see you too."

"I am less so." Ishmael walked down the ramp looking clumsy and small next to Bo. "That prisoner you left with me is perhaps the most annoying woman I've ever run across. I'm afraid to find out what you want next."

At Jones's request, Kal had contacted the Alliance member and asked for him to reach Bo and bring both him and their ship to the area outside of Chengdu. It took several hours, but the man had delivered as promised.

"Let's get inside, we don't have a lot of time." Kal gestured toward the open cargo bay of the *Salamis*.

Sampson had faded in and out of consciousness and was a long way from being mission ready. Ekon and Kanumba carried him up the ramp and into the ship's cargo bay where Ekon activated the medbot to tend to his wounds. The bot had an array of medicines and nano bots that promoted healing, eased pain, and could even perform some minor reconstructive surgery. Kal remembered all the times he'd seen a medbot bring someone back from the brink of death.

Ekon remained in the cargo bay to supervise Sampson's healing while the rest of their team went to the galley. Kal felt his grim sense of determination reflected in the faces of the others. The uncertainty and questionable morality of assisting a criminal enterprise had been replaced by resolve. They would get their soldiers back.

Sergeant Jones stepped in front of the viewscreens, a man in his element. "The Movement's facility is well-guarded, and the area where they house prisoners is in the center. Which means we can't just blast our way in."

"Well, yeah," Garcia said. "That's what we were trying to do before."

"Well now we're going to try harder, *sir*." Jones scowled at the pilot and launched into his plan.

The average Human had never met a Nasi face-to-face and was scared to death of them. Bo could easily pass as a Nasi soldier, and it was a fair bet that most Humans would be too frightened to question anything he said. Questioning any order from a Nasi was a quick way to disappear. Bo would claim that he'd caught several Humans while they were trying to attack his squad and wanted them imprisoned. They should be able to get access to the prison facility, and once there, they'd have to rely on their training and luck to fight their way out. The *Salamis* would be on standby and attack the base as a diversion once they'd recovered their teammates.

After Jones finished, the room was silent. The only sound was the thrumming of the idling thrusters. "This sounds—" Kal began.

"Like suicide," Garcia finished.

"I was going to say it sounds like a tough plan to pull off." Kal shot the pilot an annoyed look.

"You're right. It's going to be tough," Jones admitted. "But we've been through worse. We owe it to Kinawadi and Chedjou to get them back."

Garcia stretched his arms over his head, arching his back. "Not much more to say then. Let's do this."

❖

Kal hated the feeling of restraints clamped down on his wrists. It was something he'd felt all too often recently. At least this time he could take them off whenever he wanted.

"Human, where is your leader?" Bo asked in the archaic Human Standard dialect of the Nasi. Bo had spoken that way when he'd first joined them. Since then, his speech had evolved as he learned Human expressions and taken on Human mannerisms.

The young guard froze for a moment. "Er, one moment...sir. I need to get my sergeant." He scurried back through the compound gate and returned a minute later, trailed by a woman.

"What the hell is—" The sergeant stopped talking when she saw the Jadid.

Her jaw clenched and Kal could see the trace of anger pass through her eyes before she regained control. "How can I help you, sir?" the woman asked coolly.

"These Humans attacked my patrol. You will hold them

in your prison until I can have them retrieved for questioning."
Kal had to hand it to him, Bo did a great job of imitating the
imperious nature of the Nasi. He roughly shoved Kal forward
and pushed the pallet lifter, with Sergeant Jones lying on it,
forward. A bloodstained towel covered the sergeant's torso,
and his face was dripping with what looked to be sweat.

The junior guard pushed the hovering pallet lifter
through the gate while his supervisor roughly grabbed Kal by
the arm.

"Yes, sir," the woman answered. "We'll take care of it."

"Wait!" The word came from Bo like a gunshot, and the
two Movement guards froze. "I need to see your prison
facility. You Humans tend to be incompetent when it comes
to these things."

The sergeant looked indignant. "I can assure you that—
"

"Are you questioning me?" Bowen's voice thundered
down on the woman. "Perhaps I should make an example out
of you?" Kal had met enough Jadid and Nasi to know that
they rarely displayed such naked anger. The Movement
soldier would have no idea though.

"No, no." She held out her hands. "You are, of course,
welcome to inspect. I think you'll find our jail cells more than
satisfactory."

The group passed through the checkpoint and into the
narrow cleared area between the building and security
perimeter. Movement soldiers clustered in groups, talking and
laughing with each other. Kal cautiously raised his head,
searching for their two soldiers. No one looked familiar.

It was roughly twenty meters before they reached the main entrance of the building. The doorway was grandiose, with a patterned relief sculpted in the concrete around the mouth. Several soldiers leaned against the wall on either side of the door watching them curiously. As they passed into the building, a high chirping sound erupted from a small box affixed to the wall.

"Shut that thing off," the sergeant yelled at a soldier standing inside the doorway. "You can see that he has a weapon already." She pointed at the rifle slung across Bo's back. The soldier rushed to the box and the chirping stopped.

The sergeant led them through the wide corridors of the building. Kal lifted his head as much as he dared, trying to orient himself. The base was like the Foyleton base—somewhat dated utilitarian hallways with a minimalist edge. However, where Foyleton had added lush carpeting and opulent fixtures that projected wealth, the Movement was a hodgepodge of different styles and tastes. Garish holo-projectors displaying racy images were placed next to exquisite ancient Earth tables with complex inlaid wood patterns.

"Wait here, sir." the woman instructed.

In front of them was a large gunmetal door that took up the entire width and height of the hallway. Someone had placed a large holo-projector next to it, projecting the sardonic phrase, "Goodbye and good luck!" The letters changed colors and danced mirthfully—a twisted touch Kal was sure Garcia would have appreciated.

"Not very professional," Bo said to no one in particular,

his face appearing as if he'd just found a dead animal. The soldiers eyed him but didn't respond.

"Greggs! Open up!" the woman shouted.

A man's face appeared on the viewscreen on the top half of the door. "Sergeant Wu, how ya doin'? When are you gonna—"

"We have prisoners," Wu interrupted. "And a guest." She inclined her head toward Bo.

"Nasi. Er, yes, of course. One moment, Sergeant." The man's face disappeared from the door and a few moments later it opened, the two halves sliding apart to reveal the clean white walls of the prison. The bottom edge of a large security door hung over their heads as they walked into the prison area. The large rectangular room had cell doors spaced roughly three meters apart on each wall. The cell doors doubled as viewscreens, allowing them to peer in and see the occupants of the cells though it appeared the prisoners could not see out. It reminded Kal of the time he had visited a zoo with his family decades ago.

He studied the doors looking for his missing team members. *Where were they?* About half of the cells were occupied, but there was no sign of them. *Wait,* Kal thought to himself, *that's Chedjou.* She sat on a utilitarian bunk affixed to the wall of her cell. Her back was against the wall and her head raised, staring at the corner between the wall and ceiling across from her. Kal got the impression she was waiting for something. Waiting for them.

Where is Kinawadi? Possibilities, each grimmer than the last, flooded Kal's mind. The People's Movement was not known to show mercy to an enemy. He had to expect the worst.

"Welcome…er…your excellency." Greggs bowed awkwardly. Kal coughed in order to stifle a laugh. Greggs flashed him a look of pure hatred and punched him in the gut. Hard. "I'll get to you," he whispered in Kal's ear.

"Hey! Get these two into their cells," Greggs said to the soldier with Wu. He grabbed Jones under the armpits and lifted his upper torso off the lifter. The other guard grabbed the sergeant's feet when he suddenly lashed out with his right foot, striking the soldier directly in the nose. The man staggered back and fell to the ground, his hands covering his face. Bo picked up Greggs by the back of his shirt and hurled him across the room as if he weighed nothing. The man hit the wall headfirst, his body went limp, and he fell to the ground, unmoving.

Kal had already deactivated the restraints around his wrists. He reached under the pallet lifter to pull out the plasma carbine strapped underneath and sensed movement behind him. He grabbed the weapon and dodged to the side just in time.

Bullets tore through the space where Kal had been standing and sparks flew off the metal floor. Kal hit the ground and rolled back to his feet in time to see Sergeant Wu's pistol pointed directly at his head. At the same moment, Bo swept his spindly arm across his body and caught the woman in the chest. The blow lifted her off the ground and flung her back-first against the wall, causing her weapon to fly across the room with a loud clatter.

The security gate slammed down, blocking the exit, and klaxons reverberated through the room. The guard Jones had kicked across the room had his hand against one of the emergency buttons on the wall. He had a triumphant smile on his blood-covered face. Kal took quick aim and shot him in the gut, but it was too late. He heard the hiss of gas pouring into the room—they had less than a minute until they'd be unconscious.

Kal pressed a button on the pallet lifter and the top sprang open revealing a small cache of weapons, explosives, tools, and—most importantly—five electronic syringes to counteract the gas. He scooped the syringes up, gave Bo and Jones each one, and then jammed a third into the meaty part of his thigh.

"Get that door open," Kal called out, pointing to Sandra's cell. Jones was already rushing toward it with the small skeleton key he'd grabbed from the lifter. The key was a computer preloaded with cutting-edge automated hacking algorithms. Chief Kanumba had made it using her knowledge of EDF technology and security protocols. The base was not one of the more modern EDF facilities, and they hoped their security protocols were outdated.

Jones pressed the small tablet against Sandra's door. After a few seconds, the door slid open. Sandra was already standing, a smile on her face, as Jones entered. He slammed the syringe into her thigh.

"What took you so long?" Sandra asked as she recovered from the shock.

"Witty banter later," Jones replied. "Where's Kinawadi?

We've got to get out of here."

Sandra hurried out of the cell and grabbed a pistol from the lifter. "I don't know. I had just finished talking to you on the communicator when they jumped me. Next thing I know, I'm in here."

Sergeant Jones swore. "There's no way we'll find him."

Bo laughed. It was a strange sound, hysterical and high-pitched. "That's so ironic."

"I think you are misusing the term, Bo" Kal studied the Jadid. He'd never seen him this way.

"I think...I'm having a reaction to the medicine," Bo had to choke out his words between chuckles. His body shook with laughter as he tried to keep it contained. It was a possibility that they'd considered. Although descended from Humans, the Jadid's physiology had evolved for centuries in another dimension. There were still a lot of unanswered questions about how they diverged physiologically from Humans.

Salamis, Kal used his neural implant to contact the rest of the team directly. *Begin the diversion. We found Chedjou but do not know where Kinawadi is. Either way, we're getting out of here. Meet at the rendezvous point.* Over long distances, their neural implants had to use the planet's local net, increasing the likelihood that the Nasi or Movement would intercept and decrypt the message. Now they were close enough that their implants had a direct connection. They were beyond caring if the People's Movement knew they were there.

Roger, Kanumba replied, *unleashing hell. We'll meet*

you at the rendezvous point.

Jones was already working on the alloy security door blocking their escape from the prison facility. Bo, Kal, and Sandra took positions on either side. Who knew what would be in the hallway when it opened?

Kal could barely hear the faint yet unmistakable sound of missiles pounding against the building's exterior. The *Salamis* had already begun unleashing its weapons on the facility. It wouldn't do too much damage but would at least help divert soldiers away from the prison.

I'm here.

Was that Kinawadi?

Kinawadi? Kal responded.

Yes, sir, the private responded over the neural net. *We're here. We've secured the outside of the prison.*

Kal was about to ask what the private meant by "we" when the large security door blocking their exit slid upward, retreating into the ceiling. About twenty soldiers were on the other side, arrayed in front of the door. They'd brought portable barricades and set them in front of the door to provide cover. Small-arms fire and plasma rounds streaked down the hallway toward them, hitting their shields or the nearby walls.

Private Kinawadi knelt in front, a smile on his face. "Glad to see you again, sir."

"Damn glad to see you too." Kal scurried forward, taking cover behind a barricade.

"Where we goin' to?" the private asked.

The rendezvous point was directly behind the facility.

164

Based on the plans they had, there should be a route that would take them there through the building's utility corridors. Jones quickly outlined their planned route.

"Sergeant," Kinawadi said, "I have a better idea."

Private Kinawadi led the group through the broad hallways of the People's Movement base. Despite the sounds of combat outside the building, he walked confidently, and his team of Movement recruits fought back the frequent attacks by small groups of soldiers. Kinawadi and his soldiers were prepared, well-armed with rifles, portable barriers, and grenades.

What had happened to Kinawadi? Kal wondered to himself as he saw the young private order one of his fire teams to hold position. He had so many questions, but they would have to wait.

The Skulls' initial assault, combined with the firepower of the *Salamis*, had clearly disoriented the group. Many Movement soldiers were running through the hallways aimlessly, unsure of what to do. Several of them had put down their weapons and sat in their rooms with their hands flat on the bunk next to them to show they weren't a threat. When pressed, the People's Movement had been subdued in their own base by a single ship and a few dozen soldiers.

As they rushed through the hallways, Bo's laughter continued to start and stop in fits. The Jadid found everything from holo-displays to the frantic cries of soldiers humorous.

Kinawadi finally stopped in front of a large bare metal door at least ten meters wide. "Khatri, come here." The private motioned to the one of the Movement soldiers who had joined their side.

The man, perhaps in his thirties, rushed forward and placed his hand on the biometric access panel next to the door while whispering something into the nearby microphone that jutted from the wall. The large utility door ground open, and they rushed in with weapons at the ready.

The doorway opened into a large room filled with twisted webs of wires and pipes running from the ceiling and floor into a large cylinder in the center. Banks of machines— computers, Kal guessed—sat flush against the walls. The entire room hummed with energy. Kal could almost feel it coming from the Tokamak reactor sitting on an elevated pedestal in the center of the room.

"Khatri here is part of the maintenance crew for the reactor," Kinawadi explained. The man nodded his head at Kal at the sound of his name.

"Can he destroy it?" Kal asked.

"Yes, but I won't let it go critical," Khatri responded. "I've done more than enough killing. I *can't* do it anymore." He shook his head.

"It's *critical* we complete this mission." Bo laughed like he had made a joke.

Kal ignored the Jadid and kept his focus on the Movement technician. He was ashamed to admit it relieved him that the choice had been taken out of his hands. "Do it."

Kinawadi positioned his soldiers at the door in case the

Movement forces bypassed the room's security while Khatri worked on the reactor. "Give me explosives. Lots of them," Khatri called out.

Several people rushed forward and handed him small high-yield explosives—small flat cylinders only five centimeters in diameter. Despite their diminutive size, Kal knew they would produce a devastatingly large blast. Khatri set their timers for five minutes and placed them against the outside of the reactor. He ran to a workstation and the cylinder slowly descended into the floor.

"There's an emergency access tunnel over there." Khatri pointed to the wall opposite from where they'd entered.

"Lead on," Jones replied.

As they were retreating, several soldiers set a proximity mine by the main entrance to the reactor room and joined the rest of the group by the escape hatch. They entered single file and scurried through the meter-high tunnel.

"Two minutes left," Khatri called out from behind them. "We need to be well away from the building when the reactor blows. It won't go critical, but it isn't going to be a small blast either."

"Almost there," Kinawadi shouted back.

Then Kal saw the end of the tunnel outlined in red small red lights. It was an emergency exit. Kinawadi pulled the red lever next to it, and the door fell outward with a small pop. Light streamed into the tunnel and momentarily blinded Kal. He looked to the side and kept rushing forward. They were not out of the woods yet; he could hear small-arms fire outside.

The tunnel led them to a small, cluttered motor pool. The ships were arranged with no rhyme or reason, and tools and materials were scattered around. Kal couldn't tell if the mess was because the attack had surprised the People's Movement or if they just didn't have the discipline to keep their facility organized.

The soldiers at the front had already set up their portable barriers and taken positions behind them. As people streamed out of the tunnel, they quickly joined their comrades behind the barriers with weapons fanned outwards.

Kal looked to the sky but couldn't find the *Salamis*. *Salamis, where are you?* Kal asked over the net.

On our way, Garcia replied. *We had to take care of some fighters.*

We need you here now! We're pinned down.

They had their backs to the building. The Movement soldiers had taken cover behind several vehicles and poured plasma and kinetic fire on them from multiple angles. Additional soldiers continued to swarm in from other parts of the base, only increasing the fire the Skulls and Kinawadi's team were taking. Soon the enemy would get heavy weapons in place. Then it would be all over.

"You Humans really like violence," Bo said with a smirk. He seemed content to sit down with his back to one of the barriers, watching rounds fly over his head.

Not far off, Kal thought to himself.

Without warning, a stream of plasma fire coursed through the parked vehicles, causing several of them to burst into flames. The *Salamis* appeared behind the Movement soldiers and riddled their positions with kinetic fire. Chief Kanumba was in the cargo bay machine gunner's position, sending an almost uninterrupted stream of rounds in the direction from where the reinforcements had come.

"Yes!" Kinawadi cheered as the People's Movement soldiers ran.

The *Salamis* thumped down onto a landing pad in the motor pool; its ramp was already down. Jones led the way, motioning for everyone to follow him, and rushed to the ramp. Once everyone was in, the ship immediately lifted off. Kal slowly counted the people around him; they'd lost five soldiers during their flight through the base.

He looked out the back of the cargo bay just in time to see half of the People's Movement's headquarters disintegrate in a ball of flame. Dust and debris showered onto the buildings next to it, but the city escaped most of the destruction. People had died, but fewer than would've if the reactor had gone critical. Chengdu remained.

"If we had medals, I would recommend you for one," Kal said to Kinawadi. "You too, Chedjou."

After escaping Chengdu, the *Salamis* landed in the small clearing where Foyleton had stashed a civilian transport ship for them to return. The Skulls and the former People's Movement soldiers were taking a moment to savor life. Each of them processed the events in their own way. A few were laughing and slapping each other on the back. Others were softly crying, perhaps thinking of friends that had died or the things they had just seen. Most of them were, like Kal, quietly contemplating what they had just gone through.

"So what happened?" Kal asked Kinawadi.

"Well, you know most of it," the private replied.

"I don't. How'd you gather an army?" Sandra asked.

"I wouldn't call us an army," Kinawadi demurred. "After I realized they'd captured you, I knew I needed to get some help. I was sure General Norman and Sergeant Jones were coming to rescue us."

Kinawadi had been making friends with the other recruits. Most of them had been what he would have expected, cutthroats and criminals looking to profit off the war. But there were also many who felt the People's Movement, however distasteful, was their only option. They were former soldiers stranded on the planet or local law enforcement that found themselves without purpose when the government crumbled.

Immediately after he saw Sandra dragged to the prison, Kinawadi asked some of his comrades if they'd be willing to help him stand up to the People's Movement. He explained there was another option and that they could fight for something bigger than themselves and be the heroes they had always wanted to be. It was a risky maneuver, but he quickly found people who were looking for some way to fight for something beyond just themselves. In the next few hours, the word spread faster than Kinawadi had expected and even reached some soldiers who were not recruits—like Khatri. Knowing that the Skulls could arrive any second, they'd armed themselves. When they heard the alarm sound in the prison, Kinawadi's crew ran to help.

"What would you have done if we hadn't shown up?" Kanumba asked.

"That didn't cross my mind, ma'am."

"So what will you do now?" Kal asked.

"What do you mean, sir?" Kinawadi raised an eyebrow.

"You've got soldiers following you. Are you all going your own separate ways?"

The private cleared his throat. "I hadn't thought about it."

"You need to start." Kal put his arm around Kinawadi's shoulder. "You have a responsibility toward these people. They broke their oaths and risked their lives to follow you."

"The general's right. You may not have been seeking it out, but you owe these soldiers something," Jones said. "They're lost and are going to look to you for what to do next."

"I'm a private!" Kinawadi held up his hands. "Can't *you* tell them what to do?"

"That's not how it works. We're not their leaders, and we've got our own mission," Kal replied. "We need to leave in a few minutes and you need to decide if you're coming with us. If not, we'll leave the communicator with you, and Ishmael can help equip your group."

"I'll be more direct than the general. Stay and be with *your* soldiers. Cause that's what they are now." Jones stood up. "You're young, but you've proven that you're ready." He turned and strode up the ramp of the *Salamis*, beckoning

Chief Kanumba to join him. Jones always had a touch of the melodramatic about him.

"Talk to your soldiers and think it over," Kal said as he stood up. "We have a mission for you and your team if you decide to stay."

Kal walked to the Skulls' ship and found Sergeant Jones standing in the shadows at the top of the cargo ramp, looking out at the clearing, studying the people. "Things really have changed, sir." Jones said as Kal stood next to him. "I grew up in the EDF, dedicated my life to it, and then it disappeared. I didn't realize the entire galaxy was going to change." He nodded toward Private Kinawadi, who had walked over to talk with a group of soldiers. "He's young enough to be my grandson, but here he is, leading almost a full platoon in battle."

"How are you not a sergeant major?" Kal asked. Sergeant Jones was perhaps the most capable soldier he had ever met.

Jones laughed. "Let's just say whenever they started thinkin' about promoting me to a desk job, I would go off and do something dumb. I've been busted down in rank more times than I can count. Only thing is, they couldn't get rid of me."

"Why not?"

"I've got a couple Medals of Valor." The man said it matter-of-factly.

Kal whistled. The Medal of Valor had been the highest possible award given to soldiers in the EDF. It had been personally awarded by the Prime Minister of the UEG and most awardees received it posthumously. The fact that Jones had earned it—not once, but twice—and had lived through both times was amazing.

"How come I've never heard of you?" Kal asked. "You should've been in the recruiting holos."

"Sir," he slapped Kal on the back, "you should know by now that's not my style."

Private Kinawadi approached Kal and Sergeant Jones. "I've decided. You say that you've got a mission for us. Me and my soldiers are ready."

"Good decision," Jones said.

Kal pointed at the men and women in the field. "I thought most of Humanity was lost and we'd need to save them. But really, they're not waiting to be saved, they're waiting for someone to lead them. They want to do the right thing, but they're not sure what it is."

Kinawadi nodded.

"We'll get you some supplies. I want you and your people to go into the cities and the towns and let them know what we're doing. Let them know we're fighting not for ourselves or the UEG or EDF—but for Humanity. The Patagonia Front is still out there too. See if you can find them and help them. You've got the communicator so you can reach me, but you'll be operating on your own."

The private gulped. "I can handle it, sir."

"I am sure you can," Kal said. "Also, if you're going to be leading soldiers then I don't think private is appropriate anymore. As of now, you're Sergeant Kinawadi."

"Sir, can you do that?"

"Sure," Kal slapped his back, "I'm a general, remember?"

They offloaded as many supplies and weapons as they could from the *Salamis* to equip Kinawadi's soldiers. The Skulls would use the civilian craft that Foyleton had provided to return so as not to risk any suspicion, while Ishmael and Bo would return via the *Salamis*. The soldiers swarmed over the crates of supplies they'd offloaded, examining the contents.

"See you back in Foyleton." Kal gave an informal salute with his index finger. The Jadid saluted back, having recovered from the drug's side effects. "Sounds good, sir. Thank you. I think we did something good today."

"I agree." Kal hoped that it would amount to something.

After the *Salamis* left, the remaining members of the Skulls climbed into the small civilian transport. It was a simple craft with several rows of chairs covered by a large transparent bubble.

"See you later, sir." Kinawadi drew himself up and executed a crisp salute.

"Later." Kal returned it. "Oh, and a piece of advice."

"Yes?"

"Try and think of a good name for your crew. Otherwise, you'll find that they pick something ridiculous for you."

"Norman's Numbskulls, out!" Garcia yelled as he closed the ship's bubble and lifted off.

Chapter Twelve

Nicole sat cross-legged on the floor of a chamber next to the Z'Ta control room with the Samsara Fleet delegation around her. The three Z'Ta that followed her there lay across from them like a dog or horse would, their hind legs on either side of their torso and their front legs splayed out in front.

Fist-sized gems lined the walls of the room, casting an ethereal glow on the proceedings. On her way in the room, Nicole had studied one up close; it was fully embedded in the rock, a naturally occurring phenomenon. Near the wall, a small viewscreen stood on a small stand on the floor.

"So," began one of the Z'Ta, "we surprised you, huh?"

"Yes," admitted Samaha, "can you tell us what's going on here? Why are we here instead of captured by the Nasi?"

"Sure," the alien responded, "not the most interesting story but probably important for you to know."

"Yes," agreed Nicole. "But before you start, can you tell us who you are?"

"Okay, okay," replied the first Z'Ta who spoke. "My name is Y'dari. My compatriots are Y'torak and Y'kiran." They each raised one of their front legs as it said their name.

"We're the Communication Council," continued Y'torak seamlessly. "Our job is to maintain the Z'Ta communication network across our systems. At least that's what it used to be."

"Now, we call ourselves the Rebel Council. We're trying to make sure that the Z'Ta don't get destroyed by the Nasi," added Y'kiran.

"The Nasi came to T'kor'nuk about seven days ago."

Nicole's implant automatically adjusted the time frame from Z'Ta to Human Standard. As she recalled, seven Human days were about ten Z'Ta days. "Our council had figured they would come and were preparing our forces for a fight."

"However, instead of just blowing up our system, they offered to leave us alone as long as we did a few things for them." The three aliens seamlessly picked up and dropped out of the conversation. "Against our wishes, the council agreed. They said they'd notify the Nasi fleet positioned outside our planet when you arrived and agreed to not aid you."

"So you decided to rebel?" Samaha asked.

"Well, pretty much. Not just us on the Communications Council, either. The council thinks the Nasi will just leave us alone, but we know that's not the case. So we sent communications probes to our fleets telling them what was going on and to hide."

"Cowards," Zzyrian said angrily, ears flattened against his head. "You hide while everyone else dies."

"Well, we could fight them right now, I guess," said Y'torak amicably. "But that hasn't worked out too well for others," finished Y'kiran.

"You've got us. What's your plan?" asked Nicole.

"We gotta lotta Z'Ta in the H'Far system that agree with us. But we don't know about the other systems." The three Z'Ta paused and looked at each other. "So we figure we'll take the ships that agree with us to join your fleet. Then we can recruit the Z'Ta ships in other systems too."

"A recruiting mission across Z'Ta space?" Nicole asked.

"Pretty much," Y'dari replied.

Zzyrian let out an angry chirp. "This is just a plot to get our fleet. They weren't able to get us this time, but if we agree, they can just lure the Nasi to us."

"Hold on," Samaha said. "I don't think that makes a lot of sense. They could have smashed the fleet today if they'd wanted to. Instead, they stayed out of the fight."

"Relax, Tounous," Y'dari said, holding its front legs in the air. "Your general's right; we coulda totally trapped you if we wanted."

"Instead, we wanna help you," Y'torak continued.

"How many ships do you think will join?" Samaha asked.

The three Z'Ta looked at each other. "Two, maybe three, in this system. Perhaps another five outside of it," Y'dari replied. That would more than double the size of Samsara Fleet.

Samaha raised her hands in surrender. "Fine, we agree. Now how the hell do we get off this rock?"

"That's going to be difficult; we're outlaws. But if we can get to our ships, they'll take us out of here." The Z'Ta continued to complete each other's sentences. "The Nasi know you're here. The council has ordered you to be found and turned over to them. We've got to get off the planet."

"How do we do that?" asked Samaha.

"Well, that's a bit of a tough one," Y'torak replied. "However, there is a way. The council has stopped all transports to and from the planet. We need to wait until they restore them."

"How long will that take?" Nicole asked.

The three aliens chittered. "We have no idea."

"So we just need to sit down here and wait?"

"We've got plenty of food." They burbled in laughter.

❖

The Z'Ta compound was a relic from when their species first traveled the stars hundreds of years ago. The Z'Ta explained it was originally used to launch their first scout vessels as they explored the space around their home system. As ships grew in size, more modern ships weren't able to fit in the landing bay, and the entire facility had been abandoned. In the intervening hundreds of years, it had fallen into disrepair.

In the past week, the Z'Ta rebels had brought in new equipment and repaired the critical systems. They brought in small nuclear generators to power the equipment and connected it all with massive cables that ran through the tunnels connecting the chambers. The tunnels themselves were dimly lit with light coming either from the small gems embedded into the walls or small string lights attached to the ceiling. Z'Ta had relatively weak eyesight and normally used sonar so Nicole guessed at least some of the lights were for their Human visitors.

For the first few hours, Nicole sat to the side in the operations center watching the Z'Ta security feed and listening in on their network, hoping they'd get their chance to leave. It quickly became clear it would take more than a few hours before that would happen. The Nasi had sent several teams to help root out the Samsara Fleet representatives but quickly realized they weren't able to navigate the subterranean caverns and tunnels efficiently. They'd left it up to the Z'Ta and ordered all traffic to and from the planet shut down.

Initially, the Z'Ta seemed eager to find them, but their enthusiasm waned after the first day. The chatter on their network was increasingly mundane military discussions about troop transport, logistics, and even jokes about the Nasi. The Z'Ta had earned their reputation for frivolity.

The Rebel Council assigned a "room" to each member of Samsara Fleet—a tiny bare cavern with a bucket. The Z'Ta themselves slept ten to a room, dozing almost on top of each other. After some tactful feedback from Nicole, the Z'Ta produced actual beds and biological recyclers for each of the Humans. Zzyrian, on the other hand, had been perfectly happy with his bare-bones room.

On the second day, Nicole started to explore the dense networks of tunnels in the forgotten base. The Z'Ta hadn't run power to the entire compound, which meant she needed a flashlight for much of her exploration. The tunnels were a mixture of smooth-floored ones made by the Z'Ta and rough naturally occurring ones. Without her implant, she would have easily gotten lost in the dense network that seemed to go on forever. Nicole was heading back to her room when she walked to the end of a large passageway and found an enormous cavern so large that her light dissipated before reaching the ceiling or far walls of the room.

Landing bay? Maintenance area? Nicole wondered to

herself.

As she cautiously stepped forward, deeper into the chamber, she swept her light in front of her looking for some clue to its purpose. Small strips were embedded into the floor making several geometric shapes, one on top of the other and at least a hundred meters across. At the center of the shapes was a smooth dark green stone sphere that wasn't attached to the floor. Boxes and cabinets stood at the edge of the room, their viewscreens dark. If Nicole had to guess, she would have said the room was a tactical center or research facility of some sort.

The Z'Ta laughed when Nicole returned to the occupied portion of the base and asked what the room was for. Rather than answering her, they glugged happily and said she'd have to see it herself. Several Z'Ta immediately began running a power conduit to the room, bubbling happily as they worked.

When Nicole returned with the other Humans and Zzyrian in tow, her mouth dropped in shock as she saw the cavern. The Z'Ta had installed several light poles throughout the room, which cast greenish halos of light. On the floor, lights outlined a large hexagon, which changed each second, rotating through a wide pallet of colors. The boxes and cabinets were consoles, their screens flashing images and emitting strange noises.

"What is this?" Samaha asked the Z'Ta who'd escorted her to the room. "A command center? Training room?"

The alien emitted a gurgling laugh. "Ha, no. It's a recreation room."

The Z'Ta walked their visitors around the room, trying to

explain how the various games worked and pointing out their favorites. After taking them around the room, they told their visitors to watch as they played a game that Nicole's implant translated as Side Out.

Six Z'Ta started with their bodies pressed against the ball at the center of the hexagon. Each Z'Ta had a side of the hexagon they were trying to prevent the others from pushing the ball over. When the ball crossed the line, it flashed a bright white, and the shape shifted to have one less side. The hexagon transformed into a pentagon, square, triangle, and finally—when only two Z'Ta remained—it became an oval with each Z'Ta defending one half of it.

Initially, Nicole thought each player would simply push as hard as they could and the strongest would win. After a few games, she realized that the players' strategy was to eliminate the stronger opponents first. They wanted to face whichever player they considered the weakest. The player who was under assault by the others would give ground slowly and then try to shift the course of the ball laterally at the last moment—to get the player next to them out. It was as much a game of cunning and strategy as it was of strength. Word seemed to have gotten out about the recreation room and soon there was a healthy line of Z'Ta waiting to play.

"This game would drive me nuts," Samaha whispered to Nicole as they watched. "The better you are, the more they target you."

"Isn't that the case in most games?" asked Nicole. "I mean isn't the best player or team always the one the others are trying to beat?"

Samaha shifted on her feet. "It's different. This just seems so devious. Look," she pointed at where the ball had just crossed out of the pentagon, "that one just let the ball get pushed toward them and then pushed it over the opponent's line at the corner. It seems so underhanded."

"Maybe," Nicole admitted, "but it's interesting as well. What would you do? Push the ball as hard as you could away from your side? You'd wear yourself out, and soon the remaining ones would overpower you."

Their pilot, Chief Heather Ramos, was on the far side of the room, trying to understand how to play the video games. Nicole tried one and had given up after fifteen minutes of having a Z'Ta explain it to her in an increasingly loud voice. Ramos, on the other hand, picked it up quickly and was staring at the screen and emitting occasional whelps of joy.

"Yo! General Samaha, the Rebel Council wants to talk to you and Colonel Bergeron," said a Z'Ta soldier.

"What about Zzyrian?" The Tounous had refused to leave his chamber, complaining of potential treachery.

"They summoned him as well," the soldier replied.

"Well then, lead on," Samaha said.

"Okay, we got everyone here," said Y'dari.

It had taken a day, but Nicole had finally learned to tell the Z'Ta apart by the striations in their stony skin. The patterns and hues covering their bodies were different—Y'dari had thin white veins running over its skin, while Y'torak's were wider and had a golden yellow hue, and Y'kiran's skin was crisscrossed with wavy blue lines.

"We've got some news. The Z'Ta council has ordered the Military Council to send logistics shipments to the fleet in orbit. The embargo has been lifted."

"That's great news," said Samaha.

"Well, it's a start," replied Y'kiran.

"Problem is," continued Y'torak, "they are inspecting everything and everyone that goes near the surface."

"What about our ship?" asked Chief Ramos. "Why don't we just fly from here?"

The three Z'Ta derisively gurgled. "That won't work, Human. Unless your little ship is a helluva lot faster than we've seen, it won't get past our point defense system. Not to mention the Nasi."

"We need some way to get onto one of the transports to your fleet," Samaha concluded.

"We can't take just any transport," Y'torak replied. "We need to get to the right ship. A bunch of the home fleet remains loyal to our council."

"So what's your idea?" Zzyrian asked impatiently, ears twitching.

"How do you feel about us working on your shuttle?" Y'dari asked.

"Wait, why do you want to work on it?" Ramos asked. "You just said we couldn't use it."

"We can't get off the planet in it. But with some modifications, we can use it as a distraction. How attached are you to the shuttle anyway?"

"Not very. What do you want to do with it?" Samaha asked. "If it gets us off this planet, then you can fly it into a star."

The Z'Ta rumbled pleasantly. "Great! We'll need your help to modify it. We're going to install a more advanced AI on the ship. When we're ready, we'll use it to distract our fleet and the Nasi to help our escape. We'll need your help as well."

"I can help with whatever you need," replied Ramos.

"Great, it'll take a few days to make the upgrades. By then we should have a window to leave," the Z'Ta replied.

Over the next couple of days, Chief Ramos spent almost all her time with the Z'Ta modifying the commander's shuttle. When she wasn't in the landing bay, she was sleeping or playing her video game in the recreation room.

Normal ship AIs were simple and designed to ensure the ship didn't crash or veer off course. Most ships rarely had an advanced AI because it was too susceptible to enemy interference or radiation. The system the rebels were adding would act like an actual pilot and make their ship act like it was trying to escape the system. Once the Z'Ta tried to chase it or destroy it, the ship would take evasive action as long as possible before destroying itself.

"How's it coming? You done?" Nicole asked as she walked around the shuttle. She couldn't see any changes from the outside.

"Still bored, ma'am?" Ramos asked, looking up from the small tablet she was holding. "It's about ready."

"I'm not that bad, am I?" Nicole knew she had been. She'd been coming down to the cavernous landing pad several times a day to ask about progress. The chief handled it pretty well, but the Z'Ta refused to respond to her questions anymore.

"I've seen worse." Ramos smiled. "But not many. The AI should work. You never know for sure when you send an AI piloted ship into space, but I think it'll last long enough to fool the Z'Ta."

"Looks like it's time to go," Nicole said. "The Z'Ta are planning on a full refuel and replenishment of several ships tonight. Seems like the best chance we're going to have."

"She's ready." Ramos patted the side of the small shuttle and handed her tablet to one of the technicians conducting final inspections. "I'm ready."

The two women walked through the tunnels to the antechamber that separated the abandoned facility from the rest of the tunnels under T'kor'nuk. Nicole realized she'd gotten used to the dim cramped caverns in the few days she'd been there. Strange what people could get used to. The antechamber was about half the size of the game room and had small storage bins lining its walls. The Z'Ta told her the bins were used to store weapons and armor when people entered the facility, but they were empty now.

Samaha and Zzyrian were standing in the room with the Rebel Council and four Z'Ta soldiers with plasma weapons strapped to their arms. Although they had three digits on their front arms and could hold a weapon, the aliens preferred them strapped to their body so they could easily run on all four limbs. A small cable ran from the weapon, down their wrists, and to their hands, where there was a trigger pad.

The Humans and Zzyrian all had small plasma pistols in holsters which they'd recovered from the small survival kit on their transport shuttle. The small arms wouldn't help them if they came across any Nasi though. The creatures would be faster, stronger, and more heavily armed.

"So that's when the Qudoru said 'I don't worship your god!'" Y'torak cried out. The Z'Ta exploded in a chorus of mirthful burbles, and even Zzyrian chirped in laughter.

"What'd we miss?" Ramos asked.

"A joke." Samaha looked puzzled. "I think."

The Z'Ta Rebel Council glugged happily for a moment before recovering. "Yes, it's a good one. We'll tell you it later though. Business first and all that." They turned to the soldiers. "Remember, the Humans are slow and weak. We will have to stop often for them to catch up."

The soldiers burbled in laughter.

"Thanks for that," Nicole cracked a small smile. "We'll try not to slow you down too much."

The door to the outside folded upwards revealing a pitch-black tunnel. Nicole turned on her small light and attached it to her head mount, wishing she had a pair of tactical goggles instead.

Initially, she barely fit into the tunnel and had to turn and crouch down frequently to crawl through the tight spaces. Unlike the base, the floor was uneven, causing her to stumble more than once. It was a naturally occurring cavern or at least an excellent imitation of one.

The Z'Ta effortlessly scurried through the tunnels, bounding on all fours and slinking in and out of the halo of Nicole's light. Zzyrian also could easily navigate the tunnels despite being larger than the Z'Ta. He scurried forward, barely registering the rocks and chasms in his path.

"How easy is this for you?" gasped Nicole to the Tounous as she squeezed herself through a narrow gap in the tunnel. He simply chirped in laughter and ran ahead.

The tunnel widened, allowing Nicole to stand up straight, and the walls transformed from a mundane brown into a kaleidoscope of glowing colors peppered with sparkling ore. Veins of color swirled and wrapped around each other like waves crashing together in the ocean. Nicole wished she could stop and spend hours examining the natural beauty around her but couldn't look at the walls too much because she had to watch her footing as small crevices split the floor underneath her. If she didn't pay attention, she could break her ankle or worse.

"We're about to enter a hive," Y'kiran warned. "Our scouts are up ahead. Just be ready to run when we tell you."

The tunnel abruptly ended in a solid rock wall that seemed drab and dull in contrast to the multihued tunnel walls they had just passed through. "Stop here," Y'torak instructed. "And be ready to run."

"Y'kiran already told us that," Nicole replied.

Y'torak made a popping noise. "Well then, it's doubly true, Human."

Nicole crouched next to the wall, sweeping her light along its face. It was smooth and completely blocked the tunnel without any obvious way through. But the two scouts that had been in front of them were gone, so there must be some way.

The seconds stretched, and Nicole shared a look with Samaha and Ramos. "This is the most excitement I've had on a diplomatic mission," Samaha said dryly.

"Join the Skulls," Nicole replied. "Things get exciting real fast."

"I can only imagine."

A circular portion of the wall cantilevered open, and a faint light burst into the tunnel. One of the Z'Ta scouts stuck its head through the opening. "It's clear. Let's go!"

The three Humans were the first to crawl through the hole and into the Z'Ta hive. Nicole wasn't sure what she expected, but this wasn't it. The tunnel was almost perfectly circular with a small paved floor. The walls were made of the same dull rock they'd seen in the hidden passage with sconces placed every few meters. She thought she'd perhaps see buildings or at least hear something, but there was nothing except a low hum that seemed to permeate the entire hallway.

"Okay, this is the tough part," Y'dari said as it stood in front of the Humans on its back legs. "We'll have to go past the hive's center, so keep moving."

"What's it look like?" Ramos asked, eyebrow raised.

"No idea," Nicole replied.

"Guess we're about to find out." Samaha strode after

the Z'Ta.

As they walked, the hallway gently curved to the left. Small doors, no higher than Nicole's shoulder, stood at regular intervals on the inside of the curve. Next to each door, lettering had been carved into the wall. As she tried to read them, her implant translated the signs from Z'Tarian into Standard Human—these were homes; the signs were their addresses.

One of the Z'Ta saw her examining the doors as they walked along the hallway. "Don't worry; this area's abandoned. No one's coming out."

The hum grew louder as they made their way down the tunnel. Now it sounded like the thrusters of a ship in the distance.

Ahead, a section of the tunnel wall disappeared, opening up into a large circular cavern. Small writhing creatures covered the walls of the cavern, moving in almost hypnotic waves under the lights hung from the walls.

"Get ready to run," Y'dari said.

As they got closer, Nicole realized the creatures she'd seen at a distance were thousands—tens of thousands—of Z'Ta scurrying and crawling over each other. Their voices merged to create the almost overpowering hum that Nicole had heard as far back as the hallway. The room had hundreds of levels, extending as far as she could see, each with several portals, just like the one she was looking through.

"Run!"

The group broke into a sprint, crossing the open portal as fast as they could. With the even floors and high ceilings, the Humans were only slightly slower than the others. Once they passed the opening, Nicole slowed down and walked.

"What're you doing?" Y'torak grumbled. "There're thousands of Z'Ta in the hive. At least one of them saw us."

Nicole began sprinting again, keeping her eyes trained on the Z'Ta scouts in front of her. A plasma bolt streaked over her head, splashing against the ceiling and causing Samaha and Ramos to duck. Several more shots sprayed down the hallway. Nicole heard the whine of plasma guns as the scouts behind them began firing back.

A Z'Ta was waiting by a small opening at the bottom of the outside wall of the corridor. The opening was pitch-black, but Nicole didn't hesitate to slide through the it, the jagged stone edges scratching her body as she squeezed through.

"Damn, that was close," Ramos said as she followed Nicole and Samaha into the opening.

Someone closed the door after they had made it through. Nicole turned her light on to see Y'torak by the door. "What about the others?" she asked. The two trailing scouts were still on the other side.

"What about them?" Y'torak asked, confused. "We needed to seal the door."

Nicole wanted to shake or hit the creature but knew there was no use arguing. She would be a fool to expect the Z'Ta to operate under her sense of morality. Instead, she kept her mouth shut and followed the group through the narrow passageway.

They ascended through the layers of the planet's crust, and the rainbow-colored walls transitioned back into a dull gray. Sounds drifted through the tunnel in front of them, engines spinning up and equipment being moved. They were close to the landing bay.

The tunnel ended in a steel grate, less than a meter in diameter. Nicole could only faintly make anything out on the other side of the grate. The relatively smooth walls, dim lighting, and lack of activity made her think it had to be some sort of utility corridor.

"Hold here," Y'dari said, holding up an arm. "We need to get ready." It motioned to the remaining scouts who dropped the packs they were carrying. They opened them and pulled out translucent bundles, tossing one to each member of the group.

Nicole caught hers and pulled it apart. It was a large sack with four round devices attached at the four corners. The diaphanous cloth-like material appeared flimsy.

"What is this?" Ramos asked, holding hers up in front of her.

"There's no way we can safely get inside the transport vessels," Y'torak replied.

"So, we're going *on* them," Y'kiran concluded.

"You want us to stick ourselves to the side of one of those ships?" Samaha looked at the deflated bubble she was holding in disbelief.

"Yes," Y'dari replied, "it's the safest way for us to get off the planet. Our ships have security protocols to avoid stowaways."

"Won't they see us?" asked Ramos.

"Maybe. Maybe not." Y'torak replied. "But let's get

these on while we convince you that we're right."

With the help of the Z'Ta, Nicole placed the transparent suit around her body. The inside of each disk had a loop, which she placed around her wrists and ankles to keep them in place. A small control pad was on the inner portion of one disk next to her hand. She pressed a button, and the material constricted around her body until it was almost uncomfortable for her to breathe.

"Okay, we've got a good hour of air in these things," said Y'dari from inside its own suit. "Be ready to follow us."

Nicole tried to remain calm as she thought about what she was about to do. Sticking herself to the side of a ship that was launching into space was not on her list of things she was looking forward to. The suit was tougher than it looked at first, but she doubted it could withstand exiting the planet's atmosphere.

"How many times have you tested these?" asked Samaha as she examined herself in the suit.

"Oh, countless times," Y'torak replied with a casual wave of its arm.

"None successful," Y'kiran added. "But we have a good feeling about this time."

Chapter Thirteen

"I'm not sure if you're lucky or good," Lukas said. Initially, he'd been furious when he'd found out his brother's friends had only destroyed the Tokamak reactor instead of causing an explosion that would have wiped out thousands in Chengdu.

He'd considered eliminating them. They were dangerous and could be a huge pain in his ass if not managed properly. But after a couple of weeks, he'd found out that the mission had been even more effective than he'd thought.

"A little bit of both," Karl replied, leaning back in his chair, clearly feigning disinterest. Lukas's little brother had become more and more despondent the closer they came to winning the war.

Their assault into the People's Movement's territory had succeeded beyond his wildest expectations. The enemy seemed to melt before his soldiers, running and abandoning weapons and equipment. Others just seemed to have disappeared; squads took their equipment and weapons and just left. The ones that remained were the conscripts, easy fodder for his own people.

He should be overjoyed, but one thing continually nagged him. His scouts reported seeing bands of enemy soldiers in the woods. They moved in squad-sized elements but never attacked. When approached, they would disappear into the foliage. Could the Patagonia Front have reemerged? He doubted it—that wasn't their area of operations, and they would've attacked. But it still raised the question of who they were. It was a loose end, and he hated those.

Lukas smiled. This time it was genuine. "Your team seems to always be in the right place at the right time. If I didn't know what was really going on, I'd have some tough questions for you." More than that. He would have had them tortured for information and killed. Lukas believed that if you couldn't understand what was going on, it was best to cut your losses and avoid a nasty surprise.

"They're the best." Karl shrugged. "I've been talking to your new lieutenants. They could probably learn a thing from General Norman." His little brother still refused to call the so-called general by his first name. The EDF had indoctrinated him completely. That said, Karl had learned some pretty useful skills in the service as well.

"That's interesting." Lukas thought about it. He had to admit, he'd lost a lot of skilled leaders when he'd cleaned house at the beginning of the war. The new soldiers were brash and many did not have any formal training. He didn't have to deal with the scheming and back talk, but still, perhaps some additional training would be helpful. "What are you thinking?"

"You've almost got Chengdu, so you don't need us on missions. You can save us for the campaign against the PPC. In the meantime, send your top officers and soldiers to us. We'll train them and make 'em better."

"Guess that will be a salve on your conscience too. Eh, brother? Keep them out of harm's way for a bit?" Lukas knew Karl still felt guilty about going behind his friends' backs to report on their activities. After each mission they executed, he reported to Lukas what had really happened. Sometimes the warlord had to stop himself from laughing when Kal was giving his mission report. Did he think he could keep information from Lukas?

Karl didn't take the bait. "Give us some of your best troops to help them prepare for the actual fight. Leave the rookies and the burnouts for mop-up duty. With our help, you'll have a group of elite forces ready to crush the PPC and take Kasongo."

It was a tempting plan. Lukas would never say it, but he was nervous about the fight with the PPC around Kasongo—a caged wolf fights the hardest.

"Fine, go for it." He thumped the mug he was holding on the table, and the beer sloshed onto the surface.

Karl rubbed his chin. "Hey, is Deedee still around? I could use his help with training supplies." Deedee had been their family's attendant. When they were boys, he had helped raise them both. He'd been completely loyal to their parents—to a fault.

"No, sorry. Someone killed the poor guy right after the Nasi invaded. Never caught the bastard." Lukas hoped his expression of concern was at least passable.

A shadow passed across Karl's face, and he looked away, eyes moist. Karl had given Deedee his name. When he was a small boy, he couldn't pronounce the man's real name, Delun, so the nickname Deedee had been born.

Lukas pulled himself up from his chair, walked around the table, and draped his hand across his brother's shoulder. "Sorry," Lukas said gently. "This war has taken so much from us."

The boy was still weak after everything that had happened. So weak. Lukas stifled a sudden urge to slam his brother's head into the table. People like him deserved what came to them.

"Don't worry, little brother," he whispered into Karl's ear. "Soon this will all be over."

It had been a week since Lukas had reassigned the Skulls as trainers, and it was going well. They no longer had to fight in a petty war they didn't believe in, and Kal now had the chance to talk with the Foyleton leaders en masse.

Both Kal and Jones had experience training recruits. Jones and the Tac-I squad trained the NCOs and soldiers on tactics and battle drills, Kanumba and Sampson helped their tech experts and hackers, Garcia led physical training, and Kal taught strategy to the officers. During his lessons, he tried to reference the *real* war—the war against the Nasi. The students seemed interested, but Kal could never talk directly about the Nasi. He was surely being watched and Lukas had told him in no uncertain terms to keep his class focused on the fight against the other factions.

Lukas had sent them the best soldiers he had, anticipating they could make them even more effective in the upcoming fight against the numerically superior PPC. As much as Kal hated to admit it, it was a pleasure to teach them. All the cadre felt that way. Garcia even went out of his way to provide extra workouts to the soldiers who were struggling or wanted extra training.

Kal stood at the front of the briefing room in the Foyleton base. A tactical map from one of the Skulls' recent missions was on the viewscreens behind him. Lukas had sent the Skulls to destroy an energy storage facility outside of Chengdu, and they met heavy resistance. Kal went through the battle step by step, talking about what they'd done right and what they'd done wrong. Since these were officers, he tied it to the larger war against the People's Movement. His goal was to help them understand that it was very possible to win a battle and lose the war.

"General Norman?"

"Yes." Kal pointed to the major in the front row with twisting braids that trailed their way down her back.

"I don't understand. Why didn't you just wait until night and strike then? A daylight raid seems like an unnecessary risk."

"Good question." She was smart. He wondered if she was former EDF, but there were some questions you didn't ask at Foyleton. Kal held up his palms in a sort of mea culpa. "I say this with all due respect, but the Skulls are the best troops Foyleton has." There was a general murmur of agreement. "We knew that the People's Movement guards were new, just posted there after their initial training. We took the additional risk because we also knew it was relatively small. The benefit to attacking during the day is that we keep the enemy on guard. They can never relax. Over time, that demoralizes soldiers and makes them nervous. You have to vary your attacks, both in timing and method."

"Honestly, who cares?" a man asked. "We've got the superior firepower and more soldiers. The war's over."

"Bo, could you come to front of the classroom?" Kal asked. The Jadid sat in the back row of Kal's class. Since he couldn't teach, he took part in the lessons as a student.

Kal looked at the student who'd asked the question. He couldn't place his finger on it, but the man had a quality that made Kal want to punch him in the face. "So, your opinion is that since we have superior firepower to the Movement, we should just choose the most direct approach. Is that right?

The man nodded.

"It's an interesting opinion. What makes you say that?" Kal continued to speak without letting the man answer. "Ignoring the fact that you have another enemy which you are engaging in the west, there is another issue. You believe Foyleton is superior because that is what your intelligence is telling you, right?"

The man nodded again, rolling his eyes.

"What if it's wrong? You've heard of the fog of war, right?" Nodding heads. "That principle applies at the battle, campaign, and theater level. You can never be sure you know everything."

"As you all know, my friend Bowen here is a Jadid. Not a Nasi but he is very familiar with them." Several students looked away. Although Bo had been at the base for weeks, many people still had a hard time being around him.

"Bo, when the Nasi held you prisoner, you must have heard them talk sometimes. What did they consider their greatest asset?" Kal asked.

"Well, sir, they had several. They had much more advanced technology, dreadnaughts which can destroy systems—"

"Yes," Kal interrupted, "but which one did *they* consider their greatest?"

"I'd say their planning, sir."

Kal looked around the room, trying to catch each student's eye. The point he was making was rudimentary and really tangential to the conversation but his real goal was always the same—tie the conversation back to the Nasi. Make sure the students realized there was another enemy, one that was more dangerous than the People's Movement and the PPC combined.

"Yes, planning. They spent *years* planning their attack. Studying Humanity and its neighbors. We were unaware, blissfully so." Kal pounded the small lectern that he'd ordered fabricated for the classes. "They waited, watched, and attacked when we were not expecting. And that's what made them so successful. Now that advantage is gone. Perhaps we may still win this war now that they've lost that asset."

Officers shifted in their seats. The topic made them uncomfortable, which it should. A war for survival was going on and they were fighting over the scraps.

"Damnit, what are you doing?" Ishmael snapped.

"This is how you do it!" The Foyleton prisoner pulled the tea kettle away from Ishmael's grasp and continued to pour the tea. "You don't know how to pour tea. You're not even Patagonian."

Kal silently watched as the two glared daggers at each other. Finally, the woman turned on her heels and strode out of the room. "Wait this time. Don't burn yourself again!" She shouted from the hallway she'd disappeared down.

"That woman," Ishmael muttered to himself.

Kal raised an eyebrow and studied the Alliance operative.

"Ava always thinks she knows exactly what to do." Ishmael winced as he took a sip of the hot tea. "Damn!"

"Isn't it a bit dangerous to have her out of the cell?" Kal asked.

"Maybe to herself. She's the biggest klutz I've ever met." Ishmael stole a glance toward the doorway Ava had disappeared into. "Anyway, the base has a lot of protocols that protect me and keep her in."

"Still, if she gets out, this entire mission fails, and we all disappear."

Ishmael waved his hand. "The Alliance has dealt with situations like this and prisoners much more dangerous than her before." His cheeks colored for a moment. "Look. I've been by myself for a long time. It's nice to have someone around. Even if they are a pain in my—"

"You sure you know what you're doing?" Kal asked, trying to hold the man's gaze.

"Yes. Yes. I know exactly what I'm doing." Ishmael returned the gaze evenly. "Now, I hope you didn't come here to nag me. I've got enough of that."

"No, I came here to see if you'd been able to learn anything more about the Foothold. Specifically, if what we're looking for is in it."

The Foothold in Kasongo was the center of the Nasi power structure on the planet. The city-within-a-city was self-sufficient for all intents and purposes with research, barracks, homes, and most importantly, gateways which allowed the Nasi to send vast amounts of ships, soldiers, and materials between their universe and this one. Because of its importance the Foothold was also highly guarded. When the Nasi first landed, the Skulls had been able to attack the Nasi Foothold on New America. That wouldn't be possible now that the Footholds were completed.

Kal was sure a Nasi skip ship was somewhere in that facility. However, he didn't know where. Until they could learn more, they couldn't move on the Nasi even if they had the resources.

Ishmael leaned forward in his chair. "Yes and no. I've been able to get some informants on the inside. Even with that, information is hard to come by. The Nasi aren't exactly known for sharing, and your stunt a month ago made them double up on security." Kal knew he was referring to their storming of the Nasi research base.

"Well, what did you find out?" Kal asked.

"Good news is, I've had confirmation the Nasi moved all research into the Foothold. Bad news is, I don't know where."

The base was too large for them to search even with a large assault force, and it wasn't like they'd be able to sneak in. They needed to know exactly where they were going.

Fighting the People's Movement was one thing but fighting the Nasi was a completely different level. They were disciplined, ruthless, and well-armed.

"When do you think you might know something?" Kal asked.

"No idea, man." Ishmael shrugged. "This isn't an easy task even for me. Besides, do you even have a crew yet?"

Kal shook his head reluctantly. "No, not yet. But we're working on that. Lukas has asked us to teach his senior leaders. It's a chance for us to reach out to them. To find the good ones."

"And how's that going?" Ishmael sounded doubtful.

"Okay," Kal replied defensively. "We're making some progress. I've had a chance to talk with some of them outside of class. Nothing detailed, but I think if we can give them a real aim, we'll be able to get some of them to join us."

"Lukas Garcia is not a man you cross," Ishmael raised his cup and took a small drink, wincing from the heat. "I've been on Patagonia long enough to see my fair share of people die at his hands."

"Fair warning." Kal rubbed his forehead and took his own small sip of tea. "However, we're reaching the endgame with the Foyleton Syndicate. Soon they'll start moving on Kasongo."

"I know, I know. But you'll at least have a little bit more time with the storms coming."

"Storms?" Kal asked.

"Yeah, storms. Around this time of year, we get hit by big storms coming south from the ocean." He held his hands apart in front of his body. "There's one that'll hit in a few days."

"I don't think storms will stop Lukas." Even ill-trained soldiers like the Foyleton Syndicate should be able to handle the weather.

"Trust me." Ishmael raised his cup.

Kal would have to ask the Foyleton officers about this storm tomorrow. "Either way, time is running short, and we need to know where the plans or the ship is."

"I'll do my best." Ishmael drained his glass. "Never failed yet."

❖

Ishmael was right. The storm caused everything to grind to a halt.

Two days after Kal had met with the Alliance leader, Chengdu had fallen. Ultimately, they hadn't been able to mount much of a defense, and the superior Foyleton forces had quickly captured the city.

Foyleton had taken all the Movement's territory in the east, including Chengdu. But the Planetary People's Council had also captured a significant amount of their land to the west. The balance of power between the two groups was even.

Unsurprisingly, Lukas seemed overjoyed the few times Kal met with him after the victory. He had destroyed two of his enemies and was about to launch an all-out war on the last one. For the Skulls, time was becoming more and more precious. They'd been on Patagonia for almost a month without anything to show for it. They were running out of time.

The storm was like nothing Kal had ever seen. The skies above Foyleton darkened for two days before the rain started coming down in sheets. The torrential downpour turned roads into rivers and fields into lakes. Whatever wasn't covered with water was turned into brackish mud, making it impossible to get anywhere and reducing visibility to nil.

As they waited for the storm to abate, the Skulls continued to train the Foyleton Syndicate. They had thrown themselves into the training; there was nothing else to do anyway. Garcia continued to conduct his supplemental training sessions with the students despite the weather—taking them on long swims through the streets of the city.

Perhaps because he had nothing else to do, Lukas attended some of Kal's classes. He sat in the back and whispered to whichever student was next to him or laughed uproariously at inappropriate times.

Kal had completed his class on negotiations and was watching the students file out of the room when Lukas approached him.

"Interesting class, professor," he said with a smirk on his face.

"How so?" Kal already felt tired.

"Your take on negotiations," Lukas said. "Overcomplicates the entire issue. Negotiation is simple. Somebody has something you want. Negotiation is just getting that thing by any means necessary. No need to worry about the psychology crap. There's a winner and a loser. You want to be the winner."

Kal was unsurprised by the warlord's take on the subject. To Lukas, everything came down to the same concept— winners and losers. He saw himself as a winner, and he clearly felt that was all that mattered.

"Take *our* negotiations, for example," Lukas continued. "When you came here, you wanted something: to survive. And you did whatever it took to get it. Which meant working for me."

The man was needling him but Kal would not engage. He looked at the man evenly, waiting for him to continue.

"Well, my friend, we're both about to get what we want. The storm's almost over. Soon our offensive will start. You've impressed me these past few weeks, but I'm still sending you back into the field."

Kal's mind raced; they needed more time. He was only beginning to really get through to the officers in his class. "That's good to hear. But you'll need advisors during this offensive. Experienced soldiers to help your leaders."

Lukas flipped a tablet idly in his hands. "Perhaps, but that's not what you'll be doing. Finish your training. I'm sending you back to the field soon."

There wasn't room to argue, not unless Kal wanted to explain why he was so intent on avoiding the field.

"Roger. We'll be ready." There was nothing else to say.

❖

Lukas had been right. After a couple more days, the storm passed, and the tropical Patagonian sun blazed in the sky with nary a cloud in sight. The air became almost sticky with humidity as the heat burned away the standing water. The landscape, used to these deluges, quickly dried and commerce and travel started to spring up again.

Lukas quickly put the Skulls back to work in the field, sending them to a PPC fighter base. The Skulls infiltrated the facility and destroyed the power system, preventing the fighters from being able to launch. It was the first blow in a new offensive by Foyleton against the PPC.

After the mission, Kal ordered the team to regroup outside the converted Foyleton transport that would take them back. It was the only place where Lukas or his loyalists couldn't overhear.

"Perimeter secure, sir," Sergeant Jones reported.

"Thank you, Sergeant," Kal said. "We've only got a few minutes until Lukas gets suspicious. How are we looking?" Lukas tracked their missions closely from Foyleton's headquarters. If they deviated too far from the planned timeline, they would get a barrage of questions when they returned.

"Sir, there are some good ones," Jones reported. "I've been talking about the Nasi, and I can tell there are people that are ready to help us. I will keep working on them, letting them know that there is a fight still going on outside of Patagonia."

"Just be careful," Garcia warned, "my brother's a lot of things, but stupid's not one of them. You say the wrong thing, and you're gone."

"What else can we do, sir?" Jones asked, crossing his arms. "We can't dance around it forever."

"I"—Garcia hesitated—"I don't know. We'll know when the time is right."

"We're running out of time," Kanumba said, still catching her breath. The pressure of their situation had gotten to her more than anyone else. She'd become distant, spending what little free time she had alone in her room. Kal worried about her but had faith that she would pull out of it. "These people are the same as the Movement. Lots of 'em are dirtbags, but there are also a bunch that want to do the right thing. They've also got some skilled people in there. I've learned a thing or two from them."

"I hate to be the wet blanket—again." Garcia said. "If they have skilled tech folks, it means my brother could intercept our comms. Who knows? Maybe he's listening to us now."

Ekon cursed. "Sir, what's wrong with you?" Jones shot him a look of warning. "Sorry, but it seems like you don't want us to do anything."

"I hate to say it, but Sergeant Kimathi may have a point." Kal put a hand on Garcia's arm. "Maybe you're too close to this. I know you used to have friends here in Foyleton. Any luck finding them?"

The pilot averted his eyes. "No, sir. That's a dead end. My brother removed anyone who was loyal to my parents."

"Sorry to hear that." Kal knew some of those people had been Garcia's friends.

"Not surprised," Garcia replied. "He's kind of a bastard."

"I've been doing some research into the Foyleton database," Bo said. "There are still some people here who served under your parents. I can provide you more information." Kal had brought the Jadid on the mission since it was a quick strike. It had paid off tremendously. Not only was he faster and stronger than any Human, but he confused the PPC soldiers, who thought there was a Nasi joining in the attack. Bo still couldn't shoot worth a damn, but he was an asset in the field.

"What?" Garcia looked alarmed. "Why would you do that? You could cause us to lose everything."

The Jadid looked chagrined. "I'm sorry, Karl. I thought—
"

Why haven't you moved? Lukas asked over the Foyleton net. Per their request, he never used the Skulls' names and understood that they would not transmit back to him. The Nasi were fine with Lukas and his quest to secure control of Patagonia, but they would seek and destroy the Skulls if they knew they were on the planet.

"Okay, let's go," Kal instructed. "Keep working on the Foyleton soldiers. We need to plant the seed now, so we can harvest them when the time is right."

"Nice metaphor, sir." Garcia said cheerfully.

"Shut up, sir." Jones half-heartedly punched the pilot in the arm.

Chapter Fourteen

After their initial advance toward Kasongo, the Foyleton soldiers became bogged down in the hills that stretched north to south across the continent. Anti-aircraft batteries dotted the hills, preventing them from launching a direct assault at Kasongo, the heart of the PPC.

The Skulls continued to be used heavily in the operation. Kal lost count of how many times he had to conduct an aerial assault on a PPC encampment. Shrapnel had hit Garcia during one their missions, putting him into hospital. Luckily, he had been alone, waiting for them to complete the assault, so no one else had been injured. But it was a matter of time before their luck would run out.

Progress on the real mission was even slower. Ishmael still hadn't located the research lab in the Foothold. The Skulls had no time to talk to, much less recruit, other Foyleton soldiers. Things were looking grim.

"Ten seconds," Sampson called through the transport's intercom. Ten seconds until they were over their objective.

Below them, perched on a hilltop, was one of the final PPC positions in the hills between Foyleton and Kasongo. If they could take it, Lukas would be able to drive his forces through and open up the war. The PPC had fortified the camp against aerial attack and Foyleton didn't have enough offensive air capabilities anyway. The only way to take it out was from the ground.

Kal could faintly hear the anti-aircraft weapons firing at their ship over the thrum of the thrusters. Timed plasma rounds exploded around the craft, and Kal heard the occasional ping of shrapnel hitting the armored plates of the vehicle.

"Go!" Jones called out.

The Tac-I squad, plus Bo and Kal, jumped out of the open cargo door and into the night. Each one of them had a modified life pack on their backs to control their descent. The packs were designed for escaping downed aircraft but had been altered to be used for rapid descent. The thrusters would automatically engage around thirty meters, allowing the wearer to freefall and then land safely on the ground.

After he jumped out, all Kal could hear was the roar of wind in his ears. With his night-vision goggles on, the flashes of the guns lobbing shells at the retreating Foyleton drop ship looked like small suns. Shells exploded in the air, bright green blasts peppering the night sky. The landscape below expanded as he plunged toward the ground. The sharp lines of the PPC base stood out against the clumps of trees and the rise of the mountain.

The most dangerous part of any airborne mission was the descent. There was no cover, no place to hide. Kal tried not to think about it and tried unsuccessfully to make out any activity in the camp below.

Kal grunted as his pack's thrusters engaged, jerking him against the harness. He was close enough to hear the PPC soldiers calling out to one another, trying to direct their fire on the incoming Skulls. Kinetic and plasma fire erupted from the base, heading toward Kal as his pack's thruster strained against gravity to allow him to land.

Report, Jones called out over their local neural net.

Each member of the squad had landed without issue, and they were all in position. They were on the upslope from the base, arranged in a half-circle outside the perimeter. Kal estimated there were about twenty PPC fighters inside.

The base itself was small, maybe a hundred meters across. Inside was a makeshift building being used as living quarters, two anti-aircraft batteries with five guns each, and the ammunition storage bunker. The PPC had erected the base haphazardly. The ammunition magazine was way too close to the rest of the base.

Bo, you're on. Jones said.

Their plan was simple, one that they had done multiple times already. Bo would be their distraction and move toward the guns, drawing most of the enemy away. Kal would take an elevated position and provide support through well-placed cover fire. The other three would be the main effort and destroy the magazine. Explosives in the right place would cause it to blow and take the rest of the camp with it. They just needed to make sure they were gone before it happened.

Kal rushed up the hillside, looking for the firing position he'd identified during the map recon. By the time he reached it and concealed himself behind a small clump of bushes, Bo had already climbed the perimeter fence. Although the Jadid was still useless with a weapon, he made up for that in speed and strength. Any PPC soldier unlucky or unwise enough to get close wouldn't stand a chance.

The PPC fighters were smart and kept their distance from the Jadid, moving to encircle him. Bo crouched into position behind an Ultracrete blast barrier. His goal was only to distract. He lifted his rifle over the barrier periodically and let off a few sporadic shots, which missed by a mile. Kal took out the PPC soldiers in his line of sight as they cautiously maneuvered through the camp, trying to get close to Bo. He took his time and paced himself as he fired down at the PPC soldiers. Inhale. Squeeze. Exhale. He took down two of them before they realized there was a sniper above them.

Kal kept an eye on the three Tac-I squad members as they scaled the perimeter wall on the opposite side of the base. So far, they had gone unnoticed. Jones led the way, flanked on either side by Ekon and Sandra. Having grown up together on New America, the two young soldiers seemed to have an almost unspoken bond during missions.

They covered the distance to the ammunition magazine in a sprint and crouched down by the door. Kanumba had changed her skeleton key to work on the PPC locks, and Kal expected them to be cracked in seconds.

Jones cursed over the net. *Damn it, this is some new type of lock. We're going to have to do this the old-fashioned way.* That meant explosives. Which meant they would alert the soldiers to their presence. It was about to get messy.

Bo, be prepared to retreat to outside the perimeter, Jones instructed.

Seconds later, a small explosion ripped through the right side of the base. It was louder than Kal expected; the sound reverberated off the hillsides around the camp. Several PPC soldiers, realizing what was happening, turned around and rushed to the ammunition magazine.

With the soldiers distracted, Bo leaped from his position

and scaled the perimeter wall. As he was pivoting over the edge, his body jerked, and he fell to the ground on the far side.

I'm hit, Bo cried out.

Can you move? Jones asked.

I believe so. The round hit me in the shoulder. I will move to the extraction point. The extraction point was about five hundred meters on the other side of the mountain.

Luckily, the PPC did not want to have anything to do with a potential Nasi and turned around to focus all their efforts on the Tac-I squad at the magazine. Kal continued to lay down fire on the PPC guards, methodically firing whenever he saw an opening. They still didn't seem to know where his position was and only sporadically fired into the lush hillside above the camp. A few shots came close though. Kal could smell the singed underbrush as a plasma round hit a couple of meters from his location.

Charges set, but we're trapped, Jones said. *Sir, any way you can provide some sort of cover to get us out of here?*

I'm trying, Kal replied.

The PPC soldiers had positioned themselves so Kal couldn't get a clear shot. He continued to harry them while he scanned the interior of the base looking for something explosive or a way to give the others time.

We've got less than a minute, Jones said. *We're going to have to make a break for it.*

At that moment, Kal saw something out of the corner of his eye. Bo leaped back over the wall and into the perimeter in a single graceful movement. He rushed at the PPC soldiers' flank. Although he was not a soldier, he was still a Jadid. That meant the unarmored Human soldiers didn't stand a chance if he got close.

Bo took out one soldier after another at close range. He was an awe-inspiring force of nature, a tempest of destruction.

The Tac-I members used the distraction to climb to the top of the wall and direct fire back on the base. Bo was too close and too erratic for them to target the soldiers near him, but they could prevent others from getting close.

Bo, get out of there. Jones called.

The Jadid threw aside the metal strut he was using as a weapon and sprinted at the wall. He only made it a few meters before his gait faltered and he fell to his knees.

Go on, Bo called out. *I don't think I can make it out.*

Use your pack, Kal instructed. They only had seconds until the explosives would destroy the magazine and most of the hillside.

I tried, but it seems to have been damaged. It's not working.

Kal saw Jones yell something to the other two on the wall as his pack burst to life. Sandra and Ekon flew away from the base while Jones swept down from the wall, grabbed the Jadid around the waist, and cleared the wall on the other side of the base as the ammunition magazine erupted.

A green-tinged shock wave blossomed out from the ammunition bunker, obliterating everything in its path. Vehicles, trees, people—all were hurled away by its force. The solid Ultracrete walls of the facility shattered outwards, disintegrating under the onslaught of the blast. A multihued gout of flame sprung from the ground where the magazine had stood. The devastation was complete.

Report, Kal frantically called out over the net.

Chedjou and I are okay, Ekon responded.

Bo, Sergeant Jones? Kal asked. Nothing.

They found Bo and Sergeant Jones tangled in the forest canopy below the decimated base. The blast had knocked them both unconscious and flung them into the trees. Luckily, the dense canopy had stopped them from falling through to the forest floor. Sandra and Ekon were able to stabilize the sergeant using their field med kits, but Kal ordered them only to apply basic first aid to the Jadid. There was no way of knowing how their drugs might affect him. They'd had a close call in the People's Movement base in Chengdu.

The flight back to Foyleton was harrowing. Jones had sustained head trauma and had several gashes on his torso and legs. By the time they touched down at the Foyleton headquarters, blood tinged the bandages they'd wrapped around his wounds.

In addition to his wounded shoulder, Bo had a nasty-looking gash on his leg. They'd tried to dress it as best they could, but the blood continued to seep out, staining the bandages a bright red.

Several members of the medical staff placed the two casualties on medical stretcher bots. They differed from the one on the *Salamis,* which was a small bot placed next to the patient. These bots were hovering hospital beds and could treat patients, transport them, and then integrate with the clinic's systems for serious cases and long-term care.

"What happened?" Garcia asked. He must have heard their request for medical support and ran to be there when they landed.

"Jones and Bo got hit," Kal said as he watched the medical bots glide away toward the clinic with Ekon and Sandra trailing behind.

Garcia cursed and shook his head. "I coulda been there. I'm so sorry, sir."

"No, you couldn't have. You're injured, remember? You'll be back soon."

The pilot flushed. "I'm still not cleared, sir. I...I'm not sure when they will clear me."

That was strange. The pilot's wounds had been bad, but Kal had seen people with much worse. He didn't doubt Garcia though; the man had proven his resolve more times than Kal could count.

Kanumba shuffled out of the small transport, the used bandages from Bo's leg in her hands. The scar across her face stood out against her sallow skin.

"I'm sorry, sir," she said, head down. "If the key had worked, this wouldn't have happened."

"It doesn't matter," Kal replied. He looked at them both. "Injuries happen, mistakes happen. This is a war and we can't do everything. Bo and Sergeant Jones will recover. The fault for this doesn't lie with either of you. I'm going to the clinic to check on them."

Kal left the landing pad and headed toward the entrance to the headquarters. The landing area was full of a chaotic energy as ships continued to take off heading toward Kasongo through the hole in the PPC's defenses the Skulls had opened up. With a pass cleared through the mountains, it was all systems go.

The hallways of the Foyleton base had become familiar to Kal. He no longer registered the over-the-top decorations and the air of false sophistication that pervaded the base. As a man who liked things simple, Kal thought he would never get used to Lukas's ostentatious style. He was wrong, the gilded chandeliers and priceless artwork didn't faze him a bit anymore.

"Taisha?" Garcia asked, worry in his voice.

Kal turned around in time to see the chief's eyes roll up in her head and her body slump to the ground. Luckily she fell to her side, and her shoulder, rather than her head, took most of the impact from the floor.

"Get a medical staffer here now," Kal ordered.

Garcia ran to the clinic and returned seconds later with a harried young woman and a medbot.

"Back up," the woman said curtly as she knelt next to the chief. After a quick examination, she lifted the chief onto the waiting bot with Garcia's help.

The clinic was relatively empty compared to the previous times Kal had been there. The pause caused by the storm had temporarily slowed the flow of new casualties. With the new offensive, they would be busy soon enough, he feared.

"What's their status?" Kal asked the nurse on duty. The man was young, in his twenties. Dark bags hung under his eyes, and he moved with the slow thoughtless movements of someone who had seen enough for one lifetime.

"That one," he pointed at Jones, "is going to be fine. He took some hits, but he's mostly made of metal anyway. Chief concern is the head trauma he took from the blast. Should be up in a day or so."

"She'll be fine too," the nurse pointed at Chief Kanumba, who was already sitting up on one of the bunks. "Seems like she just got over exhausted or something."

"What about Bo?" Kal asked.

"The alien?" He shrugged. "Beats the hell outta me. Frankly, I don't care either. We can't use any of our medicine or equipment on him. The freakin' thing has a pulse rate of two hundred beats per minute, and his blood oxygen level is sixty percent. I have no idea if that's even good or bad."

Kal saw red. Before he had time to think, he'd lifted the nurse off the ground with his cybernetic arm. The man's eyes went wide, and he dropped the tablet he was holding.

"You will do *everything* you can to save him. He's one of us." Kal pulled the nurse's face close to his own, so close that he could hear the man's breath whistling through his nose. "Do you understand?"

"That won't be necessary, sir." Bo croaked from his bed.

Kal dropped the nurse on the ground. He picked himself up and ran out of the room.

"Bo! You okay?" Kal asked.

"I'll survive." Bo picked up the small sheet draped

across his body. He looked at his leg and then craned his head to examine his shoulder. "The wounds are bad but not fatal."

"You had us worried," Garcia said with a smile, the first genuine smile Kal had seen on the man's face in days. "You're a scientist, remember? Next time the general tells you to go out on a mission, you tell him to shove it."

Bo laughed. "Thanks, Karl, but I'm still going to be there with you. My people, the Jadid, are responsible for all of this." He waved his arm, pointing around the room. "I feel responsible. Besides, as you say, you need all the help you can get."

Kal laughed.

Kal, come to the gallery now, Lukas called through the neural net implant. *Oh, and bring my brother with you. We got's ta talk.*

Lukas's private gallery was near the bottom of the Foyleton base. He had converted one of the large bays normally used for repairing atmospheric craft into a large gallery for the art he had recovered during the war. In Kal's opinion, the large room was hideous. Lukas had ordered the walls and ceiling painted gold and had a marble floor installed over the existing Ultracrete one. Paintings hung on almost every inch of the wall space and sculptures were scattered throughout. With modern super realistic art next to older surrealistic pieces, there was no sense of continuity. Lukas didn't really care about the art itself; he only cared about their value and saw them as a symbol of prestige.

"Well, ya did it, boys," Lukas laughed as he turned around from the painting he was examining.

"See this painting?" Lukas asked as he pointed to the artwork he'd been studying. In it, a group of men were crossing an icy river in a small boat. The boat was almost overflowing with people and Kal immediately noticed the discrepancy between the men at the bottom, struggling to propel the boat forward, and their passengers. One passenger was standing in the center of the craft, looking forward with a ray of light creating a halo around his body. Kal felt a mix of emotions while staring at the painting: hope, determination, and a feeling of cold.

Kal nodded.

"It's an ancient Earth picture called *Wilson Crossing the Delaware*." A soldier leaned forward to whisper something to Lukas, but the warlord waved him away. Lukas stepped forward and craned his head forward until it was only a couple of centimeters away from the painting. He turned around and faced Kal. "Very expensive. You can even see the brushstrokes in the painting. There's something interesting about having a picture that has that kind of texture to it. Wouldn't you say? It's so much more complex than the holos and viewscreen images we normally see."

"Sure," Kal agreed. He wasn't there to talk art.

"When I heard you had destroyed the final PPC anti-aircraft position, I thought of this picture. This general, he was crossing some river. See those people at the bottom?" He pointed to the bottom of the picture, where the men pushed the boat along with determined expressions. "They're like you; they're the ones that make the boat go forward. I'm him." He pointed to the man in the center, hand on knee, looking solemnly into the distance. "The visionary looking toward the future and the goal. Both are important."

Garcia sighed. "What's your point, brother?"

"My point, dear brother, is that we are about to cross our river. We're about to become rich and famous, and you helped do that." Lukas stepped back and patted the two men on the back.

"We're in the last stage and I've been receiving word from my soldiers that we have a solid presence on the other side of the hills. The war will be over soon."

"What then?" Kal asked. His war was long from over.

"Then we rebuild this planet, my friend. I've got plans, big ones. We're going to make Patagonia the new capital of Humanity."

"Under the Nasi rule," Kal spat back.

"I'd hoped you'd gotten over that." Lukas raised an eyebrow. "The Nasi ain't going anywhere. They're like the stars and my good looks, here to stay. I'd suggest you accept that."

Kal wanted to grab the man by his shirt and shake him. He was so ready to accept defeat and eat the crumbs he was given. Instead, Kal forced himself to breath slowly and bunched his fists, trying to calm himself. "Of course, you're right. I've learned it the hard way."

"We're still in denial," Garcia said with a wry smile.

221

"Takes time to realize when you're licked."

Lukas nodded. "Maybe. But better to recognize it and move on than to keep poundin' your head against the same wall." He ambled to a modern sculpture in the middle of the room. It was a mixture of copper and holographic projection. Kal thought he might have seen it in a holo once before.

"Like I said, we're reaching the end game here. I'm going to need you to be ready to go. Sorry to hear you had some injuries on this mission. But I need you back and ready for action soon. You've got two days. By then we'll have the PPC under siege in Kasongo."

"What about the Nasi?" Kal asked. "Will they stay out of it?"

"Always have," Lukas replied. "Guess I should contact them though and let them know my intentions. The last thing we need is a bunch of battle-suited Nasi soldiers crushing us."

"We'll be ready, brother," Garcia promised. "Then you'll be the ruler of Patagonia. Something our parents never dreamed of."

"Yes." Lukas stared off into the distance, his face a blank mask. He turned to look at them. "This war is finally coming to an end."

Chapter Fifteen

Nicole knelt near the grate to the landing bay in the strange suit waiting for the group to move. The anticipation was killing her, and she hated not knowing what was holding them up. There didn't seem to be any activity in the corridor beneath them and with only an hour of air in their suits, their margin of error to get to a ship and off-planet was very small.

Finally, one of the Z'Ta scouts next to the grate turned around and gave a quick nod to the group. It was time.

Two Z'Ta soldiers pushed against the grate until it fell away from the wall with a small pop. They maneuvered the detached grate back into the small tunnel and set it against the wall. The scouts silently crawled forward and gracefully lowered themselves into the corridor while the Humans followed, sliding legs-first out of the opening and dropping onto the stone floor. It looked exactly like the one they had been in at the hive—smooth walls, level floor, dim utility lighting—except it was at least twice as wide.

The group slowly traipsed through the hallway, careful to keep as silent as possible. Their pistols were useless since the clear outfits trapped them against their bodies. If they were found, they would almost certainly be captured.

The hallway was curved, preventing Nicole from seeing the end, but she heard the faint hum of engines mixed with the faint bubbling of Z'Ta talking ahead, reminding her of the sound of river rapids. Intermittently, she heard the hiss of small thrusters, most likely from cargo being loaded onto ships using pallet lifters.

They passed several large openings leading into what

appeared to be storage rooms. Unlabeled boxes, material bins, gas canisters, and other goods filled the room from floor to ceiling.

Y'kiran turned to Nicole and the others. "Just be ready to run. We'll have to time it just right. Follow us and then press the attach button in your suit when we get on the ship. Do you remember which one it is?"

Samaha nodded. "Yeah, the triangle."

Y'kiran shook his head. "No, square." It paused. "Wait, maybe you're right."

Y'dari whispered, "Try the triangle and if you don't stick to the ship, then try the other ones until you do."

"That's our plan?" Chief Ramos asked.

"That's our plan," replied Y'kiran with a hearty glug.

Before Nicole could say anything, the scouts broke into a gallop, hurtling down the hallway on all fours. The rest of the group was forced to follow. As they ran, the already large tunnel grew in diameter until the walls stretched almost as far as Nicole could see. She realized they were at the top of a crater. Below them, hundreds of transports sat parked in even rows with loading bots and stevedores walking and gliding between them loading boxes and supplies into the ships. The stars shined in the dark night sky, giving Nicole the impression of being in space rather than on a planet.

The tunnel's rock floor turned into a walkway suspended over the landing pad. As they ran down the catwalk, several of the ships taxied from their pads, activated their thrusters, and climbed into the atmosphere with a roar. *If they look over at the wrong time, we're toast*, thought Nicole. She tried to suppress the negative thought and focused on running despite feeling like someone had stabbed a knife into her side.

The group turned down a staircase that dropped until they were less than five meters above the landing pad floor. The Z'Ta working below seemed almost close enough to touch, and she could make out bits of conversation as they guided floating pallets of cargo into ships and laughed in conversation.

"Stop! Where are you going?" Nicole's heart stopped when she heard the shout in Human Standard. A Nasi. She had to fight her instinct to drop and roll along the floor to avoid incoming fire.

She looked down. The shout had come from directly beneath them where two Nasi soldiers stood. One had their hand pointed at a Z'Ta a few meters away. *They're not talking to us.* Nicole continued to run and hoped that the sounds of the loading and ships would cover their muffled footsteps as the group ran overhead.

Without warning, the two scouts leapt gracefully over the railing onto the top of a transport ship directly below the walkway.

The ship was dark brown in color and about half the size of the *Salamis* with a large delta wing shape. It had the same smooth design as other atmospheric ships Nicole had seen, except for the large bubble near the front of the ship that protruded from its top. The ship's thrusters emitted the high whining sound that meant they were almost fully engaged, and all the landing bay bots and personnel had cleared away from the area. The ship was about to depart.

The three Z'Ta council members turned and looked at their guests.

"So make sure you are behind the cockpit," said Y'kiran.

"Otherwise, you'll roast alive inside your suit," continued Y'dari.

"Or fall off," concluded Y'torak.

The three Z'Ta then gracefully leapt over the railing and landed on the hull of the transport ship directly behind the bubble. The ship's engines raised in pitch as it lifted from the landing bay floor, turning slowly toward the taxiway next to it. Zzyrian was right behind them, leaping over the railing with a similar grace.

The three Humans stopped at the railing, looking down.

"Let's go," Nicole said. "We've got to jump now. There's no time." The other two women looked at her for a moment and then gingerly climbed the railing.

They jumped and landed in a sprawl on top of the ship. Nicole followed right behind, rolling as she landed. Despite its worn appearance, the ship's hull felt smooth and slippery underneath her suit. She felt like she was about to slide off as the ship slowly taxied from underneath the network of walkways.

Nicole realized she'd landed to the side of the bubble rather than directly behind. With the Z'Ta's words ringing in her ears, she tried scrambling toward the rest of the group, but it was impossible to get any traction on the ship's exterior with the suit on. Finally, she found she could move by inching her body like a worm. Nicole slowly inched across the top of the transport as it smoothly rose into the air. She could feel the vibrations of the thrusters grow and realized they were above the top of the crater. This would have to be good enough.

Nicole activated her suit's pads, and the four disks immediately attached themselves to the ship's hull. Turned out it *was* the triangle button. She craned her head to see if the other Humans had made it. Thankfully, they had timed their jumps better and were next to Zzyrian and the five Z'Ta directly behind the cockpit.

The ship took off from the crater at a gentle incline, gaining altitude slowly. Nicole felt a rising sense of panic. She imagined the disks slipping and her hurtling back to the planet's surface. How could the impossibly thin suit protect her? She put her head down and closed her eyes, feeling the roar of the ship's thrusters through her body as they continued to climb.

Eventually, the roar of the thrusters died down and Nicole opened her eyes. She was still alive. So was everyone else, or at least they were all still attached to the ship's hull. T'kor'nuk spread out below them, somehow more beautiful now that she was seeing it with her own eyes rather than through a ship's viewscreen. Small crevices and canyons splayed across the brown surface of the planet, making it seem fragile—like it would crumble away if she blew on it. The light from H'Far's sun fell across the world's surface like a blanket, ending in darkness on the far edge of the planet.

Nicole desperately wanted to use her implant to call out to the others, but they were too close to the transport.

Instead, she tried to appreciate the beauty around her and the sense of her own insignificance in the vast reaches of space. It was a thought that was both comforting and incredibly scary.

As the journey continued, her worry gradually changed from falling to her death to suffocation. Her implant estimated she had about fifteen minutes left of air in the suit. She wasn't able to see any ships around them though the cockpit bubble blocked most of her view in front.

Nicole forced herself to think about things other than her oxygen. She thought about Kal and wondered what he and the rest of the Skulls were doing. She had no desire to go back to Patagonia after everything they'd seen there already. At least she could breathe on Patagonia. She focused again, and her mind turned to her family. She felt the starfish pendant her sister had given her pressed against her chest. What would Sylvie say about all of this? What would she think about what Nicole had done? About her treachery? Hopefully, Nicole would be able to prove herself, to prove that one mistake, no matter how bad, did not define her.

Five minutes.

Nicole felt drowsy. A part of her mind knew she was slowly suffocating. The suit was running out of oxygen. There were no sensors or alarms, but she knew the signs. She felt too tired to care and lay her head against the side of the craft, watching the gorgeous brown planet. This wasn't a terrible place to die.

❖

"She didn't fall asleep, you idiot. She almost suffocated!"

The words caused Nicole's eyes to snap open. She was lying on the ground in a landing bay. Chief Ramos's face was centimeters away from her own. Nicole idly realized the chief was actually older than she first appeared. Tiny crow's feet spread from the corner of her eyes, and small wrinkles lay across the woman's forehead.

"Ma'am, you okay?" the chief asked.

Nicole groaned. Her head was splitting. "I've been better." She tried to sit up but failed. Instead, she turned her head and looked around the room. General Samaha stood directly behind the chief, her brow wrinkled in worry. Y'kiran and Zzyrian stood on either side of the general, looking down at her with what she could only describe as mild interest.

"I can't believe you fell asleep," Y'kiran said with a burble. "I was incredibly worried but turns out you just went to sleep. Amazing!"

Someone had cut away the protective suit around her face, but the rest of her body remained ensconced in the tight transparent material.

"How do I get this thing off me?" she asked.

"Press the circle button," Y'kiran replied.

Nicole felt a thousand times better as the suit loosened and sensation flooded back into her body. With the chief's help, she sat up and began peeling the suit off her body. The rest of the group had removed theirs and dumped them on the ground, creating a small translucent mountain next to them.

She was lying on a hard metal floor next to the ship they'd rode on. A small procession of cargo bots was emptying the ship's cargo bay and moving the contents into the storage area next to her. Identical transports in similar states of being unloaded filled the Z'Ta landing bay.

"That's so much better." Nicole gasped. She gingerly stood up with the help of Samaha and Ramos.

"Now that you're done napping, we can get to work," Y'torak strode toward the door.

"Where're we going?" Nicole asked.

"We're going to meet the Command Council of the ship," Samaha replied. "They're one of the ones that agree with us."

"Well, at least they haven't put us in restraints," Ramos said.

"Yet." Zzyrian held up a single digit.

"Hey, hurry up!" Y'dari stomped its back foot.

Part of traveling through space was getting used to the recycled air and cramped spaces. The Z'Ta took it to another level; the three Humans had to crouch down to make it through many of the fetid passageways as they followed the Rebel Council through the ship. The Z'Ta scurried through the hallway, crawling over each other as they passed and forcing Nicole to have to stop more than once and press herself against the wall to let them pass.

After an extremely cramped ride on the ship's lift, they arrived at a small room where three Z'Ta waited for them. As they'd walked through the ship, Nicole had glanced through the open doorways at the rooms, and this one was different. First, it had a door—the other rooms opened directly into the hallways—and second, they had mounted viewscreens on a wall of the room.

"There ya are. Come on in," one of the Z'Ta said with a wave of its arm.

The three parties—the Rebel Council, Samsara Fleet, and the Ship's Command Council—sat across from each other in the middle of the room.

"Glad they finally got those atmospheric suits to work," said one of the new Z'Ta pleasantly. "It was so disappointing to hear about how they kept failing so catastrophically."

"This is the battleship *L'kor* and we are the ship's Command Council," the second continued. "I'm X'har and these are X'der and X'lan."

"Thank you for having us," Nicole replied.

"Yes," agreed Samaha, "and thank you for agreeing to join the fight against the Nasi."

"Well, we haven't quite agreed to *fight* the Nasi," X'lan replied.

"It's more of a decision to *help* you rather than to *fight* them," X'der continued.

"How are they not the same?" asked Nicole, confused. "We're at war."

"It's rather simple. We don't want you to get captured by the Nasi, so we're helping you. But we haven't decided if we want to fight them or simply evade them. Never make the mistake of turning complex choices into artificial binary decisions; you limit your options." Like the Rebel Council, the three Z'Ta took turns talking, their sentences flowing from one speaker to the next.

Nicole wasn't sure she agreed. Was helping the Humans the same as fighting the Nasi, or was there a difference? In the end, she guessed it didn't matter from her standpoint. Either way, they would try to convince the Z'Ta to fight with them. In the meantime, any assistance would be helpful.

"We're grateful for your help," Nicole replied.

"Of course, of course," X'har replied dismissively. "Actually, I think maybe we will fight the Nasi."

"They're terribly boring," X'der said. "And they do tend to commit genocide."

X'lan burbled, "Nasty habit that. No good for anyone."

"So...you'll join us?" Samaha asked.

"Yes, yes, we'll help," X'har said, "I thought our Rebel Council had already told you this."

"Well, you just said you wouldn't fight Nasi."

"To prove a point," X'lan replied.

Nicole could see the color rise in Samaha's cheeks, and Zzyrian's ears pulled tightly against his head. She couldn't tell if the Z'Ta were purposely goading them, it was a miscommunication, or if something else was happening. Whichever it was, the conversation needed to end before someone said something they regretted. "Thank you. Is there a place we can sleep? Are there bunks aboard the ship?" She hadn't seen any when they were walking through the corridors.

X'har burbled in surprise. "One bunk each?"

Nicole was not looking forward to the voyage.

Samsara Fleet had instituted a mechanism to ensure their agents could locate the fleet wherever it was. Under normal circumstances, they wouldn't have needed it; the network of probes that had enabled interstellar communication allowed fleets to send encrypted communications to various systems.

Since the Nasi had destroyed the probe network, General Zhou had developed a way for their mission teams to reestablish contact with the fleet. He'd established a schedule comprising specific coordinates and windows of time where the fleet would leave a scout ship. If a ship needed to locate Samsara Fleet, they could meet with the scout ship, which would have the fleet's current location.

According to her implant, the current location of the fleet's scout ship was a five-day journey from H'Far. Since they'd had to flee from T'kor'nuk, they didn't know where the fleet might have regrouped.

In addition to the *L'kor*, the Z'Ta carrier *L'jadgr* had agreed to join Samsara Fleet after talking with Nicole, Zzyrian, and Samaha. Thankfully, their escape from T'kor'nuk had gone unnoticed.

Nicole found out their ruse with the command shuttle had worked. The Z'Ta forces guarding the planet had sent two squadrons of fighters after the shuttle they'd rigged. Nicole listened to the recording of the fleet's conversation as they declared the Samsara Fleet leadership dead when the ship self-destructed. She doubted the Nasi fully believed it though.

Once the *L'kor* began to fold to the scout ship's location, the Z'Ta crew stood down. On a Human ship, the soldiers used the time to conduct training. The Z'Ta mainly used the time to enjoy their many recreation rooms. Chief Ramos was overjoyed to discover that one of the rooms had the same video game she'd enjoyed playing on T'kor'nuk. The ship was too cramped for a full Side Out court, but they had several virtual reality systems they used to play a virtual version of the game while aboard. Nicole would have loved to try it, but the headset and haptic suit didn't fit Humans.

Instead, she spent much of her time in her cabin, reading a few of the novels that she had saved in her neural implant or in the recreation rooms, watching the Z'Ta play Side Out. The VR system had a large viewscreen above the six player stations so that spectators could watch and cheer.

"Oh, this should be a good one," X'har said as it slid next to Nicole.

"Why?"

"It's the finals!" X'har gurgled. "Haven't you been paying attention?"

"Off and on," Nicole replied. Even with her implant, Nicole hadn't been able to follow the complex rituals associated with the Z'Ta tournament.

"I so love this game," the council member admitted. "Although every Z'Ta does. There's an old saying; 'The only Z'Ta that does not like Side Out is the one without legs.'"

"Why don't you play then?" she asked, ignoring the strange saying. In her experience as an attaché, she'd heard much stranger ones than that.

"It's frowned upon for council members, especially on our own ship. Besides, once you get to my age, you enjoy watching more than playing." It pointed to a player. "That's T'der, one of our junior officers. It's my favorite in this match."

"Why do you like the game so much?" Nicole asked.

"Because it's *real*," X'har replied vehemently. "Your general, she sees everything as us versus them, right and wrong. Blah, blah, blah. That's not really what happens. There are many sides to every issue and the strongest side rarely wins. Side Out is the best representation of reality; it is true to life."

"You think there are many sides to what's going on now?" Nicole asked. "With the Nasi?"

"Of course!" The Z'Ta sounded surprised. "Don't you?"

"Not really." Nicole shrugged. "The Nasi attacked out of nowhere and are laying waste to the galaxy. They're a virus."

X'har gurgled with laughter. "That's one way to look at it. I don't think this came out of nowhere though. The Nasi are just you Humans, right? Humans that were cast away. They've just returned is all." It cursed as the ball rolled over the line. "Damn." It looked back at Nicole. "The Nasi are an explosion, quick and dangerous, but also temporary. There will be an end to this war soon. I don't know what it will look like after though."

"Explosions destroy," Nicole responded. "It's not a good thing."

"Depends on what they destroy. Some things should be

destroyed."

The Z'Ta leapt onto its hind feet and let out a loud grinding noise. "Ah crap, T'der." The Z'Ta player pulled off their headset and shambled over to join the rest of the spectators. "Better go talk to them. Remember, we're joining your fleet because we don't want to be destroyed in the blast. It's not just you and the Nasi; there are many sides to this war. Some are strong like the Nasi, and some are not. But this part of the galaxy will be changed forever by what happens. The strongest at the beginning is not the one that normally survives at the end."

The Z'Ta slunk down from the elevated stands and lay down next to T'der. Nicole thought about what the Z'Ta said. Not all of it made sense, but a lot of it did. The threads of this conflict extended well beyond Samsara Fleet, and she'd need to remember that.

The Z'Ta ships arrived at the predetermined rally point for Samsara Fleet, and Samaha asked the Command Council to be present on the bridge for the arrival. The Z'Ta had no objections. "Sure, whatever," was their exact response. After they'd flown into communications range, the *L'kor* opened a channel and provided the encrypted signature from Samaha's implant that showed the Nasi had not compromised the ship.

"General Samaha, we're so glad to see you," a young lieutenant said.

"Thank you. We're glad to see you as well," Samaha

replied, relief still written clearly on her face. "What's going on with the fleet?"

"They're less than a day's travel from here, just outside the H'Tromalk system, ma'am." H'Tromalk was a Z'Ta system at the edge of their space. Nicole knew they had a presence there but knew little else.

"Great, we've got two Z'Ta ships that would like to join our fleet. Transfer the coordinates and we'll head out."

"Roger, ma'am. You want us to land on the *L'kor*?"

"No. Stay here until you're supposed to return." Likely Samaha wanted to spare them the discomfort of spending almost every waking hour either crouched down or running into ceilings.

The officer's mouth bent up slightly at the general's words. He must have heard about what it was like aboard a Z'Ta vessel. "Will do, ma'am. Transferring coordinates now."

"Thanks. We'll see you when you return to the fleet." Samaha cut the connection and turned to Nicole.

"Interesting that they'd choose H'Tromalk," she said thoughtfully.

"Why's that, ma'am?" Nicole asked.

"It's a contested area. The Z'Ta and the Khrgylisk have been fighting over it. The Z'Ta have always owned it, and the Khrgylisk have harassed them for years."

"So?" Nicole asked.

"The fleet's going to need to resupply. H'Tromalk is not a good place for that. Fuel and ammunition are at a premium in places like that."

"It'll be hard to convince the command councils in the

system to help you," agreed Y'dari.

"Any help they provide weakens our position there," Y'torak said.

"Well, we've got to try," Nicole said. "Perhaps when the Khrgylisk realize the stakes, they'll join us too."

Y'dari chortled. "Good luck."

Chapter Sixteen

"So, glad to be back?" Samaha asked.

Nicole stretched in the chair contentedly, raising her hands in an arc above her head. They were back in Samaha's stateroom aboard the *Gedorhan's Return*. The Tounous ship didn't normally have human furniture like chairs, but the general had ordered several pieces fabricated and brought to her room.

Despite being on the general's staff, Nicole had decided to remain on the *Ofira*. The cabin she'd shared with Kal felt empty now, but it felt like home. She'd had enough of the strange feeling of being on an alien ship; it would be nice to be on a ship that was actually built for Humans.

"Very glad," Nicole replied honestly. "If I had hit my head one more time, I think I would've grown a new one."

Samaha smiled. "Agreed. I think I grew calluses on my forehead. I never thought I would look forward to returning to this ship. Goes to show that anything can change."

"General Zhou did a good job keeping the fleet together," Nicole observed. The general had taken command and ensured that the fleet started repairs and continued running scouting missions after they'd escaped the Nasi at T'kor'nuk.

"Yes, he did." Samaha leaned back. "Now we need to make his effort worth it. What do you think of the Z'Ta?"

Nicole clasped her hands together and paused before responding. "I think they could be a great asset to the fleet. They're not like the Kurz. Their motivations remain their own and they're rather upfront about it. I think we ignore that at our own peril."

"Every member of this fleet has their own motivation," Samaha said with a frown.

"We can't count on them, ma'am," Nicole replied. Samaha needed to understand that the Z'Ta were different from the other species. They were impulsive and didn't have the same motivation as the other members who had lost almost everything to the Nasi. The Z'Ta home world still existed.

Samaha sighed. "Probably true. However, I must work with what I'm given. I'll keep an eye on the Z'Ta, but I'm still going to get every single ship I can from them."

"Now that we're back, what do we do next?"

"We'll head to H'Tromalk. The fleet needs to be re-armed and refueled." She sighed again, this one bigger than the last. "The problem with this job is that you have a million decisions and none of them are good. You just make the least worst choice."

Nicole thought back to the general's decisions with the prisoner, Salah. Was that the least worst one? She knew the Nasi would have done the same, but that didn't justify it. Kal had been in the EDF for decades. Would he have done it as well? Now was not the time for that conversation though.

Samaha grabbed a tablet from the table in front of them. "I've got to go. We'll need you on the bridge when we arrive in H'Tromalk."

Nicole stood up and shook the general's hand, her mind on the prisoner. The sense of camaraderie she'd felt when she'd entered the officer's room had disappeared.

Nicole sat in her small jump seat at the back of the *Ofira's* bridge. The fleet had just finished their extensive scouting of the H'Tromalk system prior to the main body folding in. They'd sent a scout ship and then the two Z'Ta capital ships to make sure the system was completely free of Nasi. After contacting the local councils, the Z'Ta ships sent back the message, "all good," via the scout.

"Prepare to fold," Colonel Petrov ordered. The commander stood in the middle of the bridge, directly in front of her console, her eyes scanning the room. The room was a hive of activity as the officers and soldiers prepared the ship to fold. Every system needed to be checked, weapons brought online, and shield activated since they never knew for sure what they'd find when they reached the system.

The colonel could have been on a recruiting poster—if Samsara Fleet had one. Her uniform was crisp and perfectly formed, accentuating her slight and athletic frame. Her dark features appeared both commanding and approachable at the same time.

Nicole was jealous. Petrov shared the natural sense of command that General Zhou did. When they gave an order, soldiers listened. It was something she hadn't seen in many people—their strange combination of intelligence, humility, conviction, and empathy let them connect to others in a very basic way.

"Samsara Fleet, begin folding," Samaha called out over

the fleet's net.

Petrov nodded to navigation, and the front viewscreen flashed. They were in the H'Tromalk system.

Routine status calls floated across the bridge as the assorted teams began their routine checks.

"No enemy ships detected."

"No foreign obstacles present."

"Establishing comms link with fleet ships."

The reports died down and Petrov seemed satisfied. She placed her tablet on her console and walked to where Nicole was sitting.

"You're up," she said. "We can use my conference room to talk with the Z'Ta."

Nicole followed the colonel to her conference room directly outside the bridge and sat down at one end of the large rectangular table.

"General Samaha?" Petrov asked as she used her implant to connect to the general's conference room aboard the *Gedorhan's Return.*

A viewscreen on the wall popped to life revealing General Samaha in her conference room, tablet in hand. Zzyrian and the other species' commanders stood next to her. "Yes, we're here," she replied. "Let's get to it. I'm going to open a line to the Rebel Council."

While the rest of the fleet had been folding into the system, the Z'Ta Rebel Council established communications with the Z'Ta ships in the system. The Council wasn't sure how the various Z'Ta ship command councils would take their request and didn't even know if they'd received the message they'd sent earlier when the Nasi first arrived in H'Far.

Although there were no colonies in H'Tromalk, there were several mining bases. Both were on the single planet in the system and spread throughout the asteroid belt. The heavy mineral and energy deposits made the system a source of contention between the Z'Ta and Khrgylisk.

"Rebel Council, you there? This is Samaha. I've got Colonel Bergeron and my commanders on as well."

The Z'Ta connected using only voice as was normal for them. As a species that lived in dark tunnels, they weren't comfortable using holos to communicate. "Yeah, we're here. We got some problems though."

"Like what?" Samaha shook her head.

"The Khrgylisk have been raiding the system more than usual. We've got three ship councils willing to join, but they can't leave right now."

"Can we at least refuel and resupply?"

"No idea. Let's ask."

They'd agreed beforehand to patch in the command councils of the ships in the system. Nicole had assumed they would need to be more clandestine in getting the Z'Ta to disobey their own leadership, but the aliens seemed perfectly content to have the discussion in public.

There were five Z'Ta ships in the H'Tromalk system—the *L'fram* and *L'esfrom* were both carriers, and the *L'rok*, *L'gerd*, and *L'redmak* were battleships. The heavy fleet presence was because of the frequent incursions by the Khrgylisk.

"Hey!" The *L'fram* council said. "How's everybody?" Nicole stifled a smile; the Z'Ta's informal way of talking sometimes caught her off guard. She was pleased to see the name of the ship speaking appeared in the viewscreen's corner. It was impossible for her to tell the Z'Ta voices apart.

A chorus of greetings came from the other Z'Ta.

"Thank you for speaking with us," Samaha began. "As the Rebel Council has told you, we're Samsara Fleet, the only force remaining in the galaxy that is fighting the Nasi. We've come here to—"

"Ask for our help," interrupted the *L'esfrom* council. "We know, they told us that too."

"We're not exactly friendly with the Nasi, but what you're asking could jeopardize our species," added the *L'rok* council.

"I know," Samaha said, "but how long until the Nasi occupy or destroy your home world and colonies? It will happen, I assure you."

"If we join you, it'll happen a lot faster," said the *L'gerd* council.

"No," said Nicole, "it's already happened. Joining with us gives you a *chance* to recover. The Z'Ta are not going to emerge from this unscathed. The question you have to answer is whether you'll emerge at all."

"Whoever that was made an interesting point," said the *L'redmak*. "Rebel Council, do you agree? Is T'kor'nuk already lost to the Nasi?"

"You know what we think. We're here after all. The Nasi appear to be determined to conquer every species and they've been successful so far. We fear that when they meet true resistance, they'll be ruthless."

"Another reason we should just do what they say!" the L'gerd replied.

"No one's going to make you join," Nicole replied. "But if you don't, you will become a thrall of the Nasi. Once you give in to them, you will have no more choices."

An alarm that sounded like two rocks clicking together blared in the background of the Z'Ta feed.

What happened? asked Petrov over the *Ofira's* internal net. *The Z'Ta's alarms are going off.*

Six Khrgylisk capital ships entered the system, two carriers and four battleships, responded the first officer. *They're already releasing their fighters.*

"The Khrgylisk are making their move," said the L'esfrom.

"We're divided and under the control of the Nasi," the Rebel Council said. "Perfect time for them to strike."

"It's time to find out whether we're better off with Samsara Fleet or the Nasi," the L'redmak said. The connection cut off and only Samaha and her commanders remained.

"Get your ships to battle stations," she instructed. "We're going to fight."

Zzyrian turned to her. "We're going to risk our fleet for them?"

"Yes," Samaha replied, swiveling on the bench to look at the admiral. "You've been part of these talks. You've met the Z'Ta. Do we have another choice?"

Zzyrian's ears twitched. "Perhaps. They've proven themselves to be different from what I thought."

"I know you have misgivings, Admiral," Nicole said. "But ultimately, we need to secure their help. We need those ships."

"Get ready," Samaha ordered. "We'll give the Khrgylisk the chance to escape. Our fight is not with them." The screen went blank as she cut the connection.

Nicole thought about the games of Side Out she'd watched. Another player had entered the court.

Launch all fighters, Samaha said over the command net, *and keep a single squadron back for defense.* A marker appeared on the fleet's tacmap. *Head to this position at full speed.* It would put Samsara Fleet directly between the approaching enemy and the Z'Ta.

The Khrgylisk we're a relatively young species, having reached interstellar travel about the same time as Humanity. Nicole had not spent a significant amount of time studying them, but knew their history was also similar to Humanity's, one rooted in conflict and aggression. They'd spent several decades losing skirmishes against the more advanced Z'Ta.

Their ships were more advanced than the ones the EDF had before the Nasi invasion. Samsara Fleet, however, was a mixture of ships from several fleets, augmented with advanced Nasi technology. If the combined fourteen Z'Ta and Samsara ships had been facing the Nasi, it would have been a hard-fought battle. Against the Khrgylisk, it was already over.

"Khrgylisk fleet, this is General Aamina Samaha,

commander of Samsara Fleet. Turn back and fold out of this system now. Otherwise, we'll be forced to engage and destroy your fleet. We've got a common enemy. Join with us and fight the Nasi instead of each other," Samaha's voice rang out over an unencrypted open net.

"They responded via written message," one of the communications officers said.

"What'd they say?" asked Petrov.

"Nothing good, ma'am."

"Fine," Petrov said with resignation. "Looks like we're doing this." She turned to the weapons section. "As soon as we're in range, fire a full battery of missiles. If we're going to fight, we're going to end it quickly."

The Z'Ta and Samsara fleets sped toward the invading Khrgylisk. They wanted to keep the battle at the edges of the system, away from the critical mining bases. Samsara Fleet, aided by their upgraded engines, quickly separated from the Z'Ta.

The swarm of Samsara fighters sped ahead of their capital ships and crashed into the enemy. The two waves swirled around each other, meeting at points with small gouts of plasma and explosions that dotted the black void of space.

Nicole glanced up. A large viewscreen at the front of the bridge displayed the fleet status screen which detailed the condition of each fighter and capital ship in the fleet. The fighters were small dots that were either red or green, depending on their status, while the capital ships were large outlines with their major subsystems split out. Barely any of the fighters the fleet had deployed were red.

Continue to press forward, Samaha commanded over the fleet's net. *Don't cut them off though. We want to give them a way out.*

Samsara Fleet continued to close the distance with the Khrgylisk. A second viewscreen displayed the tacmap—a two-dimensional representation of the battle that played out in real time. Several concentric green circles were around each ship, showing the maximum range of their weapon systems. The Khrgylisk fleet was almost touching the outer ring of the Samsara Fleet capital ships. They were entering the range of their missile systems.

"They're in range, ma'am," reported the executive officer, Lieutenant Colonel Reddy.

Ma'am, permission to fire? Petrov asked.

Let's give them one last chance, Samaha responded. *They've already seen what our fighters can do. Perhaps they'll leave without more bloodshed.* The fleet's fighters had almost completely decimated the enemy.

"Khrgylisk fleet, stand down now and leave this system," Samaha said over the open net. "You have ten seconds to comply. Otherwise, we will attack."

The time passed with no response from the Khrgylisk. *Open fire,* Samaha commanded.

Ship-to-ship missiles arced out from the seven ships of the fleet, flying straight toward the six Khrgylisk capital ships. They streaked through the cloud of fighters—almost all of them Samsara Fleet now—and adjusted their trajectories as they locked onto the key systems of the enemy's capital ships.

The Khrgylisk point defense systems fired plasma and

kinetic slugs at the incoming missiles, detonating several in colorful plumes of green and blue. However, the incoming volley was too much for their defenses, and several missiles made it through, detonating with large fiery green explosions.

A glowing orb erupted in the middle of the Khrgylisk fleet, bright enough that the bridge's external camera viewscreen dimmed. The missiles must have hit a ship's primary reactor.

"We've got one destroyed, one disabled, and at least three damaged." The operations officer spoke in a matter-of-fact tone. There was no glory to be won in this battle.

"Hold fire," Petrov ordered. "Those missiles are hard to replace. Let's get closer and hope they retreat."

As the words came out, four of the remaining Khrgylisk ships released a barrage of missile fire toward Samsara Fleet. Nicole waited for the fleet's point defense systems to activate as the missiles got close. Instead, the missiles passed around the cloud of fighters and Samsara Fleet and continued. The Khrgylisk weren't firing at them but at the Z'Ta fleet behind them.

The missiles adjusted course as they neared the Z'Ta, bowing away from the fleet before corkscrewing back at the critical systems on each ship. The point defenses easily detonated most of them, but two missiles passed through, exploding in flashes on the hulls of their intended targets.

"They got the shields on the *L'rok* and the main thrusters on the *L'esfrom*," the operations officer reported.

Keep firing on the Khrgylisk fleet, Samaha ordered from the *Gedorhan's Return. Either we destroy them, or they withdraw. Either way, we need to protect the Z'Ta.*

"You heard her," Petrov said to the bridge. "Continue forward, engage with long-range missiles, and prepare to engage with plasma cannons when ready."

"What about our fighters?" asked an operations officer.

"I don't want to risk them against the point defense on those ships. Our weapons systems have already proved more than capable. Have them take screening positions to see if they can intercept any of the missiles that are headed toward the Z'Ta."

The cloud of Samsara Fleet fighters spread to cover more of the space between the Z'Ta and Khrgylisk fleets. The Khrgylisk continued to fire, their missiles detonating in the cloud of fighters or by the Z'Ta point defense systems. Samsara Fleet kept a steady rate of return fire launching missiles every few seconds to conserve their ammunition; the Khrgylisk posed no real threat and they would need it later.

Nicole didn't think the Khrgylisk fleet could withstand even the sporadic missile fire for much longer. Four more of their ships had been hit and at least two had exploded in blinding flashes of light. *We're easily destroying them,* Nicole thought to herself in awe. It was strange to think how the past months had resulted in staggering technological leaps forward. They were fighting with guns while the Khrgylisk still had arrows.

The Z'Ta fleet had moved close enough to engage with their missiles as well. The combined firepower of the full Z'Ta and Samsara Fleet was devastating. After a few minutes, only two of the enemy ships remained operational; their attack had annihilated the rest.

Finally, the two remaining enemy ships turned and moved toward the nearest fold point.

"The enemy is retreating," Colonel Reddy reported.

"Let them go," Petrov ordered as she sat down. "They won't be coming back soon."

❖

After the Khrgylisk had folded out of the system, the two fleets moved back toward the system's main mining colony to conduct repair and replenishment operations. The Z'Ta granted Samsara Fleet full access to their supplies and asked to speak with Samaha, Zzyrian, Zhou, and Nicole.

"Very impressive," the L'fram's Command Council said.

"Yes," agreed the Rebel Council from the L'rok. "You handled them like it was nothing."

"Working together, we're stronger than any one species," Nicole replied smoothly.

The Z'Ta burbled with amusement. "Working together? Your ability to integrate Nasi technology into your ships is more like it," the L'redmak council replied. "We barely got a chance to fire."

"So we've talked," the Rebel Council said, "and agree to help you. But only the L'rok and L'gerd will join the fleet. The rest of our ships are staying here to protect our mining colonies."

Their offer made sense to Nicole, but she felt a trace of concern. The Nasi had destroyed the home worlds of all the species in Samsara Fleet. They had nothing left to lose. The Z'Ta still had a functioning central government even if they were a puppet of the Nasi. Could they trust the Z'Ta ships to remain loyal? What happened if the interests of the fleet conflicted with the interests of the Z'Ta as a species?

"Thank you," Samaha replied. "We gladly accept your aid, but need another day until we're ready to depart. After that, we'll travel to the other Z'Ta colonies to see if we can persuade more of your fleet to join us."

"Whatever," the *L'gerd* council replied.

"Can we count on your help in upgrading our ships?" asked the *L'redmak* council. "We'll need it if we're going to face the Nasi."

Zzyrian chirped angrily. "That's what this is. A power grab, a way to get—"

"Look, you need us, and we need you," the Rebel Council interrupted. "Let's not pretend anything differently. Instead, let's pretend we're allies. Maybe it will actually come true."

The Tounous's skin lightened, but he didn't say a word.

"We'll share our technology with the ships that join our fleet," Samaha replied evenly. "After this war is over, do with it what you will."

"Fair enough," the Rebel Council replied as they cut the transmission.

"I don't like this," Nicole said. "They've only got one foot in."

"True," Samaha replied. "And providing the technology to upgrade their fleet could come back to bite us. However, we've got to do it." She cleared her throat. "Unfortunately, we used more missiles than I would have liked during the battle. General Zhou, ensure the fleet gets as many supplies as possible. This mining base may be the last time we get a chance for a while."

"Yes, ma'am," Zhou replied. "We also ran the tests you had asked about during the battle."

Interesting. Nicole wondered what they were testing. She didn't bother to ask, if Samaha wanted her to know, she would've told her.

Samaha raised an eyebrow. "And?"

"Unsuccessful."

"Well, unsurprising." The general sagged down on the bench. "See if you can get the materials to fabricate more."

Fabricators were used to build most of the weapons and ammunition on the ships. The machines could convert raw materials into almost anything. However, the more advanced the item, the more difficult to fabricate. Thanks to Bo and the work of the Skulls, Samsara Fleet had several advanced weapons and equipment designs. They'd implemented many of them but had used up almost all their raw materials. The mining colony would be helpful in more ways than one.

"Yes, ma'am," replied General Zhou, "we'll get the fleet fully stocked."

"Thank you," Samaha said, "then we'll gather as many Z'Ta ships as we can in the other systems. We have around sixty days to rendezvous with Ancient Wang. We need to make them count."

Chapter Seventeen

It took another two weeks for Foyleton to eliminate the PPC resistance around Kasongo. Despite Lukas's boasts, the PPC was well entrenched and proved to be a formidable opponent. After weeks of fighting, only the city itself remained under the control of the PPC.

The Skulls had been conducting missions non-stop during the offensive and Lukas had finally given them a recovery day while he repositioned his forces for the final assault. Waking up without a mission to go to had been refreshing and Kal decided to go to the Foyleton mess facility and grab a bite to eat. Of course, Foyleton called it a café and had replaced the standard EDF furniture with tables and chairs that seemed to have come from the governor's estate.

"How you doin', sir?" Sergeant Jones asked from a gold encrusted chair next to Kal. Jones had recovered from his wounds in only a couple of days, which made Major Garcia's absence even stranger. The clinic's medical staff confirmed there was still an issue with the pilot and refused to allow him back in the field.

"Couldn't be better. Finally have a day to get some things done. How's the team?" Kal asked. Running missions every single day had to be wearing them down. He knew they prided themselves on not showing it though.

"As well as you can expect, considering." Jones's meal was only an enormous cup of coffee. Kal was pretty sure the man had brought the mug himself; they didn't have any with the letters HMFIC in the café.

"We have to stay the course now."

254

The subtext of their conversation was difficult for Kal to navigate. He wasn't sure if the sergeant was completely reading between the lines. In the end, it was all he could do though. Lukas could always be listening.

After a heated discussion during one of their missions, the Skulls had decided they would stay on Patagonia. Samsara Fleet could survive without them, and they felt like they were getting closer to their goal of getting a skip ship— or at least plans for one. Meanwhile, the Skulls continued to speak with other Foyleton soldiers whenever they could, talking about the Nasi and Humanity's desperate struggle.

Although no one had said it, they also knew that this was still their best shot. Bao Wang and the small Jadid fleet could never stand against the Nasi nor did they seem inclined to try. Even if Nicole and General Samaha created a coalition of every species in this part of the galaxy, Kal wasn't sure they could defeat the Nasi. The Jadid would have to be involved. The stakes for their mission couldn't be higher. They had to get to Altterra and meet with the Council of Ancients.

"I agree, sir. But remember, some of them don't see it that way." He was referring to Lieutenant Sampson. The pilot had stormed away when they'd decided to remain, muttering that they clearly had a death wish. Kal couldn't argue with the pilot, though Sampson was always the first person to say they needed to leave or retreat.

"I'm going to go out to get some equipment today," Kal said. "I'll see if I can find anything useful."

What he meant, was that he was going to see Ishmael later that day. The Alliance leader had sent a coded message to Kal asking to meet. Over the past few weeks, Kal had snuck away a couple of times to see him. The Alliance representative claimed he was making progress on the location of the Nasi research lab but hadn't been able to determine anything other than what quadrant of the Foothold it was in. They still did not know which building it was or if there was even a ship.

"Hope you find something, sir."

"Me too." Kal finished up the last of his breakfast. He'd ordered a dish from Mariga that he'd eaten as a child, mashed oats and honey. Although not really intended for breakfast, he'd made it his regular breakfast meal.

"Sir, I think we're getting close to the end of this," Jones said. "I was in the operations center last night after we returned. They're planning the final push."

Kal hoped they weren't being watched; he couldn't fake any excitement this soon after waking up. "Well, we'll see what happens. The PPC has been more resilient than Lukas expected them to be."

"Yeah, they've been pretty respectable actually." Jones looked thoughtful. "I wonder if they're getting help."

Kal considered the sentiment. Could the PPC be getting help from the Nasi? It seemed unlikely. The aliens didn't really seem to care who ruled Patagonia as long as they got what they needed in terms of resources. If they assisted one side or the other, then that would be something to worry about.

"I'm guessing no, but check in with Bo. See if he has any thoughts," Kal said. Bo was almost fully healed now though Kal still hadn't green-lit him for any missions. After a few days of recovery, Bo had retrofitted one of the medbots so it could treat Jadid patients. Although he was not a doctor, the scientist knew enough to adjust the system to treat his pain and marginally decrease his recovery time.

"Will do." Jones leaned forward on the table. "Sir, something else."

"What?" Kal asked.

"Maybe it's nothing but...well, Garcia still isn't mission ready. I talked to the doctors at the clinic today." Jones's eyes bored into Kal's.

"I trust Garcia," Kal replied, returning the look. "He'll come back when he's ready."

"Maybe, sir. But we should watch him. I worry his injuries are more severe than they look." Jones's look said something else entirely.

Kal thought about it for a moment. Major Garcia had been acting strangely. He'd been distant and spending an inordinate amount of time with the Foyleton soldiers. Kal assumed that he was just doing the same as they were, trying to find allies in the ranks. But what would they do if it was something else?

"Good advice," said Kal. "I'll keep an eye out."

❖

"Ish, he's here!" Ava turned away and walked back down the utility corridor. The woman didn't seem to hold any sort of animosity toward Kal for becoming a prisoner. To be fair, she didn't seem like a prisoner anymore either.

Ishmael walked through the door and gave a quick wave to Kal. "Hey, there ya are. Long time and all that." He motioned toward the viewscreens on the wall. "Got some good info. Come over here and check this out." The viewscreens transformed into overhead maps of the Nasi Foothold. A yellow box surrounded three buildings on the map. They were relatively close to each other, within a block or two.

"So great news. We've been able to determine that one of these buildings is the Nasi lab. My sources have seen materials being brought to them that line up with what your Jadid friend said would be needed to build or test one of these things."

"That *is* good news," Kal replied. "Can they find out which one it is?"

Ishmael let out a long sigh. "I'll be honest, getting this far took every single informant I had in the capital. Men and women died to get this information to you. I...I just don't know if there's anything more I can do."

Kal looked at the man. The picture that was Ishmael suddenly became crystal clear. He was not a mercenary, not cut from the same cloth as Lukas. Kal wasn't sure how he'd ended up as an Alliance leader, but Ishmael was an idealist. He believed in what the Skulls were doing. He cared.

"I appreciate it," Kal said. "We can do something with this. It's the break we needed."

Ishmael turned away from the viewscreen and looked at him. "I hope so. Unfortunately, there's not much time left. The Nasi may move these labs again. They captured some of my agents, and the Nasi aren't known to be friendly to their prisoners. They use…oh, what do you EDF people call it?"

"Enhanced interrogation techniques," Kal replied. It was a practice that Kal hated. The EDF had used the technique on some Torgham prisoners during the war. Afterwards, the officers responsible had been tried and stripped of rank. Although it wasn't something Kal liked, he recognized the utility of it. The Nasi committed much worse atrocities than that.

Ishmael pointed at him. "Yes, exactly. As you know, the Alliance doesn't tell our sources why we need the information we ask for. But the Nasi will probably figure out why I had operatives tracking where they were having materials delivered."

He was right, the Nasi would figure it out and either move the lab, set a trap for whomever came looking for it, or both. They had to move fast.

"Thanks, Ishmael, I appreciate all you've done," Kal said. He tried to instill an earnest sense of appreciation into his words. Simply saying thank you felt inadequate.

"It's my job," Ishmael demurred, his bravado gone for a moment.

"Maybe, but it's valuable. It's got to be tough for you, staying down here and running these missions."

"Yeah, but it's been better since you came along," Ishmael smiled. "Anyway, at least I'm not alone. I got Ava to drive me crazy."

"You love it!" The woman's voice came from the utility corridor.

Kal knew she was right. Again.

❖

Kal headed toward the Foyleton compound with his mind racing. They had their chance now and needed to figure out a way to take advantage, only they were still missing the resources to execute the mission. As Kal left the neighborhood where the Alliance front was located, he pulled a small device out of his pocket and removed the disc that blocked his implant. Ishmael had given it to him to ensure that Lukas would not track him to the location of the front.

The implant rebooted, sending out tones through his auditory nerves and superimposing a calibration screen over his vision. As it finished, Kal heard the ping announcing there was traffic over the Foyleton command net. Lukas's commanders were frantically talking over one another as they spat out orders and asked for status updates.

It took a minute or two for Kal to understand what had happened. The PPC had launched a surprise counteroffensive and was pounding the Foyleton bases outside the city. Foyleton had taken heavy casualties and was launching everything they had to support their forces in the area. Kal's walk turned into a run as he realized what was going on. They would almost certainly send the Skulls out to assist, and he needed to be there when they did.

Foyleton's headquarters was in chaos. Transport ships ferrying soldiers and equipment to the front almost collided as they landed and took off minutes later. Men and women were running back and forth, shouting at each other. Groups of soldiers stood at the landing bays fully equipped and waiting for a troop ship to arrive. Their faces were grim—the reports from Kasongo were not good. He noticed more than one officer had unholstered their pistol, ready to shoot if a soldier disobeyed.

Kal ran through the landing area, into the base, and toward the operations center. Rushing soldiers and stacked equipment filled the hallway, forcing Kal to dodge back and forth as he ran. When he arrived at the operations center, the map on the viewscreen painted an ugly picture. The PPC had broken through the Foyleton defenses and was moving to encircle them. Already, there were several divisions that were completely decimated by the PPC onslaught.

"There you are," Lukas shouted as he saw Kal enter the room. His face was red and his eyes wide as he pushed past several people to reach Kal. "Your team needs to get in the air now. Those bastards are trying to break through."

To Kal, it looked like they already had.

"What's the mission?"

"You're going to take out the PPC commander and her staff." Lukas smiled grimly. "They've moved all their forces to the attack and left them unguarded." Namrata Abbas had been a small-time local gang leader. In a matter of weeks, she'd been able to overthrow the Patagonian government and create a new regime that ruled the western half of the Pangean continent. According to Lukas, Namrata had left her headquarters and established a forward operations center outside the gates of the city. For the first time, Foyleton had the opportunity to remove her from the equation. With the commander and her staff gone, the PPC would crumble.

"I've got one of my best drop ships on the landing pads," Lukas said. "Get your soldiers and get out there."

Kal contacted the Skulls via their private net. His soldiers were professionals; they had anticipated the order and already armed themselves and were moving to the landing pad. They'd also promised to bring his equipment with them. When Kal arrived to find a relatively new EDF drop ship in the landing area, his soldiers were already on board.

"What took you, sir?" Sandra asked with a smile as Kal ran up the cargo ramp.

"Let's go!" he called out to the cockpit.

The small ship immediately ascended and sped away from Foyleton. As the pressure from their takeoff subsided, Kal grabbed his equipment and put it on. Not for the first time, he wished Foyleton had battle suits. The equipment gave him some protection, but there was nothing like the feel of the self-contained armor and enhanced strength of a battle suit. The other passengers already had on their equipment and were making final checks.

"Fifteen minutes until we're at the objective," Sampson called out.

"Roger. Everyone here?"

"Everyone except Major Garcia, sir." Chief Kanumba responded. Kal looked at Jones and frowned. *How could he miss this?*

"Bo, you ready?" Kal asked.

"Yes, sir. I have still got some minor complications from

my previous injuries, but nothing that would significantly affect my performance on the mission." The scientist still drifted back into the stilted ancient Standard Human dialect when he was nervous.

Kal reviewed the bit of information that was in the intelligence brief for the mission. The suspected PPC operations center was in a dense part of the jungle immediately outside of Kasongo. They didn't know the size or exact location since the jungle canopy hid it from the air. A Foyleton scout team had noticed command ships landing in the area and discovered that a ring of anti-aircraft batteries encircled something. They'd been able to relay they'd found the commander and her staff shortly before being taken out. It wasn't a lot to go on. In fact, they weren't really sure the commander would be there. It would have to be enough though.

"Drop in ten," Sampson called from the cockpit. The rear door at the back of the ship opened, revealing an almost uniform sea of green trees. Sergeant Jones stood up and shuffled to the door to inspect the drop zone and give the command to jump. Kal stood up with the rest of the team and felt the familiar tightness in his chest that he got when he was about to do something stupid. The light next to Jones turned green. They were over the drop zone.

There'd been no time to scout for a cleared landing zone; they were going to have to find a place to land on the fly. Ekon hopped out the side of the aircraft first and the rest of the team followed with Sergeant Jones bringing up the rear. As Kal descended he used his life pack's thrusters to slow his descent as Ekon searched for a clearing. After a few seconds, Ekon founding a landing zone and plunged toward the forest. Kal cut his thrusters and dove toward the forest with the rest of his team.

❖

Kal rubbed his arm. He'd slammed it into a tree branch on his way to the ground, and it still smarted. Hopefully that would be the worst injury he got on the mission. They were literally in uncharted territory—their neural implants had no information about the area despite being so close to Kasongo.

Because of the density of the forest, they remained in a single file as they walked towards their target. Sergeant Jones used his large plasma machete to cut a path through the bush, stopping periodically to listen for enemy activity. Kal felt hemmed in by the dense multi-colored brush that surrounded them. He couldn't see anything except Sandra's back two feet in front of him. At least the thick underbrush also kept them hidden.

Sporadically, he heard the distant reports of fighting around them. Enormous booms echoed in the distance and machine guns cackled in the skies above their heads.

After a half-hour of walking single file, the surrounding brush opened up and they were able to distance themselves from each other. The dense bushes grew sparser, and small ground plants created a yellow-red carpet along the forest floor. Kal felt like he was in a building with the forest canopy as the roof and the enormous trunks as the columns holding it up. It was like they were inside one of the Nasi ships.

Jones held up his hand for the group to stop and motioned for them to gather around him in order to split them into two fire teams—Alpha Team led by him and Bravo Team led by Ekon.

The two teams crept through the jungle, apart from each other but still in eyesight. The teams moved in a bounding overwatch; one team moved while the other covered them. As they continued farther into the forest, Kal saw the forest floor had been disturbed by vehicles—brown earth peeked through the yellow foliage that coated the ground. They were close.

Jones stopped abruptly and crouched down, motioning for everyone else to do the same. He pointed at a clump of bushes. Kal squinted to see what the sergeant was pointing at—then he saw it: a small bunker. There was no entrance or markings to be seen, just a dark gray slab of Ultracrete. He adjusted his goggles and magnified the bunker. Years out in the humid climate of Patagonia had discolored the structure.

They remained crouched, watching the area for several minutes before something caught Kal's eye. A small spark, a flash of light reflecting off glass. There was something or someone in another cluster of bushes to the left of the bunker. Actually, there were several identical clusters of bushes encircling the structure. *Fighting positions*, Kal realized.

Jones pointed back the way they came, and the two teams slowly backed away. They quietly retreated a couple hundred meters and regrouped.

"That's got to be our target," Jones said.

"Did you see the fighting positions around it?" Kal asked.

Jones nodded. "Yes, sir. They've got guards positioned around the perimeter."

"I'm guessing they're probably bored out of their minds," Ekon said. "Should be easy to get the jump on them."

"Maybe," Jones replied flatly, "but I wouldn't count on it. Also, we need to ensure they don't activate the fail-safe. That bunker is a standard EDF model. There's a fail-safe that prevents any access from the outside. If that's triggered, we'll have a *very* hard time getting in."

Kal looked at Bo. "How are you at climbing?"

Bo turned out to be quite adept at climbing. He was as nimble in the air as he was on the ground and easily scaled the tall trees above the PPC bunker. The plan was for the Jadid to make his way over the bunker and drop in the center of the fighting positions. Meanwhile, the rest of the team would be arrayed around the perimeter. Bo would silently take as many of the guards out as he could. If they discovered him, the rest of the team would rush the fighting positions. The fail-safe for the bunker was next to the entrance to prevent anyone from accidentally triggering it in their fighting position. They had to make sure the guards didn't have time to reach it.

Kal could barely see the Jadid as he quietly swung between branches, slowly but methodically making his way across the forest roof. The Jadid and Nasi seemed to have every advantage over Humanity. They were faster and smarter. Kal thought it was a wonder Samsara Fleet had survived this long.

Bo swung out onto a relatively low-hanging branch only a few meters above the bunker and stopped. He was getting ready to drop. Kal gripped the stock of his rifle tightly in anticipation as his friend landed silently on the solid Ultracrete structure. There wasn't any movement in the orange bush he was watching.

Kal lost sight of Bo as he crept down the side of the bunker. He waited for something to happen. Could Bo actually disable every single soldier before they realized what was happening?

No.

Bolts of plasma shot out from the perimeter, careening wildly into the canopy overhead. Time to move. Kal jumped up and ran at the defensive position in front of him, screaming as he ran. He could hear the others doing the same. As he ran, he threw a grenade at the position and fired erratically in its general direction, hoping to confuse the soldier inside. When Kal was halfway to the position, kinetic fire shot through the air around him. It was hard for him to tell where the slugs were hitting, but he knew they weren't hitting him.

The previously quiet forest was now a cacophony of screams, explosions, and gunfire as the Skulls desperately tried to overwhelm the enemy.

Kal felt a pain in his leg and stumbled. He'd have to check that later. He reached the dark orange stand of plants and jumped through the branches. His knee collided with something—a PPC soldier's head. The impact knocked the soldier into the opposite side of the foxhole, bending his torso backwards over the lip. Kal looked up from where he'd landed to see the soldier bent over the edge of the hole, unmoving. A moment later, he collapsed, rolling off the edge and onto the ground, unconscious.

Kal examined the downed soldier. Shrapnel from Kal's grenade had sliced through his arm, staining the off-white sleeve with a curtain of crimson. The man wasn't young, maybe about Kal's age, and he'd clearly seen better days. Wrinkles lined his face, highlighted by the dirt that seemed to cover every inch of the foxhole in a brown-gray powder.

Kal slapped a restraint around the man's wrist and checked his pockets. They were empty except for an old-fashioned family picture printed on paper in his breast pocket. It was eerily familiar—Kal felt his hand touch his own family portrait. There was nothing else he could do here. He wouldn't kill unless he had to; the PPC wasn't the real enemy.

Kal threw the soldier's weapons and equipment out of the foxhole, climbed out, and crawled along the perimeter toward the sounds of a struggle. He couldn't see anything other than the tranquil forest. However, he could hear a struggle in the foxhole a few meters in front of him.

Screw it.

Kal jumped through the bushes and into the waist-deep

hole. He collided with two people, knocking them apart. As he landed, Kal's leg gave out, and he collapsed, his face grinding into the hole's metal siding. Kal twisted on the ground, trying to get back up. He looked up and found himself staring into the barrel of a plasma rifle only centimeters from his face. Behind it were the eyes of a young man, narrowed in rage.

A shot rang out.

The man's face fell as the slug passed through his head. Kal closed his eyes. He could feel the spray on his face, a warm mist that he could taste on his tongue. He dropped his head back on the dirt-covered floor and lay there, numb.

"Sir?" Kanumba's face hovered over his, her brow furrowed in concern. "You hit?"

"I'm okay," Kal said after a moment. He grabbed Kanumba's outstretched hand, avoiding her eyes, and pulled himself up. "Let's get out of here." He couldn't bear to be in the pit any longer than he had to.

They crept out of the foxhole and crawled toward the next position, listening for any movement.

Report, Jones called out over the net. *Any injuries?*

Skull Six with leg injury but still full mission capable. Kal used the handle they'd chosen for this mission since they weren't using names over the net.

He looked down to see that blood covered his right leg. A large gash extended from front to rear of his right thigh. The blood had mixed with dirt and debris, creating a pulpy russet brown mess. Kal pulled out one of his medicated bandages and gently wrapped the wound. Although bloody,

269

he clearly could still walk. The painkillers in the bandage would get him through this mission when his adrenaline wore off.

Their assault had been a success. Only Kal and Bo had sustained injuries, and Bo's were just superficial cuts to his face. The six members of the Skulls—everyone except Sampson and Garcia—huddled near the riveted metal door of the bunker.

"Any idea of what to expect when we open that door?" Kal asked Sergeant Jones. "Do you think we tripped any alarms?"

"Sir, I don't think you're going to like my answer." Jones met his gaze evenly, his blue eyes seeming to glow in the strange light of the forest.

"Just tell me, Sergeant."

"I have no idea."

Kal barked out a laugh.

"I said you weren't going to like it." Jones smiled slyly at Kal and turned to Kanumba. "Can you open that door, Chief?"

She nodded and pulled a skeleton key out of her cargo pocket. In seconds, the door was open, revealing a utility ladder that disappeared into the ground.

"Looks like we're going down," Jones said as he motioned for them to continue forward.

Chapter Eighteen

The ladder led them down into a small metal-lined utility tunnel. The walls amplified the sounds of the group descending the ladder and walking on the metal grate floor. If anyone was nearby, they would easily hear the Skulls coming.

"There'll be a command post ahead," Jones whispered. "Stagger your positions and prepare to assault when we reach the room."

Lights affixed to the ceiling created regular circles of illumination in the corridor and cast shadows on the walls as they moved forward. Kal couldn't see anything other than trails of oxidation on the metal walls.

The hallway ended in an open doorway to the command post. Kal didn't hear any sound but saw light streaming into the corridor. Jones motioned for them to take positions on either side of the passage and flung a stun grenade into the room. The metal canister pinged off the floor several times before coming to rest out of sight. Seconds later, the grenade exploded, flooding the tunnel with light, sound, and smoke.

The team jumped forward, rushing into the room in front of them. Kal held his weapon at the ready and trained on the center of the room as he ran through the door and sidestepped along the wall. There was no one there.

"What the hell?" Ekon exclaimed.

"Quiet!" Jones ordered. "Clear the room and check where that leads." He pointed to another doorway on the opposite side of the room.

The command post had clearly been occupied recently though Kal couldn't tell how long it had been. Viewscreens lined all six walls of the room, and a small control panel with chairs sat in the center. Several tablets were left on tables next to the panels. Had the occupants run off? Or were they expecting to return?

Kanumba quickly investigated the control panels and tablets before turning back to the team. "Suicide locks," she said. "It would take a while to break this. If I make one mistake, the system destroys itself."

"No time. We're here for the commander and her staff anyway," Kal replied.

"There's another tunnel," Ekon called from the other door. "A *very* long tunnel." He held his hands far apart in front of his face. "No idea where it goes."

"Sir, you want us to keep going?" Jones asked.

"Yes, there's no turning back." They had to keep going. Kal had seen the intelligence; Commander Abbas was around here. He could feel it.

Ekon hadn't been exaggerating; the tunnel stretched as far as Kal could see. The regularly spaced amber lights on the ceiling gave it a strange ethereal quality. As they progressed down its length, Kal realized the tunnel was not completely straight or level; there was a slight rise and curve to it.

Kal felt like he was in a dream and the tunnel would never end. The sound of their boots hitting the floor as they walked made a rhythmic drumming in his head as they pressed forward. Kal thought of the man in the foxhole and touched the pocket where his own family portrait was. Was that man's family alive?

Jones stopped. "There's something up ahead," he said, pointing to a door at the end of the passage.

Kal adjusted his goggles to magnify the door. The pristine white of its panels stood out against the darkness of the hallway. Bright white lights hung above it, reminding Kal of an entranceway to another world, a portal from the dank tunnel.

Kal checked his implant. They'd walked a little over two kilometers and must have passed under the walls of Kasongo by now. "I think this leads to the EDF headquarters building in the city," Kal said to Sergeant Jones.

Jones thought about it. "Damn. You're probably right, sir."

Ekon gave a crooked smile. "This is getting good. Time to take out the entire PPC by ourselves."

"Any way we can find out what's behind the door?" Kal asked.

"Not from here, sir." Kanumba replied. "But I'm not detecting any active security systems on it. If we get closer, I can check it out."

Jones looked at Kal inquisitively. Did he want to take the next step?

"Nowhere to go but forward," Kal said, motioning toward the door.

Jones led them to the end of the tunnel and positioned the fire teams for cover as Kanumba crept forward. She pulled out a small tablet and a set of three sensors that she placed a half-meter apart on the door's side. After a few minutes, the chief retrieved her sensors and walked back. "Well, it's a door."

"Thanks, Chief. Anything else?" Kal asked.

"The security system is pretty dated. The skeleton key can crack it, no problem," she replied. "As to what's on the other side, I'm not sure. It appears to be another hallway and there don't seem to be any soldiers nearby. But after that, it gets hard to tell."

"Let's keep going then," Kal said.

Kanumba nodded and returned to her position by the door. In less than a minute, it slid open and the Skulls poured through, weapons at the ready.

The style was unmistakably EDF. A clean utilitarian hallway with bright overhead lighting stretched out before them. They were in a command area—several of the doors led to conference rooms and private offices. This wasn't the main command center though. Structural supports bumped out from the walls and there was a slight musty smell to the air.

"I don't think this is the main headquarters building." Jones motioned for the team to take positions in the doorways along the hall. "I think it's the command bunker."

Each EDF planetary facility had a command bunker. It was a secondary operations center for the main headquarters and located deep underground so it could withstand intense orbital bombardment. Normally, it was near the headquarters building and connected by tunnels to allow the command team to evacuate to it in case of emergency.

"The PPC is still assaulting Foyleton's positions," Kal

said. "Abbas still has to be around here."

"Operations center is that way," Jones pointed down the hall. The EDF tried to keep a uniform layout to all their bases; Kal knew intuitively the sergeant was right.

They crept forward, waiting for someone to come out of a room and raise the alarm, but no one did. Their footsteps echoed in the empty hallways. Kal was surprised by the lack of personnel—the PPC must have thrown every soldier into their counteroffensive.

They started to hear sounds rippling down the hallway: rapid talking, equipment being moved, the beeping of terminals. They continued to creep toward the source of the sounds and Kal felt a tightness in his chest as he waited for gunfire to erupt. The hallway ended in a T and Jones pointed in the noise's direction and held up three fingers. Attack in three. Within the base, they dared not communicate through their neural net before the PPC discovered them.

When Jones's last finger dropped, Ekon threw a flash-bang grenade around the corner. Seconds later, it detonated, throwing smoke and debris across the intersection.

The Skulls rounded the bend to find two guards unconscious, shrapnel wounds peppering their bodies. The blast had also caused some minor damage to the operations center behind them. Several viewscreens had polychromatic scars across their faces, and a small veil of smoke hung above the room.

Plasma rounds swept between the two fire teams, forcing them against either side of the hallway, and splashed against the opposite door with a sizzle.

Bravo Team, get inside. We'll cover you. Jones instructed over the net. No need for radio silence anymore.

Bravo Team, led by Ekon, rushed into the room and dove for cover behind a bank of terminals while Alpha Team concentrated their fire into the room. Alpha Team rushed after them, taking positions behind the consoles on the other side of the hexagonal room. Kal estimated there were at least five PPC soldiers, and they were all bad shots. Plasma bolts were flying all over the room, most of them hitting well above their position.

Get under cover! Jones instructed over the net. He lobbed another grenade across the room. It detonated almost immediately upon landing, and Kal heard a soldier cry out in pain.

"Advance!" Jones was already up and moving along the wall toward the other end of the room, sweeping it with his rifle.

Bravo Team followed suit, hugging the periphery of the room, their weapons trained on the last PPC position as they made their way across. A low keening sound came from the downed soldier's location. When they reached his position, they found three PPC soldiers on the ground; two were dead or unconscious, and the other was on his knees crying, holding his arm close to his body.

Jones looked down piteously at the man for a moment, then pulled out a bandage out from one of his cargo pockets. He knelt down and wrapped the bandage over the stump where the man's hand had been.

"Where's Abbas?" Jones's voice was hard.

"Wha—what?" The man looked confused.

Jones pressed his hand down on the bandage, putting pressure on the fresh wound. The man screamed in pain.

"Where. Is. Abbas. Your commander, where is she?"

The man's shocked expression cleared momentarily. He pointed towards the door behind him with his good arm. "She ran down that way when the first grenade went off."

"Don't follow us."

The door opened into another corridor, bright white, like the one they had come from.

"Offices," Jones said as he examined the wall plates by the doors. "It's a dead end. She's got to be here somewhere."

The Skulls hastily worked their way down the short hallway, clearing rooms as they went. These were emergency offices, intended to allow EDF soldiers to survive orbital bombardment. They were sparse, only containing a desk, toilet, and bunks.

"Ever have to stay in one of these bunkers, sir?" Jones asked Kal as they moved between the rooms.

"Once," he replied, "during the Torgham War. I was in one of these bunkers for a couple of weeks."

Jones nodded. "Me too, for three weeks. Sometimes I wished they would just blow us up."

After checking all the others, the team arrived at the office at the end of the hall intended for the base commander.

Kanumba stood next to the electronic lock plate next to the door and looked at Jones. "Ready, Sergeant?"

Jones looked around at the group, receiving nods in return. "Open it," he instructed.

Kanumba knelt down with the skeleton key, and the door slid open a few seconds later. Before it had even finished opening, several plasma bolts launched out from the opening. They flew harmlessly between the two fire teams arrayed on either side of the opening. Kal pulled out his last grenade. "Fire in the—"

"Wait! Wait!" a woman's resigned voice called out from the office. "I surrender."

"Okay, we're coming in," Jones replied. "Stand up facing away from the door with your hands up."

"Fine."

They waited a few seconds before Jones and Ekon rushed into the room with their weapons ready, quickly followed by the other four. Commander Namrata Abbas stood behind the large desk in the center of the room with her hands above her head. She was large, about two meters tall, with long platinum hair cascading to her waist. A balding man stood next to her, his hands raised in the same position. Ekon and Jones restrained them both as the rest of the team stood at a distance with their weapons trained on the prisoners.

"So, looks like Lukas figured out what we were doing," Abbas sneered. "Guess he's not as dumb as I thought."

"I wouldn't say—" Jones punched Ekon on the shoulder.

278

"Let's go," Kal said. "We'll head back the way we came." He turned to their two prisoners. "Keep up."

Jones hurried them through the underground command complex. The PPC's base defense had yet to react to their attack. Whether it was because they were ill-trained or understaffed, Kal didn't know. The group made their way through the operations center and to the entrance of the tunnel that led out of Kasongo. Still no sign of anyone following them. The two prisoners kept up with them—despite, or because of, Sandra and Kanumba's rifles pointed at their backs.

As he rushed through the tunnel to the forest outside of Kasongo, Kal felt his anxiety subside. They could make it. Less than a kilometer left until they reached the bunker. He felt his heart skip a beat as he heard a boom behind him echoing off the metal walls. Someone had tripped the proximity mine they'd armed. Someone was following them.

"Faster!" Jones shouted, picking up the pace. They were almost at a full sprint now, careening through the tunnel toward safety.

The door to the bunker was still open the way they'd left it. The small operation center in the bunker looked untouched as well. Kal felt a sense of gratitude blossom in his chest. They were almost away. Ekon used their final proximity mine immediately outside the door to the tunnel then closed it.

They quickly climbed the metal ladder and huddled in the small chamber at the top. Jones motioned for the group to stop and knelt down.

Sampson, sending you coordinates for extraction, Jones

called over the net. *We have enemy on our tail. Hurry.*

Roger. On my way. ETA is two minutes.

"Let's get out of here," Jones said. "I'll take lead." The sergeant pulled his rifle from his back holster and stood in the doorway.

They exited the bunker and rushed toward the landing zone. Kal avoided looking at the bushes that hid the foxholes. No use dwelling on the past since he would see it in his nightmares anyways. By the time they reached the coordinates Jones had transmitted, Kal could hear the whine of the Foyleton transport's engines.

Seconds later, the converted civilian transport hovered over them. As it descended into the small clearing, the tips of its stubby wings brushed against the branches of the surrounding trees. Kal turned his face away as the thrusters blew soil and debris from the ship in a whirlwind.

Get on, Sampson called. *Let's get out of here.*

It was the best thing Kal had heard in a while.

"Kal, Kal, Kal," Lukas held his arms wide as he stood at the bottom of the transport's ramp. "Welcome back."

"Thanks," Kal replied gruffly.

Kal had been listening to the Foyleton command net on the way back to their headquarters. Their mission had the intended effect. The PPC counteroffensive had stalled. With their command center destroyed and their leader dead or captured, the PPC units had faltered and retreated into the city. Now it would only be hours until Foyleton marched in. Already there were reports of refugees and deserters trying to sneak into the countryside.

"Lukas, you pile of crap," Namrata spat out.

Lukas laughed. "Tsk, tsk. You should be nicer to the new ruler of Patagonia." He put his arm around the woman. "Come on, let's talk."

Namrata slammed her head into Lukas's face, causing him to cry out in surprise and pain. A small trickle of blood coursed its way between his nose and mouth.

"Ah, still got that fire in you." Lukas smiled, blood staining his teeth. He pointed to the other PPC prisoner. "Take him to a prison cell. Kal and Karl, come with me. Let us three celebrate the new Foyleton. As for the rest of you, great job. Go get some rest. A new day is upon us."

Lukas escorted Namrata into the Foyleton headquarters, with Kal and Karl on either side and four guards flanking them. The base was emptier than Kal had ever seen it—most of the soldiers must be at Kasongo. The ones who remained were laughing and drinking, celebrating their victory and the end of the war.

"You know, I wasn't sure I could trust you at first, Kal," Lukas said amicably. "But you came through." He chuckled. "Good job."

"What'll you do now?" Kal asked.

"What'll I do?" Lukas looked incredulous. "I'm going to celebrate. After that, I'll get to work."

"What about the Nasi?" Kal knew it was hopeless but had to try.

"What about 'em?" Lukas stopped and faced Kal. "Look, bud, you just won a war. Stop thinking about the one you lost." He patted Kal on the shoulder. "Let loose."

Kal kept his mouth shut as they continued through the base. It was a blessing that the fighting was over. Now Humans could stop killing each other and perhaps focus on their real enemy—but he wasn't sure what it meant for their mission. They still needed soldiers for the assault on the Foothold.

The group arrived at Lukas's office and the four guards arrayed themselves at the back of the room. Lukas had already placed a crystal decanter with three glasses on the ornate wood table in the sitting area. The feed on the viewscreen walls was of Kasongo, clearly taken before the Nasi invaded. Fireworks shot into the sky around them, and throngs of people celebrated in the streets below.

"Discovery day last year," Lukas said, waving his arms at the walls. "I thought it was appropriate for today." He walked over to the table and poured three colorless drinks from the decanter. "This soju was actually brought here from Earth. It's basically priceless now. I've been waiting for a special day."

Lukas gave a glass to Kal and then Garcia before raising his own. "To Foyleton." Kal mimicked taking a sip and placed the glass down on the gilded ancient credenza next to him while Lukas and Garcia swallowed theirs in a single gulp.

Namrata's face twisted in hatred. "You pampered scum. You don't know the people of Patagonia. They won't accept a buffoon like you."

"Ah, Namrata." Lukas put down his glass and walked in

front of the woman. "What to do about you." He looked at one of his guards, who nodded back at him. "I want to show you something."

A viewscreen on the wall switched to a security camera video feed. The balding PPC soldier they had captured stood in the center of the room with two Foyleton guards facing him, their weapons raised.

"It surprised me you surrendered," Lukas said, his voice so quiet that Kal had to lean forward to hear. "Surprised that they let you live after you did. That's not normally how I do things. But now," the soldiers fired at the helpless PPC commander, and his body toppled over, hitting the wall headfirst, "I get to enjoy watching this with you."

Namrata rushed at the warlord, her hands still bound behind her back. Lukas easily stepped out of the way as she jumped up, trying to kick him, and fell hard on her back.

The warlord slapped another restraint on the woman's feet as he jumped on top of her and swirled to place his body weight on her chest. He looked at her with a twisted smile. "Yes, this is much better."

Lukas turned his head and looked at Kal, smiling. "Don't you agree, Kal?"

As Lukas said his name, Kal's arms were pulled back behind his body. He tried to resist but couldn't break free despite his cybernetic arm. Whoever was holding him must also have augmentations. He felt the cool metal of restraints being placed on his wrists.

"I'm sorry, General Norman. You've been a good soldier, but the war's over." Lukas frowned in a pout. "And if the war's over, we don't need generals anymore. Do we?"

Kal looked to his friend, Garcia, for help as he continued to try and escape. The pilot's face remained impassive as he stood next to his brother, hands behind his back. "Garcia? Karl? Aren't you going to do anything?" Kal felt another set of restraints encircle his ankles.

Garcia looked at Kal evenly but didn't respond.

"You're wasting your time, General. My brother's been with me since the beginning. Actually, you're lucky he was. Otherwise, I would have killed you when you got here. He helped me see that like any good soldier, you're a tool." Lukas laughed. "You don't just go throwing away unused tools."

"Now, give me a sec and I'll get back to you. You deserve my full and undivided attention. Got a loose string I need to clip first." Lukas pulled a plasma cutter from one of his pockets and flicked the switch. A glowing white blade sprung from the handle. Kal could hear the crackle of the plasma and smell the faint whiff of burning ozone as Lukas held the blade aloft.

"So, my string." He lightly slapped Namrata's face. "You ready to be clipped?"

"Screw you."

Lukas smiled as he plunged the blade into the woman's chest and twisted it. Kal looked away. He'd seen enough death. When he looked back, Lukas was standing over Namrata's lifeless body on the floor. A blackened cut wound its way along her chest.

"Now General Norman, I want to say thank you." Lukas

walked around his desk and opened a drawer. "I can't let you live, of course. Not after you've been going behind my back and meeting with the Alliance."

"Are you just going to stand there?" Kal pleaded with Garcia.

"The war's over, sir. The Nasi have won." Garcia's voice was barely a whisper. "There's nothing more we can do."

Kal felt a tear flow down his face. After all of this, to be betrayed by someone he trusted. Jones had known, had tried to warn him. But Kal had blindly believed in his soldiers, in his friends. Humanity didn't deserve to win. They were rats, scrambling over each other to gnaw at trash.

Lukas picked up an ancient firearm. Kal was familiar with the model; it was hundreds of years old, a collector's item. "This is one of my prized items, a .45-caliber handgun. I had to pay a pretty penny to get this. I wanted to make your death special. You've earned it. You deserve a final priceless drink and death by a priceless work of art." He frowned as he held the gun aloft. "You didn't take the drink, but you will take the bullet." Lukas cocked the hammer back on the gun as he walked around the desk and stood a meter away from Kal. Garcia remained behind his brother, his face cast downward.

"I'm sorry it had to end this way," Lukas said, raising the gun. "But it always was going to."

Chapter Nineteen

"We're up to thirteen ships in the fleet," General Zhou reported, "almost doubling our size." He had a contented smile on his face. The fleet was in the H'Dreloa system near the center of Z'Ta space after traveling for two months. They'd gone to every major Z'Ta system to recruit ships for the fleet.

"Yes, but they're still being retrofitted," Field Marshall Krunalt replied. "It'll take at least a couple more months until they're as effective as the rest."

Retrofitting advanced Jadid and Nasi technology into existing ships took time. Teams of engineers had to map out the connections and translate systems so they could work together; it wasn't as simple as slapping some parts on a ship's bulkhead. Fabricators and the willingness of the Z'Ta to provide them with resources had been a great help; but nothing could speed up the painstaking engineering process of integrating alien systems together.

"We'll need to leave Z'Ta space soon," Samaha said. "Our rendezvous with Ancient Wang's fleet and the Skulls is in almost two weeks."

The mission had taken more time than expected; Z'Ta space was much larger than Humanity's. They had invented interstellar travel hundreds of years before Humanity, and their empire was not only larger but more populated and developed as well.

Nicole found herself increasingly bored since most of the time they were folding between systems. The officers and soldiers spent the time conducting battle drills and training on simulators, but she was alone with nothing to do. She tried to use the time as best she could—training on marksmanship and using the battle suit simulator so she'd be ready when the Skulls returned.

Nicole also started having a regular morning breakfast with Chief Ramos. They were both from Earth though the Chief had grown up in a middle-class family rather than the communes like Nicole. Ramos had a no-nonsense attitude toward the fleet and their situation but somehow was still optimistic. It was this combination that made their beginning-of-the-day discussions a highlight for Nicole.

"Do we have any systems we've missed?" asked General Nervaan, the Qudoru commander. The fleet had been to ten different Z'Ta systems since they left H'Tromalk.

"You got the big ones," Y'dari replied, "the rest of our systems only have orbital defenses or small cruisers."

"What about the two new ships?" asked Nervaan. "Do we have the resources to upgrade them?" They had convinced a Z'Ta battleship, the *L'hera* and a carrier, the *L'eds*, to join the fleet during their visits to the previous two systems.

"We should," responded Zhou, "the Z'Ta garrison here on Dredl has almost an entire cargo ship of raw materials." Without the right raw materials, and a lot of them, the fabricators on board the ships would be useless.

"Excellent," responded Nervaan, "that gives us enough time to fabricate upgrades so they'll have some chance of standing against the Nasi." The general's staff was growing increasingly worried that they hadn't heard of or seen the Nasi fleet since H'Far.

"We're loading the raw materials on our ships now,"
Y'torak said. "We'll be able to depart for the rendezvous in
four hours."

"Okay, commit final checks and get ready," Samaha
said. "We'll fold as soon as we've loaded the materials."

Colonel Bergeron, wake up!

Nicole's eyes fluttered open. The dream she'd been
having slowly drifted from her mind like a morning fog. She
remembered holding Kal's hand as they walked along a beach
back on Earth. It hadn't only been him there; she
remembered her family and Zzyrian standing on the beach
with them. What had they been doing? Wait, was it Kal or
Ramos that had been with her? The dream evaporated and
left only a residue of contentment.

*Nicole, I need you to get to the Commander's
Conference Room. Now!* It was Colonel Petrov. Nicole
jumped off her bunk ready to go. Thankfully, she'd fallen
asleep in her blue Samsara Fleet duty uniform.

She ran out of her stateroom and took the lift to the
command level. When she entered the conference room,
Petrov was already sitting at the table with a deep frown on
her face. The rest of the fleet's commanders were on the
viewscreens, their faces a mirror of the colonel's. Something
bad had happened.

"I don't care what they did," Emissary T'Kalu said. The

Torgham emissary's tentacles were twitching, a sure sign he was upset. "We cannot go back."

Petrov muted the microphone as Nicole sat at the table. "We received word the Nasi are systemically executing the people of T'kor'nuk."

"Genocide! Why would they do that?" Nicole asked. "They already had the planet."

"My guess? We were a little too successful in our recruiting effort," Petrov replied. "They decided to send the Z'Ta a message. Come home or else you won't have one."

"Did all of them go?" asked Nicole. She feared she already knew the answer. How could the Z'Ta remain here while the Nasi killed their people on their home world?

Petrov nodded as she unmuted the room. General Zhou was speaking. "—would make this entire mission a failure. We have to go back to H'Far."

"How would it affect our timetable?" Samaha asked.

"This is insane!" T'Kalu shouted. "We cannot return to almost certain destruction."

"You are not a member of this fleet," Field Marshall Krunalt shouted. "We *must* honor our agreement with the Z'Ta and come to their aid." The Kurz were notorious for their adherence to treaties and agreements. It was almost a religious belief among their people.

"To be clear," Samaha said, "there is no treaty. We are under no moral obligation to assist them." She looked directly at the camera in her conference room. "Is that clear, Field Marshall Krunalt?" Nicole knew what the general was doing. If the Kurz believed this was a matter of honor, they would stop at nothing to assist the Z'Ta.

"However," she continued, "I think losing five partially upgraded Z'Ta ships is too great a cost."

"What about what's right?" Nicole asked. The others stopped and looked at her. "Whether or not we survive, don't we have an obligation to *try* and stop them?" It was the piece that was missing from the machinations and discussions of the staff officers. They were thinking about ends without considering the means. If Samsara Fleet allowed this genocide to happen, were they not somewhat complicit in it? She thought of Samaha's willingness to commit torture for the fleet. In many ways, were they not one and the same?

"I agree," General Nervaan said. "We cannot let another sin cloud our future. We must act." The Qudoru believed that any sins a person or species committed would always return in the future.

Several more said words in agreement. The only voice of dissent was the Torgham emissary, and he was there only in an advisory capacity. The Torgham had declined to join despite Samsara Fleet protecting their home world, Geerlok.

"We've made our decision," Samaha said as the conversation died down. "Travel time to T'kor'nuk is approximately five days. We fold in less than an hour. We can expect the Nasi will be ready for us."

"And we'll be ready for them, ma'am," General Zhou said with a conviction Nicole wished she had.

❖

Nicole stood in the back of the *Ofira's* ready room, watching General Zhou talk in the center of the room. Next to him was a large holographic projection of T'kor'nuk with the Nasi ships highlighted in red. Commanders and officers from the other ships in the fleet filled the viewscreens on the walls. Officers from the *Ofira* filled the seats arranged in a circle around him. The general had spent the last fifteen minutes outlining their attack strategy prepared for their final fold to the planet.

The fleet had arrived at coordinates less than a light day away from T'kor'nuk an hour earlier, and Samaha had immediately ordered several scout ships to fold to the planet. One had already returned and provided data on the disposition of the Nasi ships, while the rest remained to monitor their movements. The Nasi would almost certainly realize an attack was eminent, but they had to have expected one anyway. At least now, Samsara Fleet would not fold to the planet blindly. This would almost certainly be a trap.

The Z'Ta ships that had abandoned the fleet had yet to arrive; the advanced nature of Samsara Fleet's fold computers allowed them to fold longer distances. However, the other ships should arrive soon, and there was no way for Samsara Fleet to contact them. The two fleets would be operating independently.

"Remember, as soon as we engage, launch all your fighters as soon as possible," Zhou said. "The Nasi have only recently equipped their fleet with fighters. Their tactics are still rudimentary, and their pilots are inexperienced."

He turned to the diagram and pointed to several clusters

of Nasi ships around the planet.

"The Nasi have six ships in the system. They've positioned two of them at the poles, and these four are at the equator in geosynchronous orbit. We have to assume the Nasi will immediately move to engage when they detect us. That'll work to our advantage—we want them coming toward us rather than away from us."

"We'll fold in here and—"

Attention command net. Scout reports the Z'Ta fleet has entered the space around T'kor'nuk and is engaging the Nasi. Nicole looked around at the surprised faces. Everyone must have heard the alert through their implants as well.

"You heard the message," Zhou said. "See you at T'kor'nuk."

Screens winked out as the other ships cut off the feed. The ready room was already clearing out as officers ran to their stations. Nicole joined them, sprinting through the hallways of the ship as alarms blared around her. She felt a tightness grip her stomach; this was it.

Nicole made it to the bridge just in time to see the stars in the main viewscreen blink and the brown sphere of T'kor'nuk appear.

Nicole studied the tacmap on the large viewscreen at the front of the bridge. The Nasi ships had started to move away from the planet and toward the Z'Ta fleet. The Z'Ta must have folded into the system en masse and were now spreading their ships as they headed toward the planet. The two fleets weren't in range yet though the Z'Ta would soon be in range of the Nasi missiles.

Each ship in Samsara Fleet had folded into a different location around the planet and the other two fleets, surrounding the entire area. Their goal was to constrict around the Nasi fleet, attacking from all angles. Zhou had assigned a Nasi target to each ship in the fleet except the *Gedorhan's Return*, which would act as a reserve. Their goal was to surround and destroy the Nasi one-on-one and prevent any from escaping. The flagship would launch their fighters and try to remain away from the action. As the Fleet's operations center and headquarters, they were the last line of defense.

"Damn it, what are the Z'Ta thinking?" Zhou muttered to himself. His seat was next to Nicole's on the bridge. "A frontal assault is suicide against the Nasi."

Attention! All Samsara Fleet ships, adjust your course to assault the Nasi from behind, Samaha instructed over the net.

Samaha had to change their strategy on the fly. Encircling and destroying the Nasi wouldn't mean a thing if they destroyed the Z'Ta fleet first.

Colonel Petrov ordered the *Ofira's* navigation team to continue at full speed. They were the farthest ship from the Z'Ta fleet. Other ships that were closer to the Nasi remained at their original speed.

The Tounous carrier *M'Koras Decision* and the Kurz battleship *Lokryz* had folded in directly behind the Z'Ta and fell in with their ships, matching their velocity.

On the tacmap, the fleets seemed to move at a maddeningly slow pace despite travelling at thousands of kilometers per second through space. The red icons of the Nasi fleet were in a wedge formation, moving away from the planet and toward the line of blue icons that was the Z'Ta fleet. Samsara Fleet surrounded them both, a ring of green icons on the map. All three were on a collision course.

"Ma'am, the Z'Ta are slowing down," the operations officer reported.

"They're waiting for us," Petrov said. "They don't want to face the Nasi on their own for too long."

The Z'Ta and Nasi fleets both launched fighters as they neared each other. Although too small to see through their viewscreen, Nicole saw the hundreds of ships swarming toward each other on the tacmap as a galaxy of blue and red dots.

"We've got missile launch," an officer shouted.

Missiles streaked from the Nasi toward the Z'Ta, weaving through the two clouds of fighters. She saw small flashes in the main viewscreen as the Z'Ta fighters destroyed a few of the Nasi missiles—but most escaped unharmed. The missiles changed course as they locked onto the critical systems of the Z'Ta ships, bending away in order to impact at a better angle.

"Time to see if the upgrades work," Nicole said to herself. Zhou looked her in the eye and nodded.

Flashes dotted the space around the Z'Ta fleet as their upgraded point defense systems took out several of the incoming missiles. Nicole held her breath, hoping for a miracle. She let it out in a gasp as one of their ships exploded in a ball of unnaturally white light.

"The *L'hera's* down," an ops officer shouted as if it wasn't already obvious. The ship's icon faded on the fleet status display in the front of the bridge.

"They hadn't received any upgrades," Petrov said, shaking her head. "They didn't stand a chance."

The Z'Ta fleet was now close enough to return fire. Almost as soon as they launched, their volley of missiles split with half the missiles speeding ahead of the others. It was clear which ones had been upgraded. The two waves of missiles flew through the fighter cloud toward the six Nasi ships. The first wave went past with only a handful intercepted by the Nasi fighters while the second wave was completely destroyed.

The Nasi ships fired their missiles as soon as they were ready, one by one. They streaked through space, passing by the incoming Z'Ta volley.

The ten remaining Z'Ta missiles locked onto the Nasi ships and adjusted their paths. Nicole held her breath, waiting to see if any of them made it through.

Several soldiers on the bridge pumped their arms as an explosion blossomed on the side of a Nasi battleship. Someone zoomed the viewscreen in to inspect the damage. Nicole could see a large cloud of debris hovering outside a jagged hole in the ship's side.

"What's the status of that ship?" Petrov asked.

"Still functional, ma'am. It appears—"

Another Nasi missile hit its mark, and the *L'eds*

disappeared in an explosion of light.

All ships, weapons, and fighters free. Prepare to launch with everything you have on my mark, Samaha called over the net. The fleet had closed the distance between them and the Nasi and the enemy ships were almost in range.

"Colonel Petrov, load five of the test missiles," General Zhou commanded. Nicole wondered what these test missiles were. A question for another time.

Petrov simply nodded at the general before turning back to face the viewscreens.

"Launch all squadrons," Petrov commanded. "Launch missiles on the fleet commander's order."

Over a thousand fighters swarmed out from the combined carriers of Samsara Fleet and headed at the Nasi. The swarms closed on the Nasi ships from every direction, contracting around the enemy vessels.

Fire missiles, Samara instructed, *and get your fighters in as close to the Nasi as we can. See what they can do against their defenses.*

With a start, Nicole realized what Samaha was doing. She was using the fighters to overload the point defenses of the Nasi ships, sacrificing her pilots so the missiles would make it through. She felt sick. They were sending the pilots to die.

A salvo of fifteen missiles streaked from the *Ofira* toward the Nasi. They were mirrored by five similar salvos from each ship in the fleet except *Gedorhan's Return*. The Nasi ships continued directing most of their fire at the Z'Ta, probably hoping to knock them out of the battle earlier. The remaining

Z'Ta ships' point defense systems were holding up against the onslaught. The Nasi also directed a few missiles at Samsara Fleet, most likely to slow them down.

"How long until the Nasi are in cannon range of the Z'Ta?" Petrov asked her operations officer.

"Perhaps five minutes, ma'am," he responded. Nicole estimated it'd be enough time for them to get one more volley of missiles off.

"*L'rok* has been hit," an operations officer called out. Nicole studied the fleet status screen. The icon was still active, the ship wasn't disabled.

"Our fighters are engaging the Nasi," the operations officer reported. The main viewscreen rotated through zoomed-in feeds of the Samsara Fleet fighters as they attempted to disable the Nasi ship. The Nasi's point defense system shredded them in small bursts of light, and Nicole despondently watched their icons turn red on the fleet status board.

"Damn it, those fighters aren't doing a thing," Petrov swore. The Nasi's point defense was designed to destroy missiles. The slower fighters were easy pickings. "Once the missiles hit, pull them back. I don't care what the fleet commander says."

Nicole remembered the first battle she'd seen the fleet fight against the Nasi. Kal and Garcia had actually folded a recon vessel into the landing bay of a Nasi capital ship and destroyed it from the inside. It was a one in a million shot though. As a long-term strategy, it was futile. They'd lose their entire fleet trying to replicate that maneuver.

The missiles collided with the Nasi fleet. The ships' point defense systems destroyed dozens of them despite the interference from the fighters. However, several made it through, detonating against the ships' hulls with satisfying explosions and gouts of decompression. Two Nasi ships exploded in quick succession as missiles hit critical systems, resulting in a small cheer inside the bridge.

"We've destroyed two and damaged two more," the operations officer called out. "Looks like we finished off the one that the Z'Ta damaged."

"Pulling fighters back," reported another officer. "Wait! There are ships folding into the system. Tracking eleven Nasi ships...including one dreadnaught."

The ball in Nicole's stomach exploded to envelop her entire body. Dreadnaughts were the largest Nasi ships, ones that could disrupt the fusion reaction of a star. When the Nasi had first appeared, they had wiped out several systems with their dreadnaughts, killing billions. Samsara Fleet had eliminated one of them already, but the fleet's intelligence officers estimated there were at least three more.

Nicole zoomed in on the video feed of the dreadnaught using her personal console. The ship had an air of twisted malevolence about it with a black-brown pitted hull that made it appear rotten. The dreadnaught's primary weapon, the one that could destroy stars, was an array of mismatched rods on the bulkhead, barely visible on her screen.

Attention all ships, focus all fire on the enemy dreadnaught, Samaha called out.

The Nasi ships had folded into the system on the other

side of the planet away from the Z'Ta. Samsara Fleet was now surrounded by enemy on both sides. Changing direction would require a significant amount of time for the large capital ships.

A Z'Ta ship's icon faded on the fleet status screen. Nicole checked her console to see what had happened; a Nasi missile had struck the circular vessel mid-ship, rending it in two. The two pieces drifted slowly apart, atmosphere and debris exiting into the void of space.

"Representatives of the Z'Ta, this is Ancient Esma Baykara, leader of the Nasi people." The voice came through an open net. The ancient Standard Human dialect was unmistakable. Her voice was steel, hard and unrelenting. "We do not wish to fight. You can live in peace if you power down your ships now. Your council promised cooperation, but you've violated that promise. This is the last chance for you to honor their word. You have five minutes to comply."

Chapter Twenty

Kal stared down the barrel of the ancient handgun. He pictured Nicole—her beautiful azure eyes and graceful features. Wherever she was, he hoped she was safe. She was smart and strong, stronger than him, and would continue to fight. He would have liked to have had more time with her though. She'd made him happy for the first time in more than a decade—that would have to be enough.

Kal jumped as a gunshot rang through the room. For a moment time stood still, then Lukas, eyes wide with shock, fell sideways, his head thudding against the ground.

Karl Garcia stood with a kinetic pistol in his hand, still pointed at where Lukas had stood. His face was wistful and a single tear ran down his cheek as he stared piteously at his brother's body. Kal heard fighting behind him and twisted around to see two of the guards on the ground, blood seeping from their unmoving bodies.

"Sir?" a guard asked.

Garcia jumped. "Yes?"

"What's next, sir?" the guard asked.

Garcia shook his head. "Get those restraints off the general." He paused, eyes forward, as he accessed his neural implant. "The others are safe."

The guards removed the restraints around Kal's wrists and ankles. Kal still felt in a state of shock. What had happened?

"What others?" Kal asked.

"My brother had ordered the rest of the Skulls executed," Garcia said.

"Sir, we've secured the prison complex," a guard reported.

"What's going on?" Kal asked.

"I'm sorry, sir," Garcia said. "I realized my brother wouldn't let us live and had to do something."

The door opened, and the Skulls rushed in, weapons in hand. "What's going on, Major?" Jones asked after quickly surveying the room.

"I promise I'll explain everything, but first I've got some work to do. My brother didn't get rid of everyone loyal to my parents." He looked at the body on the floor. "He cared about money and power and thought everyone else did as well."

"What can we do?" asked Kal.

"For now, sir, nothing." Garcia strode across the room. "If you get involved, it will only muddy the situation. I'm taking control of Foyleton." Garcia turned his head as he stepped out of the office. "I'll be back."

After a few minutes, they dragged the bodies out of the room and locked the door. Jones took control of the situation, posting soldiers to watch the entrance since it wasn't clear what was going on outside.

"What's going on in the rest of the base?" Kal asked.

"No idea, sir." Jones replied.

"We were walking back to our rooms when the Patagonia Front prisoners found us," Sandra said.

"Kinkaid?" Kal asked.

She nodded. "Yeah, him and the other ones, they were with a few of the Foyleton soldiers. They brought us here."

"What about you, sir?" Ekon asked.

Kal explained what had happened after they'd taken Abbas to Lukas's office.

"What is Karl doing?" Bo asked.

"I think he's taking over the family business," Kal replied.

"About time," Jones said.

After an hour, Garcia returned to the office, flanked by the same two soldiers.

"Major Garcia, what's going on?" Kal asked.

"In a word, sir? Rebellion." Garcia stepped behind the desk. "When I saw my brother again, I realized how much he'd changed. He'd always been...difficult. But since I'd left, he'd become something else entirely. I knew he'd have us killed unless I could make him think he could use us."

"You had to let him think you were betraying us?" Kal asked.

Garcia nodded. "Yes, he had to believe I was in his pocket. Lukas only understood self-interest. He couldn't understand things like honor or duty. So, I spoke his language."

"You took him down from the inside?"

"I knew there were still good people here. I did everything I could to find them and talk to them. Once I had some people in his own security staff on my side, I was free to recruit openly. So I"—he cleared his throat—"injured myself and convinced my brother I should stay here instead of going on missions." He slumped down behind the desk. "Now that it's over, it just seems so bad, so deceitful. I felt horrible, still

302

do, that I wasn't with you. But there was no other way. I had to build my support among my brother's followers. You were being watched all the time and I couldn't tell you what was going on. If he'd had any suspicion, we'd all be dead."

"I understand," Kal said. Though he wasn't sure he truly could. Garcia had been one of them. Everything he'd done, he'd done for the mission. But Kal found it hard to look at the man now. There was a part of Garcia that he didn't understand.

"As soon as you captured Abbas, I knew my brother would have you eliminated, so I made my move." Garcia looked at Kal pleadingly, perhaps sensing his disapproval. "I want you to know, sir, I never wavered. To me, it was always about the mission."

"I know," Kal replied. "And the mission isn't quite over yet."

❖

After beating back the PPC assault, Foyleton's forces had hurried in to seize the capital. Garcia rotated commanders and leaders who he knew were still loyal to Lukas back to Foyleton, separating them from their troops. He did it quietly and subtly so he wouldn't raise any alarms. Still, some commanders disappeared into the countryside before he could retrieve them.

For now, the civil war that had ravaged the planet of Patagonia was subdued. Though it wasn't clear how long the peace would last. Scouts reported unrest in the several of the cities around the continent. The missing commanders could appear again as well. It was an uneasy peace.

In the following couple of days after seizing power, Garcia immediately implemented the lessons Kal knew he had learned as an EDF officer: enforcing regulations, restricting looting, and starting a training program for his soldiers. He removed the signs and icons of Foyleton from his soldiers, replacing them with Patagonian symbols.

The Nasi continued to stay out of the Human power struggle—they still ruled the planet in the end. As long as Garcia ensured they received the resources they needed, the Nasi would leave him alone.

"Well, sir," Garcia said, "this is about as far as I've been able to think through. Anything beyond today is going to be winging it."

Kal smiled dutifully. "It's a great start."

They were sitting in Garcia's reception chamber in the governor's mansion in Kasongo. The room was enormous and lavishly styled, intended to be used to receive foreign dignitaries. Three couches were arranged around an ornate wood table with metal inlays snaking their way around each leg, and meeting in a web of silver and gold on the top. Delicate curtains hung from the four walls; cascading rainbows of pastels that swept from the ceiling to the floor. Actual windows let light into the room on one side, and large viewscreens which displayed slideshows of the Patagonian countryside sat on the other three walls.

The PPC hadn't used the governmental buildings in the city, allowing them to be taken over by squatters or "friends" of Commander Abbas. They'd been too intent on their military goals to pay any attention to the daily needs of the people they ruled. Garcia began to reinstitute the government, finding the civil servants that had fled into hiding with the rise of the PPC. He dictated that new employees should be hired based on skill rather than allegiance to any one faction.

"It's been months of war and you Humans are already rather unstable. Can this last?" Bo asked.

"We'll see," Garcia said. "Either way, I'm going to work to rebuild Patagonia for the people."

"That's how we win," Kal said. "It's not just winning the battles; it's winning the war. Show not only our people, but other species and the Nasi themselves, that there's an alternative."

"I'm going to try." Garcia motioned toward the windows. "I never thought I'd be back here. And I sure as hell never thought I'd be leading Foyleton, not to mention all of Patagonia." He sighed. "But here we are."

"You'll do well," Kal said. "You've got a planet torn by war looking to you for help. We're looking to you too." Garcia began to say something, but Kal held up his hand and continued. "It may not be fair. But that's life. We'll miss you. You're one of the best pilots I've ever seen."

"*The* best pilot," Garcia said with a grin.

Kal smiled back. "Of course. *The* best pilot. But you've got a new job now."

A guard walked into the room. He wore a surplus EDF uniform with a green armband—the new uniform of

Patagonia's military. "A Captain Ruiz is here, sir."

"Let him in." Garcia and Kal had given Private Kinawadi the name to use as an alias. Captain Esperanza Ruiz had been one of the first members of the Skulls to die in battle. She'd been one of the most fearless officers Kal had ever met. When he needed a boost of courage, he'd think of Captain Ruiz.

They'd contacted Sergeant Kinawadi over the Alliance communicator and asked him to come into the capital. Garcia didn't dare challenge the Nasi; they would remove him immediately. But he could work with the new leader of the Patagonia Front to coordinate their actions. Kal had a feeling that there would be a lot of near misses between the rebels and the new Patagonian government.

Kinawadi walked into the room and waited for the guard to leave and the curtains to slide over the windows before pulling the hood away from his face.

"Pleased to see you," he said formally. Already there was the hint of command in his voice. He wasn't just a private anymore.

"Sergeant Kinawadi, take a seat." Garcia motioned to the sofa across from him.

"I can't believe we did this," Kinawadi said, looking around the room. "We've taken over a planet."

"I wouldn't go that far," Kal said. "Remember, the Nasi still control Patagonia."

Kinawadi's face darkened. "True, but still."

"Are you ready to become the face of the opposition?" Garcia asked. "Are you and your soldiers ready to fight the Nasi-loving government?" He raised an eyebrow.

Kinawadi looked at him quizzically.

"Although Major Garcia has taken control of the Humans' government on Patagonia, nothing has changed," Kal explained. "The Nasi still rule this planet. If Garcia or his soldiers take any action against them, the Nasi will lay waste to them. We still need the resistance."

Garcia chimed in. "You will do what I can't. And I will, for all intents and purposes, try to stop you." He slyly sipped his tea. "I can't promise you and your soldiers will be safe. But I can work to make sure my forces are unsuccessful in destroying your new Patagonia Front."

Kinawadi sat back and ran his hands through his hair. It was no longer the buzzcut the man had been sporting before. He'd grown it out since Kal had seen him last.

"What about you, sir?" Kinawadi asked. "What are you going to do?"

"The Skulls are going to carry out our ultimate mission tonight," Kal replied. "We'll need help from the Front to be successful. Then we'll leave to rejoin the fleet."

"We're all grown up now," Garcia said as he looked around the room. "Frederick—I think sergeant's a little too formal considering everything—you and I will remain here and help the fleet by infiltrating and sabotaging the Nasi. I'll be the bumbling official who's always outsmarted, and you get to be the heroic revolutionary fighting for freedom."

"Sounds like you got the raw deal, sir."

Garcia laughed. For a moment, he sounded like his dead brother. "Well, at least I get to sleep in the governor's mansion. You'll have to sleep in the woods." His laugh faded, and he looked at the sergeant. "Understand though, that I will still have to hunt you and your soldiers. I'll be walking a fine line. If I am too incompetent, the Nasi will remove me. I don't think we want to risk another civil war."

"Understood." Kinawadi cleared his throat. He looked hesitant, reminding Kal of when he'd met the young man only months ago.

"This is something you can do," Kal said. "I've talked to your soldiers. You're an excellent leader. You'll also have the help of Commander Kinkaid to help guide your decisions. Just remember, they are *your* decisions. We trust you, so trust yourself."

Kal had talked to Commander Kinkaid the day before. Somehow the old man had realized from the beginning the Skulls were not willingly part of Foyleton. When Kal asked how he knew, the former professor smiled and said, "It's just not in your nature."

"Frederick and Karl, your mission on Patagonia is critical," Kal continued. "I don't know when the fleet will return or when we'll talk next, but I have faith that you'll both do the right thing." He stood up. "We have to carry out our mission tonight and I need help from both of you."

"Damn, the thing really is already complete," Ekon said as he looked over the wireframe holo of the Nasi Foothold.

The Skulls were sitting at the long oval table in the center of one of the conference rooms within the repurposed

EDF headquarters in Kasongo. A viewscreen on the far wall displayed an overhead image of the Nasi Foothold. The circular city within a city was five kilometers wide and surrounded by a perimeter wall with active security systems. An enormous twisted tower rose in the center, dominating the skyline of the compound and the city. Concentric rings of buildings radiated out from the central tower, making the camp look almost like a bullseye from above. The Nasi had only been there months—to have constructed almost an entire city in that time was a feat of engineering.

"We Jadid learned to adapt our building styles to the harsh climates of Altterra," Bo said. "Our weaves allow us to build quickly compared to the more stationary techniques you Humans use."

"Weaves?" Kal asked, "What do you mean?"

"We construct our buildings and ships through weaves. Rather than building in place as Humans do, we weave each piece and transport them into place. The weaves are light, easy to transport, and strong enough to withstand most forces. The hard part is building the frames to hang the weaves on."

It made sense. The thin walls of the Nasi and Jadid structures were, in fact, fabric. Just a stronger one than Humans could build. This technique allowed them to construct structures ahead of time and then simply put them together when ready. The Nasi must have been building the weaves for their Footholds for years. It was an indication of just how far into the future their enemy planned.

"We gotta talk about that later," Ishmael said. "Right

now, we've got bigger issues."

Ishmael's sources had seen no movement around the Nasi labs, so they assumed the skip ship or technical documents still had to be in one of the three buildings he'd already identified within the compound. Unfortunately, they were no closer to knowing which one. They would have to target all three in the assault. The Patagonia Front could provide the soldiers they needed. Over five hundred of them would rush the Nasi compound that night, armed with the best equipment they could find.

Ishmael stood up and pointed to three towers surrounding the larger central one. "We think these have anti-aircraft emplacements within them. They're there to prevent anyone from launching an attack directly at the central tower and their leadership."

"What about this?" Kal asked, pointing to an enormous sphere that was offset inside the base. It looked like it had been misplaced, its location disrupted with the neat circles of buildings around it.

"That's the gateway," said Bo. "It's what allows them to bring supplies and people between their universe and our own. Probably the most important building in there."

"Can we destroy it?" Ekon asked. "They'd be helpless."

"I wouldn't do that," Bo replied. "Only orbital weapons platforms could penetrate the exterior, and the Nasi will heavily defend it with soldiers and countermeasures. Almost any attack is doomed to fail. The repercussions for the attack would devastate the Humans on the planet. The Nasi would not hesitate to eliminate all life on Patagonia if they felt too threatened." It was not an idle threat. The Nasi still had dreadnaught class ships, capable of destroying entire systems.

Karl and Frederick looked at each other. They were responsible for what happened here more than any of them. "It's not worth it," Karl said. Frederick nodded in agreement.

"Agreed," Kal said. "Let's focus on why we came here."

"Good news is the labs are on the periphery of the compound," Ismael continued, pointing on the map. "They're relatively small self-contained buildings."

"If we can make it through the perimeter, it should be easy to get in the labs," Ekon concluded.

"No." Ishmael shook his head. "You've fought the Nasi before. You know it's never that simple, man. They've got quick reaction forces that'll be there as soon as you breach the perimeter. Once the mission starts, we'll have minutes at most before the Nasi bring hell down on you."

"So, it's pretty much a suicide mission," Ekon concluded.

Kal ran his hand over his short graying hair. "Honestly? Yeah, probably. But it's a crucial mission, one that will change the course of the war. The Nasi can attack us with impunity. With this technology, not only can we contact the Jadid, but we can also take the fight to them, to their universe."

"And we've got a few things that may help even the odds a bit," volunteered Frederick with a clap of his hands. "We're not just going in with assault troops. Last week, my soldiers found an abandoned EDF mobile artillery camp and got the cannons working."

"I'd love to hear their net when they realize they're under bombardment," Jones laughed.

"I'd love to be there," Garcia said, taking a small sip of his tea. "But I fear my army will be on maneuvers outside the city. I hear there are rebels about."

"You'd better believe it," Frederick smiled grimly.

❖

"You ready, sir?" Sergeant Jones asked as he walked into Kal's cabin aboard the *Salamis*. Kal put the photo back in his pocket and stood up.

"Tell me. Did you ever get used to this?"

"Probably shouldn't say it, but yeah," Jones replied evenly. "You crave it after a while. There's that feeling you get during the mission, the excitement. It's a drug. War ends and we return home. But the war never leaves a person."

"I still think about the Torgham War. It doesn't seem that long ago."

Jones smiled. "Only twenty years, right? Yeah, I was there. Still think about it too. I'd been in for what, ten years at that point. I was in ten years and thought I was going to stay in twenty and be done."

"What happened?"

"I saw what happened to my friends who got out," Jones stared distantly at the viewscreen behind Kal. "They couldn't handle it. Didn't know what to do with themselves." He chuckled. "Honestly, I was scared of getting out. I can handle the Torgham or the Nasi, but a life outside the EDF? I wouldn't know where to begin."

Neither soldier spoke. Kal thought about what he'd done after retirement. Nothing. He'd retired and then just drifted through the galaxy from one chem bar to another.

"Let's go." Kal's words cut through the silence. He stood up with a groan and walked out the door of his cabin with Jones following behind. The *Salamis* was in a clearing outside of Kasongo. No matter what, the Skulls would leave Patagonia that night.

"Did we receive word from Kinawadi and the Front?" Kal asked.

"Yes, sir. They're ready to go." Kinawadi's soldiers were in the woods around the city, waiting for Kal's signal to start. The five hundred soldiers were the most they could bring without raising Nasi suspicion that the new Foyleton government was involved.

Six soldiers, already in their battle suits, stood in the cargo bay, waiting for Kal and Jones. The *Salamis* had eight battle suits and only four soldiers who could be part of the assault force. The Patagonia Front had detailed four of their own soldiers to the Skulls to assist on the mission. Bo stood next to the soldiers, his life pack strapped to his back.

"Glad to see you again, General." The words came from the external speakers of one of the battle suits.

"Who's that?" Kal asked. There was no way to tell who was inside the suit with its faceplate darkened.

Koula Bhatt lifted her helmet, revealing a purple buzz cut. "Didn't think we'd meet again so soon." Koula was the first Patagonia Front soldier the Skulls had met when they had originally come to the planet.

"Glad to see you, Bhatt," Kal replied. "Glad you survived."

"You and me both," she replied. "Few did. Lukas hunted us down like dogs."

"I'm sorry."

"Well, he got what was coming to him." She shook her head. "Got a crew here to help you out. Huang, Laghari, and Raymond—they're all former EDF and know how to use a battle suit." Learning to use a battle suit was akin to learning to pilot an aircraft. It was not something that you could pick up on the fly; you had to train diligently. The suit amplified the thoughts of the wearer, and if you didn't know what you were doing, you were liable to hurt yourself or someone else.

Kal nodded to each of the four suited soldiers and stepped to the side of the bay. His battle suit was waiting, open in the back, for him to enter. As he stepped into the boots, the seams along the rear of the legs, arms, and finally back closed and knit themselves together, creating an airtight seal. Kal grabbed the helmet in front of him and placed it on his head.

The suit went through its initial diagnostic sequence, checking systems and fuel levels. Once complete, all the indicators for the suit were green on his heads-up display, indicating he was ready to go. The display also showed the location and status of the other seven soldiers in battle suits.

Sergeant Jones and Kal conducted a quick inspection of each other's suits, and Kal conducted a comms check with each of the assault elements. The Skulls were the main effort for the mission. Three Patagonia Front assault teams of over a hundred-fifty soldiers each and three mobile artillery batteries would support them. On Kal's command, the Front's artillery batteries would enter Kasongo and converge and destroy the Nasi wall and defenses. Then the assault teams would enter the Foothold via drop ship and converge on the three labs they'd identified as targets. As soon as they found the right lab, the team would radio for the Skulls to come in. Their mission was simple: enter the lab, recover what they could, and get out.

While The Skulls were searching for the skip ship technology, the Front would try to hold off any Nasi response forces for as long as possible. Karl had moved most of his forces far outside the city and assured Kal their response would be slow, so they shouldn't have to worry about Foyleton getting involved. However, the Nasi would almost surely respond quickly and decisively. It was a suicide mission for the Front soldiers. Despite that, there had been no shortage of volunteers to assist in the mission. Kinawadi had to turn people away.

Kal called out for a status check over the net, and each of the three Front teams—Sword, Arrow, and Shield—reported they were ready.

Begin movement! Kal ordered. There was no going back. One way or another, it was the Skulls last day on Patagonia.

Chapter Twenty-One

The Salamis's main engines spun up and Kal felt their vibrations in his battle suit. As the main effort, the Skulls were to remain on the ground and hidden until the Front engaged the Nasi's forces. As soon as the *Salamis* was airborne, it would be a target. Kal hoped the recent civil war would confuse the Nasi, and they would initially think the Front soldiers entering the city were targeting Foyleton, not the Foothold.

He watched the tacmap in his suit as the three Front teams entered Kasongo from different directions and converged near the north wall of the Nasi facility. When they were a kilometer out from the walls, the mobile artillery units stopped moving; they were landing and driving jacks into the ground to stabilize themselves when they shot. The three assault teams continued forward, slowing as they neared the defensive wall around the Foothold.

Lifting off, Sampson called out through the Skulls' net. Kal felt the ship rise into the air and the gentle pressure of acceleration as they sped toward Kasongo. He brought up the video feed from the cameras on the ship's hull onto his suit's display—he wanted to see what was happening outside.

The artillery batteries had started to fire on the Nasi Foothold. Their explosive and plasma-infused rounds smashed into the Nasi wall, causing the several buildings near the structure to collapse under the shock wave of the explosions. The wall itself still stood strong. Zooming in, Kal saw some damage to the parapet, but there were still antipersonnel and ship weapons active.

Fire on the wall, Kal ordered over the ship's net. If the Front's forces couldn't get over the wall, they'd be sitting ducks for the Nasi. The aliens might not be willing to destroy their own buildings and people, but Kal was sure they wouldn't hesitate to destroy Kasongo to protect themselves.

The *Salamis* launched several volleys of missiles at the Foothold's perimeter wall. As they neared the structure, a point defense system shot small streams of plasma at them, causing the missiles to detonate harmlessly in the air. If they sent the drop ships without disabling the point defense, the Nasi defenses would make quick work of them.

Focus your fire on the top of the wall, Kal instructed the artillery. *We're not going to be able to destroy the structure and we need to get their defenses offline.*

The Front's artillery adjusted their fire to focus on the antipersonnel and missile systems at the top of the wall rather than the structure itself. Bright bursts of green plasma explosions bloomed across the wall. Their light illuminated the growing curtain of smoke drifting across the city.

We've got incoming!

The cry went across the net as Nasi counter-battery fire streaked from the towers inside the compound. Explosions erupted around the artillery pieces, covering them in billowing plumes of smoke. The batteries continued to fire though. Kal saw the small flashes through the smoke and the explosions of their shells detonating against the wall.

Assault forces, you have to move, Kal instructed. He wasn't sure how many of the Nasi defenses were still active. But they had to get into the compound before the Nasi could bring out more of their forces. The drop ships flew over the city and the wall, almost touching the still smoking structures. A handful of anti-ship missiles still flew from the ramparts toward the ships. Their low altitude helped many of them cross unharmed, but missiles still hit two of them, causing them to crash into the Nasi buildings within the perimeter.

We're inside, called one of the assault team commanders. *Adjust fire.*

The remaining artillery pieces began firing into the compound, trying to disrupt any Nasi forces moving from the center of the base to engage the assault forces.

The video feed suddenly flashed white as an enormous explosion rocked the city, buffeting the *Salamis* as it hovered at the periphery. Two more explosions rattled the ship, causing them to drop precipitously before Sampson recovered and got them back into a steady hover.

What was that? Someone called out over the net.

The three mobile artillery batteries were gone, along with several blocks of the city. Orbital fire. The Nasi ships orbiting Patagonia must have fired their weapons at the batteries in the city. All that remained of the Front's artillery pieces were smoking craters and rubble.

We've got incoming Nasi air support, Sampson called. Red icons appeared on Kal's screen as the pilot was speaking. He could see the thrusters from the fighters trail through the night sky as they swarmed toward the Front's forces in the compound.

Should we abort? the pilot asked.

Damn it, no. Kal wanted to strangle the man. *We're*

going into the Foothold. *Get us through and drop us off.
Then do what you can against the Nasi fighters.*

Will do, sir, Kanumba responded.

The rear cargo door opened as the *Salamis* sped over
the rooftops of Kasongo, hurtling past the smoking craters
and over the wall. The icons for the three assault teams were
on their objectives. Their forces had regrouped after the initial
assault. Hopefully, they'd hear something soon.

Get ready, we're going to the central building, Kal
instructed over the Skulls' private net. *We'll assist the Front's
forces there and then move to the next lab if we need to.*

The ship slowed as they approached the building, and
Jones gave the signal for the team to jump. They dropped
from the rear cargo ramp in pairs, engaging their battle suit's
thrusters as they left.

Kal activated his night vision and dropped from the bay.
The drop was short, and he landed on the sloped roof of the
building after a quick second. His suit identified a group of at
least ten Nasi soldiers running through the street, heading
toward their location. They were a kilometer out and would
be there soon.

Jones saw them as well. *Bravo Team, put two soldiers
on the roof and stop the Nasi heading from the south.*

Sandra and one of the Front soldiers remained on the
roof and immediately launched antipersonnel missiles at the
enemy.

Kal hopped from the roof onto the ground, the suit
automatically cushioning his fall. It felt good to be back in a
battle suit. He felt invincible.

319

The rest of you sweep inside the building, starting with the back, Jones ordered. *Team Sword is already in there at the front.*

Kal rushed into the building, sprinting past the unarmored Patagonia Front soldiers. The irregular circular front entrance opened into a long corridor that curved through the length of the building. The floor was relatively level, but the walls were irregular and made of the weaves the Nasi used for almost everything they built. The threads embedded in them produced a multihued light that glowed brightly in Kal's enhanced night vision.

Ekon and Bhatt, the other two soldiers in Bravo Team, had already reached the room at the end of the hallway and started to search. Before the mission, Kanumba and Bo had prepared a file for all the members of the assault teams to help them identify materials that could be important. They wouldn't be able to crack the Nasi systems, but they could take materials and tablets and try to decrypt them later.

Kal entered the room to his left, the circular door dilating open as he approached. As he stepped through, a plasma bolt splashed against his suit's front energy shield. Kal immediately jumped forward, tucking into a roll, and came back up with his suit's railgun pointed directly at a Nasi scientist. The creature didn't have time to react before several rounds struck her torso, knocking her back.

Pairs of workstations straddled benches loaded with strange artifacts. The devices looked like long sticks with wires twisting around them with an irregularly shaped brown ovoid at one end. There was no way Kal was going to be able to carry the devices with him. He looked around the room for anything he could grab. A tablet was lying on one table. Kal quickly stuffed it into his suit's cargo compartment.

We've got at least three separate teams approaching, Sandra warned over the net. *I doubt we'll be able to hold this position for long.*

Sir, Jones called out over the net to Kal, *get up there with Chedjou. We need a good shot up there.*

Kal acknowledged the order—Jones was in charge when they were on the ground—and ran back through the building. He engaged his suit's thrusters and landed on the roof next to Sandra. His suit's automatic targeting system began highlighting the Nasi approaching the building. Sandra was right. It didn't look good.

Kal knelt down and took careful aim at the approaching Nasi with his railgun. There were too many for him to stop, but he could at least slow them down. Seeing your buddy take a round caused anyone, Human or Nasi, to slow down a bit. Breathe. Fire. Breathe. Fire.

In the air, at one o'clock. Kal looked at where the Front soldier next to him was pointing. Four Nasi in battle suits were flying directly at them.

Salamis, we could use some air support, Kal called. *Just identified four targets in the air. Can you take them out?*

Can do, Kanumba replied. *On our way.*

Missiles flew from the approaching Nasi, heading directly at their location. The three Human soldiers engaged their thrusters and scattered, letting the missiles hit the outside of the Nasi building. In the air, Kal could see the three unarmored Nasi teams still making their way toward the lab. They'd be overwhelmed soon.

A barrage of plasma fire streamed from the *Salamis* as it flashed over the tops of the Nasi buildings. The Nasi battle suits could absorb some blasts, but the ship's cannon was too powerful. The plasma bolts splashed into the Nasi, knocking them from the sky and sending them careening into the streets below.

Arrow, Shield. Find anything? Kal asked over the central net.

Negative, the Shield commander responded. *We had one of our ships hit on entry. We're in the lab now. Don't know what the hell we're looking at though. It's just big vats of slime or something. We're halfway through the lab.*

Keep going, Kal responded. He placed a round through one of the approaching Nasi, causing the others in its squad to scatter to cover. *Arrow?*

We're in a firefight here. The Nasi have barricaded themselves inside. We got to the first hallway and are taking fire on all sides.

Kal looked at the tacmap. A wave of red was coming toward them. The Nasi had recovered from whatever initial surprise they'd faced and were bearing down with everything they had. Time was short.

Bo. Kal contacted the Jadid via a direct link. *Any ideas? The plan is shot. We need to figure out what to do and get out of here.*

Sir, based on what we've found here—

Bottom line, Kal interrupted.

If it's anywhere, it's with Arrow, Bo replied.

Kal contacted Jones. *We need to move to Arrow's location.*

Jones switched over to the Skulls' net and ordered Alpha Team to cover Bravo while they moved to the other lab.

Kal switched to his plasma rifle and fired as fast as he could, trying to distract the Nasi from the four battle-suited Humans as they flew toward the other lab. A scream echoed through the net as one of the Front soldiers was hit, their icon going red in Kal's HUD.

The rest of Alpha Team joined Kal and the others on the rooftop. They quickly depleted what missiles and explosives they had left. Bo crouched with them, his life pack on his back, firing his plasma rifle in the general vicinity of the enemy. At least it slowed their advance somewhat.

When Bravo Team reached the other lab, Jones gave the order for Alpha Team to head out. Kal fired his thrusters, trying to keep as low as possible over the irregularly shaped Nasi buildings. As he flew, he heard the pings of low-caliber Nasi slugs hitting his suit's armor. Thankfully, this new design had a thicker armor than the old.

An alert sounded through his implant. The Nasi had locked onto him. He turned to see a pair of missiles coming toward him from his left. Kal cut his thrusters, dropping like a stone between two buildings as the missiles flew overhead.

Kal crashed into the ground and looked up to see a pair of Nasi looking at him wide eyed. The man and woman slowly raised their hands, showing they were unarmed. Rather than the gray uniform Kal had seen most Nasi wear, they wore simple pants and shirts. They seemed to be civilians of some kind, though Kal hadn't realized that could be possible with the Nasi.

Kal saw the sinuous black line of their tattoos curving around their faces and arms in his night vision. The line was almost impossibly complex, a pictograph that represented their personal and ancestral history. The single line meant they were relatively low-level Nasi, otherwise they'd have the more complex multi-lined patterns he had seen on the Nasi leaders.

He stood, transfixed. The two civilians were unlike any Nasi he'd seen—afraid and helpless, staring at him like children. They didn't have weapons and they looked out of place amidst the fighting and chaos of the battle. This was something new.

Sir, Jones asked, *are you okay?*

Yes, Kal replied, shifting his attention to the task at hand. He re-engaged his thrusters and flew out of the small passageway. The Nasi that had fired at him were close, less than a hundred meters away. He turned in midair to face his attackers while his thrusters continued to propel him toward the second lab.

The Nasi battle suit's vulnerability was its helmet. The torso and other extremities had enough armor to deflect almost anything except the most powerful weapons. Kal was out of missiles, but he still had some rounds left in his suit's railgun.

Kal took careful aim at the rutted helmets as the Nasi veered left and right. He'd have to time his shot perfectly. He breathed in slowly and pressed the trigger stud inside his suit. The round landed perfectly in the center of a Nasi's helmet. The armor plating blew apart, and the soldier dropped from the sky.

As Kal was sighting the other Nasi, he felt pain course through his left leg and screamed in agony as his suit's diagnostic system turned yellow. He'd been shot. He tried to keep firing but couldn't concentrate. Tears of pain blurred his vision despite his suit already applying pain medications on the wound. Kal did his best to maneuver in his suit trying to make himself harder to hit, but even that was difficult.

The Nasi soldier was close enough that Kal could see them training their weapon on him. He gritted his teeth through the pain and regained some control of his suit, dropping as the Nasi fired; the round streaking past him. A large plasma bolt impacted the side of the Nasi followed by two more, tossing the charred suit into the side of a building.

Kal turned around and dropped onto a roof near the lab. As he landed, his legs gave out and he fell onto his side, sliding across the rooftop before coming to rest near the apex of the dome. He heard sounds of fighting nearby through the external microphones on his suit.

Kal checked his tacmap. The Nasi had trapped Arrow Team in the building's antechamber, and reinforcements surrounded the entrance and were streaming plasma and kinetic fire into the doorway. Bravo Team had taken positions in the passages around the building, trying to attack the Nasi's flank.

Arrow, report. Jones' voice cracked through the net.

We're at about fifty percent, the commander replied. *We're trapped. The Nasi are still holed up inside the building, and we can't get through.*

Bravo Team, you're going to breach the building, Jones said. *Alpha Team, get in position behind Bravo. Be ready to exploit the breach. Once we're inside, Bravo holds the door. Give us an escape route.*

What about Arrow? asked Raymond, one of the Front soldiers.

There was slight delay before Jones responded. *There's nothing we can do. We have to get inside that building and have some chance of getting out.*

You can't abandon them and leave them there to die.

Raymond, we've got a goddamned mission to complete, Bhatt called out. *They knew the risks. Leave them so this'll mean something. Do what Jones says.*

We can't abandon them to die! Raymond shouted over the net. Kal saw his icon move across the tacmap as he went to engage the Nasi. It was a suicide mission, worse than that, it was a meaningless one. What Jones knew but didn't say was that Arrow was already doomed. There was nothing they could do.

The rest of you, move! Jones commanded.

Kal tried bending his leg. At least the suit was still responding to his commands. The pain was not as severe as before; the painkillers were working somewhat. He mustered up the strength to look down at his leg. He expected to find a cluster of twisted metal. Instead, there was a simple hole less than a centimeter across with a small trail of blood flowing from it. He didn't want to think about what his leg looked like inside the suit.

Kal rolled over and moved himself into a crouching position. He could see the firefight between the Arrow Team and the Nasi to his left. He also saw Raymond's body lying on the nearby rooftop, smoke still coming from his chest. Plasma streaked from the Nasi across the street in front of the building and landed inside the hallway where Arrow was holed up. He couldn't determine the exact location of the Nasi attackers, but based on the trajectories of the fire, they were in multiple positions around the entrance.

Kal dropped to the narrow passageway on the side of the building away from the lab and sprinted toward the breach point that Jones had added to the tactical map. The movement caused the pain in his legs to scream, and Kal grunted in pain as he ran through the narrow spaces between the Nasi buildings.

Up here, sir, Jones called.

Kal used his thrusters to join the rest of Alpha Team on the rooftop next to the lab. They lay prone, watching as a Bravo Team member placed explosives on the outside of the lab.

Bravo Team, put every single thing you got on it, Jones said. Despite their appearance, the Nasi weaves were tough. Kal had only seen them breached once before, and that was from the cannon fire of a ship. Missiles and grenades tended to be useless.

Fuse set, Ekon responded over the net.

Bravo Team ran from the breach site and took positions

at the base of the building Alpha Team was on. A few seconds later, the side of the Nasi lab erupted, pushing Kal and the rest of Alpha Team across the roof and into the alley below.

Get up, and get in there, Jones ordered.

Kal used his suit's thrusters to jump over the building and into the ripped hole in the lab's side. Jones was in front of Kal and dove headfirst through the hole. Kal quickly followed, rolling as he landed inside the building.

At least five hostiles in here, Jones reported.

Kal looked around the room. It seemed to take up the entire building. A ring of consoles surrounded a small ship about a third the length of the *Salamis*. It had a delta shape and an almost unnaturally smooth hull, unlike any other Nasi ship Kal had seen, save one. A plasma bolt shot out of the rear hatch of the ship, splashing harmlessly against the side of the hangar next to Kal.

We've got two in the ship and three over there. Jones pointed to the far end of the room, where there was a wide oval door. *They're behind the consoles.*

Bo had crawled through the hole in the building's side behind Kal and crouched behind one of the damaged consoles.

Sir, you and Bo clear out the ship, Jones said. *I'll get the hostiles behind the door.*

Kal nodded and moved clockwise around the room,

trying to get a clear line of sight into the black cavern of its cargo bay. Bo trailed behind him, sweeping the room with his weapon.

Kal's shield status flashed red as another plasma round streaked out from the side of the ship's bay and struck his energy shield. His energy shields were drained; the next round that hit him would be his last.

Sir, Bo asked over the net, *do you trust me?*

Yes, Kal replied. The Jadid had done more for Kal than almost anyone.

These have to be people I've worked with. Let me talk with them.

What? Kal turned around and looked at the scientist. Was he insane? Trying to have a conversation in the middle of a firefight?

There are only a handful of scientists that have the skills to work on this technology. I know them all. Rather than attacking them, perhaps I can convince them to stand down.

Do Nasi stand down? Kal asked, thinking of the Nasi civilians he'd seen in the alley minutes before.

They are scientists, not soldiers, Bo replied.

We have a minute at most, Kal replied. *But I do trust you. Go ahead.*

An explosion near the doorway reverberated through the room. Kal was now almost directly across from where Jones was assaulting the Nasi position by the door. He looked for an opening to see if he could help. There was nothing; the Nasi were behind cover.

"Hello!" Bo yelled. His voice echoed in the enormous

room. "This is Bowen Nguyen, who's in there?"

"Bo?" Kal thought the voice was a female.

"Yes, it's me. Is that Fen?"

"No, it is Ai. Fen is with me. What are you doing here?"

"I was the first scientist the Nasi captured. It appears they have found people to continue my work," Bo replied.

"They told us the Humans assassinated you," she cried out.

"That is not correct. I was held captive, and the Humans rescued me. I have voluntarily joined them."

"What?" The question dripped with shock.

"It is true. I am here supporting the Humans." The Nasi's stilted Standard Human was almost comically out of place amid everything else. Kal heard the sounds of combat outside the building growing stronger. The gunfire within the building continued to intensify. Jones had to be almost out of ammunition at this point. Kal doubted the sergeant would survive if the Nasi rushed him.

Bo, this is on you. Kal said. *I'm going to help Jones.*

He crept along the outside of the room between the terminals and the wall, hoping the Nasi would be too focused on Jones to notice him. Tables and stations lay in his path, providing cover from the Nasi at the door.

"I apologize, but we do not have time." Bo stood up. "We've been colleagues for decades, and I hope you trust me. At least more than you trust these Nasi who've captured you. The Nasi are exterminating the Humans."

A Jadid woman slowly crept down the ramp, cautiously peering at Bo. "I do trust you. But if you are here to steal this ship for the Humans, you will not be successful. Fen and I have already disabled it."

"Do you have the diveculum?" Bo asked. Kal knew from the mission brief that the diveculum was the critical piece of the fold drive, the part that made the whole thing work. "We can use that and your notes."

"We?" Ai asked. "Are you suggesting that Fen and I join you?"

"Yes."

The exchange of fire between Jones and the Nasi by the door died off; the room was quiet. All Kal could hear was the conversation between Bo and the Jadid scientists in the ship.

Someone crashed into Kal's side, slamming him into a console. The warning lights on his suit started to flash red; he was rapidly losing power. The attack had pushed Kal into a small clearing between several pieces of equipment with two Nasi. The third Nasi crouched over Kal with a plasma cutter in her hand. Kal tried to shove her off him, but the soldier had driven the cutter directly through the central power generator on the back of his suit. It was dead.

Sergeant Jones launched from his position toward Kal, kinetic rifle in one hand and plasma gun in the other. He held the weapons like spears, ready to throw. As he soared, almost touching the consoles of the research bay, the sergeant threw the two weapons downwards at the two Nasi next to Kal. The machine gun speared through a Nasi's chest, knocking him back against the wall, and the plasma gun hit the other Nasi in the head, knocking him back against a terminal. The soldier's body went limp, and he dropped his weapon as his body slid to the ground.

The Nasi on top of Kal turned around, plasma cutter in hand, as Jones's armored foot connected with her forehead, driving her off Kal.

"Looks like you could use a hand, sir," Jones said as he reached around Kal. The noncommissioned officer removed Kal's helmet, turned him over, and pulled the emergency escape handle on the back of his suit. The rear seam cracked open and Kal gingerly pulled himself out, his leg screaming in pain.

Kal tried to stand up, but his left leg buckled under him, pitching him into the ground.

"You're going to need help," Jones said.

Kal looked down at his leg; it was gruesome. The blood from his wound had pooled inside the suit and soaked the leg of his pants. He found his gaze wandering down to examine the wound itself.

"Sir, look at me." Jones stomped one of his metallic boots on the metal floor. "Look up. We've got to get out of here."

The sergeant grabbed his arms and gently helped Kal to stand. Kal hobbled forward on his right leg. He couldn't even feel the other leg anymore. He tried to push the nightmare of the wound from his head.

"Sir, we're almost ready to go," Jones said. "We've almost got what we need."

Bravo Team, we've located the ship, Jones reported over the net. *It's been disabled, but we're working on getting any parts and schematics we can.*

Bo, what's going on with your friends? Jones asked.

Colleagues, the Jadid corrected. *I am not sure.*

"Ai!" Bo yelled out. "What's going on? We have to leave."

Shouts and the sounds of a fight broke out from inside the ship. A Jadid, Kal guessed Fen, ran halfway down the ramp and threw a small sphere that landed at Bo's feet. The scientist stared at the device, not moving, seemingly unable to understand what was happening.

"Grenade!" Jones yelled as he pushed Kal down on the ground.

The sergeant streaked across the room in a single thruster-assisted bound and landed on the device. The grenade exploded, hurtling Jones past Bo and into a terminal bank with a horrific crash. His body had directed the explosion away from Bo and caused it to pepper the open cargo bay with plasma residue and shrapnel.

Bo finally seemed to snap out of his shock. His face contorted in rage. Teeth bared, he rushed into the back of the skip ship. Kal heard sounds of protest and screams suddenly cut off. Seconds later, the scientist emerged with a pile of parts in one hand and a Nasi tablet in the other.

Jones. Sergeant Jones. What's your status? Kal asked over the net. He knew the answer though. No suit could withstand a plasma grenade at that close a range.

Kal tried to stand, failed, and instead pulled himself across the floor toward Sergeant Jones.

"Bo, help me!" Kal cried out as he crawled along the floor. He vaguely realized that the soldiers outside were calling him over the net, but he couldn't respond. They must've seen Jones's icon turn red. He needed to know, to be sure, before he could say anything to them.

Kal was halfway to Jones's motionless body before Bo picked him up and awkwardly placed his arm below Kal's shoulder. They solemnly hobbled the rest of the way together and stood above Jones's body. The sergeant was lying on his side; the blast had seared away the front of the suit's armor. Blackened metal, shredded and melted by the plasma explosion, surrounded a gaping cavity in his torso.

Bravo Team, we've got one wounded and one KIA. Kal reported. *Sergeant Kimathi, you're running this mission now.*

Roger, sir, Ekon replied. *Salamis, we need extraction. Now!*

Roger, Kanumba said over the net, *we're on our way. We aren't gonna have time to stop, so just be ready.*

"Bo, can you carry me?" Kal asked. "We'll never get out of here alive with me on this leg."

Bo scooped Kal up and threw him across his shoulders like a child. As the Nasi strode toward the entrance they'd blasted in the building's side, a voice rang out. "Bowen, I am sorry. I did not know Fen would do that." Ai rushed down the cargo ramp.

"There's no time to talk right now," Bo replied. "We must finish what we started. You can come with us if you want."

Kal looked askance at his friend but was too tired and defeated to argue.

"Thank you." The woman replied. "I retrieved a few

more pieces that are critical to the functioning of this drive. We've made progress since the last time we worked together."

Bo didn't respond. Instead, he turned, crouched through the hole in the side of the lab, and stepped outside, carrying Kal.

❖

We're comin' in hot, Kanumba called out over the Skulls net. *The cloak works okay but we're still takin' heat.*

Roger, Ekon replied, *we're ready.*

Bravo Team knelt at the top of the building next to the lab, directing their fire at the Nasi soldiers in the passages and streets surrounding them. After fleeing the lab, Bo and Ai tried crawling up the building's side, but couldn't climb the smooth exterior.

Only five out of the original nine in the assault force remained.

Go! Kanumba called out.

The three remaining members of Bravo Team swept down from their position to grab what remained of Alpha Team. Bhatt grabbed Kal from where Bo had dropped him on the ground, cradled him like a baby, and engaged her thrusters. As they climbed, Kal felt his head snap back. The city was upside down in his view, and he stared at the skyline of Kasongo as they shot through the air. It was thick with smoke and death that floated from the Foothold's wall and the three labs.

Kal realized he'd never called off the assault. *All teams retreat*, he called out over the general net. *We found what we're looking for.*

Sir, they're gone, Kanumba replied, using a private link. *I think maybe a few of them escaped.*

Kal closed his eyes, shutting out the wind and the city. The entire force was gone. He heard the roar of an engine. They must be approaching the *Salamis's* cargo bay. There was a sudden jerk as Bhatt landed on the bay floor, her forward momentum carrying them forward several feet before she could recover. Kal opened his eyes.

As Bhatt stepped to the edge of the bay and docked her suit, Ekon and Sandra dropped into the bay and the cargo door closed. Kal grabbed onto a bracket in the floor to hold himself as the ship climbed out of Kasongo's atmosphere.

"Sit still, sir," Sandra said as she knelt over Kal and wrapped a bandage around his injured leg.

"I've got to get to the cockpit," Kal replied.

"There's nothing you can do from there," Ekon said as he placed his helmet on the dock. "Besides, trying to get up to the second deck while we're leaving the atmosphere *and* you're injured is a bad idea."

Kal knew the sergeant was right. But after everything that had just happened, he wanted to find something to keep his thoughts at bay. Anything was better than sitting there and thinking of Patagonia.

"Fine," Kal conceded. "Can you at least take me to the galley?"

Sandra nodded and helped Kal to stand. After only a

few stumbles and one fall, he flopped down on a chair in the galley and watched the last stages of their ascent.

The *Salamis's* cloak worked, and they avoided detection by the Nasi fleet around Patagonia. The ships and fighters clearly knew they were in the area but could not pinpoint their exact location. They flew in circular search patterns, trying to get a visual on the ship as the *Salamis* continued to put distance between itself and the planet.

Kal watched as the blue-green planet receded behind their ship and hoped that he'd never have to see it again.

After several minutes they were far enough to engage their fold drives and Patagonia disappeared in the blink of an eye. Kal took a deep breath and thought of Sergeant Jones. He hoped his sacrifice would not be in vain.

Chapter Twenty-Two

Nicole sat in her chair on the *Ofira's* bridge, dumbfounded. Esma was the Ancient she'd heard so much about, the one who had created the Nasi. Her voice was a nightmare come to life. She knew the Nasi ultimatum was genuine. They would destroy the entire H'Far system without hesitation if they felt it was necessary.

"Ma'am, the Nasi dreadnaught is powering up their weapon!"

"We can't get to it in time," Petrov replied. "Navigation, find us a path out of here."

Colonel Bergeron, I'm patching us through to the Z'Ta on a private link, Samaha's voice said through Nicole's implant.

Rebel Council, Samaha said, *I'll be brief. We've lost this battle. You can either give in to the Nasi or escape with the fleet. You've seen what the Nasi can and will do. Giving in to them is the same as putting restraints on yourself. You'll never be free again.*

That's true, the council replied, *but escaping means we would cause the death of billions of our people and the destruction of our home.*

It's already gone, Nicole said. *The Nasi will use it against you until you can't resist anymore.*

Already gone? the council asked. *We still see our planet in front of us. If we leave, then we'll never see it again.*

You can give in to the Nasi now, Nicole said, *and you'll survive. But they will wipe out your people whenever they want, and you will have given up any chance of stopping them. You still can fight; you are still in the fight. As soon as you give up, then you can never resist again.*

This is a horrible decision, the council said. For the first time, Nicole heard sorrow in their voices. She couldn't imagine having to make such a decision herself. There was a long pause. *We will...go with you.*

Thank you, Samaha replied. *General Zhou will provide you with our operations plan and the rendezvous point. I'm sorry.*

The ship's navigation cell was frantically looking for the nearest fold point for them to escape the system. The Nasi ambush fleet was quickly moving from around the planet toward the *Ofira* and the rest of Samsara Fleet.

"Where are the fighters?" Petrov asked.

"We've got the first squadron returning now. The other should arrive in the next couple of minutes."

The *Ofira* had spun and moved laterally away from both Nasi fleets. In order to activate their fold drive, they would need to be clear from any gravitational fields, which meant getting away from everything else in the area.

The Z'Ta had also changed their fleet's direction and were flying away from the planet with the Nasi fleet in pursuit. Despite the upgrades from Samsara Fleet, the Z'Ta ships were slower than the Nasi and had the disadvantage of having to change course.

Lokryz, what are you doing? asked Samaha over the net. The *Lokryz* had stopped its retreat and was moving between the Z'Ta and the four Nasi ships pursuing them.

We will give our allies a chance to escape, the Kurz

commander said. *They've had enough death today.*

The Kurz ship fired its full complement of missiles at the approaching Nasi. As the fleet advanced into cannon range, the *Lokryz* unleashed a barrage of plasma and kinetic projectile fire, connecting with the ships' shields in a miasma of blue and green. The battleship unloaded its missiles as fast as they could, firing them without taking the time to engage the tracking and most likely damaging their firing tubes.

The full barrage had its intended effect and the Nasi fleet slowed to concentrate its fire on the lone Kurz battleship. Nasi missiles exploded around the ship as its point defense system took them out one by one. The *Lokryz's* shield glowed in the darkness of space as they absorbed the continual stream of plasma fire from the Nasi in front of them.

Watching the valiant stand on her console's viewscreen, Nicole was reminded of the time her parents had taken her out to see fireworks as a child. The bright lights had exploded over the beach, their colors reflecting in the smoke. And then it was over; the viewscreen lit up as the *Lokryz* succumbed to the Nasi, disintegrating in a bright ball.

"How are we looking?" Colonel Petrov asked.

"Fighters have returned and we're less than a minute from our fold point," replied Colonel Reddy. Nicole could see that the fighters had taken heavy losses.

Ships continued to drop from the fleet status screen as they folded out of the system. Finally, only the *Ofira* and the *L'kor* remained.

"Ma'am!" Colonel Reddy turned from his console to look at Petrov. "Should we try the—"

A bright beam of what appeared to be pure energy shot from the Nasi dreadnaught at the sun. The beam was so bright that the bridge's viewscreen dimmed in response. Nicole remembered the video she'd watched of the same thing happening in the Sol system when four Nasi dreadnaughts had entered the system and fired into the sun. At first, it seemed like the beam would have no effect. Then slowly, the star grew brighter, and the color deepened to a dark orange. It suddenly expanded, unleashing a wall of devastation that would annihilate anything left in the system.

"Navigation, we ready to fold?" Petrov asked.

"Yes, ma'am." Almost all the Nasi ships had already left.

"Then do it."

The burnt orange ball that had been a sun flickered off the screen, leaving only the dark chill of space.

Silence hung over the bridge like a shroud. Nicole heard several muffled sobs as soldiers, heavy with failure, hung their heads. The Nasi had won. Again. Nicole held her head in her hands, thinking of the billions of lives that had just been wiped out. They'd failed. Again.

She looked up. The three viewscreens at the front of the room were empty except for stars. Colonel Petrov was slumped in her chair with her head down, staring at her console's viewscreen. She mouthed something to herself and then deliberately stood up, her back ramrod straight.

"Navigation, I need you to tell me our exact position,"

Petrov commanded in an unwavering voice. "Communications, re-establish a communication net with the rest of the fleet. Operations, continue to scan for hostiles and get me a full report on damage to the ship.

"Is the commander's flagship in communications range?" asked Petrov.

The seconds ticked by. Finally, the communications officer responded, his voice breaking. "Yes, ma'am. They're in comms range."

Petrov marched toward Nicole, her eyes looking anywhere but directly at her. "Colonel Bergeron, come with me." Nicole stood up and followed the commander through the bridge's entrance and into the conference room.

"Damn it, Nicole," Petrov sighed as she slumped into her chair at the head of the table. "Damn it!" She slammed a fist down on the table.

Nicole didn't know what to say. What was there to say?

"Irina," Samaha said, her face appearing on a viewscreen.

"Ma'am." Petrov nodded back.

"I...I know this is hard." She placed a fist over her mouth. "It shouldn't have happened. But it did. Your crew must be devastated. You must be devastated. Remember that this is not your fault and that we will stop those bastards. They're scared. That's why they did this. And we've scared them because they know we *can* win."

"We *will* win," Nicole said.

Samaha inclined her head. "Yes, we will. Get me a full rundown of your ship's systems and ammunition. We'll fold out in an hour as long as we're able to. You've got the coordinates already."

Samaha cut the feed, leaving Nicole and Petrov alone in the conference room.

"Time to get to work. Feelings later." The commander said it to herself as much as to Nicole.

It ended up taking two hours for Samsara Fleet to be ready to fold. The three remaining Z'Ta councils were understandably devastated, refusing to answer anything but the most basic questions. The rest of the fleet wasn't much better; now they were *all* orphans, species without homes to return to.

The voyage back to Human space to meet with Ancient Bao Wang would take them two weeks. As they started the journey, the time passed slowly for Nicole. She was looking forward to seeing Kal and her friends in the Skulls, but the depression of what had happened to them muted even that excitement. She suspected she was like many people on the ship, wondering what they could have done differently. They could have done more to fight the Nasi and perhaps overwhelm them. They could have left the Z'Ta alone and let them survive.

She knew that it was all conjecture. Who knew what would have happened if they'd played things differently. Soldiers didn't dwell on the past for this reason, there was nothing to be gained.

Nicole continued to have her morning breakfasts with Chief Ramos. Initially, they sat together in silence much of the time, neither wanting to voice their feelings. Around halfway through the voyage, the ice began to thaw, and their conversation turned to the future—what to expect when they met back with the Skulls and Ancient Wang's Jadid fleet.

As the journey wore on, Nicole increasingly saw signs of life among the crew of the *Ofira*. After the first day, Commander Petrov seemed unaffected by the events, continuing her duties in the brisk, efficient way she normally did. However, Nicole noticed small things were different—she spent more time asking how soldiers were doing, complimented them on small wins, and spent less time in her office.

By the time the *Ofira* completed its final fold and arrived at the meeting point, things were starting to feel normal again. She heard soldiers making jokes in the hallway and talking about what they would do if they *ever* got shore leave. The events at T'kor'nuk had been terrible, but they had survived and they still had a war to win.

The Jadid Fleet and most of Samsara Fleet was already there by the time the *Ofira* arrived. The Z'Ta ships were still en route. Unfortunately, the Skulls weren't there. Nicole tried to ignore the knot that tightened in her stomach as she looked over the tacmap.

After they'd conducted their initial checks upon arrival, Petrov asked Nicole to join her in the conference room to talk with the fleet commander.

"Colonel Petrov, how are your soldiers?" asked Samaha.

"Good, ma'am." Petrov replied. "We're holding up."

"As you probably noticed, we're still missing the Z'Ta and the Skulls, but I'm confident they'll show up." Samaha's eyes flickered, and Nicole could have sworn the commander was looking at her.

"Well, the Z'Ta haven't upgraded their fold drives and the Skulls are always late, ma'am." Petrov smiled weakly. "You know how General Norman's crew is."

Samaha laughed. "Well, we can't wait on them. Bao Wang is ready to meet with us. Per the Ancient's request, I'll need yourself and Colonel Bergeron to join me on Wang's flagship immediately."

"Yes, ma'am." Petrov nodded.

"Get your crew to do any maintenance that couldn't be done while folding and cross-load any supplies with other ships in the fleet. We may need to leave soon." Samaha closed the line.

Nicole hated traveling through empty space between the ships in the small tender. She remembered watching holos as a kid and how the ships were impossibly close to each other, almost touching sometimes. In reality, space was incredibly vast, and she couldn't see any other ship as they left the landing bay of the *Ofira*. It would have been nice to see a planet or large station near them, so she didn't feel like they were stranded, alone in space.

After arriving on the *Galaxy's Edge*, they were escorted to Ancient Wang's office. He gave a perfunctory smile as they entered and gestured to his seating area where a small carafe and cups were already waiting.

"Glad you made it." Wang sat down casually in his chair. "I don't see any other ships though."

General Samaha began to describe what had happened with the Z'Ta. The Ancient interrupted her several times to ask clarifying questions or make a comment. Nicole felt like the exchange was more of a debrief than a meeting of equals, and from the general's clenched jaw, she probably felt the same. When Samaha finished describing the destruction of the H'Far system, the Ancient's eyes widened and he leaned forward in his chair.

"Goddamn, they are bastards," he muttered. "Esma's gone too far."

"She went too far a long time ago," Samaha snapped. "And you did nothing about it."

Bao looked up at her. "Yes, you're right of course. We thought the problem would just go away. Let them leave Altterra and let someone else worry about the consequences."

He crossed his legs and leaned back in the chair. "Well, I hope to do something about that. With your help, of course."

"What'd you find out about the Nasi?" Samaha asked.

"It's interesting," Bao tapped the side of his mug thoughtfully, "how we never appreciate the effects of our actions. When you use a hammer, you are striking the nail, but the nail is striking the hammer as well. When you have enough nails..." He trailed off.

"What do you mean?" Nicole asked.

"The Nasi have changed." Bao waved his hand. "They didn't want me around, but it's hard to refuse an Ancient even if you're a Nasi. I got to go down to Wudexingqiu and see the Nasi patrols and even met with some of their fleet commanders. They're changing. Becoming more Human if you can believe it."

"How so?" Nicole asked.

"The way they speak, dress—hell, even the way they think. I don't think Esma counted on that." He chuckled. "The woman's like a machine, not surprising she wouldn't consider that her followers would change."

"They didn't seem to have changed when they destroyed T'kor'nuk," Samaha said. "They were the same psychopaths as when they destroyed those other systems and planets."

Bao let out a deep breath. "The Nasi are based on an ideology that is strict and unforgiving. That doesn't make them a monolith, at least not anymore. I would guess that there were soldiers on that dreadnaught that disagreed with the decision. I doubt that was the case when Earth was destroyed."

"So what? We convince them to stop?" Nicole asked.

"Too late for that," Samaha spat. "They're here. Nothing is going to change that. We can't just all get along."

"Well, it's an interesting change either way." Bao shrugged. "From what I saw on Wudexingqiu, they have completed their Footholds. As you say, they're here permanently. With the additional reserves they brought into this universe, they've begun expanding to the colonies and systems outside of your Human ones."

"So, they're vulnerable in the Human colonies?" Samaha

asked.

"Yes and no. Yes, their fleets have mainly left the area except for a couple of ships. But they still have the Footholds and can always bring their fleets back. If we were to capture a planet, we wouldn't be able to hold it."

"And we risk them destroying the entire system," Nicole added.

Bao pointed to her. "Yes. We've got to hope the Skulls come back with the skip ship prototype. If we can get the Jadid involved, there may be a way to close the gateways between our universes and prevent them from being resupplied from there."

"And they have ships, I assume." Samaha said.

"Yes, they do."

"So, we're in a holding pattern?"

"I think we need to wait for now," Bao replied. "If your friends don't return, then we'll need to think of another strategy."

"I'm sure they'll be here soon," Nicole replied.

"Of course, me too." Bao smiled soothingly. "I don't doubt it."

Chapter Twenty-Three

Nicole, they're back!

Chief Ramos's call startled Nicole from the book she was reading on her tablet. Samsara Fleet had been waiting at the rendezvous point for two days, and with each passing hour, Nicole felt her panic grow. Reading, exercise, training—she'd done everything she could to keep occupied and not torture herself with thoughts of where her friends may be.

General Norman is with them, but they've taken casualties, Ramos warned.

Nicole felt a tearing inside as two conflicting emotions battled, relief over Kal's safe return and sorrow over the loss of her friends. A third emotion, guilt that she could feel even some happiness when her comrades had died, joined in with the other two. How many and who had they lost? What had happened?

She rushed out of the room and toward the lifts. Nicole couldn't get to Kal and the Skulls fast enough—the lift to the landing bays seemed to take more time than she remembered.

Finally, she arrived out of breath in the scout ship landing bay. The maintenance crews and bots walked between ships, repairing the damage they'd taken at T'kor'nuk. The *Salamis* sat at the far end of the bay with its back ramp down.

"Colonel Bergeron!" Bo called out as he walked down the ramp and gave a small wave, his face solemn. "It is good to see you."

"Bo, glad to see you too!" she called back as she strode

toward the *Salamis*.

Then Nicole saw Kal hobble down the ramp next to the Jadid. She couldn't help herself and broke out in a run toward the ship—propriety be damned. Kal scanned the bay and gave a weak smile as he saw her, breaking into a run as well. The two met in the middle of the bay and Nicole was reminded of all the silly holos her mom and dad had watched when she'd been a kid. Kal picked her up off the ground in a desperate embrace. The stubble on his face scratched against her skin and his labored breath blew in her ears. She took a moment to enjoy the feeling of their arms around each other and warmth and smell of him—everything else faded away for a precious moment. They pulled their heads back and their lips met, sending a jolt through her body.

Kal finally set her down and looked into her eyes. She could see the toll that Patagonia had taken on him—clammy skin, red eyes, and three-day stubble on his face. She saw her own troubles and sadness reflected at her.

"Bad, huh?" he asked.

She nodded.

"Me, too."

The rest of the Skulls slowly walked down the ramp, jump bags slung over their shoulders. They all had the same war-weary expressions on their faces as they trudged through the landing bay.

She saw some unknown faces among them…and realized some were missing.

"What happened?" She asked.

Kal looked away. "Kinawadi and Garcia both stayed

behind. Sergeant Jones didn't make it."

Her heart sank. Jones had been the constant, the rock, that their small team had been built on. His loss was much greater than one person.

"How's Ekon?"

"Damaged." He looked back into her eyes. "But he'll make it."

"The Nasi destroyed T'kor'nuk. We lost—"

"Kal, we're glad you're back," General Samaha interrupted as she walked up to them. Kal and Nicole let their arms drop and turned to face the general.

"Thank you, ma'am. We retrieved the plans and materials to create a skip ship." He pointed to Bo and another Jadid standing on the ramp of the *Salamis*. "Bowen and Ai, another one of the kidnapped Jadid scientists, say they have enough to convert one of our ships."

"At least it wasn't for nothing." Samaha frowned and placed a hand on his arm. "I'm sorry about Sergeant Jones."

"Thank you," Kal replied. He clearly didn't want to talk about it.

"I'll give you a chance to get settled, and then we need that skip ship built as soon as possible."

"Yes, the Jadid are already working on it. They say the *Salamis* is an ideal candidate for conversion."

"They can have whatever they need." Samaha placed a hand on Kal's shoulder. "I know you've been through hell, but we're almost there."

Nicole hoped the general was right.

❖

The cabin he shared with Nicole seemed so strange to Kal. It felt enormous, a far cry from the stateroom in the *Salamis*. The generic white walls and faux high-end finishes seemed cold and unfeeling.

Since they'd returned to the *Ofira* the day before, the Skulls had spent their time apart trying to process everything that had happened. Kal spent it in his stateroom with Nicole— telling each other stories, making love, and just lying together quietly. They rarely talked directly about what they'd been through, opting to mention funny stories or how they had missed each other. Just having her close helped to lift some of the weight lift from his shoulders.

Kal woke screaming, the sound of the grenade in his dream still ringing in his ears. Nicole was still miraculously asleep next to him, her face serene and lips pursed. He fought the urge to bend over and kiss her; she deserved to rest.

Instead, he threw on a loose shirt and pair of free merchant pants and walked to the landing bays to see how Bo and Ai were faring with the *Salamis*. During their return to the fleet, the two Jadid had carefully inspected the ship's systems, making notes on the small computers strapped to their wrists. After the thorough inspection, they'd declared the ship a good fit for the experimental skip ship technology. The experimental fold drive could only work on ships of the right size and shape. With some modifications, the *Salamis* could meet the criteria.

He found the two Jadid working quietly next to each

other in the cargo bay. They'd removed several panels as well as many of the wires and devices inside the hull. They were silent as they worked, each focused on the task in front of them.

"Hello," Kal said as he walked up the bay and stood between the two scientists. "How's it going?"

"It is going well," Ai replied, standing up from the wires she was untangling.

Bo remained kneeling over a small device on the bay floor. "We're doing okay, sir. Of course, we're finding some things that are unexpected."

"You think you can still do it though, right?" Kal hated the thought of everything being in vain.

Bo waved his hand. "Yes, sir. These are normal issues. It's like battle—nothing goes according to plan. To convert any more ships may be difficult though. The materials needed are very rare and fabrication techniques needed are extremely complex."

"Once we have the drive complete, we will also need to upgrade the other systems." Ai was still standing in front of him, her back as straight as a recruit's.

"You can keep working," Kal said, "we're not the Nasi."

"Thank you." The female knelt back down and continued unsnarling the wires.

"If you remember our trip in the *Park*, the systems that work in this universe will not work in ours. We essentially need to have two ships inside the hull of one." Bo interlocked the fingers of his hands.

"That sounds like it'll take a long time."

"We have the schematics for most of the systems in the notes we took," Bo replied. "We sent them to the ship's fabrication team and they're already building the parts. If we get some more hands, we can speed it up."

"Where's Chief Kanumba?" Kal asked. Normally, she wouldn't let anyone work on the ship without her present.

Bo shrugged. "She left saying she wasn't feeling well."

That was odd. "I'll check on her. How about you two?" Kal asked. "I know Samaha said she needs everything right away, but you've been through a helluva lot too."

"We'll be fine." The scientist stood and looked down at Kal, meeting his eyes. "I'll work on this until it's done. I owe that to Sergeant Jones. He died for this—for me. I won't let him down."

"Thank you," Kal replied, "let me know if you need anything."

Bo gave a thumbs up and knelt back down, intent on his work.

Nicole woke from her nightmare with a start as her leg spasmed, kicking the bulkhead. She lazily rolled over to find the bed empty; Kal must have left while she was asleep. As she touched the starfish pendant around her neck, her dream came back to her. She'd been saying goodbye to her sister, who had been begging her not to leave.

Nicole's thoughts turned to Taisha. Normally, she was the one Nicole could talk to but she hadn't talked to her friend in months. When Nicole had tried to say hello on the landing bay, the woman had seemed as dazed and sullen as the rest of them, shuffling away without saying a word.

Nicole quickly got dressed in the loose-fitting shirt and pants that were the informal uniform of the Skulls—no more Samsara Fleet uniform now that her friends were back.

The hallways seemed more empty than usual and the overhead lights dimmer. She knew it was in her head, but Nicole couldn't help feeling like she was sneaking somewhere in the middle of the night.

She pressed the call button outside of Taisha's door, and it slid open immediately. The chief was lying on her bunk, back propped against the wall, idly spinning a small ring around her finger. From the way she stared longingly at the ring, Nicole could tell it must have come from Jae-Ho.

"How are you?" The words felt inadequate as soon as they left her lips.

"Been better." Taisha pulled the ring off her finger and tucked it in a pocket on her shirt.

"Kal was telling me about what happened. It sounds rough."

"Yeah." She seemed distracted. "Though watching a system get destroyed doesn't sound much better."

Nicole took a deep breath. Time to cut to the chase.

"Taisha, how are you, *really*?" She sat down on the bunk, forcing the chief to look at her.

"Really?" She pulled her head back and hit the wall with a solid thunk. "I don't know." She picked up a tablet lying next to her and handed it to Nicole.

There was a black and white three-dimensional image on the screen. At first glance, it appeared to be some sort of abstract art, though she wasn't familiar with the artist. Then Nicole realized what she was looking at.

"Wait… what?"

Taisha nodded, tears running down her cheeks and over her smiling lips.

"How?"

"Well, you see Nicole. When a pilot loves a chief, they—"

"I know *how*. But it's insane considering everything going on." The thought of her friend pregnant amidst everything else was shocking. "This shouldn't even be possible."

Every soldier, both male and female, in the EDF had contraceptive implants. The only way to get pregnant would to be to so intentionally.

"We figured what the hell?" Taisha laughed. "With everything else going on…" The laughter faded away and her voice dropped. "Well, we said who knows if we'll even live to see the baby."

"That ring, it's from Jae-Ho, isn't it?" Nicole pointed to Taisha's chest.

She nodded. "It was from his mother. I figure it will be something to give to the baby, a reminder of its father. You know, I still can't believe he's gone. It's like a dream. I didn't even know him that long."

"Well, I know he'd be proud of you. You're amazing." Nicole grabbed her friend by the shoulders and pulled her close. It was the most wonderful, most tragic thing Nicole had experienced. They held each other, laughed, and cried. It was a miracle.

❖

"You think this'll work?" Kal asked Ai and Bo.

It had been seven days since they'd begun working on converting the *Salamis* into a skip ship. Kal stood inside the ship's cockpit, examining the outcome of their work. They'd attached several banks of analog controls below the front viewscreens, which they had converted to work in both universes. Wires ran in bunches along the bulkhead, between the screens and controls before disappearing in a jagged hole cut into the hull's inner lining. The entire setup reminded Kal of the interior of the *Annie*, the junker he'd flown as a merchant.

"We'll need to continue to run some more tests, but it should work," Bo replied. "He ran his hand affectionately along the hull."

"This is our greatest accomplishment," Ai said, glancing at her fellow scientist.

"Yes." Bo gave a pained smile. "And to think we accomplished it under these conditions—in another universe with limited supplies."

"Good job," Kal slapped the hull. "Jones would be proud."

They three walked back through the ship, toward the back cargo ramp. Besides some bundles of wiring running along the ceiling in places, the ship looked about the same as it had before. In the cargo bay, a section of the bulkhead now bulged out in the bay, cutting into the open space. They'd had to move the battle suit docks against another wall to make room.

General Samaha and Lieutenant Sampson were walking around the ship's exterior while Chief Kanumba stood at the foot of the ramp, hands on hips, looking into the bay. Kal felt a twinge of emotion seeing her, a bittersweet sadness that was shaded with his own memories of parenthood. He couldn't have been happier for her though.

"This is amazing," the chief said. "You've ushered in a whole new era."

"Yes, I think we have," Ai replied. Kal glanced at her in time to see the small smile that accompanied her words.

"Can we make more of these?" asked Samaha as she gently touched one of the ship's wings.

"It will be difficult," Ai replied.

"There are several materials needed that are extremely rare," Bo replied. "Not to mention the complexity of building the systems. You can fabricate the parts if you have the right materials and an extremely good fabricator. But the configuration and installation are also delicate processes."

"So don't break it," Kanumba said smirking.

"One thing at a time," Samaha twisted her mouth. "We'll work on making more when we return." She slapped the hull. "Speaking of returning, when will it be ready for us to go?"

"We need to run tests, ma'am. I'd like Lieutenant

Sampson and Chief Kanumba to be present with us. They'll need to know how to fly the ship."

"Wait, do we know what that might do to me?" Kanumba asked, her hand absent-mindedly touching her abdomen.

"I do not believe anyone has ever thought about it before." Ai put her hand to her chin. "There is a chance that the fetus could mutate in the womb. I wonder what the effect would be. We'd need to do some analysis and experimentation to—"

"I think it's safe to say that we won't do that." Kal wasn't about to have his friend and her unborn child become guinea pigs. "We'll need someone to replace her for the testing and the mission."

"Not a problem. Colonel Bergeron and I already have someone lined up," Samaha said. "Finish up. We need to get out of here."

Chapter Twenty-Four

"You ready, sir?" Sampson asked. His finger hovered over the blue button that would activate the ship's experimental fold drive.

The *Salamis* was about to fold into the Jadid's universe and travel to Altterra, their home planet. The scientists were thorough, and it had taken several days for Bo and Ai to complete their tests. They even conducted a full test run, folding to their home universe and back with Sampson and Chief Ramos.

Kal didn't relish the thought of going back to Altterra. The planet, and the whole universe, was a strange mixture of the familiar and the bizarre. This strange dissonance made Kal less comfortable than if the universe had been completely alien from their own.

"Let's do it," Kal replied.

Sampson pushed the fold button, and the ship's interior went pitch-black. A moment later, amber lights on the ceiling sprung to life, illuminating the cockpit in a dim bluish glow. The viewscreens flickered back to life, revealing a splash of coral stars around them. Kal looked down at his hand; his dark brown was now tinged orange, creating an umber color.

"Still cool," Sampson gasped, holding his now peach colored hand in front of his face.

Kal felt an immediate wave of nausea as the gravity of the universe faintly pushed and pulled his body in different directions. Bo had tried to explain the differences between this universe and his own. Kal hadn't understood everything, but what he had figured out was that this universe had subtly different laws of physics than their own: gravity wasn't a constant, the light spectrum had shifted, and electricity worked differently as well. There were many differences but also many similarities. For instance, though gravity operated differently, it still existed. Theoretically, there were countless other universes, each with slightly different physical properties.

Kal flexed his cybernetic arm. It had worked last time they'd been here, but it was always good to check. The bioelectrical impulses that powered it seemed to operate in the same manner in this universe.

"Sir," Bo floated through the cockpit door, "I came to check on the systems." His skin was no longer violet, but a dark chartreuse.

"Well, we're alive at least," Chief Ramos said wonderingly. She waved her arm in the air as if trying to prove it to herself. Samaha had assigned her to the mission as a replacement for Chief Kanumba.

The ship's artificial gravity didn't work in this universe. Bo had warned them their implants and many of the ship's systems—including their shields and weapons—would not either. At least the two scientists had modified the viewscreens, drives, and other critical systems so the ship could get them where they needed to go. Unfortunately, it couldn't do much more than that.

"One moment." Bo pulled himself down and examined the network of cables and small devices that littered the floor below the viewscreens. After a few minutes of mumbling, the Jadid declared all systems were working.

"Okay, then. Next stop Altterra," Chief Ramos declared.

The voyage to Altterra only took a few hours compared to the days it would have taken in Kal's universe. The distances were the same, but the alternate universe's gravity affected the physics of the fold drive, allowing them to travel much farther between folds.

Soon Kal was looking down on an alternate version of Earth. Milky-white oceans dominated the planet and surrounded continents made from a patchwork of colors. From this distance it reminded Kal of the marbles he had played with as a kid, a glittering multicolored orb in the darkness of space.

The *Salamis* smoothly sailed through the outer layers of the planet's exosphere, passing through the wispy blue clouds. As they descended, the ocean's surface came into focus, the large chalky waves becoming visible as they neared sea level. They continued to speed through the air, and the ocean gave way to land. Patches of plants in blue, red, and green passed beneath their ship.

Bao Wang stood next to Kal's console, looking at the land beneath them with an inscrutable expression.

"Tarzirbu control, this is Ancient Bao Wang. We will land at the Palace of the Ancients."

The net was dead for several seconds. "Affirmative, Ancient Wang. You have permission to land at the palace. The Council of Ancients would like to speak with you immediately upon arrival."

Another voice cut through the line. "Ancient Wang, ignore the previous message, insurrectionists have taken Tarzirbu. We've moved our headquarters to—"

"What's going on?" Kal said.

"I don't know." Wang looked confused.

"Bao," said a woman's voice, "this is Salina. You need to head to the palace. We have had something terrible happen."

"Salina, what's going on?" Bao clenched his fist and looked around the cockpit as if searching for a clue to what was happening.

"It has all gone to crap." Kal heard the despair in her voice. "I can explain when you land. Things have become much worse than when you left. I cannot speak any more on this open line." It went dead.

"Salina, what do you mean? Salina?"

There was no response.

"Where should we go?" asked Samaha. She must've run to the cockpit from the galley.

"I—"

"Bao, this is Jian." Another voice on the net, this one male. "Salina is not telling you the full story. After you left, the rift widened and became inseparable. I am with Girish in Eden."

"What happened?" Bao asked.

"It is the Humans," Jian responded. "Richard and Salina are convinced we should help them. So are their followers. Girish and I tried to help them understand what was at stake, but they will not listen to reason."

363

Bao shook his head, rubbed his temples, then looked at Kal. "This is what you and your friend's indiscretion cost us. You broke apart a people that had been unified for centuries."

Kal snapped. He thought of all that had happened since the Nasi, a faction of the Jadid, had arrived—the people killed or enslaved, battles fought, families ripped apart—and grabbed the Ancient by his shirt, shoving him into the bulkhead.

"*We* didn't do anything; your people were already divided. Your buddy Esma started this by coming to *our* universe and destroying *our* home. You kept your people isolated and controlled them. No wonder this happened. Don't put this on us."

Bao shoved Kal backwards, causing him to stumble and fall back against the bulkhead. "We told you to stay out of sight, to help us control the situation. Now..." Bao checked himself and smoothed his blouse. "You may be right, but damn it, it hurts. Centuries. That's how long we've been here building this civilization. Now it's gone."

"No." Ramos turned away from the controls and glared at the man. "Earth is gone. Your civilization—the people, the customs, the buildings—they're still there, just divided."

"Maybe." Bao seemed mollified and sat on a small jump seat.

"Head to Tarzirbu," Samaha said. "At least that faction *wants* to help us."

"I'll need to talk with the others," Bao said. "Maybe there's a way for this rift to be mended."

"Fine," Samaha replied. "Sampson, head to the palace." She turned to Bao. "Can you give the pilots the coordinates?"

A few minutes later, they were coasting over the city of Tarzirbu. Muted colors draped every surface, making it appear like a dark stain against the vivid colors of the natural landscape. Enormous buildings dotted the cityscape, branching and twisting into the sky. Small transports snaked between the buildings, creating small rivers of light in the shadows of the towers.

The Palace of the Ancients stood at the edge of the city, encircled by a dark gray wall at least ten meters high. Colonnades connected the large complex of rectangular buildings, turning them into a single sprawling structure. The buildings surrounded three sides of a large square that was filled with Jadid—the Ancients' Market that Kal had stumbled into with Karl the last time they'd been there.

The Ancients occupied a position somewhere between gods and ceremonial figureheads among the Jadid. From what Kal could gather, they'd tried to stay out of the affairs of their "children," but their decisions were still inviolate. By the time the Nasi had decided to invade, they had removed themselves from the day-to-day life of the Jadid and retreated to their palace. But the emergence of the Nasi had forced them to take an active role in the functioning of the Jadid once again.

The *Salamis* touched down on the landing pad next to the palace with a gentle bump. The planet's strong and ever-changing gravity pushed and pulled Kal; it was a disorienting feeling. Kal walked to the cargo bay where Nicole was waiting with General Samaha and Ancient Wang. Samaha and Wang had decided the four of them would speak with the Ancients while the rest of the crew waited in the ship.

Two dozen Jadid soldiers in matte black battle suits stood in a semicircle around the ship's cargo ramp. As opposed to the bulky Human suits, the Jadids' seemed to be molded to their bodies. Several had an extra mechanical appendage extending from the back that made the soldiers seem especially alien. Each of them had a white cloth wrapped around their arm—a symbol they were part of the Ancient's personal guard—and a long twisted rod in their hands.

A female stepped forward from the semicircle. She wore a simple indigo formfitting gown that reached from her neck to her ankles. Her face was smooth and angular with high cheekbones that highlighted her deep blue eyes. Kal remembered her from last time he'd been to Altterra: Madeline Huang, the governor of Altterra.

"Ancient Wang, welcome back." Huang bowed deeply while keeping her eyes firmly on his face. "Ancients Kingsley and Musa are waiting for you in the private chambers."

"Governor Huang, thank you." Bao gave a slight inclination of his head in return. "I'm sorry things have become so fraught."

Huang's thin lips twisted in displeasure as she regarded the other Humans. "It is a terrible thing that's happened because of these Humans."

"Now, now," Bao wagged his finger, "we cannot blame them for what's happened. Much of this is on us. General

Samaha, General Norman, who I believe you already know, and Colonel Bergeron," he pointed to each of them as he said their names, "have come here to talk with the council. Please take us to them."

"Certainly, sir"

"Also, Scientists Bowen Nguyen and Ai Martinez are on board the ship. They are to be allowed to enter the city."

The governor nodded curtly and began walking toward the entrance to the palace. The guards split evenly, half moving to surround the *Salamis* and the other half stepping to flank the procession as they walked into the palace. Kal studied the ornamental spire that adorned the building over the entrance. Swirling pictographs covered every facet.

The ornate rectangular doors to the building slid open as they approached. Huang led the silent procession through the broad hallways of the Jadid palace. Guards stood at regular intervals, weapons in their hands and white bands around their arms.

"Have you noticed the Jadid are different colors in this universe?" Nicole whispered to Kal. Bo and Ai were both a green color in this universe while Huang was the same lilac color as the Jadid in the Human's universe.

"You're right," he whispered back, "Karl and I never understood how that could be."

"Also, this building has rectangular doors."

"Perhaps because of the Ancients?" Now that she mentioned it, the structure wouldn't have been out of place among the ancient temples and cathedrals of Earth.

Governor Huang stopped at the side of an enormous

door. A silver thread, inlaid in the wood, made swirling patterns across its face. It was reminiscent of the same pictographs the Nasi had tattooed on their skin.

Bao leaned in toward the three other Humans. "Okay, it's time." As he turned, the doors opened and the Ancient stepped through with a loud cry of "What'd I miss?"

❖

A man and a woman sat at a small stone table in the center of the room. Although not enormous, the room had a presence and majesty to it. Large windows at the top of the walls let in sunlight, which shined off the intricate silver threadwork covering the walls.

Nicole tried to concentrate on the two Ancients in front of her, but she found herself continuing to glance around the room. There was so much detail and information embedded in the very walls of the building. She knew from talking with Bo that the decorations told the history of the Jadid.

"It's not a time for humor, Bao," the man said, his tan face as hard as stone.

"You and your friends have caused a rift that may take centuries to mend," added the woman with a look of disapproval.

Nicole was surprised at how young they both looked. Despite having lived for centuries, they could have been her age or even younger.

Bao strode forward and took a seat next to the other two Ancients. The rest of their group followed his lead, sitting at the table across from them.

"Ancients Richard Kingsley and Salina Musa, this is General Aamina Samaha, commander of Samsara Fleet and Colonel Nicole Bergeron." He smiled. "I believe you remember General Kal Norman."

The two Ancients gave them a disapproving look and reluctantly extended their hands.

"Now with introductions over, what happened?" Bao asked as he poured himself a cup of a milky white liquid. "We didn't see eye to eye, but this is something else entirely."

"Perhaps we should talk about this later," Salina said with disapproval as she eyed the three representatives from Samsara Fleet.

Bao thumped his cup onto the table. "Nonsense. The time for isolation and secrecy is over. I've been over to the Human's universe and seen what Esma's followers are doing. We can't sit here and keep secrets while our own children kill innocents."

"You're right," Richard replied, rubbing his salt-and-pepper beard. "We cannot change what has happened, only what we do in the future."

"So I'll ask again, what happened?"

"Fine," Salina said rubbing her eyes with a single hand. "After you left, the protests got worse and turned into riots and violence. Jian and Girish forced a vote on the issue. With you and Esma gone, it was a deadlock." She sighed.

"We resolved to wait until you returned," Richard continued, "but the situation continued to escalate. Jian and Girish disappeared one day along with tens of thousands of our children. Next thing we knew, they'd declared themselves the leaders of a group called the Isolationists and said they would have nothing to do with the Humans or Nasi."

"How bad has it gotten?" Bao asked, leaning forward. "We aren't actually fighting, are we?"

"No. Thankfully, it has not escalated to full war," Salina replied. "For now, the Isolationists have secured control of a large portion of our fleet and several cities. They have declared that all they want is to be left alone. We tried to reason with Jian and Girish, but they will not even speak to us."

Bao whistled. "God, how did it come to this?"

"We knew this was a powder keg. That is why we tried to keep it contained." Salina looked at Kal. "Your friend had other ideas."

Nicole could see Kal trembling in anger and his hands balled up into fists. She had to do something before the man exploded like he did on the ship. "I don't think you can blame Kal for what happened," Nicole said, keeping her voice even. "I don't believe two people can cause an entire planet to descend into chaos simply by walking into a market."

"Yes, yes, of course you are right," Salina admitted. "But it all happened so fast. It took only moments to undo centuries of work. They were the spark that lit the fuse."

Richard laid his hand on hers in an affectionate gesture. "I think we need to accept that some of that work was flawed. We are the ones who told our children about Earth, and we gave them these feelings whether or not we meant to."

Nicole saw a gleam in Bao's eyes. "Yes. Therefore, we

have to do something about it." The Ancient gestured at Samaha. "They've been able to build one of the skip ships; we can now travel freely between the universes. We've already waited too long to save Earth, but we can still bring our ships through to the Human's universe and help them."

"How was it?" Salina asked, her wide eyes fixed on Bao. "What was it like to be back?"

Bao smiled. "Amazing. I had forgotten what things were like over there. The white stars, the strange gravity, and different colors. It felt...right."

Nicole sensed an opening. "But we need your help. It's being destroyed by the Nasi, by *your* children."

"We want to help; *our* children want to help." Richard cleared his throat. "But we have been through hell together. To fight our own people—that is something that I do not know we are ready for."

"We built everything you see around you," Salina said. "We survived a planet and universe that wanted us dead because we stayed together."

"We need to talk. I don't think we can stay on the sidelines." Bao turned to Fleet officers. "Look around. We need some privacy to discuss this."

The doors of the room opened, and Governor Huang gracefully strode through and bowed to the three Ancients. One of the Ancients must have called for her using their wrist computer.

"Follow me please," she said, gesturing to the door.

"Wait, we're not done." Samaha slammed her hands down on the table.

"General, you know that I'm on your side," Bao said. "I hope you realize what you're asking. Give us some time to talk."

Samaha reluctantly stood with her hands clenched at her side. They had done so much to get to this point and now they were being asked to wait. It frustrated Nicole as well.

"I will show you around," Governor Huang said as she walked them out the door. "There is a lot to see, and this time you do not have to remain hidden."

The Palace of the Ancients was an anomaly among the Jadid and Nasi buildings Nicole had been in. It wasn't made from the same weaves that she'd seen in their other structures and ships. Instead, large rocks that appeared to have been hand quarried had been used to construct the enormous structure. The walls were rough to her touch and had a thin coat of a sand-like substance covering them. Although not ostentatious, the palace was graceful and impressive with the flowing Jadid script covering every surface.

Governor Huang walked them through the halls, telling them about the history of the Jadid and the building itself, which had taken a century to create. As she listened to the governor talk with fondness about the struggles of the early Jadid, Nicole had a realization.

"Wait, how old are you?" she asked.

Huang smiled. "I am one of the first children of the Ancients. I helped lay the first stones for this building over two hundred years ago."

Nicole knew the Jadid did not age, but she still was in shock; Madeline Huang looked to be in her early twenties. The woman had been alive before the UEG and EDF had existed. She couldn't imagine living for such a long time.

"What do you think about all of this?" Nicole asked.

"About you Humans?" Huang asked, her smile fading. "I am of two minds about you. I hate that you came here and ruined a peace and unity of purpose that has lasted my entire life. But I also realize it is not your fault. Our people had to be as one to survive here; we had no other option. His arrival," she pointed at Kal, "did not truly split us apart. It simply exposed fault lines that were already there."

The governor turned to face the tapestry again. "This wall hanging shows the plight of our people when they first left Earth and came to Altterra. These events are the seeds that caused the Nasi to return to your world. But history has no beginning, and the end is never written. There are no villains or heroes really. Perhaps we were heroes once and now we are the villain." She shook her head. "Either way, I believe we have to do what is right despite the cost. Despite what happened in the past. I think in this case it means protecting the people, or their descendants, who cast us out, against our brothers and sisters."

"I think we're entering a new age," Samaha said as she softly touched the tapestry. "For you, for us, for everyone. Things can change gradually or all at once. However this war ends, things will be completely different from how they were at the start."

They continued through the broad halls of the palace. Nicole interpreted Madeline's narrative in a different light now that she fully appreciated the woman had lived through the events she was discussing. This wasn't someone who was reading ancient texts or watching holos; it was someone who had trod through this area when it was covered by nothing more than dirt and low-lying bushes.

"These doors are the main entrance from the market," Madeline said.

Nicole regarded the elaborate set of doors and the guards standing at attention on either side. "Can we go out and see it?"

"Yes, there are no restrictions on you. You're free to do what you want. But I should warn you: the citizens have heard Humans have returned. A crowd has gathered outside the palace."

"A crowd?" Samaha asked with almost childish wonder. "Really?"

"Yes, General." Huang regarded Samaha with cool eyes. "That's *why* I said it."

"Point taken. Let's see them," Samaha said in a more dignified manner.

The doors opened and a wave of noise and voices poured through the opening. Huang led them through the open doors onto an elevated landing surrounded by a waist-high railing. Several guards, dressed in battle suits, stood at the bottom of the two curved staircases that descended to the market. A large transparent barrier stood in front of them, preventing the jostling crowd from getting close.

The milling crowd of Jadid, pressed elbow to elbow, filled the square. They roared and surged against the barriers as they saw the Humans walk onto the landing. Shouts and screams threatened to overwhelm Nicole's sense as she looked across the sea of faces. She looked up and could see the silhouettes of Jadid looking down on them from the wall separating the palace from the city.

"Why have you come?"

"What have the Nasi done?"

"What do you need?"

Individual shouts escaped the roar of the crowd. The market stalls they had seen from the air were no longer visible, the crowd of Jadid having swallowed them up. Nicole looked above the crowd and saw drones hovering—holo cameras, she guessed.

"Was this what it was like when you were here before?" Nicole asked Kal.

Kal turned and looked at her with wide eyes. "No. This is something else entirely."

"This is great," Samaha said as she smiled and waved at the crowd. "It lets them know we're real. It's our chance to speak to the citizens of Altterra themselves." She motioned at the hovering holo-cams.

Samaha moved to the front of the landing with a smile still plastered on her face. She shouted toward the crowd. "Thank you, people of Altterra. I am General Aamina Samaha. We come here seeking your aid."

Jadid at the front of the crowd quieted down and stopped pushing against the barriers as they realized she was talking.

"The Nasi entered our universe and attacked us without warning. We—"

Plasma bolts sizzled around the group on the platform. Gasps and screams came from the crowd and several in front ducked down. Nicole felt Kal's weight as he tackled her. As she fell, she saw a green bolt of plasma strike Samaha, knocking her to the ground.

Chapter Twenty-Five

The drones in the marketplace abruptly dropped from the air as the guards activated the anti-drone interference system. Anti-drone technology was something widely used in their universe. It was the reason no one used drones in combat; they were too easy to defeat.

"You okay?" Kal asked.

"I'm fine," Nicole replied. She looked around the platform. Had anyone else been hit? Samaha was on her side, curled in a fetal position with her charred right arm pulled in against her side.

"They hit the general," she said.

"We need to evacuate this area," instructed a guard in a battle suit as he picked Samaha up in his arms and rushed back into the palace. The rest of the group followed him, crawling back through the door they had exited. There were a handful of guards waiting in the hallway who quickly helped them as they came back through.

Samaha lay on the floor where the guard had laid her down, still clutching her wounded arm against her side. Kal rushed to her and gingerly examined it, frowning.

"The hand's gone," he said. "Wounds completely cauterized, but you still may go into shock." He turned to Governor Huang. "Is there a medical facility here?"

The woman's violet face had lost almost all its color. "Yes. Follow me," she said. Huang motioned for a guard to pick up Samaha and strode through the hallway at what would be a run for a Human.

They followed the governor to a small room with several

bunks cantilevered from the walls and an enormous machine against the opposite wall. As they rushed through the doorway, a short Jadid in a lab coat—Nicole assumed he was a doctor—turned from the viewscreen he was examining to see who had entered. Samaha continued to groan, her jaw clenched, as the guard gently placed her on a bunk.

"W-w-what has happened?" the doctor asked, mouth agape.

"Someone attacked us in the market," Madeline replied. She delivered the words at a rapid pace like slugs from a rifle. "Can you help her?"

"I do not know," he replied. He looked over the general's wounded arm. "The wound is clean. The plasma cauterized much of it. I have some painkillers that we use for the Ancients."

"What happened?" Ancient Kingsley asked as he ran through the door of the medical facility. The other two Ancients were fast on his heels. The Jadid in the room bowed deeply as they saw the three Ancients enter.

"We were attacked in the market," Governor Huang said. "One of the drones was armed and fired several plasma bolts before the defensive system disabled it."

"How could this happen?" Ancient Musa cried out.

"We are not sure," Huang responded. "I have several soldiers combing through the crowd, and we are reviewing sensor data from the incident. We will find out what happened."

"This is chaos," Bao said as he looked down at General Samaha with a frown.

"They've gone too far," Kingsley said, his jaw clenched. "The Isolationists need to be stopped."

Salina touched the man's arm. "Wait, this may not be them. The Nasi could equally be responsible."

"They've never done anything like this before," Bao replied. "Why would they? They're already in the Humans universe. No, this has to be the Isolationists."

Kingsley turned to Huang. "Governor Huang, you need to find out who did this as soon as possible. Events are spiraling out of control." The Jadid nodded. "In the meantime, double security on the palace and bring the two scientists that arrived with Ancient Wang back to the palace. No one goes in or out until we know what is going on."

Nicole watched the exchange with morbid fascination. Even the Ancients with their advanced technology and wealth of experience had no idea what was happening. She wished she knew more about their politics. Would the Jadid turn on each other? Was it a Nasi agent?

She also wished her implant worked in this universe. The others on the *Salamis* would have no idea there had been an attack and Samaha was injured. They would need to get word to them.

"I would like a guard on the Humans at all times," Bao ordered. "They were clearly the targets, and until we know what is going on, they are in danger."

"Yes, sir," Huang replied.

Bao turned to the three Samsara Fleet officers. "I'm sorry, but you'll need to be restricted to the palace. You will have full access to the area, but I can't risk your safety."

"What about our team on the *Salamis*?" asked Nicole.

"They need to return to the palace," Bao replied. "They're at risk in that ship. This palace can withstand attacks from orbit. There isn't a safer place on the planet."

Nicole remembered the stories that the governor had told them while they were touring the palace about the species the Jadid had encountered. She couldn't imagine how strong the building must be to face attacks like those.

"We will put you in the best guest rooms in the palace," Huang said.

Nicole didn't like the thought of being away from the ship, and from his expression, Kal didn't either. With everything going on, it was their lifeline to safety, their way out.

"We'd prefer to stay on our ship," Kal replied. "With all due respect, it would be safer for us."

"This is not up for debate," Salina replied. "We cannot allow you to get injured."

Kal put his hands up in a gesture of surrender. "Fine. Show us to our rooms."

"What was that?" Nicole asked, waking Kal from his light sleep.

He sat up. The only sound he could hear was his own breathing. Then he heard it—the sound of explosions reverberating through the thick stone building.

"We've got to wake everyone," he said, jumping off the

rock-like bunk.

He used the small wrist computer, which he had learned was called a comeca, the governor had given him to turn on the overhead lights of the room and grabbed the small jump bag he'd retrieved from the *Salamis*. The guest room was simple but still elegant with a bunk against one wall and a small seating area comprising a padded bench, table, and chairs across the room. The high ceiling, irregular stone walls, and upright lamps casting halos of light around the room gave him the feeling of being in a cave.

Nicole used her own comeca to open the door to the hallway. They both ran out to find it empty; the guards that had been posted outside their doors were gone.

The door next to theirs slid open. "Did you hear that?" Sampson asked, jump bag already slung over his shoulder.

"Yes," Kal replied. As he said the words, the building seemed to vibrate with the sound of a much larger, closer explosion.

"We've got to get out of here," Sampson said as he inspected the hallway.

"For once, we agree," Kal said. "I'll get Bo. You get Ai," he turned to Nicole, "and you get Chief Ramos."

Kal ran to Bo's door and pressed the small call panel next to it. A second later, the door slid open to reveal Bo sitting on the bunk, his eyes half closed.

"Yes, sir?"

"Bo, get up," Kal said. "Someone's attacking the palace. We've got to get to the ship."

The Jadid's eyes sprang open. "That's not possible." He

381

jumped up. "No one would dare attack the palace. It's never happened."

A loud boom echoed from down the hallway.

"Well, it's happening, now." Kal threw the Jadid his pants from the table. "I don't know what's going on, but we've got to get out of here."

Bo gasped as he caught the pants. He stood up and hastily put them on, mumbling to himself the entire time. "How could this be? What has happened?"

Scientist Ai and Lieutenant Sampson were rushing out of their rooms as Kal and Bo entered the hallway. The scientist had the same horrified expression as Bo. For them, this was the unthinkable, an attack from their own.

"We need to get General Samaha," Kal said, "and then we head to the ship."

"Are we leaving Altterra, sir?" Sampson asked.

"I don't know," Kal replied. "We'll cross that bridge when we get to it."

Ai shot a confused expression to Bo. "Idiom," he whispered to her.

There weren't any guards or functionaries in the palace hallways as they rushed through them. Every time he turned a corner, Kal expected them to come across a Nasi or Jadid patrol, but none appeared. They must have all been called to defend the palace.

He worried what would happen if they came across whatever group was attacking the palace. They were unarmed and would be almost useless in a hand-to-hand fight against the stronger, faster Nasi or Jadid. Bo and Ai were scientists and wouldn't be much help either.

"Anything on the net?" Kal asked Bo.

The Jadid shook his head. "There's a standing order for all personnel to move to the front of the palace. No reason is given."

Kal saw the door to the medical center ahead, unguarded. He'd never heard of a doctor who would leave patients, but maybe the Jadid were different. He wasn't sure it mattered if the doctor was there or not.

"Bo, Ai, take the lead and be ready when we go through that door. We don't know what we'll find."

The two Jadid glanced back at him and gave a quick nod, their eyes narrowed and jaws firm in determination. The group rushed through the door with the two Jadid in the front to find the doctor sitting at his desk, shakily pointing a small sidearm at them.

"Oh!" The Jadid put the weapon down and slunk down in the chair. "I am very glad it is you. I heard the attacks but was not sure what was happening."

"We don't know either," Bo admitted. "But it can't be good."

Kal was already across the room, checking on Samaha. Could they carry her to the ship? A fresh bandage was wrapped around her wounded arm, and she appeared to be deep in sleep. Kal tried to shake her awake, but the general remained unconscious.

"She is still under the effect of the anesthesia I gave her," the doctor said. "She will most likely not wake for hours."

"Can you give her something to jolt her awake?" Nicole asked.

"I am sorry, but we have nothing like that for Humans," the doctor replied. "I would not recommend using our Jadid equivalent either as we do not know correct dosage amounts or if it would even work. You would be as likely to kill her as wake her."

Kal muttered a curse under his breath and turned to Ai.

"Can you carry her?" He asked.

The Jadid woman strode to the slab and carefully lifted Samaha onto her shoulders without saying a word.

"What am I to do?" the doctor asked. "This has never happened."

"Stay here," Bo replied. "You are a medical professional. They would never harm you."

"Let's get out of here," Kal said. He checked the map of the palace on his comeca. The *Salamis* was only a couple of hundred meters away in a straight line. Unfortunately, they would have to cross some of the main hallways to get there. The chances of running into someone were high, and they didn't know who was friendly or not.

"Can we have that?" he asked, pointing to the weapon laying on the desk.

"This is all I have to defend myself," the doctor replied indignantly.

Bo's arms struck out like a snake, snatching the weapon from the desk before the other Jadid had time to react. "I'm sorry, but we need this more than you." He handed the weapon to Kal.

After a quick inspection to confirm he knew how to use the pistol, Kal signaled for the rest of the group to follow. "Stay close," he said. "We don't know what's going on out there."

Kal led the group out of the medical center and jogged through the hallway, pressing his side to the wall. The sounds of explosions, thankfully, were coming from the far side of the facility—Kal guessed the market.

When they arrived at the exit to the landing pad Kal was surprised to find it was unguarded. He opened the door with his comeca, revealing the *Salamis* sitting on the private landing pad fifty meters away. A group of five armored Jadid soldiers stood between the palace and the ship, weapons pointed directly at them.

❖

Kal let out a breath as Ancient Wang and Governor Huang stepped out of the ring of soldiers and walked towards them. "I figured you'd come here," Wang said as he motioned for the guards to put their weapons down.

Kal hesitated, then put his pistol back in its holster. "What's happening?"

"The Isolationists," Bao replied, "they're attacking the palace."

"An armed group has stormed the facility," Huang added. "They set off explosives in the market as a distraction and launched a full-out attack."

"They must be looking for you," Bao said. "When we

found your rooms empty, we thought you'd come here."

"They will expect you to come here as well," Huang said. "You need to get back inside."

"No way," Kal replied, "we're getting on that ship and getting out of here."

"I thought you came here to get the help of the Jadid," Bao replied.

"We'll come back," Kal said. "It's not—"

Several missiles exploded in the middle of the Jadid soldiers before Kal had time to react to the hiss of their approach. The explosions flung the five soldiers across the open area of the compound, and Kal felt himself lifted and pushed off his feet, crashing onto the ground several feet from where he'd stood. He looked around, trying to see where the missile had come from and realized it had to be from the compound's perimeter wall.

"Everyone okay?" Nicole asked, groaning. Her voice was a relief to Kal.

"Get inside!" Kal shouted as he pushed himself off the ground and dove behind the short wall that enclosed the landing. The *Salamis* was too far away for them to make a run for it and the Jadid soldiers lay unmoving on the ground.

He ran to Sampson, helping the dazed pilot to stand, while Nicole helped Ramos. Bo and Ai moved towards the palace door and quickly backed away as a hail of plasma fire greeted them.

"I have locked it," Huang said as she used her comeca to close the door, "it will take them several minutes to get through."

"We're going to need to get to the ship." Kal pointed to Samaha's unconscious form on the ground. "Ai, can you pick her up again?" The Jadid ran over and scooped the unconscious Human from the ground.

"Grab their datons," Madeline instructed, pointing to the stick-like weapons scattered on the ground.

Plasma fire suddenly rained down from the top of the palace, peppering the perimeter of the landing. They were close enough to the door that their attackers must not be able to see them; the shots were too scattered. Kal guessed whoever was firing was holding their weapons over the side and shooting blindly.

Normally, the fifty meters between them and the *Salamis* would be nothing. But right now, it felt like fifty kilometers to Kal. There were assailants on the roof behind them and likely more on the wall in front of them. The waist-high wall that enclosed the landing was the only thing that provided any cover from their attackers.

"How do we do this?" Nicole asked.

The other members of their group, even the Jadid, looked at Kal, waiting for his response.

"Bo, on my mark, sprint to the ship and get that cargo door open," Kal said. Normally, they used their implants to open the door, but that wasn't an option on Altterra. "Once the cargo bay is open, provide cover fire for the rest of us to follow and we'll lift off."

"Then what?" Sampson asked.

Kal shot the man an annoyed look. "One thing at a time." He turned to Governor Huang and Ancient Wang.

"You armed?" The two shook their heads. *Damn it, this couldn't get any worse*, thought Kal.

He was wrong. Four Jadid dropped from the roof above in front of their group, brandishing their datons like staves. Kal instinctively pulled out the pistol he'd grabbed in the medical center and shot the male in front of him point-blank, knocking him over the surrounding wall. Huang, Bo, and Ai engaged the Jadid attackers, taking advantage of their close distance to grab the datons before they could fire. In the melee, the combatants knocked General Samaha's unconscious body off the landing and onto the ground. Kal worried about her, but there was no way for him to get close enough to do anything.

He wasn't sure about Madeline but knew that Bo and Ai were relative amateurs in hand-to-hand combat. They held their own though, wrestling with their Jadid attackers in a flurry of arms and legs that made its way across the landing. Kal looked for a clean shot, but there was nothing he could do; they were moving too fast.

"Get the weapons," Kal said to the other Humans as he pointed to the datons on the ground. "I'll see if I can get a clean shot off."

Despite his recent career as a scout, Kal had been a logistics officer in the EDF. He'd received some close combat training from Sergeant Jones and the Tac-I squad during the lull when they were folding but was no expert. He looked for an obvious opening, aware that he could be just as much a hinderance as a help to his allies.

The three other Humans ran onto the dirt-covered ground between the palace and the *Salamis* to grab the datons. Plasma fire streaked around them, singing the ground and creating small depressions as they melted the dirt. Kal watched them out of the corners of his eyes but had to focus on the fight in front of him. That, he might be able to do something about.

With a guttural yell, a soldier threw Bo back against the stone side of the palace. Kal saw an opening and reflexively pulled the trigger stud on the Jadid pistol. The small plasma bolt sizzled as it landed a foot in front of the surprised Jadid warrior.

That was the opening Bo needed.

He leapt away from the wall, arm raised, and brought it down like a hammer on his distracted adversary's head. The Jadid dropped to the ground immediately, his skull hitting the dais with a hollow thud. Bo kicked his opponent in the head in a smooth motion and then quickly checked to make sure he was out before jumping back into the fray to assist Ai.

Kal had knelt down to double-check the downed Jadid for signs of life when a large bolt splashed against the unconscious Jadid's chest, singing away his flesh in a burst of viridescent light. The unwanted aroma of burned flesh filled Kal's nostrils.

"Why'd you do that?" Kal asked, looking at Wang, who still had his weapon raised.

The Ancient was stone-faced. "Did you want to leave him?" he asked. "I don't have any way to restrain him and the Jadid can recover quickly. He'd get up and attack again."

Kal turned as he heard a scream from behind him. Bo stood panting, looking down at the second attacker, her face almost completely disfigured by the savage blow the scientist must have landed on her. Ai stood nearby, a horrified expression on her face as she looked at the scene.

"She's making a run for it," Huang cried out, pointing away from the palace.

The third attacker had broken away from the governor and was sprinting toward the wall that separated the palace compound from the city. Huang smoothly raised her daton, sighted it, and placed a plasma bolt directly in the middle of the attacker's back, sending her sprawling to the ground—dead before she hit.

Bo rushed over and knelt down to examine the Jadid female's corpse. The anger and determination that had been in his face was gone, replaced with a look of melancholy. He reached to the Jadid's arm and ripped off a white band, holding it up into the air for the rest to see.

Bao gasped. "The Palace Guard," he cried. "This is an attack from within."

"They are not the Palace Guard, sir," Huang said as she took the band out of Bo's hand. "We wouldn't have stood a chance against them. These are imposters."

A missile landed above their heads, exploding against the ornate stone wall of the palace. They ducked behind the short wall encircling the entrance to the palace.

"We need to get out of here," Kal called out. "The plan remains the same. Bo, get out there. The rest of you, fire everything you can at that wall. I don't care if you hit anything, just keep their heads down." He pointed to Samaha's unconscious form on the ground. "Ai, grab her again."

As Bo sprinted across the coarse ground, the rest of the group fired at the top of the city wall. Governor Huang's and Ancient Wang's shots traced the top parapet of the wall while everyone else's were scattered across the structure, some missing altogether. Bo hurtled through the mangled bodies laying on the ground and dove in front of the ship, using it as a shield from the attackers on the city wall. Seconds later, the back ramp dropped to the ground, and he took a position next to it, firing at the wall.

"Run!" Kal yelled as he climbed over the wall they'd been using for cover. He waited for the rest of the group to pass him and then began sprinting across the short distance to the *Salamis's* cargo bay.

Nicole sprinted toward the open bay of the *Salamis*, glad she had taken the time to use the muscle stimulators aboard the *Ofira* while they were traveling through Z'Ta space. She heard Kal's breathing behind her and the sound of plasma rounds splattering around them as they ran.

Nicole felt something from behind knock her down and felt a wave of pain in her back and legs. As she pushed herself up, she turned back to see Kal facedown on the ground, unconscious from the blast. Looking forward, Nicole saw the rest of their group had already reached the safety of the ship and Wang arguing with Ramos and Sampson on the cargo bay ramp.

Nicole made a shooing motion with a free hand. "Get

out!" she yelled, the pain from her shrapnel wounds causing her to gasp. "Get away!"

The three ran up the closing ramp and the *Salamis* took to the sky a few seconds later, leaving her and Kal alone. Nicole dragged herself toward Kal; the pain in her leg let her know she wasn't walking anywhere.

The explosion had shredded Kal's legs and blood soaked the bottom of his pants. He lay motionless, except for the small rise and fall of his chest.

Nicole heard the thuds of several battle-suit clad Jadid landing behind her. "Do not move!" one of them yelled. Obediently, she lifted her open hands above her head and lay flat on the ground.

The Jadid grabbed her arms and pulled them roughly behind her back and applied restraints on her wrists. She grimaced in pain as they pulled her legs together and placed another restraint around her ankles. Finally, the soldiers shoved a hood over her head, casting her into darkness.

Nicole felt herself lifted and then the sensation of someone carrying her through the air. The entire process was eerily quiet. The hood must not only block light but sound too. They'd left the palace. A few minutes later, there was a jolt as the Jadid holding her landed. They set her down on a rough surface. Nicole felt the ground with her hand. It was dirt. She must be somewhere outside the city.

She wondered what had happened to Kal. She assumed they'd captured him as well. They wouldn't kill him, would they? His wounds had been bad. The Jadid needed to treat them soon or he would bleed out.

She wriggled her body, trying to see if there was anyone or anything near her. After a few seconds, pain blossomed in her side as someone kicked her sharply. Wherever she was, they were watching her.

Nicole wasn't sure how long she lay on the ground blind and deaf. An hour? Two? She continued to think about Kal. Was he right next to her? Was he bleeding out on the ground outside the palace?

Finally, someone not in a battle suit—she could feel the warmth and give of flesh—lifted her again and placed her on a hard metallic surface. They ascended again—she must be in a vehicle—and flew for several minutes before descending. Nicole felt herself carried out of the vehicle. There were several starts and stops as her captors transported her. For about five minutes, they were still as the Jadid talked to someone—she felt the vibrations of their speech through her body.

Her captor dropped Nicole on the ground. She waited for several minutes to be picked up again, but it never happened. Finally, she writhed on the ground, trying to get some sort of bearing on her surroundings with her legs or hands. She could feel hard walls around her, but no one kicked her in the side again.

Wherever she was, she was trapped and alone.

Chapter Twenty-Six

Nicole woke to someone reaching under her armpits and roughly pulling her to a standing position. She immediately crumpled back to the ground as her injured leg folded underneath her.

Powerful hands grasped her ankles and dragged her along the rough stone ground which wore her hands, restrained behind her back, raw. She tried to turn onto her side, but the pain shooting through her leg made her quickly give up.

Suddenly the hands let go of Nicole's ankles and her feet dropped to the floor. She felt the air move and vibrations from explosions around her—a firefight had broken out.

Nicole felt more helpless than she ever had in her life—even more than when she'd been a prisoner of the EDF and was unable to do anything except watch the video of the Nasi destroying Earth. She couldn't see or hear and the only thing she could do was writhe on the floor. Even that was futile since she had no idea which way to go. Nicole sat still, waiting for freedom or death—it felt like the hell she'd read about in ancient books.

Light.

Ancient Bao Wang stood over her, his eyes narrowed in anger. "Release her," he said as he turned his head, "and the man too."

Nicole looked to her side and saw Kal next to her, hood still over his head. Bloodstained bandages covered the bottom half of his torso, hiding the damage from the grenade. Thankfully, he was still unconscious—she couldn't imagine the pain he would be in otherwise.

A Jadid turned Nicole on her side and disengaged the restraints on her wrists and ankles. She pulled Nicole up, causing her to stumble and fall as her leg gave way under her body's weight.

"Hold her up, for God's sake," Bao yelled. The Jadid pulled her up again and pivoted so that her shoulder was under Nicole's armpit, supporting her weight.

The room looked more rustic and utilitarian than anything in the palace. It had a large rug in the center, which looked to be woven from the same materials the Jadid used in their buildings. A table with six chairs arranged around it stood on the rug. Bunks lined a wall of the room, and storage bins lined the other two. Five Jadid soldiers stood around the Ancient, weapons at the ready.

Two Human bodies lay in the center of the floor next to the table, their glassy eyes fixed on the ceiling. The rebel Ancients, Jian Chen and Girish Khati. Multiple Jadid bodies lay scattered across the room, plasma burns denting their torsos and coating the stubs where limbs had been. They all had white bands on their arms. It was a scene of total carnage.

"We've got to get you out of here," Bao said.

"What happened?" Nicole eyed the bodies on the floor.

Bao's expression transformed; his eyes grew glassy as he regarded the fallen Jadid. "We came to get you and General Norman back. I tried to reason with Jian and Girish, but they attacked." He glanced around the room. "There was nothing else we could do. Now we've got to get out of here. The deference paid to an Ancient will only last so long. I expect the Isolationist guards to storm in here anytime."

"Where are we?" Nicole asked. The room's low ceiling and amber sconces gave Nicole the impression they were underground.

"This is Eden," Bao replied, "the first place the Jadid found safety on this planet." He held up a hand. "No more questions for now. We've got to get out of here. There are a few escape routes known only to us Ancients; though it may be difficult considering your friend's current state."

"Let me try and stand on my own," Nicole said to the Jadid holding her up. He moved back, and Nicole gingerly tried to place her weight on her injured leg. It was still painful but would be good enough for her to walk on her own.

One of Wang's soldiers picked Kal up and placed him on another soldier's back. He used the restraint that had been on the man's ankles to tie his torso to the Jadid and reapplied the other restraint to his wrists. The end result was that the general was attached to the soldier's back with his arms around his neck like a backpack.

"Follow me," Bao instructed.

Bao led them single file down the narrow hallway as fast as Nicole could hobble. The light from the amber sconces cast long shadows on the stone walls and made her feel like she'd stepped into a horror holo.

A plasma bolt struck the soldier on Bao's flank, sending the female to the ground with a hiss. Nicole almost gagged as she dropped to the ground next to the female; she could smell the burnt flesh. The bolt had come from the intersection ahead of them, but Nicole wasn't able to tell how many guards there were or where they'd fired from.

Bao pulled back as the three Jadid soldiers not carrying anyone ran toward their attacker, firing back. As the lead soldier neared the intersection, the Isolationist guard who had fired on them jumped into the hallway, rolling as they landed. They swung their daton as they came out of the roll, bring their weapon upwards in a vicious slash.

The Loyalist soldier jumped to the side at the last moment, bringing their own weapon down on the head of the guard, knocking them to the ground.

"Keep going," Bao said, waving Nicole forward.

As they crossed another intersection minutes later, several plasma bolts passed only a few centimeters in front of Nicole's face—close enough she could feel the heat from the shot as it passed. Nicole broke into an unsteady run, the adrenaline pouring through her veins acting like a temporary pain reliever.

A soldier in their group casually dropped a small device onto the floor as they ran. After they'd traveled thirty meters farther, the device exploded, causing a twinge of pain in Nicole's eardrums.

"That should slow them for a second," Bao said. "We're almost there."

A group of three Isolationist fighters, weapons readied, materialized from the shadows in front of them. They fired their datons directly above the group's heads, halting them in their tracks.

"Stop!" shouted the soldier in front. "Ancient Wang. Sir.

Please do not advance any farther. We don't understand what you are doing."

"It is okay, my children. I can explain everything. There has been a huge misunderstanding." Bao raised his arms and slowly started inching toward the three soldiers.

Abruptly, the Ancient dropped to the floor, and the three Jadid Loyalists behind him fired their weapons at the guards. The bolts hit the shocked guards in their torsos and faces, knocking all of them off their feet and melting their flesh as they hit the ground.

"Let's go," Bao said matter-of-factly, waving the group forward without bothering to look back.

Nicole was frozen in place at the man's betrayal. She'd seen the trust in those soldier's eyes; they hadn't wanted to hurt Bao.

"Let's go!" Bao shouted, his face flushed.

Nicole jumped and stumbled to catch up with the group, trying not to look at or smell the charred bodies as she stepped around them.

The corridor ended at a blank wall and Bao immediately crouched down at the end. Nicole crouched next to him while his soldiers turned around and knelt, prepared to provide cover fire. Shouts emanated from the direction they'd come. The Isolationists had found the bodies.

A plasma bolt hit a Loyalist soldier in the head, completely disintegrating it as his body hit the ground. Gritting her teeth, Nicole bent over and grabbed the soldier's daton from his grasp. She quickly looked the weapon over and then pointed it down the hallway behind them.

The deep shadows cast by the widely spaced sconces hid their assailants. Nicole thought she saw movement and fired, the bolt coursing down the hallway and through the darkness to reveal nothing there.

Another bolt shot out from the shadows, catching a second soldier in the chest. She fell back against the wall, her head hitting the stone and falling onto her shoulder.

"Bao," Nicole yelled, "we're about to get overrun!"

"Almost there," he replied without looking back.

A plasma bolt shot over Nicole's head, splashing the stone behind her. She had an idea—a crazy one, but an idea.

"Hello!" Nicole yelled while simultaneously jumping backwards and peering into the blackness, her weapon raised. A bluish-green bolt of plasma shot down the hall and hit the spot where she'd been standing. There! She pulled the trigger stud on the daton and sent a bolt into the darkness, hitting their assailant in the chest.

"Got it," the Ancient said. "The mechanism on the door was jammed."

A small door, barely big enough for a person, swung open in the wall. Bao climbed through and then signaled for the rest to follow.

"Him first," Nicole said to the Jadid holding Kal. The soldier quickly dropped the Human onto the ground and pushed him through the opening with Bao pulling from the other side. He then slithered through the opening, somehow making the motion seem elegant in the process. The other Jadid soldier continued to keep watch, examining the dark hallway with their weapon raised.

Nicole dove into the hole, headfirst, after the other three. As soon as she was through, a blast sent a wave of dust and debris after her. Bao quickly shut the small hatch and pressed a square button next to it.

"That will keep them out," Bao said as he turned on the light built into his comeca. "Follow me."

❖

"Almost there," Ancient Wang said reassuringly. "This tunnel leads directly to the surface."

They'd been making their way through the cave, slowly ascending to the planet's surface, for the past hour. Nicole felt like collapsing. But seeing Kal, still unconscious on the back of the Jadid in front of her, acted like a stimulant. She had to make sure he was safe. She had to keep going.

A faint glow of light appeared before them, illuminating the small veins of silver minerals in the rock. Nicole was too exhausted to feel anything more than relief as they climbed the last few meters to the planet's surface.

Bao tapped on his computer. "I've called for a transport. They should be here soon." He flopped onto the ground. "We've done it."

Nicole lay next to him, her leg now an agonized mess. She leaned over to inspect her wound; the blast had ripped her pants in several places and dried bloodstains covered the surrounding cloth. It didn't look good, but with a few bandages and a medbot, she should be okay.

"What happened in there?" Nicole asked.

Bao twisted to look at Nicole. "After hundreds of years, you'd think we were beyond these squabbles. We've raised children and grandchildren together for God's sake." Bao sighed. "We knew the Isolationists would take you to Eden. The remaining Ancients decided the best course of action was for me to mount an assault to rescue you. As you can see, I know passageways in and out that no one else does."

"I knew where they'd hold you. But they were waiting for me when I got there. Well, an argument ensued and"—he held up his hands—"I had to act in self-defense."

"Sir, what will happen when we get back?" asked the Loyalist still carrying Kal on his back. "Are we at war with the Isolationists?"

"No. No. We're not at war with them. My hope is now they will understand the errors of their ways. Jian and Girish led them astray."

The Jadid seemed satisfied with the answer and turned to look out from the bushes that covered their position. They were in the center of a small clearing. The trees and shrubs around them waved gently from the gravitational waves of the planet. The movement had an almost hypnotic effect on Nicole.

"It's a shame," Bao said quietly. "The Jadid have gone through many wars—at first with the creatures of this planet, then with scavengers that came from the stars—but never with ourselves. We were always as one until Esma decided she wanted to return to Earth. When she actually did, she opened this door of possibilities. I think it changed so many things. It certainly changed me."

"How?" Nicole asked.

"I realized that perhaps I'd never been truly happy before." He looked down at his comeca. "I grew up in Brazil. It was a territory in the South American confederation back on Earth. I grew up poor and never was able to escape poverty. I got caught up with a dangerous crowd, and a friend convinced me to join him on a robbery that went wrong. That's how I ended up here. The government told me I would have my debts and record expunged if I volunteered for one experiment." Bao held his hands up in a weighing motion. "I gambled and lost. Instead of folding a few light years away, I folded here. We built up this civilization and this species. I thought I was happy. I had everything: followers, wealth of a sort, and power. When Esma told us about her followers traveling back to Earth, I realized it was an illusion. I was just a kid who'd built a castle of sand to pretend he was king."

"So what?" Nicole asked. "None of this is real?" She pointed around them with her hand.

Bao laughed. "It's real. I'm not sure if it matters though."

The sound of thrusters seeped into the clearing; the transport must be close. Nicole slowly stood up, straining to keep the weight off her injured leg, and followed Bao and the soldier to the treeline.

The misshapen ovoid transport slowly descended into the clearing, and a circular door on the side dilated open. Two Jadid jumped out and helped the four of them into the vehicle. Moments later, they were off on their way back to the Palace of the Ancients.

Chapter Twenty-Seven

"Kal?"

Kal slowly opened his eyes and tried to look around. His lids were heavy, and his vision blurred. Where was he? He recognized the voice though: Nicole.

"Hey," he murmured. As he spoke, tendrils of pain shot up his side.

"You're injured. Again." She smiled down at him.

"Still not dead," he said, trying to lift his head to give her a kiss.

"I don't know if there's anything that can kill you," she said. She bent down and kissed him. He closed his eyes, enjoying the sensation and the smell of her closeness.

"What'd I miss?" Kal asked. He wasn't sure how long he had been out. He remembered running toward the *Salamis*, plasma bolts hitting the ground around him, and then nothing.

"The Isolationists captured us," Nicole said. "Seems like they were behind the attack. Bao led a team to rescue us. The *Salamis* returned back after we were captured; everyone's still here."

Kal frowned. He wasn't sure why the thought of a Jadid civil war made him sad. But it did.

Nicole helped Kal sit up. He dipped a finger into his shirt pocket—his picture was still there—and looked down to see beige bandages wrapped around the bottom half of his legs. A dull pain materialized as soon as he saw them.

"How bad is it?" Kal asked, pointing to his legs.

Nicole looked away. "Not good. We need to get you

403

back to see how bad it is. The Jadid don't really understand Human physiology."

She handed Kal a plate filled with Jadid foods. He'd seen several of them before when he'd visited Altterra for the first time. He remembered the ground dog was particularly good.

"Best thing to do is eat a little for now," Nicole said. "You've been under a while." She handed him a glass filled with a milky liquid. "Small sips too."

Kal slowly ate the meal, his mouth burning from the spices. After he'd finished a quarter of the plate, the doors opened and General Samaha walked into the room. Her right sleeve had been sewn shut, ending in a simple fold of the fabric.

"How are you, Kal?" Samaha asked. "You look like crap."

"I feel better than you look, ma'am," Kal replied with a weary smile. "Glad to see you up and about. How's everyone else?"

"Alive. The three of us got the worst of it," Samaha replied.

"You're hurt?" Kal asked Nicole. He felt a pang of guilt as he realized he hadn't asked her if she was okay.

Nicole smiled comfortingly. "Nothing serious. I'll walk with a limp until I get to a medbot, but I'll survive."

Samaha sat down at the foot of the bunk. "Colonel Bergeron and I have been talking with Ancient Wang. It seems like they're going to agree to help." She sounded hopeful. "We've been waiting for you to regain consciousness before we discuss."

"That's great news," Kal replied, a smile on his face.

"That's an understatement. Finally, our sacrifices may be worth it." She absentmindedly rubbed the end of her arm where her hand should have been. "I know you've been through hell, but we need to meet with them soon and get back to our own universe. The fleet is waiting for us."

"The Jadid provided you something to get around with," Nicole said as she pushed a floating chair to the side of the bed. It was crafted out of the typical Jadid weaves with a wide seat and four thrusters attached to the bottom. "I gave it a test run. It's pretty comfortable."

Samaha laughed. "Until you ran over the planetary governor."

Kal laughed and regarded Nicole's blushing face. "Really?"

Nicole gave a small laugh. "She has pretty slow reflexes for a Jadid."

Samaha gave Kal's leg a gentle pat, causing him to wince in pain. "Sorry." She moved her arm away. "Take a moment and enjoy your time with Nicole. We'll need to leave within the hour. Until then, you deserve a break."

"General Samaha, I want to apologize for the treatment you and your fellow Humans suffered here on Altterra." Ancient Richard Kingsley stood in front of his chair looking gravely at the three Humans seated before him. Ancients Bao

Wang and Salina Musa sat to either side of him, sharing the same stony expression.

After an all-too-short hour of rest, the Ancients summoned the Samsara Fleet officers to their formal receiving room. The walls of the large elliptical chamber soared upward, meeting in a dome above their heads. The same intricate silver patterns were embedded into every surface of the room, shining in the glare of the bright lights that dangled from the ceiling. A large oval table stood in the center of the room, appearing to grow from the floor. Six chairs sat on either side. At the far end of the table stood three Jadid, clustered around a drone holo camera, their postures stiff and formal.

"We have decided that we will join you in your fight against the Nasi," Musa said. "We will announce this to our people right now with you by our side." She motioned to the team of Jadid standing at the end of the table. "We will broadcast this message to our children hoping it will help to unite our people."

Samaha inclined her head. "Thank you. We appreciate your help. What would you like us to say?"

"From my experience, it does not matter what we tell you to say," Kingsley replied. "You will just say what you want anyway."

Nicole chuckled to herself, thinking of Major Karl Garcia.

She walked to the other side of the table to stand next to General Samaha and behind the three Ancients while Kal sat in his chair next to them. A few minutes later, the camera team signaled they were ready for the broadcast. The green spherical camera hovered eye level with the Ancients sitting at the table.

"Go ahead," Richard said to them. He paused for a moment and then began speaking.

"Citizens of the Jadid, we are broadcasting to you today with tragic news. Two of our beloved Ancients have died. Nasi forces attacked and killed Ancients Jian Chen and Girish Khati in Eden." He wiped away a tear. "This is a declaration of war by our brethren, and we can no longer ignore their actions."

Nicole tried to hide her surprise at the lie.

Richard motioned to the members of Samsara Fleet around him. "Today we've agreed that the Jadid will join the Humans in their fight against the Nasi. Although they are flawed, they are still our cousins, and we will aid them in their quest to survive. We will show that we are magnanimous in our forgiveness of past transgressions."

Samaha looked at Nicole with a raised eyebrow.

"To those children who joined the Isolationists, we ask that you come home and join your brothers and sisters in this fight. We have known peace for a long time, but now we face our fiercest enemy—ourselves. Ancient Musa and I will lead our forces on Altterra. We will capture the Nasi gateways from this side while Ancient Wang leads our fleets in the Human's universe." Kingsley nodded to Bao.

Wang stood and nodded back. "Thank you, Ancient Kingsley. As my fellow Ancient has said, I will lead our forces to victory. The Nasi have become a blight, not only on us, but on the entire Human universe. And our own." He stared at the camera and almost shouted the words. "I will need your loyalty as we prosecute this fight. Ancients Kingsley and Musa have named me the commander of our fleet and I will not let them, or you, down."

"Thank you, Ancient Wang," Richard said as Bao sat down. "Finally, I want you to hear from the Humans yourselves. This is General Aamina Samaha, the commander of Samsara Fleet, and two of her staff officers. They came here asking for our help and we want you to know what they are facing."

Samaha gave a slight bow to the Ancient. "Thank you, Ancients. The Nasi entered our universe and immediately destroyed Earth and several other planets." Nicole was impressed. The general delivered the message in a voice that conveyed both determination and vulnerability. "They have killed billions and made several species their unwilling slaves. Our forces are outnumbered but determined. We also plead with you to stop this fighting with each other and join the true battle against the Nasi."

"Thank you—"

Nicole couldn't stop herself from stepping forward and cutting the Ancient off. She heard the words she was saying before her brain had time to register that she was speaking. "Earth is gone. But Humans remain. We are here and so are you—the children of Humans. You are proof that we can overcome anything. I have seen your cities, heard your history, and marveled at the things you have done in a strange universe with everything against you. Come back and help us. Our universe is yours as well, and there is a place for you in it when this is all done."

"Thank you, Colonel Bergeron," Ancient Kingsley said, giving her a sharp look. He turned back to the camera. "Children, you have seen what has happened and heard the pleas of those less fortunate than us. We need all of you to join with us in order to save not only Humanity but our people, the Jadid." The Ancient gave a nod toward the team of Jadid operating the camera and they turned it off, the drone slowly drifting down to the ground.

"That was...interesting," General Samaha said, her eyebrow arched.

"That is one word for it," Bao said. "I don't know what our children will think of your plea or your invitation."

"I fear nothing good will come from it," Ancient Musa said, disapproval dripping from every word.

Nicole stepped foot on the rear cargo ramp of the *Salamis* and felt like she was returning home. If she was being honest with herself, it was as much of a home as she had right now. The only people that mattered to her, that knew her, were normally on the ship.

She gently touched the starfish pendant around her neck. A gift from her sister, Sylvie, when she'd left home. It was a reminder, a promise, that whatever was broken or lost could be replaced. Nicole felt a moment of peace as she looked at the familiar battle suits standing in their docks at the edges of the bay.

"So I guess we got what we came for," Kal said as his

chair glided up the ship's ramp.

"I'd say so," agreed Samaha. "The Jadid ships will need retrofitting once they come to our universe, but Bo and Ai are staying with them so they can start working on it now."

"How long until they're combat ready?" asked Kal.

"A few months," Samaha replied. "We'll need to provide them with as many materials as we can. The Z'Ta can help us with that."

"Is Ancient Bao Wang coming with us?" Chief Ramos asked, flashing Nicole a smile in greeting.

"No," Nicole replied, returning the smile. "He's staying here to lead the fleet's preparations to fold into our universe. They won't have any way to return to their own universe for at least a while. Also, there's the campaign against the Nasi in this universe. The Jadid need to draw up their battle plans to shut down the Nasi gateways."

"We're ready to go when you are," Lieutenant Sampson announced as he climbed down the ladder. "The sooner the better as far as I'm concerned."

Kal said he wanted to lie down in his bunk for their departure. He suggested Nicole watch from the cockpit so she could see the city and planet as they left and she was more than happy to comply. She made her way to the cockpit and sat down in Kal's chair behind the two pilot consoles. Samaha was there as well, seated in the narrow jump chair that folded out of the bulkhead.

As they lifted from the palace's landing pad, the city of Tarzirbu spread out before her. It looked like a dull cloud hung over the buildings, muting their red and yellow exteriors. She could see small vehicles speeding over the interlocking rings of roads, which created an initial impression of randomness in the city's layout.

As they ascended, Nicole felt nauseous from the oscillating weight of the planet's gravity combined with the pressure of their ascent. She'd gotten used to the strange and heavy gravity of the planet but would be grateful to be away from it.

From a distance, Altterra looked almost like a child's candy. The bright colors of the land mixed with the dull white of the oceans and were coated with a smattering of blue clouds. She couldn't help remembering Earth as she looked at the familiar landmasses below. She watched the planet grow smaller in her personal viewscreen as the *Salamis* sped away from the planet, gaining distance before folding.

"Preparing to fold," Sampson called out.

"Do it," Samaha commanded.

Sampson pressed the fold button, and the cockpit became pitch-black as all the viewscreens, dials, and lights went out. The viewscreens flickered back on a moment later, revealing the white stars of their own universe. Nicole felt herself pulled down as the ship's artificial gravity turned back on as well.

"Glad we're back," Sampson said as his hands danced across the viewscreen in front of him. "Conducting post fold checks."

"It was an interesting place," Chief Ramos said, conducting checks of her own. "But isn't that why you joined the EDF in the first place? To see new places. Have new experiences."

Sampson grunted in reply.

"Ma'am, we've established contact with the fleet," Ramos reported. "Ready to land on the *Ofira*."

It took fifteen minutes for them to return to the fleet and enter the *Ofira's* landing bay. The bright lights of the bay and familiar faces of the crew were a welcome relief. After they touched down, a small crowd gathered around the ship. General Samaha stood on the landing bay and announced their success to a smattering of applause.

"The war is by no means over," Samaha said as the applause and shouts died down. "We are on our back foot, but we're still swinging. The Jadid will take months to be ready, and we will be on our own until they are. But there is a light, a hope for us to win."

Less than an hour later, Nicole sat in the *Ofira's* conference room as General Samaha made the announcement to the assorted Human, Kurz, Z'Ta, Tounous, and Qudoru commanders. Chirps, burbles, rumbles, and cheers of happiness met her news. The other commanders began peppering her with questions about the timing and their battle plans. Samaha tried to answer them, but Nicole could tell the general was exhausted.

"Enough for today," Samaha said. "It's been a grueling mission, and we're still recovering. We'll start battle planning on the *Gedorhan's Return* in twelve hours."

After a few more rounds of congratulations, Samaha shut off the screens with her implant and sat back in her chair, closing her eyes. The general looked like she had aged ten years in the past few days. The lines in her face stood out against the glare of the conference room's lights.

Still leaning back, she turned to Nicole and Kal. "Get some rest," Samaha said with a smile. "If you thought escaping a Jadid prison was tough, wait until you spend five hours in a planning meeting with them." She waved at the blank viewscreens. "I still have to get back to my flagship and rest too."

"When will we see the first Jadid?" asked Kal.

"Ancient Wang said it wouldn't be for at least another month," Samaha replied. "In the meantime, we'll run scouting missions out to keep track of the Nasi and plan for their arrival."

The general leaned forward and looked at Kal. "This wouldn't have been possible without the sacrifice of the Skulls. I know what you lost on Patagonia. I hope you and your soldiers realize what you did. Once again you," she looked at Nicole, "both of you, have saved not only this fleet but Humanity. I just hope we can stop asking you to do it." She gave a wry smile. "Now get out. That's an order."

Nicole walked back to their stateroom with Kal gliding next to her in a new chair that worked in this universe. The ship's doctors had already scheduled him to be seen in the next day. They seemed confident he would walk again, albeit most likely with another cybernetic limb or two.

Nicole helped Kal onto the bunk and then flopped down

onto it herself. The mattress was so soft compared to the hard Jadid bunks that she almost moaned in pleasure.

"Good to be back?" Kal asked.

"Yes," she replied.

"Did you know that when we were going through Sergeant Jones's things before his memorial ceremony, we found a copy of his personnel file on his tablet?" Kal asked with a smile.

"Really?"

"I haven't been through the entire thing yet, but what I read was pretty incredible. Did you know he actually told the commander of the Earth Defense Force to walk out of an airlock?" Kal laughed. "Or that he rejected getting promoted twelve times?"

"He was a hero."

"There's been a lot of them." Kal's voice dropped to a whisper. "I think of Chief Kanumba and her child. That child is the future that we are trying to save."

"You think we're close to the end?" Nicole asked. She'd been pondering the thought since they first lifted off from Altterra.

Kal lifted himself up onto his elbow and gently ran his hand through her hair. "I don't know. Maybe. Either way, I'm just glad we're together."

"Maybe there really isn't an end," Nicole said, almost to herself. "I mean, we'll never go back to the way things were. The Nasi have shattered everything, including the Jadid themselves."

"It will be interesting to see them when they come to

our universe. Wonder what that'll do to them." He continued to gently stroke her hair. She could feel herself growing tired as she looked into his dark brown eyes.

"Let's get some sleep," she whispered. "All of this can wait until later."

Kal pulled her close, and they turned out the lights. As they lay in each other arms and drifted to sleep, Nicole felt a sense of peace that had eluded her for years.

Epilogue

Ancient Bao Wang walked through the dark tunnels underneath the Palace of the Ancients. A layer of dust covered the wide, poorly lit corridors. It was the kind of place most people used to store things they'd never use again. It was also the perfect place for him to set up a private study.

He used his comeca to open the simple metal door to the study. Although it seemed simple and inconspicuous, the most advanced security system on Altterra protected the door. If anyone other than him even *tried* to open it, they'd be dead in seconds.

He'd attempted to make it feel like home with bright colors and a statue of Cristo Redentor that he'd carved from memory in the corner. He'd even installed an additional heating system to make the room feel like a warm Brazilian summer.

It had all been perfect—until Esma ruined it. He'd thought her talk of returning to Earth had been just that: talk. Then she'd done it and destroyed their home planet at the same time. Bao had wanted to kill her, but her Nasi cultists would never let him get an agent close.

Instead, he'd realized she had opened his eyes and presented him with an opportunity. He'd been satisfied, thinking he'd achieved all he wanted. But now? Well now, he wanted more.

Ancient Esma Baykara's round face appeared on the screen in front of Bao. Her blue eyes stood out against her olive complexion. Bao, like many, underestimated her at first because of that innocent-looking face. It had taken him several decades to realize the full depth of his mistake.

"Bao," Esma said, "have you been successful?"

"Yes, I have," Bao smiled back. He'd long forgotten how to smile naturally. It was just a mask he put on as needed. "Jian and Girish are dead, and I will lead our fleet."

"That wasn't supposed to happen." Esma looked shocked. With someone as old and wily as her, Bao couldn't tell if it was genuine or not. "What about the Humans?"

Bao tsked. "Your anger always gets the best of you, Esma. The Humans are very much still alive."

Her eyes narrowed, and she leaned into the camera, her expression one of barely contained rage. "What game are you playing at, Bao? Is this war?"

"It's not a game, Esma. You should know that." Bao smiled broadly; he knew that would infuriate her. "I've just decided to amend our arrangement."

"I gave you those resources to kill the Humans and pin it on Richard and Salina. What you've done is treason, you bastard."

"You shouldn't talk that way to me, Esma," Bao replied with an air of nonchalance. "Not if you want me to spare your life."

"Go to hell." Esma cut the line.

Bao dropped the mask and leaned back in his chair. If he still could *really* smile, he actually would have. He found it hilarious how Esma's followers were so ready to believe the nonsense she spouted about somehow helping the Humans. He knew the truth; no one carried a grudge like Esma Baykara. She wouldn't stop until she got the revenge she believed she was owed. He was counting on her same anger being directed back at him.

Bao remembered the first time he had killed a person back on Earth. They'd caught him pilfering rations, and he'd reacted without thinking. What he hadn't expected was how much he'd enjoyed it. Since then, he'd realized he loved the power he felt when he made the decision to end someone's life. There was nothing like it. Other than Esma, none of the other Ancients really understood Bao, and he liked it that way.

Esma Baykara might be ruthless and determined, but she was no match for Bao Wang.

Thank you for reading *For the Ones Who Rebel* and the Samsara Fleet series. My readers motivate me to tell this story and make the hours of work worth it.

I loved seeing the further adventures of Kal and Nicole as they fight the Nasi. This book was especially enjoyable because we get to see some of the divisions and fractures that have occurred because of the Nasi's actions. Much like real life, there are second- and third-order effects to world-shattering events.

As an author, I make an outline for how I want the series and each book to go but then find myself surprised by the actions my characters take. I always go with it and let them make their own decisions even if it changes the path we take to our ultimate destination.

I believe every story should have an end, and Samsara Fleet is no different. We still have a way to go with them though. I find myself continuing to be drawn to this world and already have many thoughts on concepts I would love to explore in more detail in future series. Hopefully, I will have the time to put these thoughts to "paper" and explore them.

If you enjoy this series and my writing, please consider joining my mailing list and following me on Facebook. You can find a link to it on my home page: https://www.rileycollins.info. I will continue to write short stories that flesh out the world of

Samsara Fleet and add to this universe as time permits and share them via the mailing list. I do not share your information with other authors or spam you with offers, etc.

I hope you have enjoyed this chapter in the Samsara Fleet series, and I look forward to writing several more.

Thank you,

Riley